The Iron Path

Book Twelve in the Iron Soul Series

J.M. Briggs

Contents

This book is dedicated to Piere d'Aterie,
the amazing cover artist who worked with me to
make every cover in *The Iron Soul* series distinct and
beautiful! Thank you for your wonderful work
over the last seven years.

1

Declaration of War

Magic had allowed Morgana to neatly wrap up everything surrounding Merlin's death. Too neatly, for Alex's taste. It felt wrong that the community he'd lived and worked in for decades thought that the healthy, passionate man had died due to an aneurysm, but they did. One closed casket funeral later and the faculty and students who knew him were going on with their lives. They would never know that Professor Ambrose Yates had truly been the mythical figure Merlin, who had fought to protect their world for over three thousand years.

Her memories were a tangle of Merlin and grief. Alex pushed her feet against the snow-dusted ground to move the swing she'd claimed as a seat. The heavy chains connecting the cold plastic seat to the bar above her head creaked loudly at her movement. Looking up, she checked on the others. Jenny was bundled up in a thick coat with her hood up and leaning into Lance, who was a bit more comfortable in the cold weather. Avani was sitting on the edge of the merry-go-round a few feet away from the swings. Bran was leaning against a tree, his breath misting strange shapes in the cold air. Nicki and Aiden were climbing over the jungle gym that was far too small for them.

Above their heads, dark gray clouds matched the mood of the day. The winter cold had settled fully into Ravenslake upon their return, and while the days were growing longer now that the Winter Solstice had passed, Alex knew that spring was a long way off, both literally and figuratively.

Alex tried not to think about what it might mean that one of their mentors was dead. In literature and even in films, the death of the mentor pushed the story forward and gave the hero room to establish themselves. She knew that this was real and not a work of fiction, but despite everything that had happened, she was still a literature student. It was hard not to see the pattern here. If that was true, then what did it mean? What was going to come next?

She still couldn't believe that the Light had killed Merlin. It just seemed wrong. Then again, she knew from personal experience that it always felt wrong. Losing someone that you loved always hurt, and Alex could admit to herself that she had loved Merlin. There were too many warm memories of him in her mind for her not to. Even if they'd never been as close as she and Morgana were in this life, Arto and Michel had loved the old man fiercely. Lokpal, Thor, and others had deeply respected the man. There was too much history between her soul and Merlin for his passing to be accepted.

She bent her legs and swung a little. The creaking of the chain shattered the quiet of the park. Even the sounds of nearby traffic were muted. Alex scanned the trees and nearby sidewalks for any potential threats. The world was silent. It seemed at peace, but Alex knew better. There was still a chance that more of Arthur's blasted amulets were in Fae hands. The Demons seemed to have settled down, and those that hadn't were being hunted down by allied Old Ones. None of the Old Ones were going crazy, at least not yet. All of it could go wrong any day.

But the Darkness had to be her highest priority. This wasn't some big bad or great evil trying to take over. It was just a cataclysm that killed whole worlds and made powerful beings flee. Even if the world they ran to wasn't right for them; even if just being there left them in pain with no end in sight other than death. Her feet dragged across the ground, mixing snow and wood chips together. The others were quiet. Alex didn't know if they were all lost in their thoughts or afraid to speak.

A burst of noise from the jungle gym made Alex look over and blink. Aiden was standing on one platform, surrounded by red plastic and scowling up at Nicki. She was a few feet above him on the higher platform with a triumphant smile.

"Aren't we a bit old for playing pretend?" Aiden huffed. Alex blinked and tried to catch up with what they'd been talking about.

"Get off my spaceship."

A laugh escaped Alex. She couldn't help it. She'd missed most of the conversation and her mind was more than happy to help fill in the gaps. Laughter filled her chest, forcing her lungs to expand and her heart to race. Nicki and Aiden looked at her, and while Aiden pouted, Nicki grinned even wider, looking very pleased with herself. Then Avani joined in the laughter and shook her head affectionately. Nicki was all but glowing.

As the laughter faded away, Alex exhaled a relieved breath. Merlin would be happy that she laughed. He'd never been one for brooding. Sitting up straighter in the swing, Alex gave Nicki a soft smile and glanced towards the funeral home as more people departed.

"It was well attended," Alex offered.

"Yeah," Aiden agreed. "He'd been at the university for years. It was nice to see so many students."

Alex nodded in agreement, and tried not to think about the pair she'd overheard complaining that their schedules for the spring semester were messed up with Professor Yates dead.

"It was." Bran nodded and caught Alex's eye. "And no one asked too many questions."

"Whatever Morgana did certainly covered things up." Nicki didn't sound thrilled with that, but Alex didn't blame her. "I still can't believe…" She trailed off, and Alex felt Nicki's eyes on her.

"Me too." Alex watched her boots drag across the ground and drummed her fingers against the swing chains. "After all this time, he's gone." Arto's pain radiated through her head, and Alex shivered. "I just hope that Morgana's doing okay."

"Speak of the devil," Jenny said.

Looking up, Alex's gaze found Morgana walking across the snow-dusted lawn of the park. The woman's stride was long, but her pace was slow. A shadow hung over Morgana, and Alex's heart ached for her. Arto's memories of Morgana turning against the Sídhe to help him and Merlin replayed vividly in her mind. Ever since then, Morgana had at least had Merlin, even as she had outlived their mother, her husband, and all other friends. She wanted to say something, but didn't know where to start.

"Morgana." Avani nodded to the newcomer.

Morgana had aged in the past week. Her long dark hair was in its usual braid, but Alex swore that there was a sheen of gray that hadn't been there before. The lines around Morgana's green eyes were more pronounced than ever, and there were dark bags under them that even makeup couldn't cover. Dressed all in black with a heavy coat, Morgana seemed too small and frail, even though she'd always been shorter than Alex.

"Thank you for waiting."

"Of course." Aiden's voice was soft and gentle. "I'm sorry we couldn't stay."

"I was the chief mourner as his best friend." Morgana raised her chin a little. Alex hoped no one had raised a stink over that. "While it was known that you were close to him, there was no reason to create more questions than we needed to." Morgana sighed and walked over to the swings. She sat down in the empty swing next to Alex. "But it's over now."

"Except for taking his ashes to Stonehenge," Bran said. "That is still the plan, right?"

"It is. We missed our chance this year, so next year it needs to be done." Morgana nodded, but then paused. She still didn't look at Alex. "If I'm no longer here, please be sure that it is done."

Everyone tensed at the words. Jenny made a small sound of alarm but lowered her eyes and said nothing. A new chill settled into Alex's bones, and it wasn't from the winter cold. Glancing across the street at the funeral home, she noted that the last of the cars were leaving. Given that Merlin was gone, she supposed it was natural that Morgana would think of her own mortality now.

"We will," Alex promised. "But don't be in a hurry, okay?"

"Fine." Morgana straightened up, her gloved hands reaching up to hold the chains of the swing. "If you're free next weekend, I could use some assistance in moving."

"You're moving?" Nicki asked.

"Yes. As fond as I am of my house, Merlin's home is where the black-smith shop is. Either I need to move in, or a couple of you need to. I'm afraid it isn't large enough for all of you." Morgana almost smiled, and Alex wondered how difficult it had been for Morgana to find a house with five bedrooms. "My home, while comfortable, doesn't have that critical resource."

"Uh," Lance raised his hand with a hint of nervousness. "Do you own the house? Or do you need to use more magic?"

"We both maintained wills," Morgana said dryly. "Never expected... we didn't expect it to be an issue, but given that we have both faked our deaths many times, we've always kept such affairs in order." Morgana's lips twitched, and Alex thought she might smile. "There was one incident when we were living in Spain. Merlin had to take off rather quickly."

"What were you? Wife or daughter?" Bran asked.

"That's flattering, Bran, but I wasn't usually mistaken as young enough for his daughter. If Merlin had appeared as old as the stories paint him, it would have been another story. No, in that period, I inherited his property as his sister."

Frowning, Alex searched her memories, but nothing came forth. Then again, she knew that while many lifetimes were rattling around in her skull, they didn't nearly cover the whole three-thousand-year span. Merlin and Morgana had lived decades at a time without contact with any incarnation of the Iron Soul.

"I'm glad to hear that," Nicki said. Alex blinked and forced herself to pay attention to the conversation. "I mean, that you and Merlin were prepared. You're already exhausted from..." Nicki trailed off, but everyone knew she was referring to Morgana's use of magic to make Merlin's death seem normal. There hadn't been a body to bring back, so Morgana had been relying on altering memories. "I'm glad you don't have to do anything else."

"I suppose so. It can't be helped. I don't want us to lose access to the forge, nor do I want to separate you children into two houses."

"That's fair, I suppose," Bran said. His eyes jumped over to Alex. "I'm not sure that we should split up right now." There was a long pause. "Maybe we shouldn't leave you alone in the house. One of us could rotate staying in the second bedroom."

"I'll manage. Ambrose and I lived together for centuries, but we enjoyed having privacy when it was possible." A wistful smile appeared on Morgana's face, and a memory from Michel's childhood pushed itself to the front of Alex's mind. "Besides, the Light is dead. It wanted Ambrose's body. The Fae are without a leader; the Old Ones and Demons are nervous about the Darkness. I don't think that there is a terrestrial threat to be concerned with right now."

With Morgana saying the word Darkness, the atmosphere around their little group shifted. In the past week, since the death of the Light, their focus had changed. Jenny, Lance, and Bran had all canceled their holiday plans for Christmas in favor of staying with their friends. Alex had spent much of her time at Morgana's house, unwilling to leave her alone, but in that time, they'd never discussed the Darkness. Now, Morgana was bringing it up in her usual blunt manner. Alex wasn't sure if she should be relieved or scared.

"So, we're going to talk about it now?" Nicki's voice was odd, as if she'd tried to put some sarcasm or cheer into her tone and tripped to fall into terror. "The Darkness?"

"It seems that we must." Morgana sighed and rubbed her eyes. "Merlin and I were operating under the assumption that it was still a distant threat, but the knowledge that it reached Earth centuries ago is unsettling."

"I don't understand that," Jenny said. "Is it moving at different rates?"

"It could be." Aiden gave Jenny a tight, pained smile. "I mean, when it comes across a world, then that-" Aiden paused, his features paling and his mouth tightening. "It would take more time to consume a world rather than move through empty space. Depending on the structure of the Tree of Reality, it might just go around worlds in some places."

"Or there might be branches that are long gone." Bran shook his head, flexing his hands in aggravation. "Not good, no matter how you look at it."

"But where did it come from?" Avani asked. "Given how similar it is to the poison, there doesn't seem to be any sentience behind it so I don't think it's a living thing."

"No." Alex shook her head. Furrowing her brow, she thought back to the time she'd spent floating in the Tree of Reality. Her skin tingled at the mere memory. "It isn't a living thing." Certainty was solid in her chest, even if Alex wasn't sure if it was a good thing or a bad thing. "When I was in the Tree of Reality, I could perceive most of it. The Tree isn't anything really solid, at least I don't think so. The shape of it seems to be how the worlds connect to each other. I get the sense that there's some sort of energy field around it."

Bran raised an eyebrow and the corner of his mouth ticked up, but he didn't correct her. Once again, Alex wished that she'd just studied physics. Maybe this would be easier if she had. Instead, she'd devoted years to the study of literature, which meant that she saw the terrifying patterns in her own life. Not very useful, no matter how much Nicki and Aiden tried to make her more genre-savvy.

"Honestly, I'm not even sure where to start in sorting this out," Bran said. "Alex's statement about energy flowing from the base of the tree and into other worlds has thrown me for a loop."

"Are you sure, Alex?" Morgana asked. Her intense gaze settled on her, and Alex frowned. "You could be mistaken."

"That's what I saw," Alex insisted. "And it's what my instincts say is true. I don't know what that energy was exactly, it wasn't magic, but for all we know it's some kind of... I don't know, mental energy. Maybe it's the reason why all these worlds have sapient life. Maybe it's necessary. Whatever the Darkness is, like the poison, it corrodes that." Bran wrinkled his nose at her suggestion, and Alex sighed. She was out of her depth here. "All I know is that there is a connection that flows between the worlds. I think the Light was correct that it could be cut, but given that the connections carry something forth, I'm worried about the side effects."

"Yeah," Nicki agreed. "We may never get to know all the secrets of the Tree, but that doesn't mean that we can just prune it to the trunk."

Morgana sighed. "The Darkness-"

"A year ago, you didn't believe in it," Nicki reminded Morgana firmly.

"That is true," Morgana admitted. Her shoulders slumped slightly. "But we need to address the threat. But I'm not sure where to start." Then she looked at each of them in turn with a soft, sad smile. "You children are incredible. All of you have learned so much about the Iron Realm. You've come such a long way since that first day in class when the Connections formed." Morgana smiled at Lance and Jenny gently, her eyes far warmer towards them than Alex had ever seen. "You've shown your loyalty to each other, and together you've dealt with far more threats than any other generation of mages has had to. I'm sorry that I don't have the answers you need, but I have faith that you will find them."

"Yes." Alex nodded in agreement. The others didn't look so certain, but she smiled softly. "Guys, I've remembered more and more of Akule's life since his hiding spell was broken. He had no knowledge of magic, and yet he was able to heal the rip in the sky that the Darkness was coming through."

"I suppose so." Nicki tilted her head and rubbed her hands together to hold off the cold. "I've been meaning to ask: where did the iron come from?"

Now Alex's smile widened, and she climbed off the swing. The memory of the blazing object in the sky filled her chest with new strength. "It fell out of the sky. An iron meteorite hit a nearby mountain right when he needed it the most." Alex watched the others exchange stunned looks. "We've touched on it in the past, but it really seems to be something, some force directing events. It isn't always pleasant, but we've always pulled through with help. Maybe it's magic itself in the Earth, or maybe it's even bigger than that, but everything has been leading to us fighting the Darkness. We'll win. I know it."

"That's the most optimistic thing I've heard from you in years," Bran said.

"I suppose so." Alex exhaled and watched her breath dance in the cold air. "I hope you're with me on this, because I think we might have to do something a bit crazy."

"How crazy?" Morgana asked. She stood up and shifted closer to Alex, her green eyes studying Alex intently.

"Find the source of the Darkness," Alex declared, "and stop it there."

"Leave Earth?" Aiden's eyes were wide.

"Our options are to cut Earth off from the rest of the Tree of Reality, and we all agree that's too dangerous, or to do nothing and know that as more worlds fall, more and more beings are going to flee here and cause problems and that, eventually, the Darkness will break through again. Except next time, it'll be worse than the small breach Akule dealt with. Sooner or later, only the Iron Realm will remain. All branches lead here."

Shaking her head, Alex was aware of a laugh trying to bubble up in her chest. "I exist to protect the Iron Realm, but this time, I think that means taking the risk and leaving."

Morgana's eyes were wide with fear, but there was a flicker of understanding in them. Her fellow mages and the three magicians of varying skill levels were staring at her nervously. No one tried to argue. Alex figured that at this point, they'd all gotten the hints that whatever force had created her and allowed Merlin and Morgana to exist was giving them. Of course, that didn't make the idea any less terrifying.

2

Metal and Grief

Bringing Mjǫllnir down on the thin strip of iron, Alex inhaled the hot air and basked in the sharp metallic ring. Things were better in the forge. This was a place of purpose. While she was here working, the rest of the world and the problems waiting for her became secondary. Setting Mjǫllnir down on the worktable, Alex used a small set of tongs with long handles to pick up the iron. She pushed it back into the heat of the forge. Hot coals sparked with light, like stars in the night sky.

Alex's magic churned in her chest, reacting to her storming emotions and sense of purpose. She'd come a long way from freshman year when she'd struggled to use magic at all. It seemed a lifetime ago, and in many ways, she was farther from being that girl then she was from being Arto. Back then, trying to make new friends and manage classes had been her priority. She'd been foolish enough to fall for Arthur's show and, worse, fall for him. As the voices of her other selves whispered to her, Alex could admit that she felt very far removed from the girl she'd been then. Like iron, she'd been put into the fire and hammered into a new shape in the time since she walked out of the Sídhe tunnel at the dawn of Beltane.

With a quirk of her lips, Alex shifted the tongs to her left hand and picked the Hammer up for another round. Mjǫllnir hummed in her hand, a gentle sensation that grounded Alex and fought to keep her focused. She brought the Hammer down on the strip of iron, shaping it into a flatter piece and filling it with magic. A faint shimmer was rising to the surface as the metal accepted the flow of energy. Alex could only hope that all of this work would be worth it when they reached the next world.

With a smooth, practiced motion, she put the metal back into the heat of the furnace and set Mjǫllnir down. A soft sigh escaped her and she closed her eyes, letting herself breathe. The spark of her magic was flickering in her chest as her arms trembled, and a dull ache was spreading through her body. Her fingers spasmed in time with her heartbeat in a stern warning that she was approaching her limit. Opening her eyes, she rolled her shoulders and stretched her arms in front of her.

Alex's eyes shifted to a nearby worktable. Merlin's unfinished projects were pushed to the side, and Alex's heart twisted as she realized that he'd never finish them. They'd been moved to make room for the pile of small round disks of forged iron that she'd already made. All of them carried some magic, but no will or intent to give them power. They were her hope of making magical batteries just in case they couldn't use magic in the other world. Morgana had used magic in the Sídhe tunnels, but that guaranteed nothing. Alex wanted to be hopeful; she wished that she had Merlin's optimism, but she didn't. He was gone.

The thought made Alex swallow. She returned to her work, pulling out the piece of iron and striking it repeatedly with Mjǫllnir. Without a clear shape to guide her motions, waves of grief, desperation, and anger fueled Alex's actions. She just hammered the metal, shoving magic into it with every blow until it was wide and flat. It wasn't a true circle, but it had been flattened in a way that gave it a vaguely circular shape and was about four inches wide. It would be easier to pack now.

Sweat trickled down the back of her bare neck. The long blonde hair piled up on her head in a messy bun was damp. On some level, Alex knew she was probably overdue to cut her hair off, given how much time she spent in combat and in the forge. But she couldn't bring herself to. She'd had long hair all of her life, and while she had it, when she looked at the photographs of her and her family, Alex could still believe she was that girl. Almost everything had changed, and she wanted to hold on to the few things that hadn't.

Her magic gathered in her chest again, the familiar spark flaring to life at her call and promising to obey her. Through her feet, Alex could feel the pulse of the Iron Realm, and more magic being gently pumped into her easing her exhaustion. When they left, this would be gone. Terror swept in, and the voices grew louder in response. Alex pushed it all away and focused on driving the magic into the metal. She swung Mjǫllnir and poured what she had left into the iron. It shimmered, a soft gray glow traveling through the iron, and settling deep within the disk.

Lowering Mjǫllnir, Alex slipped the tool into the leather loop that was fixed to her belt. It was hanging on her left side in the leather loop holster that Nicki had made. Alex hoped that it would be enough when they started traveling, but maybe she needed to talk with Nicki about making something stronger. As she used the tongs to pick up the metal and put it in the mineral oil, Mjǫllnir gently bumped her leg. When the metal was cool, Alex toweled it off and carried it over to the stack of misshapen iron disks that were already waiting for their departure. It joined the others with a clang, and Alex pulled off her leather work gloves.

There was nothing more to do in here. Her eyes traced the stack of enchanted metal, but Alex's chest throbbed in warning. Her time in the forge was done for the day. She cleaned up the tools she'd used and made sure that the furnace was cooling before grabbing the coat she'd worn on her way over. It was too hot inside the forge, but she was grateful for it as soon as she opened the door. Scampering to the house, Alex hissed as the cold air stung her sweat-damp skin. She briefly regretted not putting her coat on, but she was too sweaty for that.

Thankfully, the back door was unlocked, and Alex quickly bundled herself inside. The house was toasty warm, and a kettle of water on the stove was beginning to bubble. It should have been cozy, but the feel of the house had changed. Alex had never realized how much Merlin filled up the space. There had always been a lingering sense of him here. The smell of him and a slight afterimage of his power. All of that was quickly fading.

It was all too sad to think about, and Alex hung up her coat. She tossed it over a chair and headed to the sink. Alex washed her hands, cleaning off the sweat and the flecks of ash that clung to her skin before splashing some water on her face and the back of her neck. As her vision cleared, she looked out the window towards the backyard. It was a sunny weekend, but snow still covered the ground. The trail she'd made to the workshop from the backdoor was apparent.

The number of boxes in the living room was shockingly low. The furniture was largely the same, though Morgana had switched out Merlin's sofa with the more elegant one from her home. It didn't quite fit the rest of the décor, and Alex wondered how much Morgana would change things.

Some of the photos had been replaced with ones from Morgana's home. Her trinkets and personal items were scattered around in the living room and kitchen. Yet, the place still felt like Merlin's home. Alex suspected that it would for a long time. She could hear Morgana down the hall, probably in Merlin's- no, her bedroom. If it was strange for Alex, it was certainly worse for Morgana.

The teapot whistled, and Alex moved back into the kitchen. She pulled the pot off the heat and reached into a cupboard for a mug. Morgana's footfalls grew louder behind her, and Alex pulled down a second mug for herself. The professor made no sound of surprise as she entered the kitchen, and Alex was reassured that her presence had been noted earlier thanks to her car out front.

"Good morning," Morgana greeted. She was dressed in jeans and an old Ravenslake sweatshirt, with her long dark hair in its usual braid. There were shadows under her eyes that Alex decided against mentioning. "No, good afternoon," Morgana corrected with a glance at the clock that was peacefully ticking on the nearby wall.

"I hope I didn't disturb you," Alex said. She poured the hot water into two mugs and stepped to the side to grant Morgana access.

"You didn't." Morgana nodded to the small kitchen table as she reached for her box of tea bags. "Have a seat."

Alex obeyed, sitting down and looking out into the yard once again while Morgana worked on their tea. Dark clouds were gathering on the horizon, hinting at the possibility of more snow.

"You've been in the workshop almost every day," Morgana said as she sat down. The professor slid Alex's mug of tea over to her and took a sip of her own. "Everything alright?"

"Yeah." Alex took a sip of the warm tea. "Just trying to make sure that we have enough enchanted iron to take with us."

"We don't even know if we'll be able to use it." Morgana sighed, her shoulders sagging, and she rested her elbows on the table. "I understand your reasoning, Alex, I do, but I can't help but worry."

"I'm worried too." Alex swallowed, and they sat in silence for several long minutes. "I wish Merlin was here."

"He never would have agreed to the plan."

"Probably not," Alex chuckled. "But at least I'd feel better about leaving the Iron Realm if he could stay here with you."

"I'm not staying. I'm going with you."

"You should stay here." Alex's protest was weak. She wasn't surprised. "You're the last Grand Mage."

Morgana snorted at the words. "Grand Mage." She rolled her eyes. "And you're the Iron Soul. We have no idea what will happen if you die in another world. We could lose you forever." Morgana's grip on her mug was turning her fingers white, and she was staring at the tea as if it held all the answers she needed. "I don't like the idea of leaving, but you're not going without me. We will contact our allies and give them the information we have." A soft sigh escaped Morgana. "I haven't always gotten along with the Old Ones, but this is their home now, and they will defend it." She finally looked up at Alex. "Do you want to take the Trishula with us?"

"I don't know." Alex took another drink to buy time to consider the question. "Maybe. I hate the idea of taking it back from Shiva. There can be no arguing that he's used it well over the centuries and kept the Demons in check."

"He doesn't need it to fight them," Morgana reminded her. "And the Trishula's purification power could be beneficial to us."

Alex shifted. Morgana had a point, but they'd never had the chance to use the Trishula on the Darkness or poison. It had never occurred to her, and now she could only feel stupid for it. Lokpal tried to reassure her, but Alex's stomach still tightened in frustration. There was too much to keep track of, and so many details that always had to be considered. Then again, the very idea of taking the Trishula back from Shiva made her nervous. He'd give it up in an instant, but with them leaving, he and other Old Ones alongside the few magicians that were alive would be all there was to defend the planet.

"Maybe," Alex said. "But what would be pure in another world?" she asked as her thoughts started working again. "I'm not sure what the Trishula's power would do in another world. Besides... I'm not sure that I want to risk taking all of the items away from the Iron Realm."

"The Urn will stay here."

"The Urn..." Alex trailed off. "I'm not sure if it has any power outside of holding the Darkness in check so we could verify our theories." That was an unsettling idea, but Akule had been sure that the Darkness was needed for something. Her left hand burned as the memory pushed through. "Anyway, you're right that we won't be taking it. I'm just sorry that we can't lay Merlin to rest at Stonehenge before we go."

Alex regretted the words immediately. Morgana tensed up, and somehow her grip on the mug tightened further. A faint spark of silver zinged along the smooth ceramic surface. It scared her: she'd never seen Morgana lose control of her magic. Holding her breath, she waited for Morgana to say something or to think of something comforting that wouldn't dig the hole deeper.

"I miss him very much." Morgana's voice was soft. "More than I expected to. I keep checking my phone, thinking that he hasn't checked in, only to remember." Shaking her head, Morgana lowered her eyes as her body trembled. "It's foolish. We had plans in the event of one of us dying, of course. There were contingencies we agreed on, but after thousands of years of war, famine, magic, and morons, I didn't think that anything would ever actually kill us."

"I'm so sorry." Alex reached out and cautiously touched Morgana's hand. The older woman released one hand from her mug and grabbed Alex's hand tightly. "I'm so sorry."

"I don't think you children can even imagine how close we were." Morgana's eyes were still downcast, and Alex had the feeling that the woman was crying. "You saw us banter and argue so often."

"You also always knew what the other was thinking," Alex whispered. "I remember so many times where you two just looked at each other and had a conversation. I'm sure that Merlin knew how much you valued him."

"I'm sure he did. He was annoying about it." Morgana chuckled, but it was a broken sound. She sniffed. "Three thousand years... we weren't always together, of course. There were many times that we separated because there was low magic and no threat. Sometimes, we just needed to get away from each other for a bit. Then we'd feel the magic rise and find each other again. Merlin had the strangest ability to track me down, even if he wasn't very good at scrying."

"I remember you raising me as Mikael."

"He was a good boy. Honestly, he was the easiest of the children I ever raised, though Merlin helping me made it easier." Affection was creeping into Morgana's voice, and she raised her face. Alex could see a few tears rolling down her cheeks. "Most people thought we were married. Apparently, most people at the university figured we were in a relationship."

Alex didn't know what to say to that. She could understand. The way they acted together had always been very much like an old married couple. Alex rubbed Morgana's hand with her thumb as memories of Merlin replayed through her mind. There were so many, and the grief of her other selves who had known him washed over her again. Arto's concern for Morgana was the most intense sensation, and kept Alex from being lost to her sorrow.

"We were lovers on and off," Morgana confessed. "Physical desire didn't affect either of us much at this point. You get to be too old. Everyone is a child to you." Alex said nothing. She really didn't want to think about that. "We always found our way back to being partners. Despite how things started between us, he trusted me. He believed in me." Morgana released her mug and wiped at her eyes, but didn't release Alex's hand. "I'll miss the old man."

"I will too."

Then Morgana pulled her hand away and stood up. Alex stayed seated and didn't follow Morgana as she left the kitchen. A few moments later, Alex heard the sink in the bathroom turn on. Holding in a sigh, Alex flexed her sore fingers and picked up her mug to take another sip. Morgana opening up had been a surprise, but Alex could already tell that they wouldn't be talking about this conversation. Gulping down the rest of her tea, Alex gathered up the mugs and took them to the kitchen sink to clean up. She wished they could take time and process their loss, but the Darkness was coming, and worlds were dying. There wasn't time for mourning.

3

Ashes and Dust

8 00 B.C.E. Northern Cornwall

There were no voices on the wind as it rushed through her hair — no Sídhe taunting her from the dark. Morgana stood on the hill, looking over what had been the field of battle below. Around her, the remaining huts of the village where she had been born were quiet. A hush had taken hold. The world was waking from a long period of fear and battle, but worrying that it was only a dream. At least, she no longer heard the distant singing and plotting of Sídhe forces from their tunnels.

The last Iron Gate was tucked out of her sight, but its magic radiated gently over the area. It wasn't as reliable as a blood protection ward would have been, but Morgana hoped that in time the magic would settle into the ground and repel the Sídhe, or at least, what remained of them. A small, brutal smile appeared on Morgana's face. It wasn't joyful. She had no joy, but there was a sort of harsh satisfaction. She wasn't happy with how everything had turned out, but it could have been worse.

Except that Arto was dead. Her little brother was gone. Rage built in her chest, and Morgana did nothing to stop it. The news that Luegáed and Gwenyvar had run off together had distracted and distressed her brother. Morgana had never liked Gwenyvar, but Arto had adored her.

The knowledge that his wife had just abandoned him had badly shaken Arto. Worse was the fact that she'd left him for his friend Luegáed. When the battle had started, Arto hadn't been at his best, and their forces had been ill at ease because of Luegáed's desertion. If they hadn't been so selfish, her brother might still be alive.

Arto wouldn't approve of her rage, the simmering anger, nor the desire to hunt the pair down and make sure that they knew what their selfishness had caused. The certainty that Arto wouldn't want her to was the only thing holding Morgana back from using her magic to track them down. If they were smart, they would have fled south, far from Morgana and Merlin, and would do their best to lead quiet lives. For the sake of Arto's memory, she wouldn't go looking for them, but if they ever crossed her path…

Morgana eyed the setting sun. The walls of the village were gone. At least one mage needed to stand guard in case of trouble. Down the slope of the hill, a pair of children were playing with a dog. The scene was so familiar from her own childhood with Arto that her heart ached. There'd been a time when he'd been young and innocent. She had never been either, but he'd helped her learn to be happy.

The crimes of the Sídhe were many. They'd stolen her childhood twice over, not even allowing the Changeling they'd left in her place as a young girl to live out a happy life, and their greed had led to the death of her beloved little brother. Their crimes against her and her family were too great for forgiveness, and that did not even take into account the generations of human slaves. Those who had been captured and groomed, as she had been. They never escaped. They lived as slaves and playthings for the Sídhe. The Queen had intended the Iron Realm to be one more world under her control.

Morgana called for the children to come in. The shadows were growing longer as the sun sank, and there was too much of a chance of survivors attacking tonight. There was no army anymore, no horde of Sídhe that could crash down upon them, but with the human forces departing for their homes, vigilance was prudent. She watched the children run up the hill and go straight to one of the roundhouses with the dog following faithfully behind.

Torches were lit before the last of the villagers disappeared inside. Morgana wondered how many would stay. Most of the dead had been cremated, and many were talking of going to join family in other villages. She didn't blame them. The walls of the village were gone, many houses had been lost, and it would be difficult for the survivors to ignore the memories. All of Medraut's worry about the bronze trade might prove meaningless.

She didn't know what would happen. It would seem that in time, iron would take over, but how long it would take Morgana didn't know. Without the valuable tin and copper to make into bronze and trade to the south, they'd have far less wealth to offer in exchange for the fine jewelry and wine that they were fond of. A new world beckoned, and more fear grew in Morgana's heart than she was comfortable with.

The sun had set. Torchlight cast flickering shadows, and she searched the darkness. Walking slowly along the ash line that marked where the village walls had once stood, Morgana stayed on guard. A few men were patrolling and clasping their weapons that were coated in dried blood. She caught sight of violet eyes in the shadows. They were all the warning Morgana needed. Raising her right hand, she summoned her magic. It rushed through her body, and silver sparks burst forth from her fingertips. A soft silver light surrounded her and pushed back the shadows that the Sídhe were slinking through.

"Go back," Morgana ordered. Sneering at a shape moving nearby, she barely resisted the urge to release her power. "I will have no guilt for killing you. It is Merlin and the humans who want this war done, but I am more than willing to finish the job."

"Traitor." She wasn't sure which Sídhe had said that. There were at least three, judging from how the shadows were moving. "Traitor. The Queen trusted you."

"Your Queen stole me from my home, from my family. When I was a traitor, it was to the Iron Realm."

"She raised you."

"She groomed me for war against my world and my family. I have no loyalty to her or her memory. My only regret was that I needed so long to find my true loyalty."

One of the Sídhe hissed and moved. Morgana turned to face it and pushed her magic forward. It was easy. The image of sharp, magical bolts sprang to mind, and the magic formed itself into her chosen shape. Three silver bolts blasted through the Síd's chest. It stumbled back, and Morgana noted that its golden armor was gone. It was dressed only in a simple tunic, and the once elegantly styled hair was in disarray. There was only a moment for it to glare at her before its body wholly dissolved.

Spinning, Morgana dodged the wild swing of a gleaming bronze sword. She flicked her fingers, almost lazily, and smiled as silver light burrowed into the second Síd's chest. There was no need for anything fancy. She told her magic how to destroy her enemies, and it did. The creature died screaming, and its body collapsed into dust as its heart was ripped out by her magic. Morgana smiled and looked to the third and final invader. The guards had come to investigate but were hanging back. That was good; they'd only get in her way.

The third did not run. That was a mistake. Morgana pulled on her magic, forming it into the familiar whip of shimmering light with a quick visualization. She did not give the Síd time to correct its mistake. With a flick of her wrist, she sent the whip slicing through the light leather armor and into flesh. The third turned to dust that the wind carried away. It was done. Three more dead, and hopefully, none coming to take their place. She and Merlin hadn't discussed it, but Morgana carried a hope that the Sídhe wouldn't be able to bear and raise young in their world. That they would do her the kindness of dying out.

A soft sigh escaped Morgana, and she lowered her hands, allowing the whip's magic to dissipate. Merlin would say that it was a waste, but a vicious satisfaction filled her chest. Perhaps she should feel ashamed by it. Arto had been a compassionate man. He'd been good in the truest sense, and Morgana knew that he would have agreed with Merlin's decision not to hunt down all the Sídhe creatures. As long as they stayed away from humans, Morgana would let them be.

Iron was spreading. Medraut had been a filthy traitor, but he'd not been wrong about the impact of iron. While all of the supplies that Arto built up had gone into the Iron Gates, the dam had been broken now. She didn't know how long it would take for the tin and copper trades to dry up, but they would eventually. Iron was superior. It was less labor-intensive, easier to reuse than bronze, and stronger. What it would mean for the merchants and regional leaders, she didn't know. She didn't care.

The guards murmured behind her, and Morgana turned to see what was upsetting them now. A new figure was walking towards them, but this one she knew well. Combing her hair back, Morgana made a half-hearted effort at fixing her braid as Merlin approached. The man was leaning on his staff heavily, and his thoughtful expression did little to mask the grief that hung over him like a storm cloud. Arto's death remained a sharp pain for her, but in her kinder moments, she reminded herself that Arto had been a son to Merlin. He had raised the boy, trained him in using magic and the history of their people. She doubted Merlin had ever assumed that he'd outlive Arto.

"More Sídhe?" Merlin asked.

"Yes. They've been dealt with."

"The attacks are becoming less frequent. That's something."

"I don't know," Morgana hissed. "I'd rather that they all stopped being cowards."

"Morgana."

"I know you want to show mercy, but they were invaders."

"I haven't forgotten, believe me, but we aren't in any condition to prolong the war. Almost all of the iron was used up, and the people are more interested in returning to their lives now. There aren't that many Sídhe in the Iron Realm."

"Any at all is too many."

"Morgana."

"I know, I understand, but... I don't want them here."

"If they attack us, then it is reasonable for us to defend ourselves. We've had luck convincing them to leave humans alone. I don't want to undo that. While their numbers are few, I still don't want to risk that fight."

"Fine." The word was nearly a snarl. "But I won't feel guilty about attacking the ones who attack me!"

"Of course not." Merlin almost smiled at her. "That would be unreasonable. Let's be grateful that most seem content to lay low."

"Information about iron has spread," Morgana said with satisfaction. "They know we know their weakness."

"Indeed." He nodded towards the path in the village. "You rest; I'll take watch."

"I'm fine."

"I'm sure your husband would like to see you."

The mention of Airril made Morgana hesitate. She looked into the darkness around the village and licked her lower lip thoughtfully. It was unlikely that there were more Sídhe hiding out there. They would have all attacked together; numbers were their best advantage. At least, it had been. Merlin was watching her patiently, leaning on his staff and completely ignoring the guards who were staring at them. Morgana supposed she should be grateful that they were still here at all. The uncharitable thought that they were only staying until they packed their homes up and their children were ready to walk crossed her mind, but she pushed it aside. She didn't care if the village was abandoned. Her father was long gone, her step-father was dead, and her mother and brother were lost to her.

So she left the ashes of the wall and allowed Merlin to escort her to her temporary home. There was still much to talk about. They walked slowly, staying near the torches, and both of them checking the darkness. Merlin's eyes were sharp as he checked for threats even as he leaned on his staff as if he were a weak old man. Many had fallen for the act in the past.

"Are you going to stay here?" Merlin asked. "What is your plan now?"

"I don't know." Morgana shook her head. Her mind spun at the very question of what came next. She'd been focusing on just making it through the last few days, but this wouldn't last forever. People were leaving the village now that the war was over. "I suppose that Airril and I should discuss that."

"Yes." Merlin nodded. They were already at the roundhouse she and Airril were using. "Try to rest, Morgana. I'll keep watch."

She entered the roundhouse with a weary sigh. A fire was smoldering in the hearth, releasing waves of heat from the glowing coals that fought off the chill of the night. Airril stood up from the bed, still dressed in his clothing, and very alert. It touched Morgana that he had stayed awake to wait for her despite his long day of assisting in repairs and overseeing distribution of what resources remained.

Airril's gentle expression warmed her, and by some magic that was all his, chased away her lingering anger. It wasn't worth holding onto. When Airril held a hand out to her, Morgana took it and pressed herself against his side. Her husband wrapped his arms around her, and she tucked her head under his chin.

It was strange. Years ago, when her step-father Uthyrn had arranged their marriage, she'd been sure that they would be unhappy. Yet, Airril had proven himself a good and compassionate man. He led his region not with fear, but with respect. People listened to him out of choice. It was a trait that he'd shared with her brother, and one that Morgana respected. Even when she had left their village to travel with Merlin, he'd been supportive, and he'd been faithful to her when she'd been absent from their home. She'd never found the words to express her gratitude and hoped that he knew.

"Any attacks?" he asked.

"Only three Sídhe. Easily dispatched. Merlin said he'd take watch."

"I'm glad. You haven't slept enough."

Morgana didn't reply. She didn't want to admit that her dreams were full of watching Medraut stab her brother while she was frozen in place. Images of the Sídhe tunnels and the Queen she'd once worshiped played out in her mind, taunting her and filling her with regret.

"What happens now?" Morgana asked. "Are we staying?"

"We could stay if you wanted to. Things are peaceful for the moment, but those who came here to help are already leaving. Soon, it will only be the farmers and traders. The biggest issue is who will be the new leader."

"Medraut was the heir through Uthyrn," Morgana sighed. "Even though my father was the one who originally led here. With mother gone...." Her voice tightened.

"I'm so sorry, Morgana." Airril kissed her forehead. "I spoke with my men. They tried to convince Eigyr to leave, but-"

"I know. That's not your fault. It wasn't your fault last week, and it isn't today." Morgana shook her head and looked into the small fire. "I miss her, but at least she was dead before having to learn that Arto was gone."

"Through you, I could claim leadership. Our village could pass to my cousin."

"No." The response slipped from her and Morgana finally settled on her choice. "I don't want to stay here, Airril. Thank you, but no." Laying down on the bed, she tugged her husband's arm. He settled down beside her, and Morgana breathed a little easier. "I want to take Arto's bones to the Great Circle. Then... then I want to go home."

Airril said nothing, but he nodded. The fire's glow dimmed, and Morgana's body relaxed into the mattress. Aches and pains that had plagued her all day eased as Airril rested a hand on her hip. His lips brushed her forehead, and tears sprang to her eyes. She didn't want to cry again. Morgana feared that was all she had done for the past few days, but her throat was tightening. Airril shifted closer. Laying her head against his chest, Morgana inhaled his warm, earthy scent. He smelled of the earth, and the smell of soot and ash was finally fading. Her eyes slid shut, and she exhaled. It still hurt, but she could hope that things would look better in the morning.

4

Doubts of the Future

Bran stumbled on the stairs and grabbed at the railing to catch himself. A yawn escaped him, his jaw cracking at the force of it, and he dragged himself up a few more steps. Coffee was his only clear thought. He needed coffee, and he could smell it. At the rate Morgana and Alex were planning, they'd be leaving soon, and coffee would become a rare luxury if they even took some.

He made it to the kitchen. It wasn't as clean as normal. Timothy was gone, passing messages to regional Fae for Morgana and keeping his ear open for any dangerous rumors. Thankfully there was coffee in the pot, and a few mugs set out and waiting. Bran grabbed one and poured himself a full mug before raiding the fridge to find some milk. It wasn't perfect, but it was just what he needed to get going. A glance at the clock after his first deep drink made him grimace. It was past ten, and he was only now getting up.

The lack of classes and a schedule were wreaking havoc on him. There were things to do, but Alex and Morgana were overseeing most of it. Lance had been going over different camping gear with Alex the night before, and jobs were assigned here and there for shopping runs, but it wasn't enough. He was a doer, but right now, he was in limbo. They all were.

Taking another sip, Bran could feel the gears in his head start to move. Letting Aiden talk him into video games last night had been a mistake. A fun mistake that had distracted him from the existential crisis trying to brew in his head, but a mistake nonetheless. Now Bran could hear voices and realized that people were in the dining room. He took another sip and let himself finish waking up before going to investigate.

Morgana and Alex were side by side at the table with their backs to him. They must have already noticed and dismissed him while he was getting his coffee. Bran could see some papers spread out in front of Alex and frowned. Maps wouldn't do any good, so he could only imagine that they were lists.

"So, you don't know for sure what the closest world in the beast branch is?" Alex asked. Bran took a step closer.

"Emrys and the White Dragon were brought through, but the extent of Cathanáil's powers to open and close portals is unknown. They might be from the closest world or another further up the tree. When portals are torn open, it's hard to control them. I don't think I need to remind you what Thor experienced."

Alex chuckled softly. "No, you don't. He spent years chasing down Frost Giants even after the corrupted Sídhe had been dealt with."

"Then you understand my point. To this day, I don't fully understand why those other holes opened. Knowing what I know now... it makes me wonder if the Darkness might have been involved."

"What?" Bran was glad that Alex asked because he'd been about to. "What do you mean by that?"

"When the Sídhe pushed through, it shocked Merlin and I. We'd been certain that the Iron Gates and their magical protection would hold, but somehow the Sídhe made a hole. But luckily, the effect of pushing through the protections scared the Sídhe, so they didn't try breaking through again. Instead, they waited for the magic of the Iron Gates to deteriorate."

"And you think they might have used the Darkness the first time?"

"I don't know." Morgana shrugged and shifted in her seat. Bran was tempted to circle the table so he could see their expressions. "Anyway, that doesn't really matter now."

"It might. I'm sure that the Sídhe homeworld has fallen, but if they have any Darkness-"

"We shouldn't assume. I shouldn't have mentioned it," Morgana stated firmly. "If they had Darkness, then I'm sure it would have been weaponized a long time ago."

Bran relaxed a little. That was a good point. He still didn't fully understand how the other races opened portals, but he was beginning to suspect that they had more magic in their worlds than Morgana believed. While she and Merlin said universes clashing created magic, the existence of the Darkness opened up new possibilities for explanations. Bran had long since learned that the Grand Mages didn't know everything.

"Good point." Alex sighed. "Okay, supplies are still going to be our biggest issue."

"They always are."

"We're limited in what we can carry and how fast we can move. Not to mention, we need to decide how much we're willing to expose ourselves."

"I don't have any answers for you," Morgana said. "The matter of exposing ourselves will depend on what we find. The Fae and Demons are physically similar to humans and can hide amongst us, but the other creatures can't. We may find ourselves in a similar situation of being too different from the natives to hide ourselves."

"I wish you knew more about the Tree of Reality."

"Merlin and I always believed that protecting the Iron Realm was our priority." Morgana's tone was dry, and Bran grimaced in sympathy for Alex. "There's nothing we can do, Alex." Morgana's voice turned gentle. "If you want to try this, then understand that we can't plan for everything."

A sigh escaped Alex. She leaned back in the chair, and Bran headed for the stairs, planning a retreat to his room. He didn't know what to say and knew that Morgana was right. It was something that he didn't want to think about too hard. Bran wished he had a brilliant idea of how to help. Nicki had been brainstorming, but Alex was right about there being a limit on what they could take with them. Despite all her hopes, Nicki had never figured out how to make transdimensional bags that could hold more than they should.

Even the major magical items created by the Iron Soul were pretty limited when you really looked at them. Cathanáil was the most impressive, serving as a weapon and able to open portals between worlds. Mjǫllnir had the ability to call lightning and functioned as a magically enhanced tool. Alex had used it to break the Queen's spell and break the Iron Chain, so it was probably the most useful. Both of them were being taken, and Bran had kept his fear that they'd lose their power away from Earth to himself. There was nothing they could do about it if that happened.

The Iron Chalice was Bran's favorite. He was biased thanks to it healing his old injuries, and he knew it. But it went deeper than that; he was connected to the Chalice. Sometimes when he woke from vivid dreams, he thought he might remember a bit about his past life in Wales with

Gofiben, but he wasn't sure. There was always a lingering sense of pride and determination, but also grief, which he didn't fully understand. He had suspicions, of course, but nothing that he was sure about. Those were their three major items. Shiva still had the Iron Trishula, and there was the Urn, but Bran knew they wouldn't be disturbing Merlin's ashes.

Bran's stomach rumbled, but he decided that he'd raid his stash of granola bars rather than go back into the kitchen. Maybe it was cowardly not to help, but he had nothing to offer. There was nothing he knew about the worlds that could help, and his attempts to scry had been useless. It was a wonder that Alex had ever seen the dying world of Sídhe. Or maybe there was more to it than that; perhaps something had helped her, and thoughts like that took him down a road that Bran was afraid of.

He felt cowardly as he retreated downstairs. This was happening, no matter how he felt about it, no matter if instinct told him it was madness. Every time they talked about it, his stomach turned. He understood why Alex wanted to go, but Bran had a bad feeling. It wasn't grounded in anything, but he couldn't shake it.

When he stepped into the converted basement he shared with Aiden, Bran raised an eyebrow at the pair of sneakers that were discarded by the door. A pair of jeans were thrown over the back of Aiden's desk chair. Books and random computer parts were jumbled on Aiden's desk around his laptop. Aiden's hamper was full of clean clothes that had yet to be folded. Normally, Aiden attempted to keep his side tidy, and Bran hadn't noticed the mess in his sleepy search for coffee.

His roommate was in a similar state of disarray. Aiden's dark hair was sticking up in random directions, which highlighted that it needed to be cut, and he was dressed in his plaid night pants and a chemistry pun t-shirt. He had one sock on and the other in his hand as he set his phone on his desk, a stunned expression on his face.

"I'm meeting Robin for lunch," Aiden said. His eyes were wide.

"Okay, so?" Bran was pretty sure he already knew the answer.

"It's a date," Aiden hissed. "An actual date, as in we agreed on it!"

"Oh." Bran paused and gathered his thoughts. "I thought you'd be happy?"

"I am... sort of." Aiden slumped back onto his bed. "Robin is great. She's insanely smart and witty. But she's also an Old One."

"Thor married an Old One. They're nice people; most of them anyway, as long as they don't go crazy."

"I know that." Aiden huffed, and struggled with what to say. Bran waited in silence to give him some time to think. "We're getting ready to leave for who knows how long. I know that we're thinking it'll only be a couple of weeks tops just based on food and trying to avoid letting the other worlds mess with us too much, but things could go wrong. It's bad enough that my parents are freaking out, but now I'm thinking about starting a relationship?"

"Robin knows what is going on," Bran reminded him. He took another sip of his coffee, grateful that he'd gotten another cup before this drama started. "You can tell her the truth, and she'll understand. Robin was born here, but she knows about the homeworld, thanks to her parents. She knows the scale of what is at stake, at least in theory."

"You're right." Aiden shook his head. "You're right." Aiden didn't seem calmed at all and inhaled slowly. Bran watched him gather his thoughts and kept sipping his coffee. "When Nicki and Avani started dating, I was happy for Nicki, but I was jealous, too." Aiden gave him a sheepish look. "I love Nicki, she's my rock, but I couldn't help but be jealous that she had someone in her life that could understand."

"You haven't dated much."

"Not since Sarah and I broke up." Aiden shrugged. "I have fun sometimes, but a relationship needs communication and honesty, and it feels like I can't give someone that."

"Except Robin knows about magic."

"Yeah, but she's not human." Aiden shifted on his bed, crossing his legs and appearing completely dejected. "Am I horrible for saying that?"

"I don't think so." Bran sat on his own bed and gave himself a moment to think of the right words. "Our popular culture might be full of hybrid creatures, but humanity hasn't had to deal with that yet. Well, not in modern times. Our ancestors, yours potentially more than mine, interbred with Neanderthals, but that's as close as we've gotten. It seems natural to be a little cautious about starting a relationship."

"She likes me," Aiden said. There was a hint of red on his cheeks. "I'm not sure why. Robin used to be Puck, THE Puck. She's an Old One with centuries of knowledge... and yet she likes me." Bewildered, Aiden shook his head. "Alex says that we can trust her, but part of me wonders if this is some kind of trap."

Bran considered the idea for a moment. "I doubt it. Morgana doesn't like her much, but Morgana tolerates her. If there was any doubt in Morgana's mind, then Robin would have already been destroyed. Besides, Sif had a relationship with Thor."

"And that's not weird to think about at all."

"I'm just pointing out that mages and Old Ones can have happy lives together. I can understand you wanting someone in your life."

"The timing is bad. We're talking about going into other worlds to stop the Darkness. This isn't the time."

"Given how the last few years have gone, there won't ever be a good time."

And there it was. The looming trip into other worlds and the shadow of their mission. Bran wished that they could have left the day of Merlin's funeral before there was time to think about it. That hadn't been possible. There were allies to alert, supplies to gather, and they had to at least try to make a plan. He sighed and rubbed his thumb against the ceramic mug as his thoughts went places he didn't want them to.

"What are we doing, Bran? Are we really doing this? Is Morgana really letting Alex do this?"

"The other option is to stay here and do nothing," Bran pointed out. "It might not impact us again. With the Light dead and Arthur long gone, there might not be any more fights in our lifetimes, but there will be more fights in the future as desperate creatures try to escape their worlds."

"So, it's us now, or other mages in the future?"

"Morgana and Merlin were blunt about us being one of the larger groups," Bran replied. He had always wondered why, and now considered that this was it. Had they always been coming to this moment? He didn't like that idea. "And we have the Sword, the Hammer, and the Chalice, so we're better equipped than most."

"Not according to Nicki," Aiden grumbled. "She's desperately trying to come up with something that will help us. Not having classes to distract her... well, if she has her way, we'll have cloaks of invisibility or something."

"Do you think she can pull that off?" Bran was truly curious. She'd managed to hide Cathanáil while it was in the scabbard she'd made. "If we wait longer?"

"I doubt it. She'll try, but I'm worried that she'll hurt herself if we let her. Besides, we have no idea how magical objects will work in the other worlds." Aiden waved a hand dismissively. "I'll keep an eye on her and remind her to ask for help if she comes up with something. Invisibility won't hide our scents or sounds anyway, so I doubt it would help that much."

"Fair point. Remind her of that."

"I will." Aiden licked his lips, and Bran got a bad feeling about what was about to be said. "Have you told your mom what's going on?" Aiden asked softly.

"Not yet," Bran admitted. "Have you told your family?"

Aiden grimaced. "I told them it's a peace conference, but we don't know how long we'll be gone. Given that Merlin died... they aren't happy about it." He shook his head. "I know Alex was right, intellectually, I know that, but I think lying would have been easier." Then Aiden jumped to his feet and grabbed his phone. "Oh shit! I need to shower if I'm going to be on time to meet Robin."

Bran blinked at the sudden 180 and watched his roommate grab clothes and his shower tote. He ran out of the room, leaving his spare sock in the middle of the floor. A small, almost sad chuckle escaped Bran. He clung to the amusement. There might not be much more of it for a while if things went wrong, and they usually did.

He was a coward. Bran put down his mug on his nightstand and stood up to gather clothing for the day. Aiden's cheerfulness rubbed him the wrong way, and he pressed his lips tightly together. He was a coward, the same coward that he'd always been and the same coward that he suspected he'd been in his earlier life. Reincarnation, it seemed, couldn't change that.

5

Reaching Through an Iron Gate

The snow crackled under Alex's feet as she climbed the slope of the hillside. Theoretically the hiking trails were closed for the winter, and she was certain that the forest service didn't think anyone would even try, but mages couldn't allow such things to stop them. Alex grabbed onto a nearby branch to keep herself steady as the crushed snow turned slick. Hoisting herself up the hill, she found a rock beneath the snow and used it as leverage to get a little further.

Behind her, the others were hiking in a line, and Alex just hoped that the snow mixing with mud didn't get someone hurt. This wasn't the best weather for a trek through the forest, but they couldn't wait for spring. It was barely January, and there was too much to do and too much at stake. Still, as her foot slipped a little with her next step, Alex did feel guilty for dragging them all out here.

Their line was oddly quiet. Everyone was focusing on staying upright or too lost in their own thoughts. Alex had no idea what she could say to lift their spirits. Merlin's absence was distinct. There was no thumping of his walking stick on the ground or soft distracted humming. Instead, there was a heavy silence that reminded Alex that her mentor of so many lifetimes was gone, and all that remained were memories and ashes in a centuries-old jar.

The ending of Akule's spell had brought new memories with it to be sorted. Alex still didn't fully understand how he had cast the spell. Akule's memories of that moment were distorted by the pain he'd been in. All she could do was chalk it up to instinct. She'd cast similar spells at this point, but nothing that strong. If there'd been more time, she would have thought to check if the spell had been anchored into the Iron Urn.

She hadn't been lying about the iron meteorite falling to Earth at just the right time. Akule hadn't possessed any knowledge of metallurgy, and there hadn't been time for him to figure it out. Instead, in some kind twist of fate, what he needed had been delivered. He'd use magic to shape it rather than relying on hammers and fire. It had been more like clay to him than metal was to Alex. While it was a relief to know that everything had worked out alright, it brought back an old question.

Was there an intelligence behind magic? Merlin had been born from a Síd raping his human mother. Such violence hadn't been uncommon, and yet, Merlin had been the only half-Sídhe. Morgana and Arthur had both been made that way artificially. Something had allowed Merlin's conception and safe delivery. Then there were the visions they were sometimes gifted with, even when they weren't looking for something. It was one thing to reach out with your magic and find an item or a person, but a prophetic vision or dream was different enough to make Alex wonder.

And Cyrridven had received the recipe for the potion from magic itself in a vision. That potion had linked Merlin so deeply to the Iron Realm that he'd seen the creation of her soul, or at least a representation of the creation. That potion had also spawned the poison that gave Alex the hint she needed about the nature of the Darkness that they now faced.

Maybe it was just a series of coincidences, but there seemed to be a plan amongst the random events and battles. Bran and Aiden weren't so sure. They'd started talking about quantum mechanics at one point and the possibility that current events were shaping the past, and Alex's eyes had glazed over. At this rate, Alex doubted that she'd ever find a satisfactory answer to this riddle.

Her path down that line of thinking was stopped when Alex caught sight of the flattened section of ground. Even the snow couldn't hide the odd flat patch the Sídhe had carved into the hillside. A soft sigh of relief escaped Alex. She wasn't sure what she'd been worried about, but the world had been on a knife's edge lately. It was good that something was right where she left it and that she knew about it. Snow covered the area in thick patches, protected from the sun by the lush evergreen trees.

The Iron Gate was obscured by the shadows of the outcropping rocks, but it was there. Alex smiled as magic brushed over her skin, radiating out of the iron that she and the others had fixed into the stone of the mountain. Walking forward, Alex looked beyond the iron and smiled. Rocks filled the space. No tunnel would likely ever be built here. She took off her right glove and gently grasped the metal. It wasn't cold. There was a warmth deep in the iron that rose to meet her touch.

"It is freezing." Avani was shifting between her feet and rubbing her gloved hands together. "I was warned about North American winters, but this is..." She trailed off and shivered again. "I was fine while we were hiking."

"That's normal," Nicki assured her. She moved closer to Avani and smiled when Avani pressed herself against her. "Physical activity helps."

"Alex, is everything okay with the gate?" Bran asked.

"Why do you call it a gate?" Avani asked. "I mean, it's more of a wall. You don't intend for them to open?"

"The gate is fine," Alex replied. She tightened her grip on the metal. There was nothing beyond the metal physically besides rock and roots, but Alex could feel something there. Once a tunnel had been here, connecting two worlds, and despite the efforts of her magic, something lingered. "And it seems, Avani, that we do intend to open it. At least, in a manner of speaking."

Releasing the bar, Alex pushed back the hood of her puffy black coat. The cold winter wind tugged at her hair, but it also cooled her down. Hiking in a heavy coat, even during the winter, was warm work. Unless you were a native of a tropical climate like Avani. Alex smiled in amusement but kept her thoughts to herself as she turned to find Nicki and Avani still pressed tightly together. They were cute, like a pair of puppies. And she would never reveal that thought to Nicki.

"Okay," Alex said. The others all focused on her. "I know that it's cold, but I'm hoping that being near a gate will make it easier for us to see outside the Iron Realm."

"Works in theory." Bran smiled and waved his hand. Yellow magic rushed over the ground and swept the area completely clear of snow. "Let's just try to stay dry."

Alex nodded in agreement and pulled a blanket out of her backpack. She rolled it out on the cleared ground while Nicki turned some snow back into water and filled the Iron Chalice. Morgana hung back with Jenny, Lance, and Avani as Alex sat down on the blanket with Bran, Nicki, and Aiden. Across from her, Bran gave her a soft smile and nodded in encouragement. The four of them linked hands, and Alex inhaled the cold air slowly.

Morgana moved closer to them, and the air warmed. Silver sparks twinkled in the air, and Alex's smile widened. It was reassuring that at least some things weren't changing. Closing her eyes, Alex focused on the others. Aiden and Nicki's bare hands were warm in hers. Their pulses were there, just beneath the surface of their skin, and she breathed a little easier.

Alex waited. Her magic gathered in her chest, and she gently urged it to build to stronger levels. The stillness of the world around them settled over Alex's shoulders, soothing her worry, but also gently urging her to protect it. Right now, the world was calm and peaceful. The plants and animals were slumbering, waiting for spring and unaware of the danger that waited beyond the protections of the Iron Realm.

Alex released a pulse of magic, letting it spread through the immediate area. Behind her closed eyes, the world changed as the energy washed across the surface of the ground and her friends. Each of her fellow mages and the magicians appeared as brightly colored outlines against the muted grays of the world around them. Alex reached further but sensed no threats. There was no immediate danger. She could focus her energies on the task at hand.

Magic flowed into her body from the hands of the others and the surrounding air. Bran's breathing changed moments before Nicki groaned softly, and Aiden panted. This wasn't easy for them, Alex reminded herself, not when Bran had to send his magic through the others for it to reach her. She kept her eyes closed and gently pulled on the new magic, summoning it to join with her own. In her mind's eye, Alex could see the different colors all shifting into the dark gray of her magic.

The color would likely always be disappointing. Alex had never revealed her feelings about it to the others; it seemed like such a small and silly thing to worry about, but she didn't like the dark gray color. It was boring. Metallic and lifeless, especially now that she knew many of her other lives had used magic with very different and much brighter colors. Alex also knew, thanks to her visions of Arthur's childhood, that a mage could make their magic another color, but Morgana would judge her for putting the effort into that. It was vanity only, and Alex knew it. Still, dark gray was hardly heroic. The only positive point was that it was literally the color of iron.

She struggled with the next step. Her mind was whirling, trying to connect stray ideas and worrying over the Darkness and what would happen if this didn't work. Slowly, Alex visualized the Tree of Reality and remembered the void that she'd floated in before. Something tightened in her chest. Her magic stretched out, reaching for something that wasn't a part of it. Alex saw it. A line of gray moving to the Iron Gate and curling around the bars. The feeling intensified, pushing against her lungs and heart. Responding to the pressure, Alex pulled the magic along the line, ordering it to connect with her. It snapped back like a rubber band, burning her skin and blinding her.

She was falling. Or flying. A weightless sensation surrounded her, filled her limbs, and swelled in her chest. There was a hint of control, though Alex feared it was only an illusion. Her heart pounded, pumping more blood and magic through her trembling body. It didn't last long. There was a sharp tug. She was dizzy, and then the darkness swirling around her took shape.

Alex was in the void of the Tree of Reality once again. Glowing worlds sparkled like ornaments on lines of silver tinsel. At first glance, she found it beautiful, but there was a purple mass slipping down the branches that laid out the tree and contained the worlds. It was hard to look at. The natural dark nothingness of the void that was illuminated only by small flickers of energy made it impossible for Alex to clearly see the edges of the Darkness. It moved slowly, almost oozing towards her, and only revealing itself in the strange purple shimmer of its surface.

Sternly, Alex told herself to focus. She couldn't stay here long. The last time she'd tried, she'd picked up a dangerous passenger who had become part of a being that had killed Merlin. Guilt shot through her heart, and it was difficult to breathe. If she even was truly breathing. Her body probably was. Alex looked down. Earth gleamed in the dim light, glowing blue and green, thanks to the lines of energy that wove through the world and split off to lead into other worlds.

For a few moments, she stared in awe of the beauty of her planet. Maybe it was cliché, but against the glittering blackness around the tree, the Earth was stunning. But that wasn't why she was here. Alex tried to move, but her feet were held firmly in place. She wasn't surprised; it had been that way last time as well. Still, it limited her view, and Alex could only see a limited scope of the Tree of Reality.

She knew what to focus on. Alex studied the worlds closest to Earth that she could see. Already, two of the branches were obscured by the Darkness. She could still see the strands of energy coming from Earth and leading into the shimmering dark mass. Straining her brain, Alex tried to remember how everything had looked the last time she was here, but the details were hazy.

Unfortunately, she couldn't tell which worlds were which. One branch looked largely intact with several shimmering worlds tied together by a glowing thread, but the one next to it was almost overrun. The Darkness was dripping down the tree at different rates. Which world was which was a mystery. Alex couldn't be sure if the safe one was one of the worlds that was home to the Dragons and similar creatures or not.

Shaking her head, Alex tried to count the worlds. It was impossible to be certain how many there were. The branches stretched out above her with sections of Darkness obscuring her view. And Sídhean was still there, at least to some extent. A world still being on the Tree of Reality didn't mean that it was safe. What mattered was that she'd gotten here again. It was possible to reach outside of the Iron Realm, even with the gates intact. She hesitated and reached for a nearby glittering world before pulling her hand back. Her feet were still stuck: she was tethered to the Iron Realm. No point in taking too many risks now.

Instead, Alex bent down the best she could and tried to see what was below Earth. There was a brilliant point of light. At this angle, she wasn't sure, but Merlin and Morgana thought that there were two lights. Two worlds, but what were they? She could see only their glow, but no colors — no shapes of landmasses or water, no clouds or mountains.

"This isn't helpful." Alex looked back at the worlds that seemed untouched. The closest was a deep brown color with hints of blue. She couldn't assume the blue was water. She couldn't assume anything. "What am I doing?"

The doubtful words were soft, and saying them out loud helped. Straightening her shoulders, Alex shook her head and closed her eyes. There was a soft hum around her that she hadn't noticed before. Alex opened her eyes again and looked down at the two points of light below Earth once more. Before she could change her mind, Alex extended her right hand towards the first one. Her muscles burned as they stretched. She extended her fingers as far as they could go, but she still couldn't reach. Then, with a twist of her body, Alex's middle finger brushed against something.

Warm air pressed in around her. The air was sweet, and the hum was stronger. Everything was bright and gleaming, but indistinct. Magic raced through her limbs, making the hairs of her arm stand on end. Then the world slipped into focus. It was some kind of hall, white floors that seemed to give off a soft glow stretched out all around Alex. There were no seams. It appeared as one large smooth room that was at least 100 feet long and 30 feet wide. The room was rectangular, and the walls were the same white material but with gray accent lines every few feet running up towards the vaulted ceiling. The hall was completely empty. There were no decorations, no seating, or anything else — just Alex.

Alex tried to move. A shock of energy made her flinch, curl into herself, and she gasped in pain. Below her, the floor rippled with flickers of color. The hum increased, weighing down on her like a heavy blanket, and filling her ears. She wasn't supposed to be here. Alex's magic sparked in her chest, growing and growing in strength, pulling at her skin and senses. Falling to her knees, Alex's hand hit the floor, and an electric jolt blasted up her arm to her heart. Below her hand, the floor opened, shrinking back but not breaking to form a round hole. It stopped at her knees, keeping her on firm ground.

Beneath her was a star. A brilliantly glowing light that turned slowly, with long trails of energy swirling around it. Lines of pale light flowed from it and reached towards her. Alex leaned back frantically as the strands spun themselves through the hole and sailed past her. They reached the ceiling, which unfolded to reveal the void of the Tree of Reality. Far above her hung Earth, and the lines of energy reached for her world. Alex watched in awe, but suddenly the hall shuddered around her. The hum turned sharp, echoing in her ears and sending pain crashing down on Alex. Closing her eyes, Alex covered her ears only to scream as the sound grew worse. The smell of ozone hit her nose.

Then the pain was gone. She wasn't on her knees. The humming was gone. Opening her eyes, Alex blinked as a snowflake landed on her eyelashes. Bran was seated across from her. His eyes were still closed in concentration, and Aiden and Nicki were on either side of her. Alex remained silent and looked toward the Iron Gate. It was still there, still intact, and she blinked in confusion.

"Alex?" Morgana called. "Are you alright?"

"I- yes." Alex swallowed and nodded. The others opened their eyes and looked expectantly at her. Nicki swayed slightly, but Bran released Nicki's hand and reached to her shoulder to keep her steady. "I was able to reach the Tree of Reality again. The Darkness is on the different branches, but I couldn't tell for sure which ones. I think we'll be okay going to the first in the beast branch, though. I don't think the Darkness has fully consumed any of them."

"That's not very reassuring," Morgana grumbled. "But it is something. And no pain?"

"No, but that was only my mind. Traveling with our bodies is sure to be different."

"Yes." Morgana nodded and stalked towards the Iron Gate. Alex thought she'd say something more, but she didn't.

"We still don't know what those lights in the trunk are," Bran said.

"No," Alex answered. She shook her head, remembering that strange place. It was something, but it wasn't... she wasn't sure what it was there for. "No, I'm sure that they aren't worlds. They're something else. I... I touched one, and I had a vision. There was a place, but it was strange. I'm not sure how to describe it. But it's not another world."

"You sound sure," Nicki said.

"Merlin and I never identified them," Morgana said. She shrugged a little, seeming just as lost as the others. "We theorized about the lights for many years, but we never had luck with finding out for certain what they were. For a time, Merlin thought they might be worlds that linked to the human notion of the underworld due to how common that idea was in mythology."

Nicki shivered at the suggestion. "Let's hope not."

"No, it's not that simple." Alex shook her head and licked her dry lips. "But they do have something to do with the energy. The one I saw overlooked the other. So, there's two. One is the source of the energy that travels through the Tree of Reality. I'm not sure what the other one is, but the Iron Realm sits between them and everything else. Between them and the Darkness right now."

She could almost hear the others thinking as they exchanged curious looks. Something was tugging at the back of Alex's mind. It was shapeless, but trying to shift itself into a form she could understand. It was like trying to recover a thought you'd just forgotten; it danced on the edge of your tongue, but never let you find it.

6

End of a Life

770 B.C.E. Somerset Levels

The roundhouse was too warm for Morgana, but she didn't complain or pull back the skin covering the door. A few feet from her, a low fire burned in the hearth, sending waves of heat rolling across the ample space of the home. Morgana cast her gaze around, taking in the items stored on the nearby shelves. There were a few pieces of jewelry that Airril had gotten her over the years, sealed jars of perfume from far away, and small trinkets that held memories.

"Morgana?"

The weak voice of her husband made Morgana look where she did not want to. Airril was stretched out on their bed under a pile of thick blankets. His hair was thin and white, wrinkles framed his eyes and brow, and his frail hand felt too ready to break in hers. Morgana forced a smile and leaned closer to him. She was perched on the edge of their bed, afraid of moving too far. Morgana's braid fell over her shoulder when she leaned forward. Her hair was still dark brown, and her skin remained free of wrinkles.

"I'm here."

"You are so beautiful." Airril raised his free hand to her face and smiled. His eyes were glazed, and his fingers trembled. "My beautiful wife."

"I'm here." Her voice quivered. Tears blurred her vision. He was so weak. Morgana could feel the life slipping away, and her magic could not stop the flow. "I'm here, Airril."

His mouth moved, but the small sounds were too quiet now. Morgana didn't think he even knew that he was speaking anymore. His chest was barely moving as his breathing grew shallower and shallower. A soft sigh escaped Airril, and his eyes slid closed. Morgana remained beside him, holding his icy hand and urging the fire and blankets to warm him up.

"Do you remember when we met?" Morgana didn't expect an answer. "You'd come south to meet Uthryn and me. He had almost given up hope that I'd accept any potential match. He complained to my mother, and she shook her head fondly at my stubbornness. I didn't want to like you. I'm sorry it took so long for me to warm up to you. We both know that when I married you, it was only to make Uthryn happy and to get away from my parents." She sighed and stroked the back of Airril's hand with her thumb. "You were so patient with me. You listened and trusted me, even if I didn't deserve it then. I know that my duty as a mage complicated our life together, but..." Her throat threatened to close as guilt and sorrow tore at her. "Thank you. I've been happy with you. Thank you for the good life."

There were more things that she wanted to say, but Morgana couldn't find the right words. How could this be the end? Looking down, she grimaced at the sight of their entwined hands. The skin of her hands was still smooth, while his hands were spotted and wrinkled. A tear escaped her eye, and Morgana quickly slammed her eyelids shut. She didn't want to cry, not now. After a few moments, she opened her eyes again and cleared her throat.

"Altan will look after the village. The people are safe and well-fed. You were a good leader and a good husband."

Airril's grip on her hand loosened. Morgana squeezed her eyes shut, desperately holding back her tears now. Her shoulders shook, but she made no move to leave the bedside. He'd had a long life. He was almost sixty, and she should be grateful. Even as the bronze trade had dwindled, they'd never gone hungry or suffered from raids. Airril had known peace and had died in his bed. She should be grateful, but she wasn't.

"Morgana."

She flinched at the voice behind her. A shuddering breath gave her enough strength to release Airril's hand. With great care, she placed his hand over his chest and brushed her fingertips over his face. Morgana tried to remember how he'd looked in his youth. When he'd been young and vibrant. It was difficult to remember that man right now. Morgana exhaled and took one more look before swallowing her tears and turning around.

The man in front of her offered her a gentle and sympathetic expression. He was a tall man with long, dark hair in a bun and dark eyes. There was a slight resemblance to Airril, but it wasn't enough to comfort Morgana. Standing up, she swallowed and tried to collect herself. Tears kept coming, and she avoided the man's hand when he reached for her in favor of moving towards the fire.

"Morgana."

"I'm fine, Altan. I'll be fine."

"There was no pain," Altan murmured. "A peaceful death. That's what he wanted."

"Yes. I know."

She didn't look back at her husband's body. Morgana wanted to let the memory of Airril when he was old and frail fade. She wanted to remember him happy and healthy instead. Her eyes landed on the bundle of hide at the side of the roundhouse. Stalking over, she scooped it up quickly and hugged it to her chest. The weight was comforting when nothing else was. Sniffing, she moved for the doorway, bracing herself in case Altan tried to stop her. He didn't.

Stepping outside into the cool air sent energy surging through Morgana. It was a stark contrast to the hot roundhouse and she welcomed it. She held the bundle tighter, suddenly cold and shivering. People stopped what they were doing outside their roundhouses to look towards her. It was midday. There was much to do, and yet they all stopped. Pity filled the eyes of one woman, while another seemed uneasy at the sight of Morgana.

She started walking, a sudden urge to put distance between her and Airril's body filling her chest. Tears were pushing their way up. She didn't want to cry, not in front of the others. They were looking at her strangely. Morgana could feel their eyes following her as she swept towards the tor. There was no one here that she wanted to speak with. Behind her, Morgana could hear voices, and Altan gave the order for Airril's body to be prepared. A fresh wave of tears threatened to take over, but she held them back. Not here, she told herself. She would not cry in the village.

Soon she was beyond the wall that protected the collection of roundhouses. Ahead of her was the tall hill where Arto had cast the blood spell over her village. Despite the spell originally harming her, she'd always felt safe there after embracing her role as a mage. Her feet carried her past the fields of the village and up the sloping hill. Her heart was racing, and it was hard to breathe, but she kept walking and kept the tears from falling.

Reaching the top of the tor, Morgana hugged the bundle to her chest and tried to breathe in the smell of the sea. The dam broke, and tears spilled forth. A raw cry escaped her chest, and Morgana's knees gave out. She didn't care about the pain that radiated up her legs. Instead, she collapsed on the ground and cried. Tears for Airril and tears for her fear of what came next mingled together, sending cascades of anger, grief, and guilt through her chest.

Even contact with the ground offered no comfort. Magic was there, brushing against her skin and reaching for her, but it couldn't help her this time. Airril was dead from old age, but she... she had barely aged. Time had slowed for her, and she hated it. As part Changeling, she was denied both children with her husband and growing old with him. She released a scream of rage, but the swamp below her swallowed much of the noise. Her hands shook as they held the bundle. A terrible stray thought hit her. Maybe she should just cast herself and the Sword into the water as an offering. It was a horrible idea, and she knew it, but what now ?

Staring out at the water, Morgana swallowed as the tears eased and finally loosened her hold on the sword. She considered returning to the village, but the soft breeze was refreshing, and she didn't want to see the stares. Morgana's mind spun. What would happen now? Altan would take over the region. His wife was a decent woman. Morgana hadn't objected when they had married, and their two young children were well behaved.

But she was an outsider. Always an outsider. Amongst the Sídhe, she'd been the exotic pet of the Queen, something that was off-limits and not understood. After fusing with her Changeling, she'd always known that she differed from the others in the village of her birth. Even Arto's affection hadn't been enough to make her feel at home there. Life as a traveling mage had been fulfilling, but the looks of awe and fear had always been there.

After it all, Airril had been the kind, supportive husband that she needed. Now he was gone. Closing her eyes, Morgana listened to the sound of the sea and focused on the smell of the salt. This was real, whether or not she liked it. This was her life now. Airril was gone, and she had to live with that.

A soft, rhythmic thumping made Morgana open her eyes. Someone was approaching her. She held the bundle tight and listened. They kept making noise as they walked up the hill. Then she heard the humming. It was soft and melodic, sending forth a familiar tune that she'd once known well. That tune had gotten stuck in her head often.

Relief and irritation warred in her. Morgana turned just enough to look over her shoulder. Sure enough, there was Merlin walking towards her. He was dressed in a long greenish cloak that had seen better days and carried his walking stick. Amulets jingled around his neck merrily, and he was still humming, but his expression was serious and cautious. Then he stopped. Their eyes met, but there was no vision this time. Morgana was grateful for that small mercy.

"What are you doing here, Old Man?"

"I had a dream about you," Merlin replied. He made no move to close the distance between them. "It left me with the impression that I should come and find you."

"And you have." Looking back at the sea, Morgana repressed the desire to lash out. He'd known of her grief before Airril's death and arrived in the village on the day of his death. "You may depart." The words were ash in her mouth, and Morgana regretted them at once, almost turning to beg him not to leave.

"Morgana, please turn around."

"Why?" Her voice did not quiver; Morgana refused to allow it.

"I wish to see if you face the same difficulty that I do."

Morgana closed her eyes and swallowed. If she turned around, he'd look the same as he had the last time she'd seen him years ago, and she knew it. If she turned around, then all of her fears would be real. Why had they never considered this? She didn't turn and listened as Merlin sighed loudly.

"I noticed a long time ago," Merlin said. "I aged, but not as I should. There is gray in my hair, and much of it I would blame on Arto, but time has been far too kind. Kind to the point of cruelty."

"You could have warned me!"

Then Merlin closed the last of the distance, resting his hand on her shoulder. New tears threatened to consume her. Shivering, Morgana wanted to pull away, but her body wouldn't move. Merlin gently pulled her into a hug, turning her so that she was facing him. Morgana allowed it and buried her face in the rough fabric of his cloak. Another sob escaped her. Morgana screamed, letting Merlin's body and the fabric muffle the pained sound.

His hands were warm against her back. There was a thump as he let his staff fall to the ground. Soft, soothing sounds reached her ears, but they offered no comfort. Airril was gone, and she was still young. She'd outlive Altan and his family the same way. She shifted closer to Merlin, wedging the bundle firmly between them.

"I'm sorry. Morgana, I am so sorry. I was in the village only moments before hearing of Airril's passing. I came to find you at once."

"I couldn't help him."

"No, I imagine not. His death, while painful, was natural."

"If I'd known, then I would have released Airril years ago." Morgana pulled herself from Merlin's arms and wiped at her tears with her left hand. "He would have made a good father with a wife who could give him children."

"I did not know your husband well, but I don't think he would have left." Merlin's voice was kind and gentle. "Besides, you had Altan. He might have been the son of Airril's cousin, but you two raised him since he was just a boy."

Morgana swallowed and blinked back tears. The words were true, but even Altan had withdrawn from her in the past few years. "He was a wonderful child, but he's a man now. He has a family of his own." Gulping in air, Morgana dropped her gaze to the greening grasses beneath their feet. "I don't know what to do now, Merlin."

"You could come with me."

The offer somehow surprised her and yet didn't. They had never been close. They had been allies for Arto's sake and, somewhere along the line, had come to trust each other. But they weren't friends. After Arto's death, Morgana had returned to this village with Airril to live out their lives, while Merlin went back to his life as a traveling priest. She'd heard about him from time to time, but that was the extend of it.

Yet, here they were. Both younger physically than they should be and without a clear future. Morgana's grip on the bundle tightened. She could feel the shape of Arto's Sword beneath the hide. Closing her eyes, she reached for her magic. It was always there, just beneath the surface, but it had grown weaker over the years. There was no war to fight. Eventually, the Sídhe had taken to building their homes underground and avoiding humans.

"To what end?"

"It's rare, but sometimes the Sídhe still cause trouble. I confronted a small raiding band last season who were stealing crops and trying to take slaves. Our magic is weaker now, as the world has less need of it, but we still possess it. I believe that means we have a purpose still."

"Do you think Arto would have grown old had he lived?"

Merlin was pressing his lips together thoughtfully when she looked up at him once more. Feeling a bit stronger, Morgana stepped back from him, and Merlin let his arms drop to his side. He didn't answer and instead knelt to retrieve his staff.

"I don't know. My grandfather, my mortal grandfather, had magic, according to my mother. She said that he was more powerful than her, so he might have been like us. He died of old age."

"So, you don't know how long we'll be like this?"

"No, I'm sorry, Morgana, I don't."

Merlin reached for her as if she was a spooked animal. Morgana didn't flinch away and allowed the older mage to cup her cheek. With his thumb, he gently wiped away the newest tears. His gaze was understanding. Morgana wondered what she had missed in their years of separation, but did not ask. Merlin glanced at the bundle but did not ask to see Cathanáil. Instead, he leaned his stick against his shoulder and gripped her arm with his free hand.

"Come with me," Merlin requested. "I don't know how long we will live. I don't know what purpose we might still have in this world, but I know it will be easier to face the coming years together."

She'd once hated this man; he'd taken Arto from her, and it had taken time for them to make peace after becoming allies years later. They'd never seen things the same way, and yet now all that fell away. Morgana didn't smile; she wouldn't smile for some time and knew it, but she nodded in agreement. The raw grief remained, but the fear eased. At least she had Merlin, for better or for worse.

Protection Agreement

There was nothing different about the hotel from the first time they'd had their little meet and greet. Given the short time period, the bottom layer of snow on the ground had probably been there then as well. Aiden knew that he wasn't entirely fair in his memories about the last meeting, but he was biased and couldn't help it. The Light had swanned in and sought to play them all like fools. That had been a turning point. He thought that he'd known it then, but just what it would lead to hadn't been clear.

Now they were back in the small hotel for another summit. Morgana had been able to call on their allies more quickly this time, and thankfully the guest list was much shorter. It had been readily agreed that not everyone needed to know that the mages were leaving Earth. He tapped his fingers against the wall he was leaning on and glared at the floral wallpaper decorating the opposite wall.

Nicki was sitting a few feet away in a cushy chair in the lobby. There was a roaring fire in the massive stone fireplace next to the reception desk, and the poor staff member already had a stunned look on his face. Aiden didn't know why and didn't want to ask Nicki what she'd said or what the poor guy had seen. Pulling out his phone, Aiden read a simple text from his sister. She was checking in, and a jolt of guilt hit him hard. He hadn't been home nearly enough lately.

There was this gap forming between him and his family. While there weren't secrets, there were truths that were too terrifying to look at. Talking about them, acknowledging them, made it all so real. He was glad that they knew, of course, and he didn't have to come up with some excuse to be out of contact for who knows how long, but that didn't make it easier. Aiden promised himself that he'd call his mom tonight and make a point of going over for dinner. Maybe he'd call one of her employees at the bookshop and check what shift she was working and sneak into the house to make dinner for the family. His mom would love t hat.

The front door opened, and Morgana stepped inside. There was a dusting of snow on her coat, and a deep red scarf was wrapped around her neck. Aiden shivered at the wave of cold that hit his skin before the heat of the room took over once more.

"Robin is in place," Morgana said. "She'll bring the guests up."

The receptionist smiled pleasantly and asked Morgana if he could get her anything. Morgana waved him off and headed down the hall towards the meeting room that she'd rented once again. Nicki stood up and followed Morgana. Aiden pushed himself off the wall and fell into step beside Nicki. None of them spoke until Morgana pushed open the door of the room and stepped inside.

It was much emptier than before. Rather than the horseshoe setup they'd used last time, they had only one large table which was draped with a dark blue tablecloth. Small folded name tents had been set up at each spot with the mages on one side of the table. There was a moleskine notebook and pen at Alex's place, but otherwise, nothing was on the table.

Alex and Bran were at a second table against the wall, organizing the meat and cheese tray and a tray of cookies and brownies. Coffee, water, and hot water for tea were all set out beside disposable cups. Small paper plates, creamer, sugar, and a selection of tea bags completed the display. It was so very normal compared to the beings that were coming.

Morgana shrugged off her coat and scarf and hung them up on the stand near the door. Without a word, she crossed the room to the refreshment table and began making herself a hot tea. Bran moved away to give her more space, but Alex lingered by the table and said something to Morgana that Aiden couldn't hear.

The last members of their group, Lance, Jenny, and Avani, entered the room a moment later. Avani was bundled up in what looked like three coats and two extra layers of pants. Aiden didn't have the heart to tell her that February was usually worse than January. She might just decide to run back to India.

"They'll be here soon," Nicki said. It wasn't necessary, but he understood her nerves. "And hey, at least the Light isn't here."

"Yeah," Alex agreed. She looked over at them and smiled. "Or worse, Arthur."

"Ding dong, the bastard's dead," Nicki sang softly. It broke some of the tension.

"You don't talk about Arthur much," Avani noted. She was eyeing everyone in the group with unsure eyes.

"Arthur isn't quite 'he who must not be named'," Nicki replied.

"But it is 'he who when is named will be followed by awkward silences'," Aiden finished. "Even in death, and isn't that just a little sad."

"No one misses him," Nicki scoffed.

Aiden glanced towards Jenny and Lance. Neither of them reacted beyond Jenny frowning. It made Aiden wonder if she missed him at all.

They'd dated for years, been lovers for years until his sick game had come pouring out. He doubted she lamented his death, but Aiden knew it could be more complicated than that. At least he and Sarah had drifted apart, and while she'd met someone, she'd broken up with him before anything happened, so Aiden knew that he'd been lucky with his love life in comparison.

Then Robin came in as if summoned by his musing on the state of his love life. Robin's long black hair was in a series of small braids that all joined to form a massive braid that hung over her shoulder. It was a style that he'd seen before, but always stunned him with how difficult it looked. Then again, Robin had some power of her own. She looked gorgeous in an elegant all black outfit and appeared calm and collected as she guided the Old Ones into the room.

Last time, they'd had Old Ones, Fae, and Demons in attendance along with the Light. Today it was a much smaller group, but Morgana had refused to let the Fae come. Instead, Timothy had been checking on the news from them and carrying messages from Morgana. Aiden wasn't sure what to think about that. On the one hand, it seemed wrong to not have them here, but on the other, he knew how bad Morgana's history with them was.

"You okay?" Robin asked gently. She had moved over to join him as the other Old Ones greeted Morgana and Alex in a formal receiving line.

"Just can't turn my brain off." Aiden chuckled weakly. "That's a problem lately for all of us, I think."

"I imagine so." Robin looked around quickly before leaning in and kissing his cheek. Her lips were warm and soft. His brain might have gone a bit staticky for a moment. "It'll be okay. No one coming is inclined to hurt any of you or the Iron Realm." Then she paused, holding her coat delicately in front of her. "Have you told the others?"

"I told Bran that we were going out. And Nicki, of course. Alex was there too. Was I not supposed to?"

Robin was smiling. "No, that's fine. I'm glad. I just wasn't sure that you'd tell them."

"Course." He nodded to the line of Old Ones. "Anyone I don't know?"

"Sif woke Odin up last week," Robin answered. She nodded to an older man with a trimmed white beard. He was dressed in a gray suit and had an eyepatch over one eye, which made Aiden stare in fascination. It was always the odd things from myths that were real. "I'm not sure how long he'll stay awake, but he's highly intelligent, so his insight could be beneficial."

Aiden nodded and checked the others. He knew all but one of them. Sif was very familiar to them, as was Shiva, who had unfolded his extra arms as soon as the door had closed, and Baldr, who he knew from the last conference. Sun Wukong looked precisely the same in his Chinese visage and bright red clothing as he shook Morgana's hand and said something to her that made Morgana swallow. It was probably about Merlin's absence.

"Do they know about Merlin?"

"News that he's dead has reached them, but they don't know the details."

Anansi cut an imposing figure in a black suit with a patterned silk scarf. He nodded gravely to Morgana and offered Alex a gentle smile. Satisfied things were going smoothly, Aiden looked to the last of the Old Ones, a woman that he didn't know. She was tall with long red locks that made Nicki's seem dull, and wore a simple green dress with no detailing. Robin shifted a little further away from him.

"That's my mother, Brigid," she said. "I woke her up. She's been asleep since the late 18th century."

"Your mother..." Aiden fought back a wave of panic.

"I haven't told her about us," Robin whispered. "Nothing against you, Aiden. I didn't think you and other mages needed that complication right now."

"Good thinking." It pleased Aiden when Robin relaxed. He wasn't offended; he was grateful. Aiden knew he was a mess right now and in no state to be meeting Robin's mother, who was a major Irish Goddess that he'd grown up hearing stories about from his grandfather and the likely inspiration for a Catholic saint. "My life is weird," he muttered.

They took their seats around the long table. He was beside Bran, who was beside Nicki, with Aiden on her far side. Morgana was on Alex's other side with Lance, Jenny, and Avani beyond her. He almost laughed when he realized their numbers were balanced. There were eight Old Ones and eight of them. It limited his ability to see the others, but at least he was in an excellent position to watch their visitors without being the center of attention himself. Scratching his fingernail against the table, Aiden eyed each of the visitors before looking at Robin, who was seated across from him. She caught his eye but revealed nothing. Brigid had sat down next to her.

"Thank you for coming," Alex said. "I know it is a long way for some of you and that two of you have only recently woken up to the modern world. What we're discussing won't take very long, but it isn't the sort of conversation to have over a phone." There was a teasing note in Alex's voice, but it sounded practiced. "And some of you don't have phones."

"I recently acquired one," Shiva remarked. He sounded proud of himself.

"I'm trying not to use mine," Sif replied. "I confess that mobile gaming is very addictive."

"It's designed to be," Aiden offered. He couldn't help but smile.

"Yes, to human brains. I had hoped that I would be less affected, but no such luck, I'm afraid." Sif gave him a warm smile.

With the ice broken, everyone relaxed a little, though curiosity and worry still filled the air. Odin cleared his throat, and all attention turned to him. He was seated across from Alex, with Shiva beside him, and across from Morgana. Aiden hoped the Old Ones wouldn't take offense at the seating order.

"I cannot help but notice that Merlin is absent," Odin said. "Forgive me, but there are rumors."

"I'm afraid that Merlin was killed by the Light a few weeks ago," Morgana stated. "Alexandra destroyed the Light in the battle immediately after."

"My condolences." Odin nodded deeply to Morgana. "He was a good man. It is a substantial loss."

There was a round of condolences from all the Old Ones. Morgana and Alex took them in with tight expressions and nods. It was painful to watch, and he was grateful when Shiva cleared his throat and drummed on the shaft of the Iron Trishula, which was awkwardly placed between him and Baldr.

"Last time we met, there were many concerns about the Darkness and how it was affecting this world and others. Given that the Light is dead, I suspect he attempted to force his solution on you?"

"You would be correct," Morgana said. "He attacked shortly after we learned of a successful defeat of the Darkness in our world. I confess we were low on magic at the time." There was a warning in that; a reminder from Morgana not to think them weak. "It changes nothing."

"What are you planning?" Shiva asked. He folded his pairs of hands neatly in front of him and turned his gaze to Alex. It was curious, almost warm, and not threatening. "What are you comfortable telling us?"

"We're leaving the Iron Realm to investigate and hopefully stop the Darkness at the source," Alex answered bluntly.

No one spoke. There was no sudden murmur of voices. They were all looking at Alex with hints of shock and understanding. Sif simply nodded with a hint of sorrow and worry flashing over her face before a calm mask slid back into place. Robin was watching the others too, and glanced his way. Their eyes met, and Aiden's cheeks warmed, but he managed not to react. This wasn't the time, but he was grateful that he'd warned her.

Robin was their ally. Bran had been right to point out that while Morgana wasn't fond of her, she didn't consider Robin a threat. She had spoken little about when she first met the Iron Soul, Merlin, and Morgana, but had revealed that she'd done something idiotic. Sometimes it was easy for him to forget how old Robin was when they were talking about a movie, and Robin's eyes lit up with glee at the jokes or effects. Other times, like right now, the full weight of her age settled into place. Sharp brown eyes were watching the other Old Ones and weighing them.

"I see," Shiva finally said, breaking the silence. "I admit my surprise. I would not have thought that you would ever risk leaving your home realm."

"I'm not happy about it," Alex said. It was oddly reassuring, and Aiden wished that he could see her face. "Our information about other worlds is limited."

"I urge you not to go to our homeworld," Odin said. "I'd be concerned what effect being there would have on you. There is little matter there to support your human bodies."

"That's been a point of concern for us," Morgana agreed. Aiden almost gave in to the urge to lean forward so he could see Morgana's expression. "You are correct about the potential danger of going into that branch. Given what happened with the Light, we do not plan on it."

"The Darkness is coming from somewhere," Alex said. "Long ago, the Darkness was stopped from coming into Earth by repairing the hole it had created. The issue is that we know very little about it."

"And you're still unwilling to break the connections between worlds?" Anansi asked. The male shaped Old One raised an eyebrow, but Aiden didn't think he was really judging them.

"Not unless I find something that assures me that is the only way to save Earth." Alex's voice was calm. She sounded so reasonable, but it also seemed rehearsed. "We are still suffering from a lack of information. This mission is to correct that."

"I can't say that I think this is a good idea," Brigid said, speaking for the first time. "But I can understand your thinking. You cannot make plans with no information."

"What do you need from us?" Shiva asked. "I'll gladly go with you-"

"No," Alex cut him off. "Thank you, but no." Aiden heard Alex inhale slowly before she spoke again. "This is your home. Even though many of you weren't born here, it is your home. I need you to protect it. To make sure that nothing bad happens while we're gone. Shiva, Sun Wukong, you've been keeping the Demons in check for years, and I need you to keep doing it."

"That's not a problem," Sun Wukong replied. He was smiling and seemed pleased.

"But you, all of you, need to monitor the Fae, and each other," Alex said. "Three magicians and Robin will remain in Ravenslake, but it's a big world."

"Robin?" Anansi asked. Robin waved to him. "Oh, I see. As you wish."

"We can manage that," Odin said. "Most of the Old Ones are still asleep, but if they do wake, Shiva has the Trishula to help with any madness that may take hold."

"And the Fae have taken heavy losses recently," Sif added. "I can't see any of them other than the Red Caps being a problem."

"Africa is largely clear of threats," Anansi said. He tented his hands in front of him. "But I shall, of course, remain vigilant and assist others as needed."

"Thank you," Alex said. Relief filled her voice, and the Old Ones all looked pleased. "This is a dangerous undertaking; I am grateful that the Iron Realm has so many allies to turn to."

"Are you sure that Morgana should go?" Baldr asked. "In case the worst happens. None of us are qualified to train mages."

"If the worst should happen, the Desai family in India would fill that void," Morgana said firmly. Aiden doubted that they'd really be able to take Morgana's place. There was a power gap between mages and magicians that would create issues. "The Iron Soul is not leaving the Iron Realm without me. It is my role to protect them."

"And I have to go," Alex said. "I understand your concerns, but the Darkness is a raw force of power that is destroying worlds and eroding the Tree of Reality. Now that we know the threat is out there, we cannot ignore it."

"And you are still unwilling to break the connections between worlds?" Baldr asked.

"I am not destroying the fabric of the Tree of Reality," Alex said.

And that was the last word on the matter. The Old Ones didn't argue with her further. Their allies agreed to support them and keep the Iron

Realm safe, removing the last of the barriers in Alex's way. This was happening. This was really going to happen. Timothy had spoken with a few of the Fae clans, and they had the agreement of eight Old Ones to stand guard over the world while they were gone. There was no turning back now.

8

Forging Ahead

Sweat rolled down Alex's back under the light t-shirt she was wearing. The band of the leather apron dug into the hot skin of her neck. Even with her long hair tied up in a tight bun, Alex was sweating and feeling each wave of heat from the furnace. Mjǫllnir glittered in the fiery light, and Alex reached over to touch its warm surface. The heavy leather gloves dulled the sensation, but Alex could still feel the hum of magic traveling from the metal into her body.

She was alone in the workshop again. The others had never enjoyed this work as much as she did. Alex wasn't really sure if what she felt when smithing was enjoyment, but there was a rightness to it she couldn't ignore. It was fulfilling, even if it wasn't fun. The ringing of the hammer drowned out the voices for the most part, and her magic seemed stronger in here.

Morgana hadn't set foot in the workshop since Merlin's death, to Alex's knowledge. Over the last week, more of Morgana's things had been unpacked from their boxes, but they were alongside Merlin's possessions rather than replacing them. If she hadn't known better, Alex would have assumed that they had simply moved in together. Of course, Merlin was gone, but there was a harmony to Morgana's taste and Merlin's preferences. One more reminder of how close and in sync the pair had been.

Shaking her head, Alex turned her attention back to the iron. She had left it in the furnace too long as it was. This wasn't the time to get lost in her thoughts. Alex pulled out the long, thin metal shape that was bright with heat. Pulling on her magic, she gave up on the tongs when it proved too difficult to keep hold of the small piece of metal. Alex's gray magic settled around the iron and slowly brought it over to the anvil, holding it in place.

Using the smallest pair of pliers, Alex twisted the metal around the thinnest point of the horn. It was so small, almost too small for her to work with. But she slowly turned and bent the metal, forming the spiral. The delicate turn of the triskelion spiral was a thing of beauty, and Alex allowed herself a moment of pride. But she had to focus. Exhaling, she pushed more of her magic into the metal, watching as it shimmered dark g ray.

That was the last spiral done. Alex watched it cool and looked over to where the first two spirals were sitting on the worktable beside Mjǫllnir. She'd done a good job making them all about the same size. In her mind's eye she could already see them joining smoothly and hoped that it would work out as well as she envisioned.

Gathering the three, Alex lined them up on the anvil. They were still rough, with tool marks visible in a couple of places and lacking a smooth polish. Alex debated with herself for a moment before dismissing that. She could use a little more magic at the end if it really bothered her. Grabbing the torch, Alex pulled on a pair of goggles and double-checked that her gloves were fully intact. The flame burst to life, and Alex adjusted it to create a narrow band of intense heat. She watched with satisfaction as the ends of the three spirals slowly melted together and joined.

Picking up Mjǫllnir, Alex hesitated for only a moment before bringing the narrow side of the head down against the iron. The Hammer glowed brilliantly, and electricity flared across the smooth metal. The Triskelion symbol melted into the metal of the tool gleamed in the corner of Alex's eye. Magic flashed from the Hammer into the small pendant.

"Translate for me," Alex said out loud. "Magic, bind my will into the metal."

She felt silly, saying the words out loud. Even with Arto's memory of Cathanáil, Thor's knowledge of gradually creating Mjǫllnir and Gofiben's experience with the Chalice, Alex wasn't sure how to do this. Merlin and Morgana had enchanted items for short-term use in the past. Merlin's old pin came to mind, and Alex knew how to store magic in iron, but this was different. The metal needed to hold her intention and do something complex, and she needed the magic to linger and recharge.

They were going into another world. There was so much that they didn't know, so much they couldn't know or plan for, so Alex desperately wanted to have something, anything, that could help them. Something small that was easy to take with them. Between Cathanáil, the Chalice and Mjǫllnir, there was already a lot going with them.

She brought the Hammer up again and smiled. Mjǫllnir hadn't damaged the shape. The metal looked smoother now, and there was the subtle glow of magic in the metal's surface. Alex was happy with the shape of the small triskelion. It was remarkably even for being formed by hand rather than with a mold. It was barely over a square inch in size, with one piece still in need of bending. Perfect for hanging on a cord around her neck. Alex just hoped that it would do what she wanted it to.

Maybe it was too small, she worried. It was much smaller than any other Iron Artifact. Then again, she had memories of a brooch and simple seal that had helped her other lives, but those had been one-use items. They were like the batteries she was trying to make.

Alex just didn't know. She knew she could ask Morgana, but it had been Merlin who was the genuine expert at working with iron. Besides... Alex hesitated to ask Morgana about anything too closely related to Merlin. It was a minefield, and while the last time she'd been over here Morgana had seemed willing to talk, Alex wasn't going to push it. Grief was something she was familiar with now.

Alex brought Mjǫllnir up again and pushed her magic into the Hammer. It received it smoothly, and outside thunder rumbled. Lightning crackled around Alex's fingers, and the air took on the sharp smell of ozone. Alex relaxed at the scent, calmed by the sensation and the memories it drew forth.

'That's it,' Thor said. 'You're doing it.'

'One more time,' Arto added. 'Not too much.'

It was impossible to visualize languages being translated. Historically, it had been something that happened mostly by accident when Alex was confronted with an unknown language. But if they were going to another world, she couldn't expect English, and relying on her magic to translate was dangerous. She needed something to help her. Alex's magic thrummed, and she brought Mjǫllnir down with a gentle swing. Lightning flashed across the anvil, but it didn't harm Alex.

She set the Hammer to the side and pulled off her work gloves. She extended her hand over the triskelion, letting the heat guide her and keeping her eyes closed. It was easy and difficult at the same time. The iron welcomed her magic, soaking it up like a sponge and much more readily than before. Her surprise made it challenging to stay focused on what she wanted. With her eyes closed, Alex could see the magic twining around the triskelion and repeated her wish for what it was to do over and over again in a frantic mental chant. The magic was there. Mjǫllnir had ensured that. She needed to tame it, to bind it to the purpose that she needed. Cuthbert scoffed at her.

She still wasn't done. Alex knew the triskelion shape was where she wanted the most magic to be centered, but the shape alone wasn't what she was looking for. Alex found another small piece of iron from the scrap pile and began heating it. She used one of the workshop towels to dry off her sweating face and looked out into the yard. The snow outside did nothing for the temperature in the workshop. Alex glimpsed Morgana moving past a window, but that was it.

Making the outer ring of the necklace didn't take long, and Alex used Mjǫllnir to push a little more magic into the metal as she used the horn of the anvil to shape it. Her hands sweated badly in the leather gloves, and she wished that she could have kept them off longer. Exhaustion was settling in, and a slight burn radiated through Alex's chest. It worried her. She wasn't completely exhausted, but she was trying to enchant a new Iron Artifact.

Searching her memories, Alex couldn't find a straight answer to if she'd done this right. Arto had made Cathanáil after years of training, while other artifacts resulted from slow enchanting without the mage even being aware of it. Frowning, she pushed more magic into the curved metal as if her willpower alone could lock everything into place. If she did it right, maybe it could.

'It will work,' Gofiben reassured her. His voice was warm.

'You did well,' Thor added. 'Mjǫllnir is a tool of creation.' He sounded smug.

The circle wasn't perfect, but it was a good fit for the triskelion. After both pieces were cool, Alex fitted the triskelion into the ring and grabbed the blowtorch. It was anti-climatic. There was no rumbling of thunder in the sky or flash of magical power beyond the shimmer deep within the metal to mark the moment. This time, she didn't need it, and she was out of magic as it was.

But Alex smiled. The new pendant hummed with magic, a softer melody than Cathanáil, but comforting and singing of magic. Watching the red heat fade from the iron where she'd joined the two pieces together, Alex started to believe that maybe she'd managed it. Pulling on the flicker of magic that remained to her, Alex lifted the pendant and commanded the magic into the metal.

"This will allow me to understand all languages," she said out loud. It wasn't visualization or a spell following a familiar pattern, but it was what she had. If she'd been in a more creative mood, she would have tried a rhyme. "This is my will."

Alex grimaced at that last part and was grateful that she was alone in the workshop. Morgana would have raised an eyebrow at that lame statement, and Nicki would have giggled at her. It wasn't her fault that magic was hard to pin down. It relied so heavily on instructions that sometimes Alex didn't know how to give. Still, she had a good feeling about this below her churning nerves. Optimism was an almost forgotten sensation, and Alex basked in it for a bit.

While the shimmer of magic was stronger in the triskelion itself, there was a flicker of magic in the outer circle as her energy spread through the pendant. Slowly releasing her magic, Alex quenched the pendant to finish cooling it and stepped back. Her muscles ached, and she couldn't blame all of it on the hammering.

Then she went around the workshop for something to protect the new pendant until she could find a sturdy chain or cord for it. In a small chest of drawers in a dusty corner, she found a small leather bag that was holding old nails that Merlin had probably meant for some project. Alex dumped them out even as her stomach twisted a little at the thought of Merlin and another thing he'd never do. The pouch was a bit large for the pendant, but it would do. Alex paused as she carried it over to the anvil. She wasn't sure if it was a pendant or an amulet, technically. It didn't bestow protection like traditional amulets, but it had power. Hopefully.

The voices returned loudly, with most reassuring her she'd done an excellent job and only a couple expressing doubts. Cuthbert was grumbling, but thankfully said nothing negative. Timur cautioned her not to get too excited before trying it out, and Alex found herself agreeing with him. Their plans were almost finished, and it would be time to leave soon. With care, Alex picked up the pendant, dried it off and slipped it into the small bag. Alex rubbed the pendant thoughtfully through the soft leather. She was torn. Part of her wanted to find something to hang it with right away, while another part of her was nervous.

'Stop doubting yourself,' Josfa scolded. He rarely spoke. Alex knew from their memories that he'd been the strong and silent type. 'Many of us never learned to use our magic at all. Those that did have faith in you.'

"Other than Cuthbert," Alex answered out loud.

'Cuthbert is an arse,' Gottfried snorted. 'Ignore everything he says.'

Alex was surprised to feel herself smile. The voices were… she was getting used to them. They were like roommates that she was stuck with. She slipped the leather bag into her pocket and pulled on her coat, shivering a little as she recalled the Light's attack on her mind. She'd been worried that the memories of her past lives would be destroyed. They hadn't. It hadn't even shut them up for long.

'That's rude,' Michel huffed. She could hear him pouting.

Walking across the lawn, Alex checked the windows for any sign of Morgana and hoped that the back door was open. It was one thing to go the long way when she first arrived, and another thing to come out of a hot forge and have to walk through the cold. When she tried the knob of the back door, Alex found it unlocked and let herself into the house.

The kitchen was warm, and a kettle was on the stove. A container of cocoa mix was out alongside two mugs and a box of tea. Alex took off her coat and hung it by the door before moving to the stove. The water was already being warmed at a low heat. Alex turned up the temperature and pulled out a spoon from the drawer. She scooped a generous amount of cocoa mix into one mug.

"Alex?" Morgana called from down the hall.

"Yeah, it's me!"

When the water was hot enough to proceed, Alex filled both of the mugs, including the one loaded with cocoa. Using the spoon, she mixed it up as Morgana walked in and selected a teabag. They worked on their drinks in silence before walking over to the small kitchen table. Alex hoped that today's conversation wouldn't be as raw as the last time she'd sat here. She took a long, nervous drink as she sat. The chocolate flavor danced on her tongue.

"Did you finish what you were working on?" Morgana asked.

Hesitation took hold, as silly as it was. Alex felt her cheeks heating up, and she debated even showing the pendant to Morgana. Compared to the other artifacts, it seemed so... unimportant. She didn't even know if it worked. Morgana raised an eyebrow, her eyes sparkling with interest and amusement. Alex hadn't seen that look since Merlin's death, and relaxed.

"Yeah, I think so." Alex reached into her pocket and retrieved the small leather bag. "I was trying to make..." She hesitated again. The doubt that had plagued her in the workshop returned in full force. "With us working on going into other worlds and not knowing if our magic would work, I thought that a utility piece of magic would make sense." Placing the bag on the table, Alex watched Morgana open it and palm the small pendant.

The older mage looked at her curiously. "It translates. I mean, at least I hope so. That's what I was trying to do when I made it. Something that would let the wearer understand and connect with other creatures."

Surprise filled Morgana's eyes, followed by consideration and then pride. Alex's chest expanded with happiness at the sight. Then she reminded herself that she didn't know if it worked and said as much. Morgana opened her hand and Alex took the pendant, letting it rest against her skin and feeling a slight warmth seeping into her hand from it. Alex gulped down some of her cocoa, letting the sugar fortify her.

"Well, that's an easy enough thing to test," Morgana said gently.

Then she smiled and started talking about some of the old photographs that she'd found tucked away in Merlin's room. Apparently, one was of the two of them at a World's Fair, and Morgana made a comment about her dislike of the dress she'd worn in the photo. Blinking in confusion, Alex wondered what Morgana was doing.

"What does an old photo have to do with anything?" Alex asked.

Morgana smiled brightly. "I was speaking in my native tongue, Alex. And I switched to Arabic half way through my explanation."

Surprise and glee filled Alex's chest. Her lungs were ready to burst at the sudden pressure and she felt a giddy rush. Morgana's smile softened, and she reached out to touch Alex's hand gently. That smile was familiar, and Alex swallowed. That was Morgana's proud smile. Alex's chest was too full, and she smiled back sheepishly.

"I just hope it works in the other worlds," Alex said.

"If it does, it's going to make this a hell of a lot easier." Morgana released her hand and sat back in her chair, still smiling. "I've finished the arrangements I needed to see to." Alex noted Morgana didn't say what those arrangements were. "And Timothy has reported that the Fae, even the Red Caps, are pulling back from the area." She took another sip of her tea. "The only thing left now is to pack."

All the pride and contentment left Alex in an instant. Raw terror took its place. This was it. They were really going to go on this crazy quest. Nothing in any of her books had prepared her for standing on the precipice as she was now, but it was still their only way forward. Unable to speak, she nodded and downed the rest of her hot cocoa.

9

Unknown Shore

721 B.C.E. Unknown

Water ripped past her. There were flashes of strange places, buildings that Morgana had never seen before, and people dressed oddly. Water united all of it. Water was the only constant in the images, but it failed to reassure her. Morgana would have screamed, but she didn't dare open her mouth. Merlin's grip on her hand tightened, and she was grateful that he was there.

The tunnel shuddered around them. It twisted and turned, with Morgana occasionally losing sight of Badb. Morgana was useless, but green magic glowed and flared around Merlin. She couldn't see his face, but he was at least a little in control. What had possessed them to follow Badb into the water? This was new, and it was terrifying. How could she have been so foolish?

But then she caught sight of Badb again, and gold glittered in the low light flickering off the water that surrounded them. Cathanáil. Anger took the place of Morgana's fear. That was why she'd run after the Old One. It would not have her brother's sword; she would never allow it. Protecting the Iron Sword was her- their duty.

She grabbed onto that thought and pulled on her magic. The water shuddered around them. It was closing. Splashes were hitting her until Morgana pushed the magic outward. The sound changed. What had been a rushing of water took on a strange chiming noise. Merlin's grip on her hand tightened. They sped up, and the gap between them and Badb shrank. The Old One didn't look back at them. Magic flared around them, illuminating the dim tunnel. Morgana struggled to keep her eyes on Badb and not look around. More images were flashing past, and she kept catching sight of them in the corner of her eye.

Was this how Cyrridven traveled? Was this what it meant to be one with the water, or was this something else entirely? Morgana didn't know, and her stomach didn't want to learn any more. At least Merlin was with her. His magic rippled around them, blending with hers in a protective shell as the water's churning grew rougher and rougher. Then it collapsed. Water crashed down on them, pulling at Morgana's body, and trying to fill her lungs.

She hit the ground, coughing up water and gasping for air. Morgana opened her eyes and blinked. They were on a shoreline with bright sand and warm water washing up over her legs. That wasn't right. Her head was still spinning. Merlin was beside her, already climbing to his feet even as he coughed a little. He was in better shape than she was.

"Morgana, prepare yourself," he said, low and dangerous.

Struggling to ignore her stomach, Morgana rose to her hands and knees. Her clothing was soaked through. Saltwater stung her eyes as it ran down her face, but Merlin's tone had stressed urgency. Climbing to her feet, she was grateful when her body held the upright position and straightened her spine.

Badb was standing a few feet away from them, glaring with a vicious expression that promised pain. Morgana hated the shiver that went down her spine, but this was a mad Old One. This one embraced death. At least the boys weren't here. She was grateful for that. Gofiben and Bran were talented students, but they were not ready for this kind of fight.

"Silly mages," Badb cooed.

"Return Cathanáil," Morgana ordered.

"So silly." Badb shook her head. "And so far from home."

The Old One gave them a nasty smirk. Babd's eyes were glowing dark red and darkening towards black with each passing moment. In her hand, Cathanáil was glowing a sickly shade of blood red. Rage bubbled up in Morgana. She wanted to claw the Old One's eyes out for daring to lay a hand on her brother's sword. Somehow, she stayed still beside Merlin.

They weren't where they had been. The tunnel had moved them. She didn't know how the Old One had made it, but they had moved. Her eyes darted around to take stock quickly. They were on a large wide beach with pale warm sand. The sun was beaming down on them. Strange trees were a few feet up the beach, with rough trunks that looked like a spiral was carved into them. Their branches were very different, coming only from the very top of the tree with small leaves sprouting from both sides of each branch. The pattern they formed almost made it look like one giant leaf. And it was warm. Far warmer than where they'd come from.

Badb was observing them, holding Cathanáil tightly. Dark red magic flickered in the air around her as the Old One released more and more of her energy. Morgana viciously hoped that the Old One ripped itself apart in its efforts. Badb, however, appeared calm and in control. She towered over them, standing more than a foot in height taller than even Merlin. Dark lines were painted over her dull gray skin, and her ratty, long black hair increased her gaunt appearance. One might have thought her a corpse, but Morgana knew better. This was the crow. The only thing keeping her from transforming and flying off was Cathanáil.

"Surrender the sword, Badb," Merlin said calmly. "We've proven that we will not give it up easily."

"Yes," Badb hissed. "Throwing yourselves into my tunnel, that was a surprise." She stroked the hilt of the Iron Sword with a smile. "But I shall not surrender my prize."

Morgana still wasn't sure what had happened, but her focus narrowed on the Sword. They had to get Cathanáil back. Morgana's chest burned. Her magic was low. She'd used too much in the water tunnel and trying to get Cathanáil from Babd earlier. Sweeping her eyes across the strange beach, she searched for anything that could help them. Morgana saw nothing. There were no houses or boats in sight. It was an empty patch of beach, and she didn't think the shells were going to help them.

"You have caused enough harm as of late," Merlin said. He took a small step towards the Old One. Somehow, he was still holding his staff, which impressed Morgana. "Your plagues have killed many."

Badb chuckled and shrugged. The feathers of her mantel shifted in the soft breeze. "It was fun, but there are bigger things." Her gaze fell to the Sword, and more of Babd's energy rippled across the blade. "So much more interesting things. You are blind mages. I am not."

Before Morgana could move, vines burst up through the sand and twisted around Babd's legs. A squawk escaped the Old One, and Merlin lunged forward. Badb shrieked and slashed Cathanáil through the air. Merlin stopped and dodged back. Morgana summoned her magic and called it forth as a whip. It flashed through the air and struck Babd's arm. The Old One kept hold of Cathanáil and drew back with bared teeth.

Cathanáil sliced through the vines, and Badb twisted back. Her feet left footprints in the sand as the vines shriveled up. Morgana shifted her magic, releasing her focus on the whip and instead summoned bolts. It was easy; the magic knew her will easily and shot through the air. Babd threw up her free hand. Dark red energy gathered, spilling from the Old One's form and blocked the bolts. However, Morgana's attack gave Merlin an opening. He tossed an orb of green magic into the air, but rather than moving straight, it swung in an arc around the shield and struck Babd's arm.

The Old One shrieked, the sound inhuman and high pitched. The shield flickered, but Badb wasn't done. She threw a wave of power forward. Morgana was ready. Magic clashed in the air, sending waves of pressure bouncing back at the mages and Old One. Dark red coiled around silver as the shields collapsed, and bright green illuminated the sky. Morgana gasped for air, the edges of her vision flickering to black. She barely noticed Babd's left arm fading. The Old One clutched the Sword to her chest protectively. The gesture enraged Morgana. The ache of using too much magic was fading away under the drumming roar of her heartbeat. Beneath her feet was the soft hum of the world, and Morgana drew comfort from it.

At least the boys were safe; she reminded herself again as she glared at Babd and tried to figure out the Old One's next move. Running away on foot wouldn't work, and she couldn't fly away with Cathanáil, but maybe she could do that trick with the water. Morgana took a slow step forward, reining in her anger and trying to put herself between Babd and the sea. The Old One shifted its position, and they stood off against each other.

Merlin was moving as well, but he was inching towards Babd with green magic flaring around him. It was mostly for show, Morgana knew. She was tired from that tunnel, and Merlin had been the one truly guiding their path. Risking a glance at him, Morgana wondered what he was planning. Babd lifted her flickering left hand, and a dark red glow erupted forth and encircled her like a mist. Her eyes darkened, and the lines around her face seemed to shift.

Unwilling to give her an opening, Morgana summoned her magic again and let it dance around her fingertips. Babd's attention was focused on her. A green bolt hit the Old One in the side. Merlin lunged forward once again and grabbed Cathanáil's hilt. The world slowed down to Morgana's eyes. The Old One fought to keep her grip. Morgana brought up her hands and sent her magic flying towards Babd's face; her mind focused on the image of the flesh being ripped apart. Morgana's heart fluttered.

Babd screamed and thrashed wildly, trying to dodge away from Morgana's attack. Cathanáil shifted as she and Merlin fought for control, but Babd had the better grip. Dark red magic flared out of Babd's body, dissipating some of Morgana's attack, and the Old One twisted to the side. The skin of Babd's face changed, becoming darker and shimmering with silver magic, reassuring Morgana that her attack had connected.

Merlin hit the ground, clutching at his side and groaning loudly. Morgana's eyes widened. There was blood on Cathanáil's blade. Merlin kept making noise and was trying to stand up, but the sandy ground was giving him trouble. His movements were sluggish and dazed. She hoped it was just a graze. Badb moved, and Morgana tensed, turning her attention back to their enemy.

The Old One stared at her. She did not need to breathe, so Morgana was denied the satisfaction of seeing Babd pant. Instinct warred with her. Merlin was down. She didn't know how badly he was hurt, but his groans and attempts to sit up reassured her he was still alive.

"Stay down, old man," Morgana barked. "Don't make it worse."

"The Sword-"

"She'll not be leaving with it," Morgana swore. Her voice promised violence, and she was pleased to see a flicker of worry in Babd's eyes.

The Old One took a step back. Their form was different now. It wasn't fading exactly, but Morgana had a distinct sense of weakness. Whatever Babd had done when she stole Cathanáil had drained her and then she'd immediately created the water passage. Morgana drew closer. Her magic was still weak, but it was gathering at her silent command. The ache in her muscles was growing worse, but Morgana fought through it. Babd's dark eyes were hesitant now, and the Old One's gaze was jumping between Morgana and Merlin.

"Stupid mages," she snarled. She took a step back, and Morgana took a step forward. "Don't you know what I did? I opened a path to another world! Who knows what came through?"

"You're lying." Icy fear gripped Morgana's chest. The Old One had to be lying, but if she wasn't- "There'd be no point."

Babd smiled again, her confidence returning. "Such a narrow view."

Then the Old One's magic flashed, a wave of sand rose into the air, and Morgana flinched back on impulse, covering her face. The hot sand stung her hands, but none entered her eyes. When she lowered her hands, she found Babd running down the shore. Morgana raced after her, stumbling in the sand as Merlin weakly called to her. Babd looked over her shoulder and then waved her hand towards the sea.

Water swirled up into the air. Morgana forced her tired body to move faster, pulling on her magic and swaying dangerously as she followed the Old One. The water spun like a whirlwind, turning on its side in front of Badb and opening another tunnel. Morgana's stomach turned at the sight of it. She closed the distance as the Old One stumbled. Throwing her arm forward, Morgana pushed her magic and ignored the sharp pain that radiated out of her heart. A silver bolt struck Babd's arm.

Cathanáil fell. Badb lunged for the sword with a shriek. Morgana's silver magic twisted around the blade, giving it a cold glow. With everything she had left, Morgana ordered her magic to bring the Sword to her. It sailed through the air towards Morgana. Sparks of silver magic faded away as Morgana's control failed, and exhaustion took hold. Striking the sand with a soft thud, Cathanáil glinted in the sunlight, only a foot from Morgana. She admired the Sword as relief flooded through her. The last of the reddish glow was fading fast.

Babd's shriek snapped Morgana back to the issue at hand. She grabbed the Sword in her right hand and moved back towards Merlin and away from the water. Babd's eyes were black, and her skin was shimmering. Morgana hoped that was a good sign. She tightened her grip on Cathanáil. She dug her feet into the sand and braced herself. Heat licked over her muscles, warning her not to push herself further.

The water tunnel collapsed, and Badb hissed, retreating up the beach. Morgana almost smiled. The Old One was too weak. Her mind itched to finish the job, but her body protested every movement. They stared at each other, green eyes meeting dark red ones in a silent challenge. Badb's eyes darted over towards Merlin. The reminder of his condition was like a splash of icy water down Morgana's back.

But Badb didn't attack. The Old One glared at her, eyes flashing bright red, and wrapped her arms around herself. Badb's body shimmered, and Morgana brought her hand up just in time to shield her eyes from the flash of light. A crow cawed and flew into the air. Morgana glared after it, considering pushing her magic to attack it one more time. A groan from Merlin made her stop. Turning back to Merlin, she rushed over and knelt beside him, desperately hoping that his wound wasn't severe. She didn't know where they were or what Badb had done. Morgana could only hope that the boys were alright.

10

Last Minute Doubts

The storm was Alex's element, but it offered her no comfort. Dark clouds churned overhead, and the air smelled of ozone. Confusion curled around her mind, a strong sense that she was forgetting something or had forgotten something, but it wasn't the time. Arthur was only a few feet away from her, watching her with those sharp blue eyes that she'd once thought were beautiful. She was holding Cathanáil in her right hand, the sheath on her back, and Mjǫllnir in her left hand.

"Alex, Alex, Alex, what are you doing?" He shook his head as if disappointed in her. "You can't deal with this, you know. Going into another world? Dealing with whole other species and the ugly events that'll unfold. That's beyond you. You couldn't even cope with the Fae you killed."

"That's on you and your mother!"

"But you struck the blows. You valued your own life over their innocent ones." His tone was mocking in its softness. "What sort of hero are you? A killer, one who values their own life above all others."

"We didn't know, and there were limited choices."

"Keep telling yourself that, sweetheart," Arthur said. "That's the thing about you, though, isn't it, Alex? You love stories. The grand tales of heroes, adventures, and love. You were so afraid of what magic would mean, but embraced the adventure in the end. And you were so happy to be my love interest in the story."

"Trust me, Arthur, that will be my most embarrassing moment from college."

"Oh, the things we got up to. You were such a giving-"

"Stop, Arthur, just stop," Alex snarled. Holding back a sigh, she fought back a flush of embarrassment and a rush of anger. He wanted to upset her, to hurt her, to make her lose her temper. "That isn't going to work, and you're just going to make me roll my eyes." Shaking her head, Alex swallowed. "What are you after?"

"Mother wanted Cathanáil to let the Sídhe escape into Earth," Arthur said. "She's got it in her head to play the hero." Arthur narrowed his eyes on her. "And now, here you are, thinking that you can stop the Darkness as if you're some kind of hero."

"Heroics are only worth so much. And you shouldn't talk about the mother you killed like that."

Arthur shrugged. "She should have known really. Should have seen it coming. After all, I have a history of betraying my family and my lovers. And she was both."

Arthur moved then, his appearance shifting as his eyes darkened, and his smile became too sharp and vicious. Black sparks flared around his hands. A stray thought of how appropriate the color was crossed Alex's mind. She twisted her torso, avoiding the beam of black that shot past her. Her heartbeat echoed. She could hear only that. Magic hung in the air. Small glittering flickers that outlined the trees, hillside, Arthur, Mjǫllnir, and Cathanáil. Beautiful and deadly. She kept moving, gripping Cathanáil and Mjǫllnir tightly in her hands. The Sword glowed with a soft light just before lightning arced out of the tip.

The beam struck Arthur, sending him stumbling back. He screamed; the beam remained fixed on him. Bringing up his hand, he shoved a wave of his magic towards her. It held off her own magic, but wasn't much. She saw Arthur's lips moving but couldn't hear. There were flashes of other colors of magic in the distance. The others were fighting.

Shoving Cathanáil forward, Alex gasped as the blade sliced into flesh. For a moment, a heartbeat, she was both hopeful and dreading what it meant. Arthur screamed something. Light flashed in front of her. Magic struck her chest, throwing her back. She hit the ground, but her fingers were still tight around the Iron Artifacts. Black sparks rippled in the air above her. Alex's ears popped painfully.

"You'll fail," Arthur mocked. "You're good at it, Alex. Merlin is dead, Morgana's a mess, and you want to go after the Darkness. Mother was a fool, but even she knew to run from the Darkness, not try to fight it."

Above her, the sky rumbled. There was no smell of rain, but Alex was sure it would come. The clouds twisted around each other, but the color and texture were shifting. Alex's eyes widened. It was the Darkness. It was at Earth! She needed to find the others-

Alex's eyes opened. Her heart was racing so hard she felt it in her throat and ears. She was choking on panic and- and- she was in her bedroom. The room was still and quiet. There was no sign or sound of Arthur. Her gaze went to the ceiling. It was too dark for her to see clearly, but there was no Darkness.

Surprise overtook her for only a moment before the realization that she'd only been dreaming settled on her. Exhaling, she closed her eyes and focused on breathing slowly. It had been so real, and yet, she'd been aware that something was off. Arthur was dead. How could she ever forget that? Then again, he'd died either possessed by part of the Light or in partnership with it. She'd never found out for sure which it was.

Opening her eyes, Alex sat up and reached for her phone. The harsh glow illuminated part of the room, and Alex grimaced. At 4:30 a.m., it was early enough to make her regret being awake, but not so early that trying to go back to sleep made sense. The house was quiet, and Alex fought down the urge to check on the others.

She was dreaming of Arthur. Why the hell was she dreaming about a dead enemy when there was so much else to worry about? A more rational part of her suggested she lacked closure about his death. She'd been unconscious when Nicki stabbed and killed Arthur only for the Light to then parade around in his body. She knew Arthur was dead, but he'd been dead before. Maybe that was why. A sigh escaped her. There was too much going on for her mind to be playing with her.

Alex climbed out of bed and turned on the light to a low level, grateful to have a dimmer. Soft white light filled the room, and Alex relaxed a little more when she found Cathanáil and Mjǫllnir in their rightful places over her bed. Everything was as it should be. Her laptop was on the desk, and all of her textbooks had been put away on the shelves. Over the last few days, they'd been cleaning the house and getting the little things organized.

A mostly packed heavy-duty backpack was sitting on the floor. It was only a little larger than Alex's school bag and not nearly the size of the massive backpacking packs she'd seen in stores. The debate over storage and ease of carrying had dominated dinner one night. Lance hadn't been thrilled with their inexperience and the limited gear they could take, but had acknowledged that they might need to run.

Making her bed quickly, Alex changed out of her PJs and redid her braided hair. She lifted the backpack onto her bed and opened the top as far as it would go. The disconnect between what Alex wanted to take and could take was vast and terrifying. There was one spare set of jeans, a couple of shirts, five tightly packed socks, and undergarments. Her sweatshirt and coat would be worn on the trip through to save space. A mess kit was packed up, matches, a utility knife, some backpacking food packets were all in the front pocket of the bag. A tightly packed tent that Alex knew she'd never get packed up so tightly again, and a rolled-up sleeping bag designed for backpacking were the finishing touches. Her flashlight and bottle of water were already in place.

Somehow, it all fit even with the iron they all had stashed at the bottom of their packs despite Lance's weight concerns. It was amazing, and still not enough. There was a little space left in the bag and so many things Alex wanted to bring. Bran was going to carry the Chalice while she'd have both Cathanáil and Mjǫllnir, so Lance had cautioned her against anything heavy. There wasn't much variation in anyone's packs. Aiden and Nicki were going to have small filtration systems in theirs. Morgana had a first aid kit and extra food.

Alex unpacked and repacked everything nervously. She grabbed her toothbrush, a comb, and a small case of soap and found space for them before reviewing the checklist again. There was more she wanted to take, but it might not help. Would bug spray work against bugs in another world? Would it poison the entire world?

Pushing away that thought because they'd have to fear taking anything, Alex went to her closet and opened the doors with a soft creak. On the floor was a simple large shoe box. Ironically, the same box that her pair of hiking boots had come in over a year ago, the same pair that she'd be wearing on their expedition. Alex didn't pick it up and instead opened it. The pieces of the Iron Chain were coiled up neatly, and just enough light entered the closet that Alex could see the individual links.

She hesitated. It was probably unwise to add more weight to the bag, and the Chain didn't seem to have any power anymore. The new Pendant around her neck warmed her skin while the Chain was cold to her touch when Alex reached out. Yet... yet, Alex couldn't shake the sense that there was still power there. Just beneath the surface of the metal was a soft shimmer that whispered to her. Even her disdain for Cuthbert didn't change that.

She unpacked the bag again, laying all of her gear out on the bed. It had all been checked for good quality, and they'd practiced setting the tents up in the living room. Still, Alex didn't feel ready. As she took out the last of her socks, Alex returned to the closet and picked up the Iron Chain. It wasn't all that long really, despite Cuthbert using it on the slave ship. This section, the magical part, had only been about five feet long. Other chains had linked to it and held the slaves, but this was the source of the ma gic.

Old anger flared in Alex's chest, but she was too tired for it to burn for long. She tested the weight of the Chain with a frown. It was only a few pounds, but right now, every pound mattered. Alex put the Chain into the bottom of her pack before she could change her mind and packed her socks around it. She only returned about a half of the prepared iron into the pack and instead put most of it to the side. All the others had iron; they'd be fine with this amount.

A gentle tap on the door made Alex jump. Then it opened, and Lance poked his head in with a curious and worried expression. His eyes took in the pack, and the gear still waiting to be returned to the bag. Alex gestured him inside, and he left the door open only a crack.

"Nightmare?" Lance asked gently. He didn't touch her, and Alex was grateful for that. She nodded. "Was it about the Darkness?"

"No. Not at first, at least." Alex snorted and shook her head. She rolled up a t-shirt and shoved it into the pack. "Arthur. It felt so real. A confrontation that we might have had, but didn't. Sorry, that probably didn't make sense."

"I dream about him too." Lance stepped further into the room and carefully closed the door behind him. It barely made a sound, and Alex slumped down onto her bed. "Sometimes it's memories and sometimes its things that never happened. Sometimes, I can forget what he was and what he did."

Alex wasn't sure how to take the confession. On the one hand, she was glad to know that she wasn't the only person haunted by Arthur. But Alex didn't want him to harm her friends from beyond the grave. She almost asked about Jenny, but couldn't voice the question. It wasn't a contest, but after her, Jenny had probably been the one that Arthur hurt the worst.

"Jenny does too," Lance said, as if reading her mind. "I have to wake her up sometimes from them." Lance's jaw tightened, and his Adam's apple bobbed in pent up rage. "They aren't as often now, thankfully, since the Light died."

"Good. I mean, not that she has nightmares, but that-"

"I know what you mean. I'm just glad that we share a room now. I hated it when we slept apart, and I had to worry." Lance shuddered, as if restraining himself from taking or hitting something. Instead, he flexed his fingers and watched Alex pack. "I don't think they'll ever go away for either of us, so don't beat yourself up for having dreams about him."

"I loved him," Alex whispered. She hated the words as soon as they slipped out. "And I just can't help but look back and want to hit myself."

"You're not the only one that he fooled." Lance sighed loudly and sank into Alex's desk chair. He slumped forward, resting his forearms against his knees. "Do you want to talk about it?"

"No, we were fighting. He was my enemy." Alex sniffed and shook her head, trying and failing to smile. "Not a very complicated dream, just my mind toying with me."

"That's not surprising." Lance sounded far too reasonable. "I understand why you don't want to wait, but I would have been happier if this could have been put on hold until you all went backpacking a couple of times." Alex glanced at him and found Lance shaking his head. "At least Morgana accepted the survival book I gave her. The information on plants obviously won't help, but if you get stuck, maybe it will give you a clue."

"Yeah." Alex swallowed at the reminder that they were going into unknown territory. "Are you okay with this?" Alex asked. She licked her lips nervously and folded her hands to keep them still. "Us going and leaving you, Jenny, and Avani to deal with any threats? I mean, so much has been happening, but-"

"I'm nervous," Lance confessed. "Scared and worried, but I understand. We'll be okay. The spell on the Fae is broken, and without Arthur egging them on, things have been more peaceful lately. The blood protection is in place around town, and Jenny and I can do some magic ourselves now. Not a lot, but it's better than nothing. Plus, we've been practicing with our daggers and talking with Avani's grandfather for more training advice."

"You have?" Alex blinked, and guilt welled up in her chest. "I didn't know that."

"You've been crazy busy. While we aren't advancing quickly, Avani's grandfather is nice, though he asked a lot of questions about our reincarnations that we couldn't answer."

"I'm glad you two don't have the memories."

"So am I." Lance tried to hide it, but Alex could see his hands tremble as he shivered. "Just the idea of remembering terrifies me. I can't imagine that we didn't live in guilt for the rest of our lives."

"You might not have ever found out what happened. There weren't exactly news sites back then."

"That's worse."

"No, I hope that's what happened. I hope that in the various lives, you two were able to just live in peace somewhere."

Memories rippled over the surface of Alex's mind as if it was water. She knew some of the lifetimes and some of the faces, but there were so many. Women that she was certain were Jenny and men that were Lance with different skin, different hair, and different eyes. They never meant to cause harm, but something bad almost always followed in the wake of them running off together or her finding them. Sometimes Merlin and Morgana were there; sometimes they weren't.

Alex doubted she'd ever know all the stories of how the tragedy played out, and that didn't bother her at all. This time, she'd dodged the bullet by being an embarrassingly straight woman. Jenny was beautiful, but Alex could honestly say that experimenting with her had never crossed her mind. Of course, part of that might have been Arthur. Alex hated the very thought, but he'd been everything she'd ever hoped for in a guy on the surface.

"Don't think about him," Lance said.

"What?"

"Arthur," Lance said. "Don't think about him. He's gone."

"How did you-" Alex cut off the question.

"You get this look on your face when you think about him," Lance admitted. He gestured to his brow. "You furrow your brow, frown, and get this look in your eyes. It's the brooding about Arthur look."

"Well, shit." Alex slumped down on her bed on the other side of the backpack. Galahad was knocked to the floor.

Lance chuckled at her reaction and smiled. "He's gone, Alex."

"Yeah, but the shadow of what he did lingers." Alex bit her lip, letting the thought stew.

There was nothing good in that direction, and she could feel Lance watching her. Clearing her throat, Alex placed the last of her gear into the bag. It was a tight fit, but there was a little space at the top. She glanced at Lance, but he was calm, and his face gave nothing away.

"I've never asked," Alex said. "But I feel I should. Do you love her?"

"Who? Jenny?" Lance blinked at the change in subject.

"Yes." Alex met Lance's surprised brown eyes. "Do you love her?"

"Yes." Lance smiled, easing the tension in the room. "I love her. I love the way her nose crinkles up when she's been looking at her phone for too long. I love the way she mumbles in her sleep. I love her giggle and smile." His posture was relaxing, and he lowered his face, trying to hide a sappy smile. "I'm sure that part of it was the reincarnation thing at the start, but now she's just Jenny to me. That's all I want her to be."

"Good." Alex exhaled, releasing something that had been weighing her down. "That's good to hear." She managed a small smile. "It probably wasn't fair for me to push you two together, but I'm glad it worked out."

"Well, I'll remind you that even after I found out about our past lives, I chose to go after Jenny. I knew she was worth it. I'm glad I did."

"Me too."

Lance reached down and picked up Galahad, lifting the small stuffed dog so they both could see it. For a moment, he said nothing and studied the old toy. Tears prickled at Alex's eyes, and she wasn't sure why. Then he held the stuffed dog out to her.

"You should take this with you."

"What?" Alex took Galahad without thinking and let her fingers sink into the familiar coarse material that had been well-loved. "Seriously?"

"Yeah."

"You're the one who was lecturing us about weight limits."

"He doesn't even weigh half a pound," Lance said. He shrugged a little, but didn't take his eyes off of Alex. "Besides… you don't know what's going to happen. Having something to comfort you isn't a bad idea." He snagged Alex's hand and squeezed it quickly. "I'm going to make some coffee. Come down if you'd like some."

With that, Lance left and closed the door softly behind him. Alex appreciated the distance, him giving her space to think and process. Galahad was still in her hand, and Alex rubbed her thumb over the fur of the beloved stuffed dog. Long ago, he'd guarded her against the dark at night. She smiled at the memory. Turning to her bag, Alex gently tucked the stuffed dog into the top of the backpack. A soft exhale escaped her. Maybe she was ready for this now.

11

Farewell to Ravenslake

The time had come. All the preparation was finished. Alex was both grateful and nervous about this. They were taking the steps they needed to hopefully strike back against the Darkness before it reached Earth again, but there'd been little time to think about anything but the plan lately. Maybe that was good, but right now, with her backpack on and the water pool in Merlin's backyard filled for them to make a water tunnel, Alex's stomach was trying to make her ill.

Merlin's back yard was cold and dark, with only the back porch and workshop lights providing any illumination. Overhead, thick gray winter clouds blocked out the moon and stars. Ravenslake at midnight was quiet. Alex hadn't heard a car since she woke up from her pre-travel nap an hour ago. Rolling her shoulders, Alex inhaled the cold air and willed herself to wake up the rest of the way. She'd showered and had breakfast with the others, but the darkness was telling her body to go back to sleep despite their attempts to prepare for the time zone jump.

"Okay, it's about 8 in the morning in Wales," Bran said. He was staring at his phone while his whole body twitched nervously. "Sunrise is a little after 8, so we'll be able to start the hike as soon as we arrive."

"That's better than hiking in the dark," Nicki agreed.

"Hey, I got us there," Lance huffed. He was off to the side, dressed in a heavy winter coat and barely holding back a scowl. "Just be careful. It's the mountains in winter. You're not used to the weight of your packs yet."

"We'll be careful," Alex promised. She nodded to herself. They'd be fine; they'd made the hike once before in the winter. "We'll be hiking during the daytime, at least."

Lance still didn't look reassured, but Alex didn't blame him. If she'd been in his shoes, she'd be uncomfortable with this plan. He caught her eyes, and Alex gave him a small nod. At least he'd hid all this worry earlier this morning. Of course, Lance had probably stayed calm for her sake. A rush of affection warmed Alex's chest.

Then her eyes moved to Jenny, who was standing silent and stoic beside Lance, hands in the pockets of her long, dark coat. While Lance's worry was now on his face, Jenny had masked her emotions. Something was brewing in Jenny's dark eyes, and her lips were pressed together in an expression just shy of a scowl.

Nicki bent down to check her backpack. "We've all got all of Lance's assigned gear, clothing, a bit of iron, and our daggers. I don't think we're forgetting anything."

"I've got the Chalice," Bran said. "Alex has Cathanáil and Mjǫllnir."

Alex nodded and shifted her backpack. She felt the weight of the last items she'd grabbed shift, and her stomach turned once again. The Iron Chain was bundled up at the bottom of her bag, adding extra weight and making Alex wonder yet again why she'd packed the thing. In theory, it provided her with a little spare iron, but they were all carrying at least one decently sized ingot. So, if there was another reason, Alex wasn't sure what it was yet. Maybe she was just scared about someone getting the magic that still lingered in the metal, or maybe it was something else. She wasn't sure about anything anymore.

Morgana strode over to Lance, Avani, and Jenny, pulling on a pair of leather gloves. Like the rest of them, she was in jeans and hiking boots, with several layers of shirts on under a coat. A pack with supplies was on her back, and her long hair was not only in its usual braid but also secured as a bun. She looked ready for anything. Alex's eyes jumped to the walking stick leaning against the workshop. It was the last one that Merlin had used, and judging from Morgana pulling it out, Alex was sure that Morgana was taking it with them.

"We do not know when we will return," Morgana said. Alex focused her attention on Morgana, who was speaking with Avani, Lance, and Jenny. Her features were calm, but the dullness in her eyes lingered. "I'm trusting you to stay on your guard and if-" Morgana's voice broke. "If there is a problem, do what you can to protect the Iron Realm."

"We'll keep an eye on things," Robin promised, joining them. She raised her chin as if daring Morgana to argue with her. "I was born in this realm. It is home."

"Thank you, Puck." Morgana nodded in return, and something passed between them. Robin seemed uneasy, but her expression only grew more determined. "I hope that we will return soon."

"Just say hello to the Dragon for us," Lance said. He looked over at Alex with a forced little smile. "I hope everything goes according to plan."

"I have alerted my family to the situation," Avani added. "While they aren't as powerful as me, our combined abilities are nothing to ignore."

"Arthur is dead, the Demons have been knocked down, and with luck, the current Old Ones will monitor each other." Morgana sounded more like she was trying to reassure herself. "Watch out for each other as well."

Morgana listed off a few more things to watch out for. Only Avani and Robin seemed to really listen to her. Jenny was looking over at Alex. There was a firm set to her jaw that told Alex she had something to say. Alex had the feeling that she wasn't going to like it. Then their gazes locked.

Alex was frozen in place as Jenny walked towards her. Jenny's features were soft, worry shining in her dark eyes, but her jaw was set stubbornly. Bracing herself, Alex couldn't imagine what Jenny had to say that would put that expression on her face. Her friend and wife of multiple lifetimes stopped just over a foot from her, meeting Alex's gaze head-on.

"Hi, Jenny."

"I don't think I'm ever going to see you again," Jenny whispered.

Alex's throat tightened. It was a negative sentiment; she should have dismissed it, but the words settled in her stomach, and she recognized the ring of truth to them. Swallowing, Alex said nothing. There was nothing she could say. Jenny tilted her head and blinked. A few shimmering tears appeared, but they did not fall. Jenny pressed her lips together tightly and reached forward to take Alex's hand. She sniffed as her thumb caressed the back of Alex's hand.

"Jenny..."

"There is so much... we have so much history, even if I don't remember it. You've never told me about the other lives, all the other times that I've betrayed you."

"They don't matter anymore. By the time I remembered, you were just Jenny to me." Alex forced a smile and focused on the familiar curve of Jenny's nose and jawline. "You, Jennifer Sanchez, have stood beside me. That was more than enough."

"Doesn't feel like it."

"It is."

They stared at each other. Alex felt a shift in the air. A chapter was over, an act of a play was closing, and the song was fading out. This was the end of something old and long. Jenny was right. She didn't know how Jenny knew, but perhaps she was linking into the magic of the Iron Realm in an unexpected way thanks to her magician training. Maybe someday, Alex would learn what this was. She was the Iron Soul. With luck, if she died on this mission, she'd be reborn soon. It wouldn't be the same, but maybe she'd see her friends again in another form.

"Be careful while we're gone," Alex said. "You're supposed to marry Lance and have a wonderful life together." Reaching out, she touched Jenny's cheek. They both leaned forward, touching their foreheads together, which left Alex leaning over Jenny. "Without guilt."

"I don't know if I can do that."

"Try. If you and Lance don't work because it doesn't work, then that's okay, but don't let it fall apart because you can't let go."

"I'll try." The promise was barely a whisper.

Kissing Jenny's forehead, Alex told herself that it was time to join the others. They wouldn't wait forever. They had a plan, and Alex was the one who had pushed for action. She couldn't be the one to falter now. Shifting back from Jenny, it did not surprise Alex to find that Lance was walking to join them. She released Jenny's hand with one last squeeze and smiled at Lance, hoping her gratitude showed in her eyes.

He stepped forward and hugged Alex before she could even take a few steps. His shoulders shuddered, and a soft sob escaped him. Gasping softly, Alex felt her own tears being renewed. Wrapping her arms around him, Alex smiled and accepted the affection that rolled off of Lance. Jenny must have told him, confided in him. That made her ridiculously happy, despite the circumstances.

"Look after each other," Alex said. "You're a good man, Lance. You always have been, and I have nothing but faith in you." He pulled back, letting Alex see his red eyes. She grasped his face in her hands and leaned up to kiss his cheek. "You were forgiven long ago."

"Thank you."

"Thank you," Alex returned softly.

Alex released Lance and watched with a smile as he put his arm around Jenny. Both of their eyes were shining with grief, but she found herself smiling. They'd helped her in this life; in so many small ways, they'd helped her stay focused and brought her happiness.

"I love you both."

"We love you," Jenny promised. "And if we are reborn again, then I hope we meet once more under better circumstances."

Alex nodded, but she doubted it. Instinct told her that Lance and Jenny were finished with their cycle of rebirth now. She didn't know what that meant for them. Hopefully, it was good. If they were reborn, she was certain that they were no longer tied to her soul. They were free. Alex's shoulders slumped, and she made no move to leave Jenny and Lance. Blinking away tears, she looked over at the others.

Robin and Aiden were standing very close to each other now. The Old One was smirking, looking like the cat that got the cream rather than a chipper bird, while Aiden was grinning like an idiot. They leaned close and whispered to each other. Alex looked away to give them privacy. That relationship was further along than she'd thought it would be, but then again, the knowledge you are about to throw yourself into another world probably served as an excellent motivation to get moving.

Avani was hugging Nicki. Fear and worry flickered over the magician's face, but when she released Nicki, she smiled and looked more confident. Lokpal glowed with pride in Alex's mind, and she watched the pair for a moment longer before nodding to Lance and Jenny. They both smiled at her and shifted to the side to give her a clear path to the pool. Walking past them was a sucker punch to her sternum; it left her breathless and her knees shaking.

The desire to turn around spiked in her chest. What was she doing? Why had she pushed for this? Leaving the Iron Realm could be a disaster, and that was if their stop in Wales went according to plan! What were the odds that things would go according to plan? She eyed Nicki and Aiden again as she joined Bran by the pool. If she was a better friend, she'd have them stay here just in case of trouble. It was foolish, maybe even suicidal, for all the mages to leave the world. Alex was afraid of what they were going to find.

"I hope you're right about this," Bran said. "Us having magic."

"I had some kind of power when I touched the light and was in that other place." Alex licked her lips nervously. She was dizzy, and tears were valiantly fighting their way out of her eyes. "I don't know what to expect, Bran. I'm tempted to tell Morgana to stay."

"She wouldn't. Protecting you, helping the Iron Soul is the only solid ground she has left." Bran shook his head. "I can't imagine what she's feeling. The one thing in her world that didn't change is gone. She's seen centuries; kingdoms, hell empires, rise and fall while she and Merlin lived on. By most standards, they were basically married."

"He was her partner." Alex's eyes teared up, and she wanted to turn and hug Morgana. "I know. I know that."

And she did. Memories echoing with grief flitted through her mind. It was always Merlin and Morgana. She knew that from time to time; they lived separate lives, but it had always been them. If she knew one of them in a life, she knew them both.

Bran took her hand. The warmth of his skin, even through their gloves, was grounding. He was real, and he was here with her. He wasn't running away like he should. Then the guilt came. Bran had a mother who loved him dearly, who had already lost her husband, and now he was leaving the Iron Realm. She knew Bran well enough to know that he hadn't warned his mother about what was happening. That was one more thing that she didn't want to think about.

"Breathe," Bran said. "We know the risks, Alex."

No, they didn't. She didn't know the risks, so they couldn't. Still, she followed his advice and slowly caught her breath. Now was not the time for a nervous breakdown. On her back, the Iron Chain's weight seemed to increase.

In front of her, the water in the pool was rippling as the winter wind rushed across its surface. Sooner or later, it would freeze, and she wasn't looking forward to jumping in this water tunnel. Bran squeezed her hand again and then released it. He didn't ask questions about what she'd been talking about with Lance and Jenny. He was a good friend like that.

"We're ready." Nicki stepped up beside them. "Shouldn't keep delaying."

"It's not too late to back out," Alex said. "You don't have to come with me."

"We don't know what to expect." Nicki shook her head and smiled sadly. "Can't let you go off alone."

"If this goes well, I won't be alone," Alex reminded her. "And maybe a mage should-"

"I'm seeing this through." Nicki's eyes narrowed, daring Alex to argue with her. "We started this together back on that Halloween night. All scared and confused, but also a little excited while Merlin and Morgana explained the Tree of Reality." Nicki's lips quirked into a soft smile, and she looked at the pool of water. "And here we are, getting ready to actually see it. I'm scared, but also excited. I wouldn't miss it for the world."

"I don't know," Alex whispered. "The world's a huge thing. It is a great price for a small vice."

Bran chuckled, and Alex figured he knew the quote. Nicki raised an eyebrow in confusion but didn't ask. Good, it was healthy for her to be the one who missed a reference occasionally. Morgana put a hand on Alex's shoulder and raised her hand. Silver light spilled out across the yard as Morgana's magic swirled into the pool. Looking over her shoulder, Alex swallowed as Avani, Robin, Lance, and Jenny lined up behind them.

Avani nodded to her and smiled, her hands glowing softly as she cast an unknown spell. Robin held her gaze, and Alex could feel the weight of a silent promise. Even if she was leaving Ravenslake empty of mages, she could know there were at least those who would look after it in her absence. It was almost enough to make her feel better as the water in the pool splashed up and formed a whirlpool in the air, opening the path to Wales.

12

Far From Home

721 B.C.E. Gulf of Guinea, Nigeria

Merlin's breathing was wrong. He was struggling to move. His eyes were wide with fear that was quickly turning to panic. Morgana violently suppressed her own nerves to focus on the old man. She hadn't even looked at the wound yet, but the state Merlin was in told her a great deal, and none of it was good.

"I'm here," Morgana said gently. "It's me, Merlin."

"Morgana." His voice was raspy. "You should- you should go."

"I'm going to pretend you didn't say that." Morgana's hands shook as she reached out to Merlin. "Stay still, you old fool."

"Morgana, strange place," Merlin groaned. "No magic. She might come back. Cathanáil-" Merlin coughed, and his body spasmed.

Morgana gently pulled back the fabric of Merlin's cloak. His tunic was soaked with blood in one large spot, but he was still breathing and groaning. She was tempted to smack him for worrying her, but there were other concerns. Gently laying Cathanáil across her lap, Morgana made herself comfortable and began rolling back the sliced fabric so she could get a better look. Merlin had a deep cut in his side, but thankfully, by some miracle, it hadn't struck any of his organs. A sigh of relief escaped Morgana, and Merlin turned his head to look at her.

"I'm not leaving you."

Defeat flickered in his eyes, but Merlin seemed to listen finally. "Moving hurts."

"She sliced muscle," Morgana said. "I don't have a lot of magic, but I can at least start healing you."

Merlin nodded and closed his eyes. Blood was still oozing out of the wound, and Morgana found herself grateful that he had stayed down. If Merlin had tried to fight, she didn't doubt that he would have lost even more blood. There was blood on his hands, indicating to her he'd held the wound and likely tried to heal it himself.

"I'm out of power," Merlin admitted. "That tunnel... it was difficult to protect us and follow her."

"I see." Morgana grimaced as another pulse of blood came pouring out of the wound. The edges were beginning to clot over thankfully, but she needed to focus. "Stay still."

Her chest ached as she pulled on her magic. Her limbs trembled, and beads of sweat rolled down her back. There was a small flow of power that responded to her call. Not much. She was fatigued, and Merlin was exhausted. She lifted her right hand and brought it towards the wound while protectively clutching Catha nail's hilt with her left. If she helped Merlin and Badb came back, they would be doomed, but Merlin would likely die if she didn't. They were in a strange place. She didn't know the plants, and if the locals were dangerous, she couldn't protect a man who couldn't move.

Morgana's silver magic was dim in the bright sunlight as it beat down on them and reflected off the golden sand. It was so bright, and Morgana was already longing for the more familiar lands of home. She put her hand close to the wound and closed her eyes tightly. It was difficult for her to focus, but a few deep breaths helped center her mind. She needed to take care of Merlin first, everything else could wait. Morgana opened her eyes and watched the silver magic sink into the flesh.

Merlin hissed, and Morgana narrowed her eyes at the wound, pushing all of her willpower into a single command to heal and imagining the flesh knitting together. The cut was clean, if long and deep. Her magic pulled the two sides of the wound together, and a silvery glow surrounded the area. Morgana's hands trembled. Her lungs struggled to expand, sending her into a coughing fit. Morgana slumped to the side and the last of her magic slipped away as she gasped and coughed.

It took her a short time to recover. Everything hurt, and she wanted to curl up in the shade and sleep, but there was more to worry about. She'd closed her eyes at some point during her coughing fit and kept them closed as she desperately swallowed and tried to wet her mouth and throat. They needed to find freshwater soon. Without their magic, the saltwater would do them no good.

Merlin sounded a little better. His breathing wasn't as ragged, and Morgana finally opened her eyes. Her knees protested every movement, but she shifted to examine Merlin's side. The wound wasn't completely healed, but the flesh had been bound together to stop the bleeding. Red angry skin met Morgana's gaze, and she regretted her inability to do more. She had no doubt that the wound still hurt badly. Merlin groaned, but carefully sat up.

"Thank you."

"It's far from healed."

"We can help it along as we recover," Merlin said. "But thank you for stopping the bleeding." He didn't touch the wound, and Morgana noted he hadn't even looked at his side yet. "Let's move into the shade."

Morgana nodded and stood up slowly. She kept her hold on Cathanáil, but also helped leverage Merlin up. Thankfully, his staff had made it through with them, and once he was on his feet, it was of great help to Merlin as he limped across the beach. They headed up into the trees, which Morgana eyed suspiciously. None the less, they provided much-needed shade from the sun. It seemed roughly the same time of day as it had been when they first entered that strange water tunnel.

Slowly, they got Merlin propped against one of the strange trees. Glaring at the odd trunk, Morgana almost kicked the thing as a way to get out her frustration. But her body was too sore as it was, and she knew better than to add a stupid injury to their problems, especially with Merlin watching. He leaned against the trunk and sighed in relief as Morgana helped him get off his outer layer of clothing so he could cool down.

"That thing she did with the water, how did she do that?" Morgana asked.

"I am not sure." Merlin's voice was soft and breathy, warning Morgana that he was still very weak. "I suppose we could try to do it ourselves, but even following Badb was incredibly difficult." Merlin shook his head, only to hiss in pain. "I'm not sure if we should risk it."

"Still, can you imagine being able to go anywhere?" Morgana smiled a little at the idea, her mind spinning with possibilities. "I assumed that Cyrridven's ability was due to her being an Old One."

"She has all but merged with the waters of this world." Merlin's muscles were finally beginning to relax. "I confess that it has never occurred to me to attempt such a feat."

"But we were able to move through the tunnel," Morgana said. Then a rough laugh escaped her. "What a pair of fools we are. We rushed in after Badb without a second thought."

"She took Cathanáil. We are a bit protective of it." Merlin chuckled a little, only to sigh. "I hope she stays gone. We're in no condition for another fight."

"I don't think she is either." Morgana wasn't certain, but Badb had been struggling there at the end. "But, where are we?"

"I'm not sure." Merlin looked up into the tree. "I've heard about trees like this. Far to the south in the old trading days."

Morgana nodded slowly. Now that he mentioned it, that was familiar to her as well. There'd been many tales in their homeland of far-off places to the south when the bronze trade had connected them with the whole world. They were south then, but where and how far from the boys?

"We need a plan," Morgana said. She glared up at the strange branches of the tree. "We've recovered the Sword, but I doubt Badb will be done with whatever she is planning."

"No." Merlin shifted and hissed in pain. Morgana put a hand on his shoulder to still him and gave the old man a sharp warning look. He settled with a soft grumble. "I'm not sure if I'd rather she keep her focus on us or not. She can travel much faster than us with that raven form of hers."

"And the water tunnels." Morgana grit her teeth and tried to think. "We survived following her through it. Perhaps, we can manage something similar with our magic. Once we recover somewhat," she added quickly. "It could prove very useful."

"Perhaps." Merlin hummed thoughtfully, resting his hands on his chest. Discomfort rolled off the man, but he was staying still, which Morgana appreciated. "Though I'm not sure how it truly works. We went into the tunnel in one body of water, even if it was a smaller one, and came out in the ocean, which suggests that it connects through the water. But what are the limitations or is it simply a question of control?"

"You were exhausted when we arrived."

"Indeed. Keeping us safe and following her was difficult." Merlin shook his head a little. "It is worth exploring, but we must be careful."

"Agreed." Morgana looked around one more time and settled herself a foot away from Merlin to give him space while still being in the shade. Her legs were grateful at the change, and her sore muscles began to ease. "I just hope that Gofiben and Bran are alright."

Her fingers itched to draw her scrying mirror and try to see them. Her visions were never perfectly clear, but over the years, her skills had vastly improved. But she had no magic to spare. The ache in her body burned with a warning not to go any further.

"Don't," Merlin said firmly.

"I'm not doing anything." Morgana gave up and flopped back on the ground. It was firm under her back, but the shade was lovely, and it was better than supporting herself.

"Don't try to use your magic. I'm in no condition to build a shelter and try to keep you alive for days on end."

"That only happened once," Morgana sighed. "I won't risk it again. I remember."

"Good, see that you keep that in mind. We need to be smart right now, Morgana. Babd may leave us alone long enough for us to recover, but we can't be sure."

"I'm confident that we'll recover faster than her." Morgana closed her eyes and inhaled deeply. "We are mages of the Iron Realm, while she is its enemy. Her use of power clearly affected her physical form. I suspect that she's in worse condition than us."

Morgana meant the words. The odd flickering in Badb's limbs had been disturbing to see, and only her knowledge that the Old Ones were masses of power with a mind had kept her from being horrified. Still, that information did not sit easy on her mind. Cyrridven was not Morgana's favorite being in the world, but she knew that the Old One was a staunch ally and gave them truthful information.

"Badb has also clearly lost her mind," Merlin said darkly. "She may not care. And today is a season day. At least... I think it still is, so our power is at its weakest."

Morgana held back a curse and a snarl. Merlin was right. It had been a season day when they jumped into the damned tunnel, and it felt like the same day. Such thoughts took her back to their battle with Badb before the tunnel. The Old One had set much of a forest on fire and had wrestled Cathanáil away from them. She'd done something with the Sword, putting it into the ground and releasing power.

"She said that she'd done it," Morgana said uneasily. "When she had Cathanáil."

"I remember."

"What do you think she did?"

"I saw nothing," Merlin said.

That was true. There had been a fog of dark red magic, but no apparent changes. Morgana hoped that the Old One's glee had been premature. After all, she pulled Cathanáil free and started to run. Surely that meant that whatever she'd been attempting had been a failure. Morgana ran her fingers over Cathanáil's hilt, just to reassure herself that they still had it. She rubbed her chest, finally recalling that her pain wasn't just exhaustion, but that Badb had gotten a powerful blow before the blasted tunnel.

"We need to move on," Morgana said. She hated the words as soon as they left her mouth. "We need fresh water and shelter. This sun...." Morgana groaned. "I hate it." Merlin laughed, but it was a humorless sound, reassuring her she wasn't alone in her feelings. "And we need a plan."

"We travel north." Merlin's voice was firm, and she heard him move. "We rest for today, regain our strength. Tomorrow, we hike north and try to recreate that water tunnel."

"Really?" Morgana frowned as she sat up. Her wet hair was sticking to her neck, and she was certain that bugs were crawling through it. "We don't know how to control it."

"Small attempts first," Merlin said. "Perhaps across a lake to start with if we find one or along the shore." He nodded to himself and gently touched his side. Morgana's eyes dropped to it. There was no change in the wound. The red had yet to fade, but they hadn't been able to wash off the blood — one more reason to find clean water. "But we have to get back. If Badb did manage something with Cathanáil, then we can't leave Bran and Gofiben to face it alone."

The very suggestion made Morgana's skin crawl. For the first time since they'd jumped into the tunnel, Morgana second-guessed herself. Protecting Cathanáil was essential, and letting a mad Old One have the Sword was out of the question, but now she couldn't help but worry. They were far to the south of home. They had to be based on the trees and the heat. Cathanáil was now oddly heavy in her grasp. Arto wouldn't be happy with her. He would have wanted her to protect her students more than Cathanáil.

Still, what was done was done. She and Merlin had pursued Badb, and now they could only address the situation as it stood. Morgana firmly told herself that they couldn't stay here. Water was an immediate need. The heat of the sun was rapidly drying their clothes, and soon they'd start to feel more effects from the heat.

Morgana shifted her body closer to Merlin and let the older mage lean on her. Between her and his staff, he could stay upright, and they wandered up the beach, looking for freshwater and shelter for the night. With any luck, they'd be able to avoid Badb and regroup. Once they did, the first order of business was to find a way home. Morgana was confident that the boys would be alright for a little while without them, but she didn't want to entertain thoughts of what would happen if Badb made it back before she and Merlin did.

13

A Cave in Wales

Alex couldn't be sure if Wales was warmer or not. They were still in the northern hemisphere, so it was still winter, and there were a few inches of snow on the ground. It wasn't as deep as the snow in Ravenslake, but the air was more humid, making the winter chill sharper. Still, it was daytime in Wales, and the sun was rising higher and higher into the sky as they hiked. Her new pendant was warm against her skin beneath her clothing, and Alex burned to test it out again.

They'd all made it out of the water tunnel from Ravenslake to a river near the mountain where the Dragons were hidden away without getting too wet. Some quick magic had dried off their feet, so there was no reason to complain. But a sense of unease and fear lingered over the group. Aiden was leading the way, following a magical guiding orb that made Alex wish they'd been better at such magic the first time they'd come here. It would have made everything easier on Lance.

Nicki was behind Aiden, Morgana behind Nicki, then Alex, and Bran was at the rear. No one was talking. Morgana was using the walking stick, and it hit the ground over and over with soft thumps. That was it. Alex kept thinking about her parting with Jenny, which only made her want to cry. Perhaps the others were feeling something similar, a sense of loss and awareness that things were different now.

Why she wouldn't see Jenny again was a dark question. Alex didn't want to think about it, but it taunted her with every step. The landscape was pretty enough, but not enough to distract her. If Jenny was right, then it was most likely that she was going to die. That was okay. It was better than Jenny dying. She and Lance were finally happy together, and Alex didn't want them to lose that. Jenny had a family while Alex didn't anymore. Her stomach turned; her mother would hate the very thought that Alex was okay with the idea of dying. Of the possible reasons they wouldn't meet again, it was the one she most preferred. After all, she'd come back and, with some luck and mercy from the magic of the Iron Realm, would remember her other lives next time.

"Almost there," Aiden called.

His voice made everyone jump. In the cold winter day, there were almost no animals around, and there wasn't even much of a breeze. Up ahead, Alex saw Aiden flinch at his voice and snorted in amusement. They kept hiking, following the trail which curved around the mountain. It was longer than Alex remembered it, which was really something since last time they'd been hiking at night.

"Do you hear the ringing?" Bran asked.

"Ringing?" Alex frowned before she remembered the strange bell sound that had guided them last time. "No. That might have been a onetime thing, or connected to the Chalice rather than the cave itself." She wasn't sure, but that sounded reasonable.

"I suppose so."

Aiden stopped, bringing their small party to a standstill alongside a looming rock face. Alex stared at it as the others looked at her expectantly. It didn't look familiar, but she trusted that the magic had brought them to the right place. Pulling off the glove of her right hand, Alex held out the hand and skimmed it across the surface of the stone. She wasn't sure what she was looking for and searched her memory with little luck.

Sending out a small wave of magic, Alex was about to close her eyes and search when the magic tugged her a few feet forward. She ignored the others and followed the magic, letting her fingers brush over the stone and icy packed earth. When magic pulsed beneath her hands, Alex stopped and rested both of her hands against a patch of rock.

The stone melted away under Alex's palms. A narrow entrance opened, and Alex shifted her hand to summon an orb of light. Tossing it in ahead of her, Alex silently commanded it to float in the air. Another light was created behind her as Alex stepped into the mountain. It was cool and humid. A low rumbling was echoing against the stones all around Alex. She walked further into the cavern, following the rocky outcropping that she knew hung over a deep cavern. The stone pedestal at the end that had once held the Iron Chalice was empty. Despite knowing at the Chalice was in Bran's bag, the sight still seemed wrong.

"Emrys!" Alex's voice echoed off the walls.

Stillness met her call. She turned slightly to look at Morgana. Her remaining mentor was creating another light orb to illuminate the cavern. Between the three floating lights, Alex could see the dark local stone and the scrapes in the rock that could only be from dragon claws.

"The Iron Soul."

There was a rush of air and scraping of stone against stone. Shadows flickered at the edge of the outcropping, and Alex stepped back to leave the edge. Something large was moving below them in the dark. While she knew it was the red Dragon, the more primitive part of her brain urged Alex to run. A small voice whispered that it could be the White Dragon, that it might be free.

Then a long reptilian head with gleaming red scales came rushing into view. Light danced off the scales of the Dragon as it landed gracefully on a rock ledge. Long talons dug into the stone, and large wings folded down against its back. It lowered its head to prevent its horns from scraping on the rocks of the ceiling. Smiling, Alex stepped forward and tightened her grip on the bag's strap.

"Hello, Emrys."

"Greetings, Iron Soul. I was not expecting to see you again in the flesh so soon, old friend." Emrys's eyes shifted from Alex to Bran, who offered a small wave. "And greetings to you, Bran."

"Hi. How are you?" Bran asked.

"I am well." Emrys chuckled, his deep tones filling the space. "Yet, I doubt you came here amid winter for social pleasantries."

"You'd be correct." Alex licked her lips and hesitated. The plan was straightforward, but she was unsure how even to explain her reasons for coming here. "Things outside are bad, Emrys."

"I have seen no reason to panic in my viewing pool."

"Humans don't know yet, but that Darkness I asked you about, it's real and even more dangerous than I feared."

"The force that drove the Demons to invade? I remember you asking me if I knew of it. I do not."

"You don't, but we've seen it." Alex struggled for a moment. "We know that it's in most, if not all, branches. It seems to be a force of nature or maybe from another universe. Something truly alien. We don't know for sure, but it's already reached Earth once, and we don't know what will happen if it keeps consuming worlds."

"Why are you here?" Emrys asked. "I hear you, Iron Soul, but I cannot help you."

"Maybe you can." Alex shrugged off her bag and set it on the ground. "I have something that should kill the White Dragon. That would free you from your prison in this cave."

The Red Dragon's nostrils flared, and a puff of smoke swirled into the air. Alex's heart jumped as a memory of the Dragon breathing fire sprang to the forefront of her mind. She didn't move back and stayed still as the Dragon studied her.

"To what end?" Emrys asked. "What is your plan, then?"

"I want to go into another world, to investigate the Darkness and stop it before it reaches the Iron Realm again. Even if it does not consume my world, there have to be consequences to such a thing."

The Dragon's head stretched towards her. Heat radiated off the scales, and a low rumbling escaped Emrys as his bright eyes studied Alex. Staying still, Alex stared into the closest eye and waited for whatever conclusion that the Dragon was going to draw.

"I am surprised, Grand Mage, that you are allowing such a plan to proceed."

"Merlin is dead." Morgana's words were blunt, and Alex flinched. "The world has already changed thanks to that great loss. If he were alive, I'm sure that he would want to stop Alex's plan."

"My condolences." Emrys bowed his head for a moment. "What do you think, Grand Mage?"

"I don't know." Alex didn't turn around, but she could hear the doubt in Morgana's voice and imagine the distance in her eyes. "The Iron Soul was made long ago by an unknown force to protect the Iron Realm. I believe Alex knows the way to achieve that. She has the memories of her former lives and a genuine desire to end the danger. She's not wrong that this Darkness is the root of all the evil and conflict between the worlds."

"Yes, that seems possible," Emrys agreed. "But leaving this world, a realm where you have power and knowledge for the unknown, is a risk."

"It would be less of a risk if I had a Dragon," Alex answered. She couldn't help but smirk.

Emrys laughed. The sound echoed around them, and he pulled his head back. Horns scratched across the ceiling, but he didn't seem to notice or care. A hint of hysteria slipped into the laugh, and Alex licked her lips nervously. Then, the tone shifted to one of relief, and Emrys slowly stopped laughing. His large golden eyes were a darker shade than she remembered.

"I suppose it would be." Emrys lowered his head to look into the darkness below. "I cannot return to my homeworld, but there is no law that would prevent me from going into other worlds under the circumstances." He looked back at Alex thoughtfully. "You truly believe this to be the best option."

"Our world has been suffering invasions due to other beings running from the Darkness," Alex said. "It's just going to get worse from now on. If there's even a chance-" Alex stuttered and needed a moment to breathe. Everyone waited, and she swallowed. "If we can slow down the Darkness or even better, seal up wherever it is coming from, we can protect the Iron Realm and other worlds. Otherwise, of course, beings are going to run to this world." She shook her head and tried to ignore the stab of guilt with no success. "What else can they do?"

Emrys stared at her, his gold eyes boring into her very being. Her knowledge, real knowledge, of his abilities was limited. Gofiben's time with the great creature had been short, and the Dragon had easily amazed him. Not that Alex blamed him, it was a real Dragon! Then Emrys nodded and pulled his head back.

"You have a good point, Iron Soul. Alex, if you can destroy my prisoner and free me from my obligation to keep him contained, I will help you however I can."

The words were an immense relief to Alex. Morgana had pushed her to make a backup plan, but Alex just couldn't imagine their crazy scheme being successful without the literal firepower of a Dragon. His ability was physiological, and Alex was confident that it would work in worlds where the magic might not. Then Emrys leaned forward, resting one great taloned foot on the end of the outcropping and lowering his head. She blinked dumbly at him, and the Dragon chuckled.

"The White Dragon is far below; I will take you down."

Alex blushed, but nodded quickly. After a moment of debate, she opened her bag and pulled out the two jars of poison and placed them gently in the pockets of her coat. Her gloves added an extra layer of protection, but that didn't stop Morgana from giving her a worried look. Doing her best to appear confident, Alex smiled at the others.

"We'll be back soon," she promised.

She climbed onto the Dragon. Alex barely held back a hysterical giggle as she carefully turned around on Emrys'... shoulders and gripped tightly to the lowest horns on his neck. A quick glance at the others revealed that Nicki, Bran, and Aiden all looked as startled and overwhelmed as she thought. Her legs were spread wide around Emrys' bulk, and she didn't feel steady. It reminded her a lot of being on a horse during a trip in her high school years. That hadn't gone great now that she thought about it.

Then Emrys moved. He dropped straight off the ledge. A scream filled Alex's mouth, but her jaw was clenched too tightly for it to escape. Below them was only blackness. They were dropping like a stone. Suddenly, Emrys opened his wings, and they slowed with a mighty rush of air against Alex's face. Her hands ached as they stopped.

"Light would help you." Amusement filled Emrys' voice.

Nodding, Alex opened her mouth and gulped in a few breaths. Then she cracked her hand off of the horn and flexed her fingers. Thankfully, her magic was calmer than her, and making a light orb was a familiar process. The orb sprang into being, and a pale glow spilled forth around Alex. She looked around curiously, never having seen this far down into the cavern as herself or as any other life.

It was far larger than Alex would have estimated. A football field would have easily fit down here, and the roof was high above them. The walls were smooth, with a slightly concave shape. A large pool of water was in the middle of everything by a slab of rock that formed what looked like an odd table. It took Alex a moment, but she realized it was for the Dragon to lounge on. There were no personal effects, just shaped stone and water.

"It's... nice."

"It has kept us contained." Emrys didn't sound distressed. "One thing we need to be aware of is that by returning to my branch of the Tree of Reality, I may need to eat again."

"Right, you don't eat."

"I could, but I do not require it."

Alex glanced at Emrys nervously, wondering if the Dragon still felt hunger. After centuries, if he did, then the pain would be terrible. Then again, he had a prisoner that he needed to kill- she put a stop to that line of thinking immediately. Still, he was calm and in full control. Then something moved beyond her light orb. Alex waved her hand and moved the orb closer to the far side.

The White Dragon lay at the bottom of the cavern with rocks pinning it to the ground. Large pale wings were ripped to shreds, but Alex could see that they were already knitting themselves back together. Emrys landed alongside a pool of still water. A growl escaped the White Dragon before it turned its face away from the light. She braced herself, wondering if it would speak, but it merely huffed and stayed silent.

"He'll say nothing," Emrys said.

Alex nodded to show her understanding. She couldn't speak. The sight of the White Dragon brought old memories forward even as her inner child rejected the idea of hurting a Dragon. These two poor creatures had fallen through a hole created by Babd using Cathanáil. Merlin and Morgana had taken off after her, leaving the Iron Soul to deal with the reality that there were Dragons in the world.

"Are you sure you're okay with this?" Alex asked Emrys. "I mean, he's been the only company you've had for centuries."

"He was vicious before we came here." Emrys' tone made Alex shiver. She knew that Emrys was some sort of law enforcement Dragon, but had little information on what the other Dragon had done. "And his repeated deaths have taken a toll."

There was a story there. Alex swallowed back a rush of bile and nodded again. They'd been trapped here for centuries, the White Dragon trying to escape and Emrys having to kill him over and over. It wasn't a pleasant situation. Hopefully, the Red Dragon's mind was as intact and rational as it seemed. Otherwise, this could be a very bad thing.

Her hands still shook as she pulled out the first jar. It was one of the modern ones made of thick glass, and Alex tested its weight thoughtfully. Despite Nicki's hopes, they'd never had enough of the poison after making the connection with the Darkness to figure out how to weaponize it. At that point, it had become a valuable research substance. Now, however, she was looking at a Dragon that she was supposed to destroy and lacked a safe way to deliver it.

There were two jars. Surely even the poison in one would be enough. Then again, they couldn't die. If this went badly, then she'd only be torturing the creature. Alex's memories of their arrival and the White Dragon's actions were jumbled. Regardless, she didn't want to torture it. Lacking options, Alex lifted the jar and threw it as hard as she could at the Dragon.

The poison exploded over the pale shimmering scales in a shower of dark liquid and glass, spilling everywhere, and Alex instinctively drew back. Horror and curiosity fought for dominance, and she hated it. The Dragon roared, turning its golden eyes on them. It tried to move, but the poison was already eating large sections of its back legs. A cry of agony, a sound that echoed in her memory escaped the beast. Another smaller growl left Emrys, it sounded pained and pitying. She swallowed again and, despite the urge to look away, made herself watch as the beast collapsed on the floor, its body twitching.

It wasn't enough. Alex brought out the second jar as the poison slowed. Parts of the Dragon's ribs were exposed, and pale pink muscles were turning black and crumbling right before her eyes. She took a few steps forward, certain that the Dragon would not move. Carefully opening the lid, Alex swung her right hand to spill the liquid in an arch forward. It splashed across the White Dragon's neck. A low groan was the last sound the creature made before the poison spread across its body. There was still a little left in the jar, and Alex crept forward to pour it out over the Dragon's head. A few dark purple droplets hung dangerously on the edge of the glass.

Backing away, Alex forced herself to watch. If she was going to play executioner in order to free Emrys so he could help her, then she had to witness what she was doing. The Dragon thrashed a little more, but its throat was gone, and it could make no sounds. Claws scraped against the ground, and its tail slapped the wall before it dissolved. Soon there was nothing but a mess of dark liquid that quickly faded away, leaving a shallow hole in the stone, almost like a grave.

"It is done." Emrys exhaled, the sound long and low. "I wish there had been another way. That was not the method I would have chosen."

"I hope…" Alex stopped herself.

"His crimes merited his imprisonment," Emrys assured her. "But I had to tear him apart daily to keep him from escaping. It took a toll on us both."

There were questions she wanted to ask, but it occurred to Alex that the psychology of a Dragon might be very different. She could not assume that the Red Dragon would react as she or another human might. Still, centuries of daily fighting was a terrifying idea. Then again, they were about to enter another world with no certainty of how it would affect them. Nausea took hold of Alex even before she climbed back onto the Dragon's back and let him carry her back to the others. It was too late to turn back now.

14

Dragon's Burden

Alex wasn't sure how to react to Emrys. There was a warm feeling of friendship from Gofiben, but none of the others except her had ever interacted with the Dragon. He'd been in their world for centuries and yet had never been a part of it. While she'd met Sif, Odin, Puck/Robin, and Shiva over and over in different lifetimes, her interactions with Emrys had been singular. He'd only ever been part of Gofiben's life and hers and only briefly at that.

When her soul had first met the Dragon centuries ago, things had been very different. Emrys had been a simple law enforcement officer pulled into their world, along with a dangerous prisoner. Gofiben had been his guide to the new world he was trapped in, while Emrys had been proof to Gofiben that not everything magical was out to destroy him. They'd gotten along, and Emrys' fire had helped craft the Iron Chalice when Gofiben had been desperate to stop Badb's plague. There was gratitude there, along with guilt that Gofiben hadn't been able to help the Dragon in return. Had Gofiben lived longer, Alex had no doubt that he would have spent years trying to find a better solution for their Dragon ally. She didn't know what he might have done, but had he been alive when

Merlin and Morgana finally returned, maybe a better solution would have been found.

Alex could imagine Merlin revealing the poison years earlier and them using it to kill the White Dragon. With him out of the way, maybe Emrys would have been able to go somewhere else. Perhaps the Old Ones would have had suggestions. It was a silly exercise in her imagination because even with the White Dragon gone earlier; the law forbidding Emrys to go home would have still been in effect.

Now the Dragon was curled around her, lounging on the edge of the rocky cliff and purring gently. The cave mouth was still open, and a soft icy breeze was flooding the cavern. Alex had debated closing it with magic for a moment, but the sight of how Emrys was basking in the fresh air had given her pause. It was one more reminder that the Dragon had been locked up for centuries. Honestly, that knowledge alone made Alex wonder how Emrys was as sane as he was.

The others were scattered around the cave. Aiden and Nicki had braved the hillside and found some wood. A small but energetic fire was gradually warming up the cavern despite the constant influx of much colder air. The decision to wait for nightfall to let the Dragon outside had been quickly made, but Alex was regretting it more and more as time crawled by. Bran was writing in a small moleskine journal, and Aiden and Nicki were sharing a paperback book that one of them had apparently brought with them. Morgana's eyes were closed, and she was resting near the doorway, likely meditating and standing guard.

"And now more waiting," Alex complained. Her right hand was toying with the new necklace she wore, and her fingers traced the triskelion symbol. "It's the worst."

"I understand," Emrys chuckled. "You could scry for entertainment as I do, but I'd advise you to save your magic."

"I'm glad you could at least manage that," Alex said. Her fingers tightened around the pendant. "I suppose I can handle some boredom. If it gets really bad, I'll roll out my sleeping bag and nap."

"Indeed." Emrys paused for a moment and shifted his head closer to her. "That necklace, I do not believe that you had it the last time you were here."

"No, I didn't. It's new, made of iron." Alex adjusted her grip and showed it to the Dragon. "Triskelion."

"Alex made it," Nicki said, voice glowing with pride. Alex nearly jumped. She hadn't realized that the redhead was both reading and listening in. "Only a couple of days ago. It translates for her."

"Hopefully," Alex said quickly. "It works on Earth, but there's no guarantee that it will work in another world."

"Still, it is an achievement." Alex could hear the smile in Emrys' voice. "When I first came here, it was difficult. Gofiben and I had to use our powers to understand each other. Through my scrying pool, I was able to see out into the world and learn some of its languages, but it took time." The Dragon shook his head. "Let us hope it will work. If it does, then it will be a great boon in this quest."

"Are you sure that you're okay with going with us?" Alex asked. Memories of Emrys' arrival in this world were vivid in her mind. "You told me once that you weren't allowed to go home."

"The changes that travel between worlds inflicts on our bodies frightened my people," Emrys explained. "I do not know for certain how it happened the first time or what the results were, but I believe it was traumatic for my people. Thus, the law was put into place. It is taboo to return."

"Are you sure the changes would even linger?" Alex asked. "I mean, that seems weird to me."

"Perhaps." Emrys shifted, and Alex had the odd impression that he was shrugging. "I have had a long time to think about it. I now wonder if they worried about ideas that might change us as well, how exposure to other worlds and their ideas might impact society. I think that is very possible as well."

"Yeah." Alex grimaced. "That makes sense, I guess. It doesn't sound good, but we keep magic a secret for a reason. You can't put the evils back into the box once you've opened it."

"Indeed, I understand, though I do hope that was not the reason." Emrys shook his head, and his horns scraped the roof of the cavern. "Still... it would grieve me."

"And your family? You must have had someone waiting for you?"

"I have often thought of them. If time moves the same between worlds, then they are long gone." Grief filled Emrys' voice, and Alex reached over to touch his scales gently. "There were times... I thought of leaving this cavern, leaving the prisoner behind and seeking out the Iron Soul. My pleas were fully formed in my head, and I dreamt of it often."

"Why didn't you?"

"My return would have meant my destruction. My family... better for them to hope that I am safe and happy in another world than to make them witness my death. I told myself that for a long time, so long that I realized they would be dead." He lowered his head. "I do not know if the law is even in place any longer. Maybe I could have returned home centuries ago, or maybe it would have been even worse."

"What's different now?"

"My world is not closest to yours," Emrys reminded her. "I can aid you without returning to my world." A soft sigh escaped him. "And... in truth, I am eager to leave. Staying here is a burden." He looked towards the cave entrance. "Even now, despite knowing the risks of being seen, I just what to push through the opening and spread my wings." His voice was both wistful and eager, almost childlike.

"I still can't believe that you've willingly stayed in here for centuries," Alex admitted. Already, the cave felt empty, cold, and far too small to her.

"My presence would have greatly disrupted your world. I am inclined to believe that in the past, creatures like me occasionally came to your world, but as humans have advanced, I believe we would have done more harm than good had we been known. I never wished to harm this world."

"That even after centuries, you still feel that way is amazing."

"You give me too much credit," Emrys said softly. "There are many times you would have been disappointed in me."

"How so?"

"I have had many moments of weakness."

Alex wasn't sure how to translate that. There were so many ways to take it, and her imagination provided her with several ugly scenarios. Emrys sighed and shifted, making his scales scrape across the stone floor. Nicki looked up at them and narrowed her eyes. Alex shrugged and shook her head. Morgana's green eyes had opened and flicked over to them as well. Thankfully, both of them seemed to calm a moment later and turn their attention elsewhere.

"Did you and the White Dragon ever talk?" Alex asked softly. "Being here alone for so long, I mean, did you ever just talk?"

"Rarely." Emrys sighed. "I don't know why the difference between us, but this world... it had a worse impact on him. He'd never been the sanest creature, but after the first century, it was like he was going feral. Part of that was me constantly having to put him down to keep him from escaping." Guilt, sorrow, and resignation blended in Emrys' voice, telling Alex that it had never been simple. "He was a murderer, a vicious one, long before we fell into this world. I knew what he would do to the humans if he had free rein. Compared to us, you're such small and powerless creatures. Back then, it was easy to agree to be sealed away."

"And later?"

"After the first year… I tried to see if I could reform him. I hoped to convince him that if he changed his ways, we could guard this world and be free." Emrys shook his head. "I was desperate and lonely. I hadn't made peace with my fate."

"What happened?"

"He killed me. Ripped my throat out and tore my wings. I had often done the same to him, but he tried to eat me." Emrys shuddered. "You don't need details, but it wasn't pleasant for either of us. I came back to full awareness to him trying to break out. That incident made me cautious for a long time. But from time to time, I'd try again, but the result was always the same." Emrys shifted and moved his head away from Alex. "I confess… it became easier to kill him every day than have to hear him taunt me or worse, have him ignore me, to punish me. It was easier to put him down as soon as he awoke and avoid injuries and the pain of resurrection myself."

Alex swallowed and licked her lips. The shiver that wracked her body had nothing to do with the winter wind. The heat from the fire was still warm on her legs. She hated Emrys' confession. She hated that he told her, but she understood. He'd been alone for so long, too long and now… now she wanted him to leave this cave and help them. Maybe this was his way of warning her to be careful around him. She wondered if the old Dragon even trusted himself anymore.

Aiden stood up, leaving Nicki to read alone, and stretched with a loud groan. It echoed in the cavern and reminded Alex that it was likely the others could hear her and Emrys talking. Rubbing the back of his neck,

Aiden grumbled, but headed for the mouth of the cave. Alex watched him depart with a small frown before realizing that nature was probably calling. She turned away and caught Nicki watching her over the top of her book. Her friend quickly lowered her eyes and Alex resigned herself to this. They were going to be living in each other's pockets for the foreseeable future.

"I might have done the same," Alex whispered. "I'm sorry that you've been alone for so long. I wish Galath had told Merlin and Morgana about you."

"I do not blame your brother. He was grieving. I doubt that it would have changed much."

"Merlin had some of the poison, though," Alex said. "He might have-" she cut herself off.

"What? Been able to put me out of my misery?" Emrys asked teasingly. "A few centuries ago, I would have taken that offer, but then I would not be here today to help you. This mission will take me to new worlds beyond this cave. I am grateful not to rot here."

"Do you want to go home when this is over?" Alex asked. Her mouth went dry at the thought, and her stomach tightened. It might have been excitement or nervousness. "If this works and we can go to other worlds, then when it's all over, maybe you could go home?"

"I- we'll see. This Darkness you speak of, I do not imagine that this will be an easy battle. A raw force will be difficult to defeat. Especially if you do not have magic."

"Do you think we will?"

"I am uncertain. Many creatures have some sort of magic, at least in small parts of the population. I cannot say for certain if it is always tied to beings from other worlds."

"Morgana could use magic in the Sídhe tunnels," Alex said. "In the Sídhe realm and they've had some soldiers who could use it in our world."

"Yes, I suspect it is far more complex than we know."

"So, you don't know what to expect?" Alex asked.

"No, I don't. I think you are correct to enter the beast branch first. Our worlds are wilder, so it may be easier to avoid detection. Then again, my knowledge is outdated. I fear that we are all plunging into the unknown." The Dragon shook his head and everyone looked towards them as his horns again scraped the roof. "My apologies."

"All will be well, old Dragon," Morgana said. "You've survived a plunge into the unknown before."

Nicki blushed and the corner of Bran's mouth twitched up, confirming that they had all been listening. Alex held back a sigh. This was the new status quo. Aiden came stumbling in and made a brisk noise as he headed straight for the fire. He was carrying a few more broken off branches that were wet. His hands were glowing, and he glanced around the cavern as if aware that he'd missed something. More red magic surrounded the wood, and he set the branches down by the fire.

Emrys lowered his head and rested it on the floor. Aiden pushed the branches closer to the Dragon, letting the red glow around his hands fade. They weren't dry, but Aiden had started the process. A deep sigh escaped Emrys, releasing hot air over the wood and making the flames of the lit fire dance wildly. The shadows they all cast shifted on the wall, and Alex watched them as the fire slowly settled.

Reaching over, she tentatively touched the Dragon's head. He was still curled up around her, his head on the ground. A soft sound escaped Emrys when Alex's fingers brushed over the ridge above his left eye, but he stayed still and allowed the gentle stroking. Closing her eyes, Alex focused on the smell of the smoke and the crackling of the fire. This wasn't home, but at least it and the Dragon were familiar. She'd enjoy it while she could. Nightfall would come soon enough, and the real adventure would begin. Alex just hoped that Emrys was up for this.

15

Lost to the River

721 B.C.E. Niger River Shore, Nigeria

They had been marching north for thirty-two days now. A wide river was to their left, and the surrounding landscape was green and lush. So far, the natives they'd encountered had been willing to leave them be, but Morgana still kept Cathanáil tucked away. There was no sign of Badb's plague in the small villages they came across, but Morgana wasn't sure if that was good or bad.

Morgana still wasn't sure how far they had to go, but Merlin was finally recovered after a very long and exhausting week of healing. He was moving faster now, but it wasn't fast enough. On foot, they were limited how far they could go, and the need for food, water, rest, and getting out of the sun had only slowed them down. Add to that the detours they'd taken to avoid area settlements, and Morgana's fear that they would return too late was growing stronger and stronger.

Cathanáil hung on her back, its weight comforting despite the heat of the sun, that it helped channel directly against her skin. They'd shed their heavier clothing as much as possible, turning their cloaks into packs to carry supplies and adjusting the fabric to cover their heads. Morgana's eyes moved across the landscape, and she frowned at every unfamiliar plant.

"We need to try the tunnel again," Morgana said. "We aren't covering enough ground!"

"Morgana, it went poorly last time," Merlin argued. "We were merely trying to cross a river, and you almost drowned."

"That won't happen again." Morgana's stomach twisted at the memory of the tunnel collapsing around her and the current pulling her under. "I have a better idea of what not to do."

"But not what to do." Merlin shook his head and sighed. "It's not worth the risk."

"There's been no sign of Badb; for all we know, she's attacking the villages and Gofiben and Bran while we walk our way home."

"Killing ourselves won't help!" Merlin glared in her direction, but he was too tired to put much effort into the look. Shifting off the trail, he moved towards the nearest tree. "I'm worried too."

Morgana's shoulders slumped. They needed a plan, but so far, this was the best they could manage. "We could try calling for Cyrridven again," she offered. "We don't know why she didn't respond."

"She may be sleeping," Merlin grumbled. He leaned against the thin trunk of the tree. At least the trees further inland were more familiar to Morgana. "We can try again, but we can't put all of our hopes on her hearing us."

"How have you reached out to her in the past?" Morgana asked. She joined Merlin in the delicious shade and watched a small black and red bird swoop past.

"I usually don't. Cyrridven finds me, or we make a plan in advance. Calling her from so far away... I'm honestly not sure if we can manage it, Morgana."

"There has to be a way," Morgana argued. "We can't keep this up forever, Merlin."

"I know," the old man admitted. "We seem to be much further south than I first assumed." He shook his head and peered out at the worlds around them. "I am trying to remember the old stories of the lands to the south."

"And?"

"There is a great desert, south of the sea where Rome was. The lands beyond the Nile River of Egypt." Merlin furrowed his brows. "I had hoped that we were near the sea, but now I believe we are on the other side of the desert. If we keep going north, we will find ourselves in an even harsher environment."

Anger filled Morgana, threatening to erupt towards Merlin, but she stilled it. Somehow, she closed her eyes and breathed slowly. It wasn't Merlin's fault. At least he remembered some of the stories. She'd never been interested in learning more about the world outside of her village as a child. To her young mind, it was all destined for the Sídhe. She hadn't understood the size of it all.

"So, what can we do?" Morgana asked.

Merlin nodded towards the river. "We keep following the river. I know it is turning to the west, but following it is our best chance to stay safe."

"It likely will lead us into the mountains."

"We can handle mountains."

"Yes, but all of this will take time," Morgana argued. "Merlin, we need to get home."

"Let us rest," Merlin said. "Then, we will use our magic at the river and try to reach Cyrridven again."

Morgana wanted to argue. Worry for their students gnawed at her, but Merlin was right that they needed to rest. With a huff, she sat in the shade and glared at her strange surroundings. Memories of stories that she had heard whispered to Morgana, and she wished that she'd paid more attention. Something large moved through the grasses across the waters, and Morgana tensed.

"I believe it is an animal," Merlin assured her. "It is not a threat to us."

The creature came closer to the water, heading for the trees, and Morgana leaned forward. It was large and grey. The sight of it called forth old stories that she'd heard from her mother. The large gray creature moved its long nose into the trees as it strolled along the path. It was almost seven feet tall with large flopping ears and wide feet. Morgana's jaw dropped a little as she watched it pluck something from the branches with its nose. Then it curved its nose to put the food in its mouth.

"I believe they are called elephants," Merlin said. "I heard traders talking about this once." He chuckled softly. "Stunning."

"Yes," Morgana agreed. Her eyes took in the creature with amazement. "It reminds me of how little of the world we've truly seen."

"It is difficult to navigate quickly. Especially now that trade is slowed."

"We may need to turn to the locals," Morgana said. "We've been seeing more of them lately."

"Yes, but have you seen any iron?"

"No." Morgana sighed and leaned her head back against the tree. "No, I haven't."

"Are you prepared to risk Cathanáil? We may have magic, but neither of us is fond of using it against humans."

Morgana thought he was being unfair with that question. Scowling at him, Morgana didn't point out that he was making a big assumption about the locals. Just because the fishermen they'd come across the last few days didn't use iron didn't mean that there wasn't iron in the area.

Then again... Cathanáil would be a prize. It was a sword fit for a king, the king that Arto had been in principle even if not in name.

She hated that Merlin had a point. They were strangers here. The locals had much darker skin, so they'd never be able to go unnoticed in a more populated area. Those they had spoken with had been friendly, but all it took was one person getting the drop on them. They didn't have time to be prisoners or need to negotiate for passage through a tribe's lands. They needed to keep moving. Guilt gnawed at her, and Cathanáil felt a little heavier than normal when she thought about Gofiben and Bran.

Morgana watched a small boat come sailing down the river. Three strong and slim men were paddling in the narrow wooden boat. There was a cover over the middle that from this distance looked like it was made of woven fabric, though Morgana couldn't be sure. Staying in the shadows, she searched their boat for any sign of metal. There wasn't any. The men wore some jewelry, and at this distance, she couldn't tell the material, but there was no reflection of the sun off metal.

Lingering in the shadows, Morgana and Merlin didn't move until the boat was out of sight. Merlin sighed loudly and stretched his arms, allowing a loud yawn to escape him. If they hadn't needed to cover ground, Morgana would have been tempted to take a nap in the shade of the trees. Merlin strode towards the water, waving one hand to bat away the large flies that seemed to be everywhere around here. Morgana smacked a mosquito off her neck and snarled. She was becoming one giant welt.

They had to be careful as they approached the river. Everything here was bigger, lusher, and harder to know where it ended than their familiar terrain. Long grasses helped to hide the extent of the water, and Morgana was glad to let Merlin go first. Even after spending half a lunar cycle following the river, she still wasn't confident about how safe the water was. They'd approached carefully and used their magic to draw water for drinking and bathing, but now Merlin seemed prepared to get close and stay close.

"Careful," Morgana told him.

"Give me Cathanáil," Merlin said. "Maybe if I channel my magic through the Sword into the water, that will be enough to get her attention."

"And what if you drop Cathanáil in the water?"

"Then, I have no doubt; you will torment me until I retrieve it." Merlin smiled boyishly at her, but he made no move to grab Cathanáil off her back. "We're a long way from our homeland," Merlin reminded her. "It will take quite the signal to draw Cyrridven here."

Nodding, Morgana drew Cathanáil out of the makeshift scabbard she and Merlin had made from the hide of that strange deer they'd killed and eaten ten days ago. Merlin accepted the Sword with a respectful nod and gave Morgana a chance to step back. Then he moved closer to the water. Morgana grimaced as she heard his feet hit the shallows. Wet shoes were never fun.

She moved to the side and found a higher spot that would let her watch Merlin. He dipped the tip of the blade into the water and closed his eyes. Merlin's magic flared around his hands in a green aura. It shimmered along the golden hilt of Cathanáil and slid down the surface of the blade, making the metal glow. Morgana could see the magic stored in the Sword responding, and the faint white magic of Arto that continued to linger in the blade came to life.

Magic flowed down the blade into the river. Ripples of green washed over the surface of the water. Around them, the world seemed to still. The sounds of animals in the underbrush faded, and the soft churn of the water in the river became muted. The air around Morgana quivered, the smell of a thunderstorm rolling in around them. She said nothing and watched Merlin carefully. Pulling on the spark in her chest, Morgana enjoyed the warm, reassuring rush of her magic down her limbs and prepared herself to step in should anything go wrong.

Merlin released more magic. Morgana tensed. Green sparks filled the air before being pushed into the Sword. The river's color was changing, and a semi-circle of bright leaf green was evident on the surface of the water around Merlin. Her eyes swept across the river, searching for any sign of Cyrridven. A bead of sweat rolled down the side of Merlin's face. His breathing was shifting towards being labored, and she was about to tell him to stop when something shifted.

Morgana narrowed her eyes at the spot on the river where she'd seen movement. The waves were moving incorrectly. Rather than going downstream, some were twisting upstream. She didn't allow herself to get excited just yet. It could be a fish or some debris, but then the waves grew. They formed a circle and rolled outward. Merlin laughed victoriously and the bright green flow of his magic continued.

Water pushed into the air with a sloshing sound, twirling and twisting into a pillar that quickly took the shape of a humanoid figure. Merlin finally stopped using his magic and stumbled back from the river. Morgana leapt forward and took Cathanáil from his hand before he could drop it in the water. The hilt hummed in her hand as Merlin's magic clung to the iron.

The water settled, and Cyrridven smiled at them both. Cyrridven looked exactly the same as she had the last time Morgana had seen her. The Old One's bronze skin shimmered thanks to small droplets of water that clung to her and the glowing circlet that she wore illuminated gentle features. Water lapped around the bottom of her gown. Morgana smiled, she was truly happy to see the Old One.

"Merlin," Cyrridven greeted. She smiled at him before her eyes moved to Morgana, and she nodded in greeting. "Morgana. I am pleased to see you both well."

"I'm grateful that you heard me," Merlin said. "We've found ourselves in a difficult situation, I'm afraid."

"Yes." Cyrridven turned her body, making the water shimmer in the sun. "You're much further south than you've ever been before. What has happened?"

"Ah, yes, of course." Merlin cleared his throat. "I fear that the Old One Badb has gone mad. We encountered her, and she stole Cathanáil. She created some strange tunnel made of water and vanished into it."

"And you followed her." Cyrridven nodded, unsurprised by what they were saying. "Did you understand what it was, Merlin?"

"In a way," he confessed. "I have seen you travel through water." He didn't mention that they'd never seen her out of water. "And she was trying to escape. It was rather obvious. I was a bit surprised that we traveled with her."

"What possessed you-" Cyrridven expression shifted between horror and fond exasperation before settling on relief. "You are fortunate, Merlin. I hope you understand that. It was foolish."

"We couldn't let her escape with the Sword," Morgana reminded Cyrridven.

Amusement over how Cyrridven was scolding Merlin rippled through her. Merlin, for his part, looked embarrassed and pleased. The relationship between the pair was one of the strangest things Morgana had ever seen. She hesitated to assign a name to it and knew that Merlin wouldn't want her to. The tips of Merlin's ears were red, and Morgana was fairly sure it wasn't from the sun.

"I understand your concern, and I agree with you," Merlin said dutifully. "It was instinct, I fear. I won't claim that I knew we'd be alright, but I had a feeling that we'd manage. Once in the tunnel, I used my magic to cushion Morgana, and myself and focused on reaching Badb. While I don't fully understand it, my magic did as I needed."

"I suppose in a way that is reasonable," Cyrridven allowed. "The waters of this world are part of the Iron Realm. Still, even when I travel through the waters, it can be difficult to control. The tide and currents pull and push you, threatening to sweep you away. I do not require breath and thus am much safer than you. Badb, as an Old One, has the same protection."

"So, you know what she did?" Morgana stepped closer to the shore. "You travel through the waters. How can we? We must return to the north. There are a pair of young mages there; we cannot leave them alone longer than we already have."

"I become water," Cyrridven replied. Her expression was thoughtful. "I have never formed a tunnel." The Old One paused, and Merlin and Morgana stayed quiet to let her think. Birds flew past, and Morgana checked the river for any sign of more boats. "I am not sure how to begin."

"We've tried," Merlin confessed. "We had little luck."

"What did you try?"

"We tried opening a tunnel up the river," Merlin explained. "But it collapsed on us."

"Allow me to try." Cyrridven shifted back, the water rippling around her as she moved. "I am more familiar with water than either of you."

Morgana offered no argument and glanced at Merlin. He was already looking better, and the worry she'd been fighting about him exhausting himself eased. She slipped Cathanáil back into the scabbard and double checked that it was tightly secured to her body. The sound of crashing water drew her attention back to the river. Waves were being pulled into the air in front of Cyrridven's outstretched hands. A faint glow surrounded the Old One, but Cyrridven's back was now to Morgana, so she couldn't see her face. The water spun rapidly in the air. It looked right. It looked like what Badb had done.

Merlin's face lit up with excitement. The water churned, and Morgana crept closer. Through the spinning water, she saw flashes of unfamiliar landscapes and felt hope blooming in her chest. The portal was a few feet away from the shore, and Morgana eyed the water carefully. Before Merlin could start wading, she waved her hand, and silver magic spread across the surface of the water. Merlin made a surprised and then pleased sound when the magic formed a thin ice bridge across the gap.

"Well done, my dear Morgana. It looks perfect, Cyrridven!"

"I am not sure if this is right." Cyrridven sounded uneasy. "I tried to focus the magic on the place we wish to go, but..." Morgana paused as she stepped out onto the ice. She had never heard Cyrridven so uncertain. "This is a new use of power to me."

"If we can make it work, it will open many new pathways to us," Merlin said. He, on the other hand, was excited and cheerful. Then he turned to look at Morgana over his shoulder. "Shall we?"

"The tunnel only goes up to the bend," Cyrridven assured Morgana. She nodded up the river. The bend was a fair distance, but Morgana supposed it was a decent first test. "And I will be with you."

Merlin grabbed her hand, his palm solid against hers and reassuring. Still, she wasn't prepared for him pulling her into the water tunnel with him. Remembering at the last second that Merlin was low on power, Morgana reached for her magic. It exploded around him in a frantic release of energy. Morgana kept her lips clamped closed as water splashed into her face. Images flashed around them, too fast for Morgana to keep track of. Pushing her magic out, she tried to imagine it wrapping around her and Merlin, keeping them safe and together.

The tunnel churned. Her body wasn't supported. She was falling forward. More water fell onto her, cold against her neck and back. Gasping in shock, Morgana inhaled a mouthful of water. The tunnel shuddered and water poured in around them. Panic stabbed her, and she kicked her legs uselessly. Then a wave hit her side, tearing her away.

Water pressed in on all sides. Morgana scrambled for anything to grab onto. The water was cloudy, but she saw light and kicked her legs as she reached for it. Someone grabbed her and pulled. Morgana turned her head. It was Cyrridven. The Old One was right beside her with a calm and controlled expression. Seeing that eased Morgana's panic.

Cyrridven hoisted Morgana up. They broke the surface, and Morgana gasped for air. It filled her lungs, and she coughed weakly. Cyrridven felt warm and real beside her, gently guiding her towards the shore. The firm touch surprised Morgana. While she'd seen the Old One touch items before, Morgana had never been touched by her. Deep down, she'd always assumed that Cyrridven was truly just a mass of moving water. Coughing, she wiped her eyes and climbed further onto the shore.

Merlin grabbed her hand and pulled her up the rest of the way when Cyrridven released her. He was safe. Morgana hiccupped in relief. Water was still running into her eyes from her soaked hair. Another coughing fit helped dislodge some of the water in her lung. Looking around, Morgana grimaced at the sight of the plants and small animals that were running about. They had moved and only to the bend as intended. No further.

"I am sorry," Cyrridven apologized. "I've never tried to take another with me."

"It's alright," Merlin said. He coughed and leaned on his staff. How he still had it, Morgana didn't know. "We can try again."

Cyrridven seemed uncertain, but after studying the pair of them, nodded in agreement. "We'll try again," she said. "I'll do everything I can to help you return to the north."

Morgana nodded and held back a groan. She had faith that Cyrridven, Merlin, and herself all together could figure out how to create a stable water tunnel, but the question of how long it would take hung in the air. Licking her lips, she reached up and touched Cathanáil's hilt to remind herself of why this had happened. It didn't dispel her worry or her guilt. All she could do was hope that Gofiben and Bran would look after each other, and Badb wouldn't cause more trouble before they returned.

16

Brave New World

They didn't leave the cave except for quick jaunts to answer the call of nature in the winter landscape and to find firewood. It was just as much fun as it sounded in Alex's head. Emrys told them what he knew of the other worlds in his branch, but it wasn't much, and the information could be horribly out of date. Still, he was confident that there were oxygen atmospheres and similar gravity so they wouldn't suffocate or be crushed the moment they passed through.

Alex had never given it much thought, and now she felt stupid. Of course, it would take something major to get a species to fling themselves into the unknown. The impact of the Darkness was becoming more and more clear. She felt like an idiot, but then if she felt that way, how had Merlin and Morgana felt about learning about the Darkness. Merlin's resistance made more sense to her now and she hated that. She hated that he wasn't here to help and that Morgana was just... existing.

Nicki had taken over logistics in her usual creative and determined mode once afternoon arrived. It had been decided that Alex would use Cathanáil to "cut" an opening to the beast branch, and just to be on the safe side, Emrys would carry them through. The issues with the plan were the fact that Alex could only hope that Cathanáil could direct where they ended up and that they couldn't all ride a dragon with their backpacks on. So, Nicki had pulled out the stashed rope from the bags and anything else that was useful to her and started building a big net with Aiden's help. That had at least kept them busy for a bit.

"Not much longer to sundown," Morgana said. She was standing at the mouth of the cave, officially keeping watch for any hikers. After her words to Emrys, the older woman had retreated once again. "We'll be able to leave soon."

"Great." Alex shivered and leaned closer to the small fire they'd been feeding all day. "Waiting is the worst."

"Yes," Morgana agreed. Thankfully, she didn't ask if Alex was certain about their plans.

A nervous and yet excited energy had charged the air. There was a hint of electricity that made Alex wonder if she'd lost control of her magic. The absence of the weight of her cellphone was distracting. It had been left behind in Ravenslake, but Alex now wished that she could look at the photos that were stored on it. They were leaving technology behind them except for the walkie talkies that Nicki had picked up for them.

The sun was setting when Alex stood up and stretched. Nothing made the day pass slowly like needing time to pass. At least the days were short in the dead of winter. The others followed her example, rising from around the fire and gathering their things. Morgana eyed Emrys and then, without a word, raised both of her hands and hummed softly. Silver magic erupted forth and swirled around the cave entrance. A strange grinding sound echoed around them, and the entrance widened. Aiden laughed in pleased surprise, and Emrys put a foot on the outcropping.

Even with her magic, Morgana barely made the entrance big enough for Emrys to slip outside. The dragon inhaled deeply, swished his tail and spread his wings. His long, reptilian head gave him limited expression, but his face could only be described as rapturous. His claws dug into the ground as he kept himself steady on the slope of the hill. Trees were already being bent over by the size of his wings as there just wasn't space for a dragon. With a sigh, Emrys tucked his wings against his back. Nicki and Aiden rushed forward with the net of their gear and started lashing bags together in a bundle.

Pulling Cathanáil out of the sheath, Alex ignored the tremble in her hand and got to work. Fear was threatening to take over, no matter what she told herself. The others were watching, and Alex did her best to ignore them and focus on the sword. Pulling on her magic, she gently pushed a flicker of power into the blade, hoping to spark it to life.

Arthur had said it was the key, and it was what had opened a portal for the Dragons and the Demons. Alex was sure that Arto hadn't intended that. Maybe it was a side effect of him making the Sword to stop the war with the Sídhe. He'd made it as a tool to close the paths between worlds, and maybe that meant that it could open them as well in some sort of magical balance. That was a question of magical philosophy that Alex wasn't about to bring up.

The metal glowed from within, magic pushing out from the heart of the blade. Memories of making it, of pulling the iron from stones and using magic in a cave to create Cathanáil came rushing back. Alex's grip tightened on the golden hilt, and she slowly brought the blade up. There was no image that she could call upon to direct the magic; she didn't know enough about where they were going. The humming grew louder, echoing in her ears, but it was reassuring. The magic was reacting to her purpose, her intent now, and didn't need direction. At least she hoped s o.

A quick slice through the air and a pale shimmering rip appeared. Stepping forward, Alex watched it slowly grow and expand. Light was spilling out of it now, a warm golden glow, and she heard a gasp behind her. The rip stopped opening, and Alex carefully brought the sword up again. She delicately touched it to the edge of the rip and jumped as a jolt of electricity traveled through the sword to her. Jarring Cathanáil, she cut the rip open further. Alex barely held in a hysterical laugh at the reality of what she was doing.

The tear opened further, revealing flickers of color and more light, but no clear details. Looking over at Morgana, she found the older mage just as uncertain as she was. Emrys, however, nodded and shifted closer.

"Let's prepare."

"Is this enough?" Alex gestured at the opening. "It's not that big, only a few feet across, and you're much larger than that."

"A little more," Emrys agreed. "But don't risk making it too large. With you mages leaving, you must not allow a threat to enter the world."

Cutting the rip open a little more, Alex's stomach was turning, and her emotions were a mess. Panic and sorrow were fighting for dominance. What if she was wrong, and they were killed going through instantly? What if something came through? What if she couldn't seal it behind them? Every question she'd had about this plan came roaring back.

Would she ever return to the Iron Realm? Jenny's words haunted her.

The light spilling forth from the hole grew brighter and brighter. There was nothing left to do. It was time to go. She didn't want to. But they had to. Alex tried to shift her features into a neutral expression and then turned around.

"Shall we?"

No one was fooled, but Nicki nodded. Part of the net system was tied to Emrys' front right leg, and the Dragon was also gripping it in his foot. He lowered his body down and adjusted his wing as best he could to grant them access to his back. They had tied the last of the rope around the base of a horn. Alex wasn't convinced that it wouldn't slip off.

She climbed up first and settled at the back of Emrys' long neck. It wasn't comfortable, and she could feel every shift of the Dragon's body beneath her. The others climbed up behind her, and Alex passed the end of the rope back to them. Morgana wrapped one arm around Alex's waist and her breath brushed over Alex's neck.

Once the others were in place, Emrys brought up his wing, and there was a moment of stillness. Then the wings came down with a roar of moving air. Another flap made Emrys' front feet leave the ground. Alex heard a cheer behind her, but the flap of the wings was too loud for her to pinpoint the source. They were lifting off the ground, their center of gravity shifting, and Emrys brought them closer to the rip. Emrys was barely off the ground due to the height of the rip, but then they were rushing towards it.

Alex braced herself as the arm tightened around her. Light blinded her for a moment. Everything changed all at once. Colors exploded around them, driving off the lingering blackness of the crossing. Sweet air with a strange taste to it, hit Alex's tongue and warm air brushed over the skin of her face. Alex looked up at the sky in awe as she saw that it was not the sky of Earth.

The golden sky overhead had puffy blueish clouds with faint hints of purple. It was familiar but alien in a way that Alex wasn't sure how to process. In her hand, Cathanáil's hum dimmed, and she looked down at the Sword in alarm. The Sword appeared the same, but it only took Alex a moment to understand that she'd drained away a good portion of the magic stored in the blade. Maybe half, but she wasn't sure. Emrys' massive wings flapped, and a triumphant laugh escaped the Dragon. Alex gripped the horn at the back of his neck tighter. Morgana's arms around her waist tightened, and a small whimper escaped her mentor.

Alex didn't dare lean too far over, but she couldn't resist trying to look down. Far below was solid ground with tall trees with green leaves and green vegetation as far as she could see. There were strange rocky patches against tall cliffs here and there, but nothing that Alex recognized immediately as a city. Emrys' body tilted, and Alex yelped in alarm. She leaned the other way as Emrys turned them around, trying to keep herself stable.

"What are you doing?" Aiden yelled.

"Turning back to the rip." Emrys' voice rumbled around them, and Alex was relieved that he could still hear them.

Everyone held on and Alex wished she had use of both of her hands. Emrys quickly completed his turn, and Alex acknowledged that it was pretty steady and graceful. They just needed some kind of warning system and to not have five people holding on by their legs and a rope. Swallowing down her alarm, Alex searched the air for the tear. It took a moment, but she found the ripple of white against the pale sky. Even now, it didn't look large enough for a dragon and his wings to have passed through.

"Do you think this will work?" Morgana asked. "Using the sword?"

"I've fixed holes before," Alex huffed.

That wasn't totally true, and it wasn't completely wrong. Alex wasn't sure that this would be as easy as it had been in India. Morgana adjusted her grip on Alex's waist to give her more flexibility. Alex carefully brought Cathanáil up and licked her lower lip. She wasn't sure about having Emrys fly any closer to it; there'd be too much chance of a wing moving through the portal.

Time to test if she had any magic. Closing her eyes, Alex breathed slowly and tentatively searched for the spark in her torso. For one terrible, long moment, she didn't feel anything. It was empty, she felt disconnected, but then there was a flutter. She froze, listening to the sound of Emrys' wings against the air. The spark grew, and magic rippled down her arm to the hilt of the Sword. It was slower than normal, but it was there and just as warm. There was a hint of something else... it was sharper than on Earth, but still very similar.

Opening her eyes, Alex dismissed those thoughts for the time being. There were more important things to worry about. She lifted the tip of Cathanáil towards the edge of the rip as if it were a wand and pushed her magic forward. Keeping her eyes open, she did her best to visualize the rip closing up, the two sides merging, and her magic responded.

Cathanáil shimmered, and the magic rippled out across the sky, almost like waves on the surface of a lake. She was at least six feet away from the rip, but her magic streamed toward it rather than slipping away. Nicki made an excited squeal behind her, and she thought she heard a sigh of relief from Morgana. A memory of something similar tugged at her. Alex smiled as the rip slowly, very gently closed, and the sky ahead of her became uniform.

A collective sigh of relief escaped all the mages at once, and Alex giggled. Emrys gently propelled them forward through the air as the laughter spread throughout the entire group of mages. It started off hysterical but transformed into a gentler release of tension. Alex suddenly felt faint. Morgana's arm around her tightened.

"Are you alright, Alex?"

"Yeah, that just took a lot out of me." Alex shook her head and blinked, telling herself to stay awake. "We have magic, but it seems to be harder to use here."

"How can we have magic?" Nicki asked, her voice just shy of a shout. "I mean, we were all hopeful, but still, it seems weird."

"The energy in the tree flows through Earth and out into other worlds," Bran yelled. "Maybe that's part of it."

Maybe, it was a workable theory. Alex didn't really care if they figured it out or not. She was just happy that they could still use magic. If they'd come through and hadn't been able to close the opening, she didn't know what she would have done. Still, it might be a weak point, and she just hoped that nothing broke through to Earth there. She couldn't build an Iron Gate in the sky.

They flew in silence for a short time. Every so often, the rope would tighten in Alex's hand as someone risked leaning over to look down. The green vegetation was reassuring, and they were breathing okay despite the different color of the sky. Alex could only imagine what was running through Aiden's mind. Then Emrys angled towards the ground.

"There is an open area ahead," the Dragon said. "Hold on."

Emrys' wings flapped and sent dirt flying into the air as he descended. The open patch wasn't very large, and Alex glanced nervously at the Dragon's wings. However, despite being out of practice, Emrys adjusted his wings and narrowly avoided the trees. A moment later, his back legs hit the ground, and he gently fell forward to land on his front legs. The impact jarred Alex and the others, but no one fell off of Emrys' back.

"Well," Morgana sighed. "That worked. Everyone alright? Sound off."

"Alex."

"Nicki."

"Aiden."

"Bran."

"Good," Emrys said. "I'm glad that all of you are alright, but if you would please dismount." The Dragon shifted beneath them. "Five humans on my spine is a bit much."

His words sent everyone scrambling. Alex heard the others hit the ground and waited until Nicki had let go before releasing her own grip. Carefully, she slid down the side of the Dragon, using the ropes to keep herself stable. Her knees quivered when she hit the dirt, but Alex could only sigh in relief. Everything had held and they'd made it through. She quickly returned Cathanáil to its sheath, grateful to release her painful grip on its hilt.

Inhaling deeply, she looked up into the trees and marveled as the reality of what had happened settled in. They were in another world. A completely different world. One with slightly different rules that they'd hopefully not have the time to learn about.

"Wow," Aiden gasped. "I know that this isn't a sightseeing trip, but we're in another world."

Nervous and excited giggles escaped everyone except Morgana. The older mage smiled a little at them, but then shook her head and turned her attention to Emrys to unload their gear. Alex checked the trees with more caution now. The leaves were similar to what she was familiar with but much larger, more like tropical trees. There was no sign of animals or any sapient beings yet. The world seemed intact, and there was no sign of the Darkness. Still, they'd made it and had a chance to investigate this brave new world.

17

Reaching

Bran inhaled the air of a new world, marveling at the very fact that his body still seemed to be functioning as normal. The scientist in him wished that they'd had room to bring equipment. It would have been fascinating to break down the exact chemical composition of the atmosphere here. Part of him wondered if it was truly that similar to Earth or if some kind of magic was at work. Maybe their magic was helping them survive, filtering out some dangerous chemicals in the air, or maybe the Tree of Reality linked worlds that were mostly similar.

Then again, that wouldn't explain the homeworld of the Old Ones. Bran almost laughed. Excitement, nervousness, and dread were bubbling like a whistling teapot in his chest. He didn't know what to do with himself. While waiting for sunset in the cave, he'd tried to prepare himself, but now he had to admit that there was just no way to prepare oneself for this! It was too much, too fast!

"Crazy isn't it," Aiden whispered. He stepped over next to Bran, looking around with wide eyes. "Being in another world. God, I wish we had some lab toys."

"Lab toys? Your father would be so proud." Bran laughed, but he was glad it wasn't just him.

"Shut up; you know what I mean." Aiden was looking up into the sky. "It's a different color than ours, but we can breathe. Maybe space is different here." His eyes widened. "Maybe it's a thicker atmosphere or has a completely different composition or-"

"That's not what we're here for," Bran reminded him sadly. "Maybe someday..." He doubted that they'd ever have that luxury.

"Yeah, maybe someday."

They slipped into silence, both of them staring out at the new world. Bran was certain that Aiden felt the same curiosity as him. It was one more amazing thing that they would have to keep a secret. That still burned, even if he understood it. Lifting his eyes to the golden sky, Bran savored the sight of it.

"Please tell me you're as terrified as I am," Aiden said.

"Oh, don't worry," Bran whispered. "I'm petrified. We're in another world, looking for a world-destroying force."

"Yeah, I'm pretty sure that's not the safest plan."

"Alex is right. We couldn't just wait on Earth forever."

Aiden smirked a little, but nodded. "I know, I know, I've been telling myself that for days. Doesn't mean that it isn't scary."

"Scary, yeah." Bran knew that word wasn't enough to encompass the terror, the thrill, the worry, the responsibility, and desperation that coming here represented. "Let's go with that."

They shared a look. Bran saw Aiden swallow and nodded to his friend. He was pretty sure that they were both desperately trying to figure out how their lives had come to this. Then Morgana and Alex started to talk, and Bran turned his attention to them. This wasn't the time or place to get lost in his thoughts.

"It's difficult to see the sun's position," Morgana said. "The cloud layer is very thick, and I'm not sure what to look for."

"You're worried about the dark?" Alex asked. Then she sighed and nodded. "That's true. We don't know the sun's schedule here." She looked up at Emrys, but the dragon shook his head.

"I have no knowledge of such things for this world."

"So, the question is, do we keep moving, either by flying or on foot, or stop here and try to gather information," Alex said.

"I saw nothing in the area that stood out to me," Emrys offered. "There were rock formations, but we cannot assume that cities would look as you might expect."

"True." Nicki nodded, and Bran noted an excited glint in her eyes. "They could have nests or live in caves!"

"They might." Morgana's tone was completely serious. "We can't make assumptions. Be ready for anything."

"No sign of the Darkness," Nicki said. "At least not yet."

"I hope that is a good thing," Emrys said. He was stretching his wings all the way out and looking very pleased with himself. Raising his nose into the air, he sniffed loudly and flicked his tongue out. "This is not my homeworld, but I believe I smell Gryphons."

"Gryphons?" Nicki's voice went higher than normal, and she grinned. "Real Gryphons!"

"Likely." Emrys looked down at Nicki almost fondly. "I am not familiar with the exact arrangement of worlds in my branch. There was some communication between worlds, but the details escape me I'm afraid. I believe... I think I remember learning about a war thousands of years ago between two of the worlds. My ancestors invaded a world, but I don't think it was this one." He shook his long head. "I am sorry; history was never my strong point."

"That's fair," Alex said. She smiled at the dragon. "Thank you for agreeing to take us. I'm very grateful for your help."

"I am grateful for my freedom from the cave." He shifted his wings again. "As you noticed, even the lower cavern was confined."

Alex grimaced and Bran raised an eyebrow. How was the dragon still sane? He must have a little magic of his own to watch the outside world, but still.... He studied Emrys as the dragon lifted his face towards the sun. Then again, Emrys wasn't a human; Bran needed to be careful about putting assumptions based on human psychology on a Dragon. Maybe it had been difficult, but not traumatizing. Given that they were relying on Emrys, he really hoped that it wasn't something they needed to worry about.

"I'd like to scry," Alex said. She looked at him, hopefully. Bran blinked, a bit thrown by the sudden announcement. "I think it's a good way to get a feel for if our magic works differently and test our limits without a combat situation."

"Did it feel different earlier?" Bran asked. "When you sealed the portal?"

"I don't think so, but I was using Cathanáil. The Sword holds a lot of magic." Alex frowned a little. "But my power felt weaker. I had to rely on Cathanáil a lot more than normal. I think I drained it a lot when I resealed the portal." Alex touched Cathanáil's hilt thoughtfully. "It still carries power, but the battery has been drained."

"So, the question is, do we have the magic we brought with us only," Nicki said. "Like a tank of gas. We can use it, but it won't recharge."

Morgana frowned, and they all looked at each other nervously. That was almost as bad as their fear of not having magic at all. It could lure them into thinking that they had magic only for them to discover they didn't at the worst possible moment. Bran's insides twisted. He wanted data, but they only had theories, and every experiment they could try could put them into a dangerous position. He hated it, and the urge to head for home was strong, but they couldn't jump back and forth.

"I'll help, Alex," Bran said. He relaxed his shoulders and tried to breathe normally. Freaking out wouldn't do any good. "She closed the portal, so I don't want her to scry alone, but I think the rest of you should conserve your magic just in case."

"You sure?" Nicki asked. She tugged at the end of her long red braid.

"We have to be careful." Bran shrugged, trying to ignore the nervous pit in his gut. "I'm the seer, remember? And Alex is the most likely to narrow in on the magic. It makes sense without risking too much of our magical capability."

"That's valid." Aiden put a hand on Nicki's shoulder. "Still, be careful. Both of you."

Morgana looked like she wanted to say something, but stayed silent. Her green eyes were fixed on Alex, more intently than Bran had ever seen before. He watched Alex give Morgana a reassuring look before she gestured to a flat patch a few feet from them. Obediently, Bran walked over with her and set his backpack to the side.

Bran sat down on the ground, noting that the dirt was warm from the day's heat, and mostly packed down. It made him think Emrys might not be the first creature to use this spot for landing. Hopefully if they were in the Gryphon world, they were not larger than Dragons. That was a terrifying thought. Any childish excitement he might have been able to have about it a few years ago had been well and truly killed over the past year.

Pushing that thought away, he steadied himself and rolled his shoulders. Even with all the meditation techniques he'd learned over the last few years, it wasn't easy to calm himself down under the circumstances. Alex sat down in front of him and took his hands in hers. The warmth of her fingertips against his skin made his heart beat a little faster for a moment before he centered himself again.

Bran closed his eyes and tentatively reached for his magic, intending to give it to Alex. There was a change in his magic. When he pulled on it, there was no sudden warm rush from the world around him to refill his supply. The sudden absence made him realize how used to that sensation he'd become. Their bodies gave out from channeling the energy after using too much, but they didn't run out of magic, not really. With all the threats in the Iron Realm, there was always more magic being generated.

For a terrible moment, Bran was certain that he was using all the magic he had, all the power that he could wield in this world as long as they were there, but then a slight trickle of energy reassured him. It wasn't the flow he knew, but it was there — a soft and slow pulse of energy that helped him calm.

"Do you feel it?" Alex asked softly.

"Yeah." Bran tightened his grip on her hands. "That's... that's good to know. I don't understand it."

"I'm not sure either, but it's there."

He opened his eyes and found Alex smiling at him. Her gray eyes were soft, and while the shadow of worry was still there, her gaze was brighter than he'd seen for some time. He gave her hands a gentle squeeze and watched silently as her eyes closed. Exhaling, Bran closed his own eyes and quietly told himself to focus on the mission at hand. When they got back home, maybe he could try to sort out his personal life.

His magic shifted, almost rippling as the shape of it changed. It was slower and slipped around his grasp like jam, solid, but difficult to hold. As it threatened to slip away, Bran followed it with his awareness, trying to pull it back. There was too little magic, and he couldn't afford to be messy with it. His magic spread out against his will, reaching for something. In his chest, Bran's heart fluttered.

A sweet scent hit his nose, and Bran opened his eyes to look around. He wasn't in the clearing anymore. Magic hummed over his skin. Around him were high white walls and floors that glowed with an inner light. Something about it was familiar. Then his eyes landed on a figure across the room.

Taking a step forward, Bran tried to move towards them, but the distance of the hall just stretched out. He couldn't get any closer. Their back was to him. They were dressed in jeans and a simple gray long-sleeved shirt. Long blonde hair hung past the shoulders, and Bran thought it was probably Alex. They didn't turn to look at him, and he couldn't get close. There was something balanced on their head, a dark gray crown with sharp spires. It glowed with magic, standing out against the pale w alls.

"Alex?" he called. The name echoed off of the great white walls. "Alex? Is that you?"

They started to turn. Bran braced himself as dread crept up his spine. The crown's glow brightened. The figure's face was obscured as the glow threatened to blind Bran. Raising a hand, he shielded his eyes and tried to look into the face.

It was gone a moment later, and his magic snapped back into his body. Vertigo and confusion flooded Bran's head, and he was grateful to find that he was sitting down. His chest burned, and Bran panicked. Alex's hands squeezed his, and he relaxed. More magic flowed away from him. For a moment, he was lost. What had he been doing?

"I see it," Alex said. He kept his eyes closed. "There's something.... I think it's a rip with the Darkness. It's a long way, but it's there."

"Can you see beyond it?" Morgana's question startled Bran. "That's only the source of where it is coming here? Can you see beyond it?"

There was a long pause, and Bran finally opened his eyes again. The brightness made him blink. Everything around him was brighter now, more vivid, and he shivered at the memory of that vision. What did it mean? Alex had talked about the worlds beneath Earth in the Tree of Reality. Had he seen that? But why? His eyes jumped back to Alex as she pulled her hands away and rolled her shoulders.

Her eyes were sharp and aware. If she was afraid, she was hiding it. That figure... Bran was almost certain that it had been Alex, but what did it mean. His mouth was dry, and his lungs felt compressed. If it had been Alex, then why had she been there? Was it the future or symbolic? After all, his vision of being stabbed in the back had no doubt been referring to Arthur, but he hadn't been the one stabbed. His visions were either terrifyingly clear, or frustratingly abstract.

"What about you, Bran?" Morgana asked. "Did you see anything?"

"I think I saw..." He trailed off, trying to find the right words. "I think I might have seen the same hall that Alex saw."

"The white and gray one?" Alex straightened up, curiosity shining in her eyes. "Did the floor open for you?"

"No, no, nothing like that, but I thought I saw you there."

"Me?"

"Like you saw Alex while she was having her vision?" Nicki asked.

Bran tried to work out how to answer that question, how to describe what he had seen even as the details tried to slip away from him and nodded slowly. Alex raised an eyebrow at him, and he nearly snorted at the similarity it gave her to Morgana.

"It was Alex," Bran said. "She was…" The last of the images were fading like he'd woken from a dream. "Her back was turned to me, but it was her. She was in the hall."

"I wonder if we'll have to go there too," Alex said thoughtfully.

"That's very interesting," Aiden said loudly. "But guys, we don't know how the day works here. We should get organized for the night just in case and get our bearings."

"But-" Alex started to protest, but Nicki nodded her agreement with Aiden.

"He's right. We need to get our feet under us first," Nicki said. "Otherwise, we won't be good for anything." Nicki smiled encouragingly. "And we can see if Alex and Bran's magic recharges. We need to know that before we find too much trouble."

Bran conceded to their wisdom with a nod. Emrys made a sound of agreement before taking off into the air with a quick promise to scout the immediate area. That left him and the others with their gear, standing in a small clearing in an alien world. It should have been exciting or at least terrifying, but Bran only had a strange feeling that he was missing something.

18

Introduction to Demons

6 21 B.C.E. Northern India

Morgana disliked going to the southern lands. She had ever since that terrible incident with Badb that had left her and Merlin stranded too far from Gobien and Bran. They'd returned home to find both of their students dead, strange stories spreading across the land, and a furious Galath who refused to answer any of their questions.

The heat of the south brought back too many ugly memories of that era for her to be comfortable, but this land was even worse. Here it was humid in addition to hot, and every time they came across another human, they had to use magic to even understand them. Using a water tunnel had helped them reach this area far faster, and she had to admit that discovering that use for magic had been useful many times over.

Still, the south still made her think of their failure to return home quickly, and she hated it. Morgana was carrying her cloak over one arm, and the bag on her back weighed her down. A glance up at the sun confirmed that it wasn't even at the zenith yet, it was only to get hotter.

Sweat was rolling down her back underneath her shirt. Yesterday, she'd secured a red tunic made of the lighter fabric favored by the locals, and while it helped, it still didn't completely stop the heat. It sank into her bones and tempted Morgana to use her magic to cool herself down. She didn't give into the temptation. They had to use magic every time they came across a local to communicate with them, and if something happened, she couldn't risk being completely exhausted.

"We're making good time," Merlin said. He was panting a little, even if he was trying to hide it.

They were following a long road through a thickly forested area full of plants and animals that had been completely new to Morgana when they stepped out of the water tunnel two days ago. A sound of something moving in the jungle made Morgana jump and call on her magic. Silver sparks surrounded her hand, but a moment later, a strange creature with thick fur simply jumped across the road to reach a tree on the other side. Merlin had the gall to chuckle.

"Try not to worry, Morgana. Magic is guiding us."

"Guiding us further and further away from everything familiar," Morgana snarled. She slapped her neck as something bit her skin. "I hate this place."

"It was your scrying that pointed us here. It is only a pity we couldn't narrow it down more. Water tunnels are unpleasant, but I would have preferred it to more hiking."

Morgana rolled her eyes and held back a sigh. She wished that too, but there was no point in talking about it. She adjusted her arm and glanced down at her cloak. While part of her wanted to put it back on to shelter her from the sun, the heavier fabric was too much for hiking in the heat. And they were still going south!

"We're lucky with the great distance that I picked this up at all," Morgana said.

"True, you're right, of course. It is fortunate for the world that you have such a talent with scrying." Merlin shook his head. "My successes have always been far more limited."

He'd been good enough to find her brother, Morgana almost pointed out, before stopping herself. The heat was making her uncomfortable and angry. Arguing with Merlin wouldn't help matters. Still, hopefully, what was going on in the area wasn't too dangerous. It might be nice to see all the new and different things this land had to offer.

Ever since Leugio's death, they hadn't strayed far from each other. After surrendering Cathanáil to the care of Cyrridven, they'd gone south across the water into the Roman Empire. Morgana had grown up hearing about the land from the bronze traders, but never had the chance to explore it herself. For a time, things had been peaceful. She and Merlin had learned a few languages and more of the culture, but had always known that their duty would call once again.

It had only a few days ago. Merlin had noted that their magical powers were growing once again, leaving them capable of performing more impressive acts of magic, and Morgana had set out to find the source. She'd been expecting that the Sídhe back home were causing trouble, but the magic had directed them east, far beyond where they'd explored in the past few decades.

"I can't believe that the Sídhe had moved this far south," Morgana said. "It doesn't seem like their climate."

"They have proven to be stubborn creatures and more adaptable than I thought they would be." Merlin's walking stick stumped along the path with each step he took. "I expected them to die out decades ago."

"Their numbers are low. Perhaps migration is the reason."

"Perhaps. There were rumors of them moving further south, but I'm not sure they are the source of this new..." Merlin trailed off and struggled for a moment. "Incident."

"Incident," Morgana repeated. "Charming, Merlin. We do not know what to expect."

That was the problem. They were far from their homeland and lacking information. Morgana only seen vague clues. Their magic had pointed them east and then further east. A desperate scrying attempt after months of travel had given Morgana an image clear enough for her to make a water tunnel.

That was it. Nothing else she'd seen had been helpful, and Merlin's attempts at scrying had been as weak as ever. He just lacked the talent, and under other circumstances, Morgana might have teased him about it, but yesterday when she'd tried, he'd pointed out just who taught her. Merlin rarely brought up Queen Scáthbás with any real bite in his voice. He'd apologized this morning, but it had been a warning of how uncomfortable Merlin really was.

"I wish we had more time to study the plants," Merlin said. His tone was light and conversational. He was searching for something to talk about. "They are a bit different from the trees at home."

"We're a long way from home. I suppose it is only natural."

Merlin made a small sound, and when Morgana turned to look at him, he was eying something off the path. There was a rustle in the leaves, and she realized almost too late that he hadn't been trying to make conversation. He'd seen something. Morgana didn't have time to be frustrated with herself. Dropping her cloak, she pulled on her magic harshly. Silver sparks spilled forth from her hands as green magic manifested around Merlin's hands.

The plants shuddered. A large shape appeared, but it was human enough that Morgana hesitated. Then three creatures lunged out at them, swinging weapons at her and Merlin. Dodging the attack of a rough cudgel, Morgana waved her hands and sent a rush of sparks forward. They snapped the cudgel in two. The creature blinked in surprise, and they came to a stop, examining her and Merlin.

The creatures were unlike anything Morgana had seen before. They were a similar shape to her and Merlin, but even with the variation of skin tones she had seen in the past few days, she'd never think they were human. The skin was a strange reddish color that didn't seem right, and the texture of the flesh was wrong. Fierce red eyes that promised violence glared at her. Most inhuman, were the two long fangs, almost tusks, that protruded from the creature's lower jaw. Something twisted in her gut at the sight of them. They were like the Sídhe; they didn't belong here.

"Tasty meat," one of the creatures said. It grinned at them, a bit of drool escaping its mouth, and Morgana curled her nose in disdain.

"How did you come into this world?" Merlin demanded.

Morgana almost rolled her eyes; the creature had just threatened to eat them, and he thought it would cooperate. She glanced at the three creatures critically. Two of them still had their weapons, and the third seemed to have recovered from the shock of her attack. Raising her hands, she made the silver sparks flare and smiled when they backed away.

"How did you come to be here?" Merlin repeated.

The three creatures glanced at each other. One snorted and shrugged. Morgana tensed in preparation for an attack.

"No weapons," one of them said.

The one that had lost its weapon frowned and narrowed its eyes at her. Morgana smiled and released more silver sparks, letting them swirl around her hands. They were debating what to do. Two wanted to attack, but the third one seemed uneasy. They weren't Sídhe; they had probably never seen mages before. At least they were on equal footing in their ignorance.

"Not gods," another said. "Don't smell right."

"We are not Old Ones," Merlin agreed. "But we can defend ourselves. What are you, and where are you from? How did you get through the Iron Gates?"

"Demons don't answer to humans!"

That was the only warning Merlin got before an axe was swung at his head. Morgana shifted back and blasted her magic through the chest of the nearest Demon. The magic hit the rough tunic that the creature was wearing and shot through with little resistance. Shrieking, the Demon stumbled back, clutching at its chest with long fingernails. A squeak escaped it as the others looked at it in horror. The body collapsed in on itself and crumbled. Calmly, Morgana turned her attention to the next one.

Merlin had used his magic to catch the axe, but there was a hint of surprise on his face. The Demon was snarling and trying to force the axe down through the green shield between it and Merlin. They were strong then. Morgana didn't like that and pulled her dagger out of its sheath with her right hand as more magic circled her left hand.

She expected the creatures to withdraw. One of their number was dead and rather than frightening off the Demon that had been nervous before; it only seemed to enrage it. With a howl, it raced at Morgana, drawing her attention away from the one fighting with Merlin. She heard Merlin make a sound of warning to her, but she was ready.

Slashing into the Demon's flesh, Morgana smirked and started to back away. But the Demon's body didn't dissolve, and it didn't howl in pain.

It snarled and lunged towards her. Shock followed by fear filled Morgana. A green blast knocked the creature back. She looked towards Merlin. He had one hand extended towards her but was still holding the other Demon back with magic.

Anger overwhelmed the fear, and Morgana commanded the magic forward. The silver spark spun into a long spear that slammed through the chest of the Demon, still trying to break through Merlin's shield. A wet sound escaped it as the Demon fell back. Merlin panted and nodded to her. Morgana's eyes returned to the last Demon as it clamored to its feet.

"Iron didn't work," Morgana said. She eyed the cut on its arm. There was dark blood, but no sign of further injury from exposure.

"Finish it!"

Morgana snapped her hand forward, envisioning her magic as a whip. It formed in her hand, pulsing with power and gentle heat. Lashing it forward, she watched it strike across the Demon's flesh. It burned into the skin, reassuring her it wasn't that strong. The Demon ran, but a green bolt of magic blasted through its chest. It fell to its knees. Then its body crumbled into dust.

Looking into the trees, Morgana braced herself for another attack. Sídhe were rarely in such small groups. Merlin's back pressed against hers, their bags jangling. Both of them were on guard as they listened and watched. But only the wind disturbed the trees. Sweat trickled down Morgana's face, and the breeze cooled her slightly. Nothing came.

"I think it was only the three," Merlin said.

Morgana nodded and tentatively stepped away from him. She adjusted her bag and stretched her arms. Her limbs were warm from the use of magic, but thankfully, there was no dangerous exhaustion. Sauntering forward, Morgana kicked the nearest pile of dust and considered it carefully. She wasn't sure if it was more like dirt or ash and had no interest in touching it. At least there were no corpses to worry about. The Iron Realm didn't want them, even in death.

"Well, they weren't from around here." Merlin brushed off the sleeve of his tunic.

"No." Morgana tilted her head to look back at him. "It fell apart like the Sídhe and Fae creatures do."

"So, likely it is not of our world at all, but from another world like the Sídhe."

"They weren't familiar to me," Morgana said. Shaking her head, she checked the trees again. "I saw nothing like them in the court." Her throat tightened at the mere mention of that place. She'd gone years without mentioning it. "It didn't react to the iron." Morgana looked down at her dagger with a frown. She disliked the fact that it hadn't been useful. That was wrong, fundamentally wrong. "At least our magic worked."

"It seems that we now face an enemy rather different from anything we've faced in the past." Merlin sounded excited about the idea. He hummed thoughtfully and leaned on his walking stick, looking into the trees with sharp brown eyes. "Very interesting."

"Interesting. Really, Merlin? That's how you'd describe this?" She went to collect her cloak and brushed the dirt off it the best she could. "I'm not thrilled with their references to what we would taste like. Clearly, they're the threat that is causing magic to grow stronger."

"Yes... they weren't what I was expecting." Merlin studied the nearest pile of remains that the wind was carrying away.

Morgana hesitated before speaking again. "Demons. That was what they called themselves. Have you ever heard of that?"

"No, I've never heard of such creatures. You're right, they are similar in shape and appearance to the Sídhe and us, but they are different. They must be from another branch of the Tree of Reality, like the Old Ones."

"Strange."

"Pardon?"

"We are both half-Sídhe," Morgana said. "I don't know. I suppose I always thought that was significant to the threats we would face. The battles we would fight."

"We may be beings created through the foul deeds of the Sídhe, but we are mages." Merlin shrugged and nodded forward to the road. "It is our lot to fight battles such as this."

She rolled her eyes, but Morgana joined Merlin in continuing on their way. Reaching to her belt, she found the bag hanging over her hip and felt the outline of the polished bronze mirror that remained her primary scrying tool.

"My dear Morgana, I think it would be best if we made a point of speaking with some of the locals," Merlin said. He glanced her way pointedly. "They may know something, and I'd rather not reach the source of the problem with no information. There's no telling what we might or might not find."

Unable to argue, Morgana nodded. She hated the idea of slowing down to stop in the villages, but Merlin was right. They were stumbling blindly towards where they sensed the strongest levels of magic, but without information. If these creatures had spread this far, then maybe the locals knew about them. If they were really lucky, maybe they had their own weakness. She could only hope so.

19

Camping

Camping wasn't Alex's thing. She'd gone with her family more than a few times, usually paired with a trip to Lake Coeur d'Alene, and what they called camping was a good measure nicer than her current situation. Her tiny tent had been chilly most of the night but was getting warm as the sun rose higher and higher in the sky.

Groaning, Alex turned her head into the small inflatable pillow that had come with her sleeping bag. Beneath her, a layer of leaves provided a padded surface, but not much in the way of comfort. It had taken far too long to fall asleep last night, and now she really didn't want to get up. Clutching Galahad to her chest, Alex sighed and squeezed her eyes shut.

Someone walked past her tent, and that did it. If someone else was up and moving, then she needed to do the same. Fumbling her way out of the sleeping bag, Alex gently returned Galahad to her backpack and retrieved her clothing. She wanted coffee but knew that they didn't have any. Still, it was hard to put away the desire. The tent wasn't big enough to even sit up in, so she had to do acrobatics to pull her jeans on and switch out her shirt. Once that was done, she packed up everything she could in her backpack and rolled the sleeping bag up as tight as she could. It wasn't as small as it had been last night, but it was a decent job.

Crawling out of her tent, Alex climbed to her feet, stretched her arms, and yawned. She bent down to tie her boots and once again lamented the lack of coffee. Inhaling the air, she noted the same sweet scent that she detected yesterday, but nothing stood out that would make her realize she was in another world if she didn't look at the sky. Overall, it appeared to be a lot like Earth, which was both good and terrifying at the same time. They had solid ground they could walk on, they could breathe, the vegetation looked promising as a source of food, and Nicki had found a small stream nearby, and the water in it had passed Morgana's inspection. Lance's major concerns for their health and safety had been met. Nothing had attacked them here so far, and the weather seemed pl easant.

The thing about Earth was that humans had walked over most of it. Alex supposed that there were a few places like Antarctica where no human had ever walked, but even in the tundra of Russia and Canada or the deep rainforests of the equator, she was pretty confident that at least once in history a human had walked there. In this world, it was the opposite. She looked up into the sky and watched pale silver clouds gently float by. No human had ever been here before. A small thrill of excitement ran down her spine. Maybe in her own way, she was as much of a nerd as Nicki, Bran, and Aiden.

That little thrill, and the way her mind was spinning at the scope of what they'd done helped keep the panic and fear at bay. Yesterday, exhaustion had set in after camp was set up, and Alex had crashed hard soon after their meal of some of the food they'd brought with them. She vaguely recalled Emrys flying away to go hunting for the first time in centuries.

This morning, Emrys was in the center of the clearing, stretching out in the sun like a great cat and purring softly. If a Dragon could smile like a human, Alex was certain that he would. The steady rise and fall of his back as he breathed fascinated her, but her mind quickly went to the question of if he'd even breathed in the cavern. Shivering, she turned to look at the small firepit Aiden had built last night and found Morgana sitting on one of the logs they'd dragged over to serve as seating.

The older woman had started the fire again and was staring into it. She didn't seem to have even noticed Alex. The metal kettle that Morgana had brought with her, which doubled as a pot, was near the flames. Alex couldn't hear bubbling yet and hoped that Morgana hadn't been up alone for too long. She glanced at the other tents and could hear soft snoring from Nicki's, but nothing from the boys.

"Morning, Morgana," Alex mumbled. In the stillness of the morning, every noise seemed to be magnified.

Morgana looked up at her. For an instant, Alex thought she saw tears in the older mage's eyes, but Morgana blinked, and they were gone. Alex sat down on the log next to her, letting the heat of the flames wash over her. At least it meant that she didn't need to get her coat from her tent.

"How did you sleep?" Morgana asked.

"I was unconscious," Alex said. "I'm sorry I didn't take a watch."

"You used the most magic yesterday, by far," Morgana replied. "Speaking of which, how do you feel?"

Alex didn't answer right away. Closing her eyes, she inhaled slowly and reached for the spark of power in her chest. It was burning brightly and seemed stable. Alex didn't call on it, but couldn't ignore the rush of relief that she felt.

"My magic is strong," Alex said. "I think that I regained some last night." She frowned a little. "I can't... I don't feel it around me like I do on Earth. It's not quite right, but I think we will recharge a little if we have to use magic."

"That's good." Relief filled Morgana's face, underscoring how insufficient her words were.

Noise from one of the tents made Alex look back towards them. Nicki's snoring had stopped, and she was moving around in her tent. A series of soft curses made Alex smile. Morgana chuckled and shook her head fondly. A few minutes later, Nicki crawled out of her tent with her hair in a messy braid that had done little to prevent tangling.

"Not a word," Nicki growled. She stood up and began struggling with her boots. Alex walked over and bent down to tie Nicki's boots. "Thanks," Nicki sighed.

"Bad night?"

"Couldn't turn my brain off." Nicki dug into the pocket of her jeans and pulled out a small comb and released her hair from the braid. "Still, it could have been worse. I wish there was coffee."

"We have some tea," Morgana offered. "The bags are much easier to deal with than coffee."

"I know, I know," Nicki grumbled. She and Alex walked back towards the fire.

Suddenly, Aiden and Bran came tumbling out of the trees and back into camp. Aiden was carrying something in his coat, thankfully the outer side, and had a gleam in his eyes that made Alex nervous. They went straight to the fire pit and plopped down on a log. Alex was very afraid of what they might have.

"I hope you didn't go too far," Nicki said. She frowned disapprovingly at Aiden. "We don't want anyone getting injured and not knowing where they are."

"We didn't go far," Aiden promised. "We were just checking the snare."

Nicki sighed, but she was inching closer to the boys and fire "I can't believe you convinced Lance to teach you that."

"Hey, Lance was glad to," Aiden huffed. "Anything that might help us pull this off and all that." The words were flippant, but there was an undertone of truth in them. She hadn't been aware of these lessons, but she could completely believe that Lance had been brushing up his skills and passing on anything that he thought might be useful. "Let's see what we've got."

The coat was put on the ground, and both Aiden and Bran made odd interested noises. Alex walked a little closer only to grimace. A dead creature was on the coat. Bran pulled out a medium-sized moleskine notebook with a pen firmly attached. With a grin, he flicked open the book, pulled out the pen, and readied it for use. Unable to resist, Alex walked around behind them and looked over Bran's shoulder. He was drawing the creature and already had a list of bullet points about its size, coloration, and foot structure. She blinked in surprise and held in a laugh. Alex wasn't the biggest nerd amongst the group, after all, not by a long shot.

"The small claws could be for gripping trees," Aiden said. "I mean, the snare was on the ground, but it could be kind of like a squirrel. Lives in trees and forages for food."

Shaking her head, Alex moved around to the side of Aiden and Bran so she could get a better look at the creature. It was roughly the size of a rabbit, but instead of hair, there was a strange pattern over its skin. It had small front legs and much larger back legs. Both had the tiny claws that Aiden had remarked on. Nothing from mythology jumped to her mind, and she was truly unsure what she was looking at. Small eyes were fixed on the front of the head rather than on the sides like a rabbit. She remembered from a documentary that such a trait usually marked a predator, but she didn't know it that held true here.

"Look at the texture of the flesh," Bran murmured. "Almost like scales, but not exactly." He ran his hand over the creature's side with a thoughtful hum. "I'm not sure. Pity we don't have a microscope."

"Seriously?" Alex curled her nose at the boys as they studied the creature. "This is getting a bit creepy, guys."

"Maybe a little," Nicki agreed. She'd finished combing out the tangles and was starting to rebraid her hair.

"It's interesting," Aiden insisted. "Besides, we need to understand what we're dealing with in this world. We have some food, but not enough to last us forever."

"Don't eat it," Morgana said firmly. "We haven't had a chance to see what the native animals eat. It could be poisonous."

That got Bran and Aiden's attention. They glanced at each other nervously, but neither sprung back from the dead animal. In fact, after only a brief pause, Aiden picked up a stick and began to poke at the thing to carefully move it around. Bran resumed his drawing and notes. Alex just hoped that it didn't turn into a dissection. Neither of them were biology majors, so a girl could hope.

"Speaking of animals," Nicki said. She deliberately turned her gaze away from the creature. "I keep hearing small things in the underbrush, and there are some insects, but I haven't seen any birds."

"Birds?" Bran blinked and looked up from his notebook. Alex almost laughed at the way he flipped through the first few pages. "Yeah, I haven't noticed any either."

"You needed to consult the book for that?" Nicki asked dryly.

Alex tilted her face towards the sky and frowned. No birds. Nicki was right now that she thought about it, so far there hadn't been any sign of birds. They were in a forest that seemed lush enough, so it was a bit odd. She sniffed at the air, but other than the sweeter scent it carried, there was nothing that seemed alarming. Then again, this was a different world.

"You can't make assumptions," Morgana said. "There may be birds, or there may not be. Don't fixate on it."

"You're right," Bran said. He smiled sheepishly. "It's just…" he waved his hands around. "It looks similar enough that you start expecting things to be similar."

"Well, the snare worked, but if we can't eat it, what should we do with it?" Aiden asked. He glanced at Bran.

"Maybe bait for the stream," Nicki suggested. Then she paused and sighed. "Then again, we don't know if the fish would be safe to eat or if there are fish."

"This is a lot harder than Star Trek ever made it look," Aiden whined. "How did they manage it?"

"Tricorders," Nicki replied. Then she looked at Morgana. "We're going to have to risk it at some point, Morgana. We'll have to drink the local water and eat some local food."

"I'd just like to see animals eat it first," Morgana said. "That was how Merlin and I managed it whenever we traveled far from the plants that we knew."

"That's fair," Alex agreed. "Emrys, what do you think?"

The Dragon had almost turned his belly up towards the sun, and his wings were folded tightly against his body. Alex bit her lower lip and tried not to think about how much their fierce Dragon companion was reminding her of Anne, her family dog.

"What?" Emrys asked.

"Can we risk eating things here?"

"Likely." The Dragon rolled over and righted himself. Emrys cleared his throat and looked around. "This world is very similar to your own. You drank the water last night," he pointed out. "You won't be able to be too paranoid for long. Besides, I ate several creatures last night."

"We could make stews by combining things," Nicki suggested. "Cut the new materials down with food from our world."

"You'll have to risk it at some point," Emrys said, not unkindly. He sniffed at the air. "There are many small creatures nearby. Try to see what they eat."

"That's what I said," Morgana grumbled. She looked back at Aiden and Bran. "Did you check the berries we left out last night?"

"Yeah, everything was gone from the rock." Aiden shrugged. "No bodies nearby, but taking the berries off the plants might have confused animals, so I'm not sure how good a test that is."

Alex nodded. There wasn't anything else she could do. Emrys flipped his tail around, catching a nearby tree. There was a rush of twittering, and another small creature like the one that Aiden's snare had caught ran across the clearing to her right. Alex turned quickly and tried to follow its path, but it had vanished into the trees and underbrush. Her eyes scanned the woods carefully, and she wondered what else might be out there.

"I'm glad that something ate them," Morgana said. "Though I would have preferred to know what. There's no sign of larger mammals yet either," Morgana added. "In my experience, if you're out in nature for even a few hours, you're going to see something."

"Maybe there isn't a lot of fauna in this world," Nicki said. "Emrys, what do you think?"

"Well… in my world, Dragons are the dominant species. Most of the other species in my homeworld are much smaller than us. It lets them hide and flee more easily." He shook his head. "While there is diversity, it isn't to the extent of your world."

"Interesting," Bran said. He was writing something else down. The sun was rising higher in the sky and he was leaning to keep his shadow from obscuring his notes. "On Earth, a lot of creatures used to be much larger and then got smaller. Biology isn't my thing, but it probably relates to having such a dominant predator."

"Or the dominate predator hunted larger creatures to extinction," Alex pointed out.

"Don't go there," Nicki huffed.

"This is the branch that Dragons come from," Alex said. "Who knows what is in this world."

"I'm hoping for unicorns," Nicki said.

Stifling a laugh, Alex couldn't decide if Nicki was serious or not. With their luck, any unicorns they did find would have the temperament of angry rhinos. In fact, she was pretty sure that rhinos were the source of the stories about unicorns and similar creatures. Then Emrys drew her attention back to him, and Alex smiled as she reminded herself that they were traveling with a Dragon. All bets were off.

"We should get moving," Morgana said. She stood up. "Boys, get rid of the carcass, and we'll make some breakfast."

"I can help with that," Emrys said. He slid closer to the fire and tilted his head expectantly.

Bran blinked but picked up the edge of the coat. Emrys opened his mouth, and Bran tossed the creature in. The Dragon's jaw snapped shut. He chewed twice and then swallowed. Alex shivered. The sound of crunching bones was not an attractive one. Emrys settled back and stretched out his body and wings away from them.

"Pack up your tents and get the gear ready for transport," Morgana said. "I'll-"

Emrys stood up and sniffed the air, drawing all of their attention. Looking into the sky, he tensed and folded his wings tightly against his back. A loud shriek made Alex jump, and her eyes widened as several large shapes flew into view overhead. Her breath caught in her throat. High above them were seven large winged creatures circling in the sky. There were Gryphons, and they had found them.

20

Gryphons Flight

Primitive instincts that weren't buried as deep as modern humans liked to think screamed for Alex to run. Some part of her recognized that the massive creatures circling over her head were much larger than her, and despite the distance, she was certain that she could see the sharp talons on their feet.

"Stay calm," Emrys ordered. His deep booming voice broke through Alex's terror. The Dragon raised himself off the ground and turned his body to form a wall in front of Alex and the others. Lifting his head, he called up to the creatures. "We mean no harm. I request an audience."

"Alex?" Bran asked softly. "Did you understand that?"

Alex's fingers went to the Pendant around her neck. "Yeah, I heard English."

"He wasn't speaking English," Bran said. "I hope they understand him."

Alex did too. If they didn't, then she'd need to step in with the Iron Pendant's power and try to talk to them. At the sight of them, Alex wasn't sure that she wanted that responsibility. She glanced nervously at Emrys, but the Dragon remained still in front of them.

"Be careful," Morgana said gently. "Remember that using your magic to translate will drain you even with the artifact's help."

Nicki grabbed Alex's hand and pressed close to her. "I want to see if contact will share the magic," Nicki whispered.

Unsure how to respond, Alex stayed still and swallowed as three of the Gryphons left the formation and swooped down towards them. Alex's stomach tightened, and the urge to run threatened to overpower her once more. Suddenly, she was very grateful that the Fae creatures were all land-based. While the Red Caps were very good climbers and jumpers, they couldn't fly, and that could only be a good thing.

The mages all huddled close to Emrys. They didn't have to discuss it. Being close to the large Dragon was a comfort when three large creatures landed with soft thumps a few feet away. They were Gryphons. Alex had known it was a possibility, but seeing living Gryphon was- it was a bit much. She didn't dare look at the others for fear of what sounds she might make. Too many emotions were crashing over her, and Alex could only hope that she wasn't going to find that unicorns were real too. That might truly be more than she could take.

Eagle eyes narrowed on them, and the beaks looked dangerous as the sunlight glinted off their smooth surface. The front part of their bodies was like an eagle with their chest puffing out due to the mass of feathers and a pair of giant wings rising from just behind their necks. Every feather of their wings was sharp and crisp, with clearly defined smooth lines. Their hindquarters were vaguely shaped like a feline's, but all of their feet were similar to a raptor's. They each had four toes, three pointing to the front and one facing back, and all had vicious looking talons.

But there wasn't thick fur on their back half like the images Alex had seen. Instead, it was rich golden skin with a layer of thin follicles that, at this angle, looked a bit more like what made up feathers than hair. Her fingers itched to reach out and brush over the area to confirm if it was feather or fur, but Alex kept her hands to herself.

The Gryphons were twice the size of a horse in mass, and their backs were higher off the ground than a horse's would have been. They were each only about a quarter the size of Emrys, but none of them seemed distressed by the Dragon. There was no indication of fear, and the remaining four Gryphons overhead kept circling.

Alex held her breath, wondering what she should do now and hating her hesitation. Coming here had been her idea. Emrys lowered himself back to the ground and crossed his front legs calmly. Alex glanced at him, wondering if he wanted to handle this or if he was waiting for her.

"Identify yourself," one of the Gryphons ordered.

"It works!" Nicki hissed.

Alex tightened her grip on Nicki's hand, unwilling to let the redhead jump around in her excitement just in case the Gryphons were twitchy. There was a flair of pride in herself for the Pendant once again that Alex couldn't ignore.

"I am known as Emrys," the Dragon said. "As you can see, I am a Dragon. We have entered this world from another on an important mission."

"And what are these creatures?" One of the Gryphons tilted its head and peered at them over Emrys' back.

"These are humans. They come from the Iron Realm."

"Do they speak?"

Terror threatened to pull Alex down. How much information did the Gryphons have about the Tree of Reality? So far, they hadn't reacted badly to Emrys' appearance or statement.

"We're sorry if we trespassed," Alex said. She wrestled her hand away from Nicki and stepped around Emrys slowly so she could come up beside him. Alex kept her hands where the Gryphons could see them. "This may sound crazy, but we are investigating a dangerous substance that-"

"The Consumption," one Gryphon said. It tilted its head, elongating its neck and peered at her.

"Hush," another Gryphon scolded. This one had darker feathers along the crown of its head that glinted of green when the light caught them. "Explain yourself."

"We are the protectors of the Iron Realm; it is the world... uh, do you know about the Tree of Reality?" Alex asked. It suddenly occurred to her that most people in her world wouldn't have a clue what that meant if someone tried to speak with them. "I'm not sure what you might know and what you might not."

"The Tree of Reality," the Gryphon repeated. Something shifted in their eyes, but Alex had no idea if it was good or bad. "I know the name, but not of what it is." The Gryphon shook its head and eyed them all critically. "This is above me." Alex wasn't sure about how the Gryphon was looking at Emrys and hoped that nothing had happened with Dragons recently. Then the Gryphon turned its head enough to look at one of the other Gryphons. Both of the other two had been silent throughout this entire exchange. "We will take them to the Nest."

"Are you certain that is wise?"

"No, but the things they speak of are unknown to me. If they have information on the Consumption, then we would be remiss in our duty if we did not take them for questioning."

"What's going on?" Nicki whispered behind her.

"I don't think they're going to hurt us," Alex answered. "Just... don't make any sudden moves."

The Gryphons were whispering amongst themselves. The leader who had been speaking with them nodded and stepped closer.

"You will come with us."

"We can't fly," Alex explained. "We were riding on Emrys."

Exchanging confused looks, the Gryphons were eyeing them in consideration, and Alex had a distinct impression that they were being found harmless. That was probably good. Being seen as a threat was definitely worse. Emrys remained still, and Alex glanced at him. The Dragon gave her a tiny nod. The Gryphons were watching him with a great deal more concern, which made sense; he had wings and claws like they did, while Alex and her fellow humans did not.

"Dragon, you may carry these humans, but be warned. Any act of violence will bring the wrath of the Nest Guard down upon you."

"I understand." Emrys lowered his head, almost bowing to the leader of the Gryphons. "I thank you for your patience. I hope that the humans and I will be of service to your world."

Alex waited for more to be said, but Emrys told them to pack up the tents and get their gear ready for a trip. The Gryphons studied the tents with interest but made no moves towards them, which Alex was grateful for. Morgana seemed uneasy and pressed her lips together so tightly that a thin line of white appeared on them, but even she obeyed.

"What's going on?" Bran asked as he closed up his backpack.

"We're going to see their leader," Alex answered.

"Shit. Is this good or bad?" Nicki asked as she joined them.

"Hopefully, good. We can't assume that we can avoid the locals the whole time we're here." Alex tried to smile and reassure them, but they couldn't talk long. The Gryphons were already shifting impatiently and wouldn't understand what they were saying.

It was the fastest packing up of a camp Alex had ever seen. She ate a granola bar while rolling the tent down as tightly as she could manage. Aiden took over to make it even smaller, and Nicki reassembled their gear net from the previous day. Things weren't as neat as they should be, but it was good enough to load everything back up in the net. Glancing towards the Gryphons, Alex found them waiting, but their impatience as the humans scrambled back onto the Dragon was apparent.

She hadn't thought about this part very much, Alex had to admit that to herself. There'd been no real plan for how to deal with the different residents of the worlds. Panic clawed at her chest, and Alex tightened her hands around the lowest horn of Emrys' crest. Not now, she told herself. This wasn't the time to lose control. Nicki's grip on her tightened as the Dragon braced himself and flapped his great wings. Air whirled around them, and then Emrys launched himself up into the air. There was a brief instant when she felt like she was falling, but then they were rising into the sky.

With a cry, the three Gryphons on the ground leapt into the air and closed in around Emrys. If the Dragon was bothered by them, he didn't let on. Rising above the trees, Alex inhaled the fresh air slowly and closed her eyes. The air rushed over her face, cooling her down rapidly, and her panic eased.

"It'll be okay," Nicki said. Her breath tickled the back of Alex's neck. "It'll be okay."

She hoped so. The flapping of Emrys' wings and the soft twittering of the Gryphons as they spoke to each other washed over her. Releasing her magic, Alex stopped worrying about translating the Gryphons' words. There'd be a need for her magic soon enough. She watched one of the Gryphons fly out ahead of them with a shocking burst of speed and vanish around the curve of a nearby mountain.

Below them, the forest seemed to stretch out forever with sharp mountains and the occasional clearing. A wide river cut through the trees. This was a wild world. The absence of any industrial smells made Alex light-headed and giddy. Even the air in Ravenslake was never so clean. The trees cleared a little ahead of them, and Alex squinted into the sun, trying to see better where they were going.

The landscape shifted slightly, with fewer trees forming the green carpet below. She saw more exposed rock up ahead that gleamed red and gold in the sunlight. The Gryphons descended, and Emrys followed when one of them made a sharp sound at him. Alex wondered if Emrys knew their language or if the Dragon was using some kind of magic of his own to understand them.

They swept down into a deep canyon carved from red and gray stone that revealed layer after layer of color. An old memory of a trip to the Grand Canyon made Alex smile wistfully. Then she caught sight of more Gryphons as they swooped around a curve in the canyon.

Nests were dug into the side of the canyon, creating shelf after shelf stacked one above the other. As they flew past, Alex could see into many of the shelves. There were large rounded nests built of grass and wood, but also shaped tables and shelves built into the stone. Gryphons looked out towards them, some large like their guides and others so small that Alex knew they had to be children.

"Wow." The word escaped Alex without her even thinking about it.

"It's beautiful." Nicki sighed.

If the others said anything, Alex could not hear it as the Gryphons called to each other and filled the canyon with melodic chirps and cries. Alex turned her head, trying to take in as much as she could. There were splashes of color everywhere, with blue banners hanging out of some shelves, and rich shades of vegetation woven into nests. There were no signs of curtains or anything for privacy. Alex wasn't sure what to make of that.

The Gryphons kept flying, and Emrys followed them obediently, his great wings flapping slowly and leisurely. The Dragon didn't seem concerned, and Alex really hoped that it was a good sign. They had allowed them to keep riding on Emrys rather than carrying them in their claws as prisoners, which gave her hope.

Then a column in the canyon came into view as they turned a bend. It was massive, standing almost as high as the canyon walls, with a large open cavern entrance leading inside. Gryphons were sitting on small stone shelves all around the entrance. Large carvings were dug into the stone of the column, showing Gryphons and other animals along with symbols that meant nothing to Alex.

Emrys shifted to the side, making them all hold on extra tight as he was directed towards the cavern entrance. As they approached, more color came into view, and she could see Gryphons backing away to give Emrys more space to land. Her breath caught again, and Alex's stomach turned. Thankfully, her brain took pity on her and didn't slip into a panic attack.

Emrys carefully lowered the net of their supplies onto the landing area. Then he shifted his position and gently landed a few feet to the right. Exhaling in relief, Alex glanced around and noted the Gryphons were giving them space. She rubbed Emrys' neck in a silent thank you before slipping off of his back with the others.

The cavern had a high ceiling and more carvings decorated the sides with elegant swirling shapes and more images of Gryphons. Carved stone benches, similar to the one in Emrys' cave, except smaller, were arranged in a semi-circle. Upon each one, a Gryphon was resting. They all differed slightly in appearance, with some having darker feathers or small variations in beak or eye shape.

Opposite to them, at the peak of the semi-circle was a slightly higher raised bench. The Gryphon sitting there was missing one ear. A drape of rich blue hung around its neck, and two Gryphons were positioned behind them like guards. Alex swallowed her nerves and focused on the small weight of the Pendant against her skin. There was a soft hum of magic. It wasn't as strong as Cathanáil, but it was there.

"I am Farilan," the lead Gryphon said. The voice was slightly feminine to Alex's ears, but she wasn't going to risk making an assumption that would offend. Nor was she going to check. "Welcome."

"Thank you," Alex said. She was beyond grateful that she'd managed to make the Iron Pendant. "We apologize for coming to your lands unannounced."

"We will discuss that later if needed. My scout reported what you said to me before your arrival. What do you know of the Consumption?" The Gryphon spread its great white and brown wings behind it. Farilan's eyes promised violence if they weren't answered.

"It has entered our world in the past," Alex said quickly. She licked her lips and stepped forward, keeping her back straight and her chin up. "Our world has been invaded by many species, many of them driven to flee to our world because of the Consumption. We know it as the Darkness, but it is the same force. It is destroying worlds."

The assembled Gryphons broke into chatter, their voices becoming higher and higher pitched as they tried to shout over each other. Farilan slammed their front right leg down on a sheet of metal before their bench, and a rattling sound made everyone fall silent. The sound echoed in the cavern for a few moments before finally falling silent.

"Why did you come here? Is your world lost?"

"Uh, no, in the past, a mage was able to seal the rip," Alex explained. She saw Morgana relax a little at her caution in the corner of her eye. "We came because we want to see if we can stop it."

"You seek to end the threat?" Another Gryphon asked, tilting its head at them. "Surely that is a risk."

"It is," Alex agreed. "But the longer the Darkness damages other worlds, the more likely beings are to flee to my world. We wish to go to the Darkness and stop it at the source."

"We lose nothing by sending you north," Farilan said thoughtfully. Another Gryphon leaned towards Farilan but shifted back at a sharp warning look. "I don't know what you think you can do, but word from the northern clans has not been good. Already thousands have fled into our lands. They speak of terrible things, and we have lost contact with other clans in the area completely."

"I swear to you that we are here to help, not harm," Alex said. "My goal is to stop the spread of this into your world, but I'm also looking for a way to stop it for good."

"How does one stop a force of raw destruction?"

"I can seal the passage that it is using," Alex explained. "When we came here, I closed the way behind us, and another mage, long ago, closed the path that the Darkness was using into our world. It can be done."

"You know more than we do," Farilan admitted. Their gaze turned towards Emrys. "Long ago, there was some contact with worlds similar to ours. I do not know if this danger plagues other worlds."

Holding back a flinch, Alex did not look at Emrys. She remembered that the Darkness had already enveloped many worlds. In some places, it might take time for it to kill everything. The world of the Dragons wasn't the closest to them on the branch, so she didn't know what condition it was in.

"I hope my homeworld is safe," Emrys said. "But I have been in exile in the Iron Realm for centuries. There are... side effects to traveling between worlds that are difficult to predict. My home had a law forbidding those who left from returning. I believe it was put into place following a war between worlds."

"I do not know," Farilan said. They shook their head, and Alex wished she knew how to read emotions on the face of a Gryphon. "These things we speak of are old histories to us. I know there are other worlds, but it has never been relevant in my lifetime."

"It is now," Alex said. "The Darkness is consuming the whole of the Tree of Reality. We're not sure how it moves since it seems to interact with each world a little differently, but I don't believe it is part of the Tree of Reality. If it's coming from somewhere, then it can be stopped."

"And all you want from me is permission to go north?"

"Yes."

"You don't want assistance?"

"Uh..." Alex hesitated again and glanced at Morgana, but her mentor's expression gave nothing away. They were letting her take the lead. She missed Merlin fiercely right now. "We are having to use our magic, a power that we were gifted with to protect our world, to understand you. We don't speak your language. Any help you sent with us would force us to keep draining ourselves."

"You are interesting creatures. I think I understand your concern, but I cannot send you alone. With the Consumption or Darkness spreading, my fellow Clan Mothers are panicking. An escort will help prevent further delays." Alex was pretty sure that the expression she was seeing now was a frown. "And they will ensure that what you say is true." Dark eyes were fixed on Alex. "I'm sure that you can understand my caution."

"I- yes." Alex could do nothing but nod. "Yes, I understand."

Three of the Gryphons that had brought them here shifted closer to them, and Alex swallowed. This was fine. Probably good even. Nicki had proven that skin to skin contact allowed her to share the Pendant's power. Then her stomach grumbled, drawing strange looks from the Gryphons.

"Sorry," Alex said quickly. "Your patrol found us before we'd eaten breakfast."

Something a lot like laughter echoed through the cavern. Alex smiled a little, feeling that maybe that was a good sign. At least the Gryphons might be able to give them more ideas of what was edible here and what wasn't.

21

Promised Alliance

620 B.C.E. Mazagaon, India

Most of the village had survived the Demon's last assault. Several buildings were charred husks, but the citizens were already working hard on cleaning up. There had been only a few casualties, less than Morgana expected, but more than enough to leave Lokpal grieving. At least his family had been safe. His wives had kept the children calm and quiet as the village below burned.

Lokpal's house was currently serving as a shelter for three different families besides his own. Materials for new buildings were already being collected, and a sense of victory filled the village. The proclamation that the Demon King was dead had brought cheers, and the communities had seen how the Demon forces had fled the area. Still, Morgana wasn't willing to consider the danger past. She remembered too well the aftermath of the war with the Sídhe when they'd hoped that the conflict was over. In truth, the war never ended.

Heema stepped onto the porch of Lokpal's house and smiled at them all. She handed her husband a leather bag and kissed his cheek before hurrying back inside. Lokpal smiled and nodded at the road that ran along his house. Morgana and Merlin walked side by side behind Lokpal, letting their student lead them into the trees.

They didn't go far, and Morgana raised an eyebrow when they approached a small clearing. The Old One that Lokpal had renamed Shiva was sitting crossed legged with his eyes closed. The Trishula was leaning against a nearby tree, and Morgana inwardly raged at Lokpal for not treating the magical artifact with more respect. She kept her lips pressed tightly together. It wasn't her place.

Lokpal reclaimed the Trishula with a smile and sank to the ground beside Shiva. The area was quiet and provided them with privacy from the guests in Lokpal's home, Morgana supposed. Merlin led the way and sat down across from Shiva. Morgana sank before Lokpal, trying to make herself comfortable on the vegetation-covered ground while Lokpal adjusted the Trishula so he could hold it more comfortably.

The Iron Trishula was a sight to behold. Morgana couldn't help but admire the way it shimmered in the sunlight filtering through the leaves of the trees. Below the surface of the metal, magic churned and hummed, giving the Trishula a soft inner glow only mages would notice. It was a remarkable piece, given that Lokpal had created it from an existing iron weapon rather than slowly building the magic into it. Despite the variation, Morgana had great confidence that the magic would hold for a very long time.

What he had done with it was unexpected. Morgana's eyes jumped over to the newly named Shiva, who was sitting cross-legged on the ground beside Lokpal. The pair were chatting as if they were old friends. Shiva had shifted his physical appearance so that he only had one set of arms, which made Morgana feel a little better. However, his blue-tinted throat and face against the sharp pale white of the rest of his skin marked him as not human. His long dark hair was tied back, and he was smiling warmly at Lokpal, calm, and at peace.

It shouldn't bother her. Morgana was irritated that it did. They'd had allies who were Old Ones before, but the scale of Lokpal pulling Shiva back from insanity was new to her. Only recently, he'd been Rudra, the terrifying Old One that hunted Demons and was feared by humans. He'd even injured Lokpal, but their student hadn't given up on the Old One. His culture and his desperation had pushed him through the dark and allowed him to pull the Old One through with him. It was... different to Morgana.

The relationship between them confused her. Morgana wasn't sure what to think or how to feel about it. The pair were sitting close together with no signs of unease. The awe that Lokpal had showed towards Shiva had vanished over the last few days. Given the brutality that she'd seen Shiva display when slaying the Demon King, she couldn't understand that.

She'd killed plenty of things in her time. Hundreds, if not thousands, of creatures, but Morgana could admit to herself that there was a difference between destroying something with a spell and driving a spear into a skull. Beside her, Merlin agreed with something that Shiva said, and Morgana tried to bring her attention back to the conversation.

"I'm pleased that the Demons are withdrawing," Merlin said. "But they are still a point of concern."

"I agree," Lokpal said. "And judging from the number of boats that are missing, at least twenty got away, and that's only if we estimate two to a boat. Likely there were more."

"Do you have thoughts about what they will do next?" Shiva asked Merlin.

"I suspect they will keep raiding, but they'll likely split into small groups." Merlin rubbed his neck thoughtfully. "It's possible that another Demon may try to take over. We don't know enough about their military structure and culture to say for sure."

"The Sídhe organized themselves into small communities," Morgana offered. "More than one species came through with them, so it was a bit of a mess."

"These Demons are fairly used to the Iron Realm," Merlin added. "So, they could theoretically disappear into the fringes with little effort."

"I'm not sure if that sounds good or bad," Lokpal admitted. His fingers tapped the shaft of the Trishula uneasily, once more drawing Morgana's gaze back to the weapon. "I don't... I hesitate to go too far from my home. My family needs me." A long sigh escaped Lokpal, and he looked at Morgana and Merlin. "What is the next step?"

"The immediate threat is dealt with." Merlin's voice was kind and patient. Morgana was grateful for that. Lokpal was the first time that an Iron Soul had children to consider. A familiar small pang hit her, but she was able to push it away. "The reality is that our world will probably never be empty of invaders. Our task is to keep them in check. That is the role of the Iron Soul."

"The Iron Soul... you never told me much about it," Lokpal said softly. "I know it is my duty to protect the Iron Realm from outsiders, but there is much I do not understand. You've referred to things, but I haven't understood. When the Demons were attacking, it didn't seem important, but now I'd like to know more."

"You carry the soul of my younger brother," Morgana confessed. "We travel the world and seek out new incarnations of him. The Iron Soul's first life was born to my mother. You are reborn again and again."

"Reincarnation," Lokpal said. He blinked and then smiled. "I've heard of it, of course, but I confess I wasn't certain if it was true."

"I have only a little knowledge of the Iron Soul," Shiva said. "What determines when and where they are born?"

"We do not know that for sure," Merlin answered. "I'm surprised that you are familiar with it, Lord Shiva."

Shiva smiled at the use of his new name, his eyes brightening, and his face becoming almost boyish. "Prior to my... slipping, I kept in contact with some of the other Old Ones. We don't frequently speak due to the great distances of this world, but some are better at reaching out than others."

"I suppose that's understandable. Even with water tunnels, the world can be difficult to cross," Merlin said. "But yes, Lokpal is the current Iron Soul. It is his duty to protect the world."

"What is the difference between the Iron Soul and a mage?" Lokpal asked. "You told me that a mage protects the world, so why have an Iron Soul?"

Morgana tensed at the question. She wasn't sure how to answer that and glanced towards Merlin, who was watching Lokpal thoughtfully. He was the one of them who understood the most about the magic of the Iron Realm and the Iron Soul.

"The Iron Soul has the ability to create far greater pieces of magic than any mage." Merlin nodded towards the Trishula. "I have tried in the past to create items such as that, but... the magic fades within a few years. While reenchanting is not impossible, it differs greatly from what you can do. I have no doubt that the magic of the Trishula will endure long after you are gone. Because it was created by you, it will gather and store magic from the world around it."

"And is that the purpose?" Lokpal pressed. He was examining the Trishula, holding it gently, and turned it, so it caught more of the light. "The creation of artifacts like this."

"If there is a greater purpose at play, I am not aware of it," Merlin admitted. "I cannot fathom what it would be, but years ago, the power of this world gathered to create the Iron Soul. It may have been the natural flow of magic, or it may serve a still unknown purpose, but today that does not matter.'

"I remember nothing of any other lives," Lokpal said. He was frowning again. "Not even in dreams." Shaking his head, he tried to smile, but the expression failed to gain any spark of realism. "Seems odd that I wouldn't."

"I agree," Merlin said. "But as old as we are, there are many mysteries still hidden from Morgana and myself."

"Indeed." Morgana's throat tightened, but she pressed on. "You have proven yourself an exceptional mage, Lokpal."

"But what is the point?" Lokpal shook his head and sighed. His gaze went to the Trishula, and some of the tension eased. "I suppose you may be correct, though I wish I understood these events better." Lokpal's spirits seemed to rise, and he smiled gently. "Now that the Demon King is defeated, what are your plans?"

Morgana and Merlin shared a thoughtful look and came to an agreement without a word. They could not leave Lokpal so soon. He was talented, but he was only one mage, and if things turned sour, they could not leave him alone. The ghost of their failure to help Gofiben properly haunted them both.

"Our work is here for now," Merlin answered.

"I'm grateful for that, but from how you speak of the Sídhe in the west, it sounds as if they need close guarding. I would not want others to suffer in the west because you are guarding my homeland. I can take the lead on protecting this land."

"I understand that you are an adult," Morgana said. "And a very capable mage, but I still hesitate to leave you alone here. You are the only mage that we have found in the area and if something goes wrong-"

"I am here," Shiva said firmly. "I owe a great debt to Lokpal. I will speak to the other Old Ones in the area about establishing a system to ensure that someone is always ready to deal with the Demons should they become aggressive."

"It's a pity that they've already started reproducing," Lokpal admitted. He shuddered at the idea, and Morgana had to fight to contain a chuckle. "I don't mind fighting the adults to keep them from upsetting the balance of the world, but children... they didn't choose to be here."

"We understand," Merlin said seriously. "It is the same conflict that Morgana and I found ourselves in long ago. Slaves from the Sidhe worlds escaped into ours. It felt wrong to destroy those who were only trying to escape slavery, and the Sídhe had children who hadn't committed crimes." Merlin shook his head, and Morgana scowled at the memories his words conjured. "It is a complex situation. The best you can do after a certain point is to watch them and ensure that they don't become a danger."

Lokpal was frowning thoughtfully now. His body had tensed, and Shiva was regarding him seriously. No one said anything, and whatever thoughts were going through Lokpal's head, he decided to keep to himself. The wind tickled at Morgana's skin and tugged at her hair, but she was grateful for the rush of cool air it created.

"You said once that your mother and grandfather could use magic," Lokpal said.

"I probably did," Merlin said. "Why?"

"My children may not be mages." Lokpal was looking towards his home again. "But I think I will try to teach them to use magic, even if only a little. It may help them in the future."

"It might, with Demons in the area, this region will likely have slightly higher levels of magic than others." Morgana studied Lokpal and wondered what he was really thinking. "But Lokpal, Merlin, and I are always alert for the next crisis. If something happens in these lands, we will quickly return."

"You are strange creatures," Lokpal said. His voice quivered a little, and he looked at Shiva as well. "All three of you. Immortal and prepared to fight forever. I am just a mortal man. Even knowing that my soul will be reborn to protect this world, I still feel like a mere slip of a being next to you."

"You bring clarity of the plight of humanity," Shiva said. He was smiling, and Morgana found herself drawing nearer to pay closer attention to the Old One. "You have a family to consider, children to seek a better world for, and an understanding of what is at risk. We do not, at least not to the same extent. There is power there. After all, you had the capacity to wish to help me."

Morgana wasn't sure what to think about all this. Merlin was smiling broadly and seemed very pleased. He nodded in approval while Lokpal seemed a touch embarrassed. That was good, she decided. Arto's humility had been critical to his success as a leader. Arrogance turned away potential allies and made a mage blind to danger.

"I will aid Lokpal," Shiva promised. "And I will watch over these lands against the Demons and anything else that may seek to harm those who dwell here. Now and beyond the time it comes that you move on."

The promise hung in the air. Shiva met her gaze, unflinching and determined. Morgana was unsure what to believe. Cyrridven could be trusted, time had proven that, but Badb had cost them. The Old Ones lived on the edge of a dagger with strength to rival a mage if they gave up their concerns for their own lives. Her stomach tightened and turned, but Lokpal was smiling.

He wasn't naïve. Lokpal had fought and suffered against the Demons before they came. He'd trained from his youth to protect this village, and he had a family to fight for. It was dawning on Morgana that he was correct. Sooner or later, she and Merlin would return to the west to keep watch on the Sídhe and the Old Ones there. The world was larger than she'd understood as a young woman and suffering under the burdens of far more enemies than she'd known. Meeting Shiva's gaze, she nodded to him once and made a silent promise to herself that she would destroy the Destroyer if he ever proved false.

22

Gryphon City

Aiden was a geek and a nerd. He wasn't afraid to admit that he not only enjoyed the glory that was science fiction and fantasy, but he also enjoyed putting them up against science and trying to analyze them. This usually worked better with science fiction, but even fantasy allowed for analysis of things like how a culture worked, what the inspiration was for certain things, and the like. In the mithril is aluminum argument, he'd come down on the side that it wasn't aluminum since aluminum tarnished, for instance, even if the theory that pure aluminum couldn't be found in nature because it had been mined up by the dwarves in ancient times was amusing.

The point was that Aiden couldn't help himself now that he was in a Gryphon city. There were actual living, breathing, and talking Gryphons around him with a surprisingly sophisticated society, given that they didn't have opposable thumbs. Then again, his brain reminded him of ravens which used tools to get what they needed, could sometimes talk, and could remember events enough to reward or punish. Thumbs weren't a requirement; they just helped.

He found it hard to focus on any one thing for too long. His eyes swept over the fluttering banners with interest. They were bold colors with an even shade across, indicating a good dying process, and the fabric looked like good quality, so they had some kind of a weaving system that worked with their physical shape. The designs were largely geometric and made him think of middle eastern architecture. The room itself and the "furniture" was carved out of stone. There were small nesting areas in the corners built of pillows and blankets, but nothing like the more portable furniture he was used to.

Thankfully the layout of the room made it clear who the most important Gryphons were. The one in the center of the horseshoe shape was the one that was talking the most and where Alex was directing most of her attention. Aiden wasn't sure if he was supposed to be looking at the leader or not. Anthropology was Nicki's thing, but he knew on Earth that there were plenty of variations when it came to manners. As he wasn't the spokesperson for their group, him watching the leader could be in bad form.

"Isn't it amazing?" Nicki whispered. Her voice was full of barely constrained excitement.

"Yeah." There was no other response that he could give.

Aiden tried not to stare, but his eyes found their way to the new triskelion hanging around Alex's neck when she turned her body towards them. It wasn't as impressive to look at as the other Iron Artifacts, but right now, it was the perfect thing. He only regretted that she hadn't managed to mass-produce them. Then again, something in Aiden rebelled at the idea of a cookie-cutter magical item like that. Some instinct whispered that it wouldn't have worked the second time. After all, there was only one Cathanáil and one Mjǫllnir. One Trishula, one Chain, and one Chalice. All of them had been born out of some circumstance that the Iron Soul found themselves in. He was probably attaching too much romanticism to it, but he couldn't shake the notion.

Alex was gesturing at them, blushing softly after her stomach had grumbled so loudly and reminded him that they hadn't managed breakfast. It was strange. He could understand her words, understand one side of the conversation, but not the words of the Gryphons. Clearly, she was still speaking English, but the power of the Pendant allowed the Gryphons to hear their language. What was the range on that? Did she have to think about it, or did the Pendant activate from a subconscious command? The power could clearly be spread out as Nicki had understood them when touching Alex, but was there a limit to the number of people that could use it? Given that it was so new, how often would she need to charge it up?

So many questions, but this wasn't the time to answer them. Gryphons were watching them with keen interest. One tiny creature, a baby Gryphon with small puff for wings, peeked around an adult in one of the corner nests. A soft breath escaped him as he beheld the little creature. It was so cute, and his mind wondered if they were born like mammals or hatched like baby birds. Was it even reasonable to imagine that Gryphons fit into categories like that?

Then Gryphons moved towards them, and Aiden's attention was firmly shifted to them. The rhythm of conversation that he couldn't understand changed, and Aiden tensed. His magic flared at the rush of fear, and it was tempting to use it to translate. Magic warmed his arms and fingertips, vibrating just beneath the surface of his flesh and ready to react if needed.

"It's okay," Alex said. "Just go with them."

A pair of Gryphons guided them towards the side of the cavern. They didn't say anything that Aiden could understand, but Alex's body language was calm, even if she was still tense. The Gryphons on their thrones were watching them curiously, but none of them were making any move to attack. Looking back to Emrys, Aiden was distressed to see Emrys shifting away from them and towards the entrance. The Dragon caught his expression and lowered his head to avoid hitting the ceiling.

"I will fit no further in," Emrys informed him. "Don't worry, Aiden. I will see you soon. There was a shift in the Dragon's features, and his teeth flashed. "I've been granted permission to hunt beyond the valley. Apparently, there are some larger animals there."

The Dragon's voice betrayed his glee. One of the nearby Gryphons made a sound that Aiden was certain reflected amusement. He wasn't sure if they understood the words or the tone. Nodding, he hurried after the others. So far, things had been going well, and the Gryphons seemed friendly even if he couldn't understand them, but no reason to make a pest of himself.

The room they were shown to was through a carved archway and had one side open to the canyon. It was small and stuffed with small nests made of twisted branches and padded with thick leaves and scraps of fabric. They were large enough for a human to curl up in, but not to completely stretch out. Bits of bright fabric were visible through the sides, and the far side of the room was already dark with no direct light. Aiden stood frozen in the doorway and watched suspiciously for a tiny Gryphon to pop out of the nearest nest.

"It's alright," Alex said. She was peeking into the small nests and smiling to herself. "This is where babies stay when their parents are in the council. They cleared it out for us."

"So, are we staying here today or leaving?" Nicki asked. "We couldn't understand, Alex."

"Right, right, sorry." Alex backed away from Nicki. "They're willing to send us north, but they want us to be escorted. They're going to bring some food while they decide who will escort us."

"Be careful with the food," Morgana cautioned. "Knowing they eat it likely means it is safe for us, but be mindful. Maybe only eat a little of everything they bring just in case."

Aiden nodded in agreement. She had a point. The internal structure of a Gryphon could be very different, and what they could eat might not work for humans. He honestly wasn't sure if they were mammal or bird.

"How are you holding up?" Bran asked Alex. "With the translation?"

Alex's hand went to the Iron Pendant, and a soft expression of awe overtook her face. Her grey eyes seemed peaceful rather than stormy for the first time in months. Bran straightened up a little, and a soft exhale escaped him. Aiden held back a chuckle and a sigh.

"I'm okay," Alex said. She gave them a soft and real smile that instantly helped Aiden relax. "Honestly... I feel its warmth and the magic shifting, but so far, I'm not having to use my magic."

"And Cathanáil?" Bran pressed. "How does the Sword feel?"

It was Aiden's turn to chuckle. "There's something you didn't expect to ever say," he teased.

Reaching back, Alex touched the hilt of Cathanáil and closed her eyes. "It... there's not as much magic as there normally is, but I think it is recharging a little. Slowly, but it feels stronger today than it was yesterday."

"That's a good sign," Nicki said. She was toying with the end of her braided hair. "So far, so good."

"Don't jinx it," Aiden hissed. "Honestly, just don't."

"So, they're going to assign us an escort," Bran said. "Then what?"

"We go north towards where I sensed the Darkness. They've lost contact with clans in that area, so they were willing to believe me that something is going on." Alex paused and glanced at the doorway. Her hand went to the Iron Pendant once again. "They don't trust us, but the leadership seems desperate for some kind of answer."

"I must admit that I'm pleasantly surprised at their friendly response." Morgana looked out the open side of the room. "But stay vigilant."

Soon after that, a pair of Gryphons came into the room carrying cloth bundles filled with fruit for them to eat, he wondered again where the cloth came from. These pieces of fabric were brightly colored, one red and one a rich blue. They carried them knotted up like bandanas in their beaks.

"Don't stare," Nicki hissed to him. "They're being nice."

"Thank you," Morgana said. She took the bundles from the two Gryphons and bowed her head slightly. "Be polite, children. We need them."

"Hey, Alex?" Aiden said. "Can you ask them if they make the cloth themselves?"

Alex gave him an amused look, but turned to the Gryphons and asked. The two seemed shocked at the question, with their eyes widening. He really hoped the question hadn't offended. One of them made a series of twittering and growl noises. Alex nodded and told them, thank you. The Gryphons watched them curiously for a moment before leaving the room.

"They have something that sounds like a loom," Alex said. "But very large and designed for their beaks, though some can apparently manipulate it with their talons. They are very rare artisans and are held in high regard. They're the ones who make the more ornate designs."

"Okay, thanks."

"That was bothering me, too," Nicki admitted. Aiden felt better hearing that. "I hope we didn't offend them."

"They didn't seem to mind. Our hands are weird to them. I get the impression that they have no stories of humans here. Whatever Gryphons came to Earth and inspired the myth, must never have gotten back here."

That was both a reassuring and sad thought. Aiden was honest with himself that he preferred the notion that the Gryphons had never meant to go to Earth and had no knowledge of it. Then again, it made them being here dangerous in another way. If the Darkness spread too much and they failed to stop it, then the Gryphons might now turn their attention to the Iron Realm. Morgana was frowning deeply, and Aiden suspected the same thought had occurred to her.

There was no table or even any kind of platform to put the food on, so Morgana simply set the bundles on the floor. Aiden picked up the bundles and gently opened them to reveal the full scale of the fruits and berries inside. They looked similar to fruits on Earth, and Aiden turned one over slowly, remembering Morgana's advice to be cautious. The one in his hand had a smooth reddish finish, a bit like an apple's but was softer under his grip. Others were much smaller than apples or oranges and looked like the berries they'd found in the forest.

"Looks okay," he said. "I wonder if they collect it wild or if there are orchards somewhere."

"Probably orchards," Alex said. She was the most relaxed of them all and had dropped to the floor and adjusted Cathanáil without a second thought. "They seem to have a complex society, even if it differs from ours."

Morgana eyed the fruit carefully. Her lips were pressed together thoughtfully. For a moment,

Aiden thought she might change her mind about trying the food. Instead, she picked up a large blue berry and popped it into her mouth. Everyone waited. Morgana's eyes widened, and she nodded approvingly.

"It's good," she said. "Take it slow. There's no rush. We'll keep an eye out for any adverse reactions, but we still have to eat. Try a little of everything rather than eating too much of one thing," she reminded them.

Everyone sat down in a circle around the sheets of fabric piled with fruit. It reminded Aiden of a picnic. A picnic in the nursery of a Gryphon City. Laughter threatened to bubble up inside of him, but then Nicki handed him a slice of a purplish bulbous fruit that she'd cut off with her knife, and he took a bite. It was very sweet, a bit like blueberries, and he grinned. She passed him another piece for Bran beside him, and they all started in on their breakfast at last. He managed not to laugh when Bran pulled out his journal and began taking notes on the fruits. Honestly, it was a smart idea. It was sinking in that they were going to be in this world awhile.

Scooting closer to his friend, Aiden leaned over to see the journal as Bran made a quick drawing of one of the more bulbous berries and noted down its vibrant blue-purple color. Nicki leaned closer on Bran's other side and made a few suggestions of her own. He glanced at Alex and Morgana, finding them deep in conversation with Morgana pressing Alex on everything that was said. He kept one ear open for any details he needed and glanced at the open side of the room once more. Hopefully, their escort would be assembled soon. As fascinating as a Gryphon City was, there was a long way to go, and it would be much easier to focus without having so many fascinating distractions. Sometimes being a geek and nerd was a recipe for trouble.

23

Masters of the Sky

The golden sky stretched out before them. The wind whistled as they flew forward, and the mountain peaks cradled them with the promise of solid ground below. Thick forests covered the mountains with only the rivers and occasional canyon breaking up the landscape. It was a wild world, raw in a way that Alex had only seen on her one backpacking trip in high school. There were no roads, no cities, and no farms to break up the forests.

Flying was a dream that Alex had let go of pretty quickly after learning she was a mage. The threat of magical exhaustion while high in the air was enough to scare her off, but Aiden and Bran had also hit her and Nicki with the hard science facts of how cold the atmosphere was, how thin the oxygen quickly became and most horrifically, the consequences of a bird strike. Add to that the danger of being detected while having a lazy flight around Ravenslake, and Alex had never tried even lifting herself off the ground. Bran probably could do that if he really wanted to. He was still the best at moving objects.

Gryphons, on the other hand, were the clear masters of their world's skies. There was still no sign of other winged creatures, and even the insects stayed low in the treetops. Despite rushing through the air, Alex had yet to have a single bug fly into her face. Alex hadn't asked if there had once been other birds in their world that had been hunted to extinction. It seemed like a rude thing to ask, especially since it was possible that evolution in this world had simply kept other creatures out of the Gryphon's skies.

They were staying low so the poor little humans could breathe, but every so often, one of the unburdened Gryphons would zoom up high into the sky and perform feats of acrobatics that even a Blue Angel would be jealous of. The group of seven Gryphons escorting them was helpful enough, but even after two days of flying, Alex still only knew the names of three of them. It was clear that this was a mission to them and nothing more. Her Pendant let her understand them, but they weren't talkative with the humans. Morgana had pointed out that they were likely there to observe the humans and didn't want to get too close to such strange creatures.

A shiver traveled through Alex's body, and her teeth chattered. It was cold. They were flying faster than Emrys had on their first day here, and Alex was grateful that they'd packed coats in their gear. The wind stung her cheeks as Alex peered around them and tried not to get airsick. She kept a tight grip on the rope tied around the Gryphons neck and wished once again that they all could have ridden on Emrys. Sadly, the Dragon had been honest with them that he dared not go too fast with all of them on board.

Emrys was flying ahead of them, the Dragon occasionally doing a trick of his own and laughing with glee. In his claws was gripped the large net holding their backpacks. Every time he spun, Alex's heart jumped in worry of losing their gear, but his childlike joy also made her smile.

She was grateful that he was with them and enjoying himself, but it only underlined the centuries that he'd spent locked away underground.

Freed of his duty, Emrys was very different, and Alex wasn't sure what to make of that. So far, he seemed determined to help them, but she worried it wouldn't last.

Alex slowly released one hand from the rope and dug into the rough cloth bag that Nicki had made them before leaving the Gryphon city. In truth, it wasn't a bag. It was a square of cloth that tied to their belt loops and sat in front of them like a pouch so they could keep a couple of things with them in flight. Alex's had a water bottle, which she pulled out and took a quick drink from, a snack bar, and some berries. She glanced towards Bran as she closed up the water and returned her right hand to the rope. He was carrying the Iron Chalice with him today. At least, she was pretty sure it was his turn.

Mjǫllnir sat awkwardly against her hip. The original holster wasn't proving good for flying as the Hammer kept shifting the first day, leading to complaints from Braken, the Gryphon she was riding, so today, Alex had tied the handle to her leg. It was awkward, and she wouldn't be able to draw it fast, but at least Mjǫllnir wasn't accidentally releasing sparks of magic or shocking a member of their escort.

At least their magic did regenerate. Morgana had no explanation for it but had admitted to using magic in the Sídhe tunnels long ago. Now, Alex wasn't so sure if it had been the tunnels or if Morgana had truly been in another world and not understood that. Her own theory was that the lines of energy that she'd seen carried some magic from Earth out into the branches. It would explain why they were regaining their magic, even if a bit more slowly.

Deep down, it did not surprise Alex to learn that it wasn't as simple as the different worlds rejecting collision. That was part of it. How magic reacted to beings from other worlds proved that, but there was more. These worlds were connected by some power, some thread that linked them all together. Why, she didn't know, but it was there, and it was real. It was something that bound the worlds together, something that they all shared, and she was sure it was helping keep them safe with magic.

Far ahead, there was something wrong with the sky. Narrowing her eyes, Alex leaned forward and tried to see the distortion. The colors of the sky were wrong; even with only her short experience in this world, she could notice that. Instead of the goldish tint that the sky normally carried, there was a cloud of dark blue. In her world, it would have been hard to notice, but here it stood out.

The Gryphons made sounds of alarm. Alex almost used her magic to listen in before dismissing the idea. That was the Darkness. That was the hole that she'd found by scrying. As it turned out, she needn't have used the magic. Each flap of the Gryphon's wings brought them closer and closer to it.

Thin dark lines spread across the sky. It was more than the crack she remembered from Akule's memories. This had spread further than what he had dealt with. Fear gathered in Alex's chest. Akule had dealt with the Darkness on a day of greater power and had been on Earth. She was in a totally different world, and there was no day that would give her greater power.

Alex shuddered. Too many unpleasant memories were surging forward. Her hand ached with phantom pain from long ago. Old lives were clawing their way a bit too close to the surface right now, given that they didn't have any useful information to share. Nothing in any of her prior experiences had prepared her for going into another world to fight the Darkness.

Unable to keep looking at the Darkness, Alex glanced at the others in hopes of being reassured by them. She was looking at Morgana and Bran's backs as their Gryphons led the way, and Aiden was behind her.

Only Nicki was in a position that Alex could really see. Nicki was looking in her direction. Alex nodded and wished that they were close enough to talk. Her fingers tightened around the rope so hard that her skin burned. She couldn't ease her grip.

'Breathe,' Thor ordered. 'Calm yourself.'

'We've beaten the Darkness before,' Akule said. 'We'll manage. You know more than I did.'

That was both reassuring and not at all. Still, she inhaled slowly and held the air in. It helped a little, and she finally eased her grip. Nicki was still watching her, and Alex gave her another nod, trying to show that she was okay. The steady flapping of the Gryphon's wings was soothing.

'Stay strong,' Timur huffed. 'You're the Iron Soul.'

It dissolved into arguing after that. Arto was trying to scold Timur for being insensitive, and Alex just tuned them out. There were too many of them. All male, all thinking they knew best, and all of them lacking in advice that she could use. Amusement at her thoughts radiated through her. She wasn't sure of the source but suspected that it had been Michel. Or maybe Thor. He had died an old man and didn't take himself too seriously anymore, even if he loved knowing that they had named a god after him.

The Gryphons shrieked at each other, and the sounds rang in Alex's ears despite the wind. With no warning, the Gryphon she was riding changed position and descended. Alex's stomach swooped as if she was on a roller coaster. Looking around, she searched the sky for any threat that might have triggered this. There was only the churning Darkness eating up the sky ahead of them.

They touched down in the small clearing, and Alex exhaled. Her head was swimming; her limbs were quivering. Somehow, she let go of the rope and slowly dismounted, knees buckling as she hit the firm ground.

"Alex?" Bran was next to her in moments, holding her up. "Are you okay?"

"Yeah." Alex swallowed. "I'm fine. Just a bit dizzy." Forcing a small smile, she shrugged. "Guess I might have locked up my knees."

Bran frowned. He was too smart to believe her, but she didn't want to admit to fighting off another panic attack at the sight of the Darkness. She didn't want to admit that part of her was ready to pull Cathanáil free from the sheath and make a portal home. Over her head, the sky twisted and shuddered like a storm was rolling in, but it was breaking apart. It was being torn open like an animal with claws, and teeth was trying to get in.

A sudden blast of wind sent dirt flying into the air and tugged at the hair in Alex's braid. She looked up with shaded eyes to see Emrys coming down for a landing. They all backed away to clear enough space for the large creature. Emrys first set down the net of packs and then landed with a soft, almost delicate thump beside the net. If she'd had a sign, Alex would have written a nine on it to hold up. The acrobatics of the mythical creatures around her were a sight to behold.

Alex barely paid attention as the Gryphons and Emrys spoke briefly. It wasn't worth the magic. Their tones were calm and she stretched out her arms and shook her hands out. One of the Gryphons drew her attention with the confused tone of its voice, but that quickly passed. All but one Gryphon took to the air and flapped their powerful wings.

"What is going on?" Morgana asked.

"They are going to scout around," Emrys answered. "They are concerned about the lack of air traffic they are seeing. The Gryphons have been evacuating the area," Emrys explained. "I'm not sure how long this has been here. Time can be difficult to translate. They say it started a season ago."

"But we don't know how long a season is here," Alex finished. Examining the nearest tree, she noted the large shining green leaves but knew it would tell her nothing. For all she knew, they were like this year-round, and this was a tropical environment. "We don't have the context we need."

Ignorance wasn't bliss. It might be their death.

"So, what is the plan?" Aiden asked Emrys. "Are we stopping for the night, or is this just a break?"

"A break. It won't be dark for some time." Emrys laid down and delicately crossed his front legs as he folded down his wings. "The Gryphons have noted that you're heavy. Please keep in mind that there are no creatures like you. They've only ever carried their young on their backs."

"Fair enough," Nicki said. She beamed up at Emrys. "Thank you for carrying our stuff. With how heavy we are, that would have been a great burden for the Gryphons."

"Weight is less of a concern for me." Emrys shifted his body, almost shrugging. "I can handle more weight than they seem to be able to. They are rather curious creatures."

"Yes." Morgana looked at the nearby group of Gryphons who had settled on the ground. "I do wonder when and how some of them entered Earth."

"You and Merlin never came across them?" Nicki asked.

"No. I believe that the first stories of them predate me. The myths spread from Ancient Persia if I remember correctly." Morgana tapped on the plastic of her water bottle. "It wouldn't be the first time that a species came to Earth and died out. The only reason the Fae have such large numbers are that the Sídhe used both male and female soldiers. If they hadn't, then we likely would have been spared many problems." There was a growl in Morgana's voice now, and she gripped her water bottle a little too tightly. Then she took a drink and seemed to calm down a bit.

Watching Morgana drink water got the rest of them to pull out their water bottles and drink. So far, they were using a filter straw Aiden had brought to clean the water they took from streams or the Gryphon cistern. They couldn't know for sure if it would clean everything, but it was better than nothing. At least that was the theory.

Sitting in the shade of a nearby tree gave Alex a chance to stretch out her legs and muscles. Deciding to treat the break as lunch, she and the others foraged near the clearing to find more of the berries and fruits that so far had proven safe. There had been no sign of farms yet, and Alex didn't want to seem insulting by asking. She kept reminding herself that her human experience on Earth wasn't a valid point of comparison.

Before they could get too comfortable, a screech sounded from the Gryphons. Getting to her feet, Alex rushed back to the clearing to find Emrys looking into the sky. Large shapes were in view over the trees, maybe a mile or two away. The massive shapes sped towards them, and Alex's eyes widened as the forms became more and more familiar. She glanced over her shoulder to confirm that Emrys was still behind her. He was, and a sound of surprise escaped him.

"Dragons," he breathed.

A cry went up from the Gryphons that didn't sound good. The first Dragon landed with a thud, shaking the trees all around them. It was twice the size of Emrys, with fierce horns growing along its head and down its spine. Blue scales shimmered in the golden light of the sky, and a thin line of smoke rose out of both nostrils. The Gryphons shifted into a tight formation, raising their backs and hissing like great cats.

Two more Dragons stayed in the air above them, their long bodies casting shadows down upon Alex and her fellow mages as they circled.

They were all larger than Emrys, and she suddenly wondered if centuries in a cave had prevented Emrys from reaching his full natural size. More hissing came from the Gryphons. Alex's fingers itched to draw Cathanáil, and Mjǫllnir hummed on her hip.

"Steady," Morgana said. "Steady."

The Iron Pendant hummed against Alex's skin under her shirt. Alex's right hand trembled as she pulled gently on her magic. Panic was threatening to take hold, and she had to be ready for any attack. Aiden stepped up next to her on her left, and Morgana came up on her right. Morgana was frowning deeply at the new Dragon. Emrys stood and stalked in front of them, mostly blocking Alex's view.

"Where did you come from?" Emrys asked the Dragon.

"We fly to freedom," it answered. Even with the Pendant, its voice was rough and difficult to understand. There was the sound of the Dragon sniffing the air.

"You smell of Gryphon blood!" Tarfil snapped. Alex identified the Gryphon only thanks to the slight lisp they had. "You will surrender yourself, Dragon. This is our homeland, not yours."

A low rumble escaped the Dragon. It sank into Alex's bones, and every instinct screamed to run from the predator. Already, her mind was creating terrible images of what the Dragon might have done to smell of Gryphon blood.

Alex tried to move around Emrys. Morgana grabbed her arm in an iron grip. She stood on her toes and tried to see over the Dragon. Alex only caught a glimpse of the larger Dragon moving and shifted back, letting Morgana grab her bare hand so she could understand what was being said.

"You will be taken to the nearest Nest," another Gryphon said. Alex couldn't be sure which one it was without being able to see. "There you can speak with-"

"No! We don't take orders from your kind!"

Alex blinked, trying to piece together what she had missed, but the Gryphons lunged forward. The new Dragon roared, and one of Emrys' wings was over them. Alex's magic snapped back into her chest like a rubber band as she lost all focus. Morgana's hands kept her steady, but the sounds of screeching and snarls made her nervous. The thin skin of Emrys' wings kept her from seeing what was happening.

"Stay down, mages," Emrys ordered. "I'll see if I can calm them!"

Protests rose in Alex's throat, but another pair of hands joined Morgana's in pulling her back. Someone had grabbed her bag and was adding their weight to leveraging her back. Emrys' body tightened and coiled before he leapt into the air. Dirt went flying, circling around them at the force of his wings, and Alex couldn't see thanks to dust in her eyes.

"What happened?" Bran shouted.

"Invaders!" Morgana snapped. She and the others let go of Alex. "The Dragons came through!"

"How?" Nicki asked.

If anyone had an answer, Alex couldn't hear it. Roars overhead made her turn her face up. Blinking and wiping at her eyes, Alex fought to clear her vision and see what was happening. Emrys had flown up between the Dragons and Gryphons. There was more snarling, but she didn't dare use her magic. Instead, she flexed the fingers of her right hand and waited.

"Steady," Morgana said again. "Don't panic."

"Shit!" Nicki gasped. "Morgana-"

"No, let Emrys talk to them. He has more in common with-"

A pale green Dragon lashed out at Emrys, catching the red Dragon's left wing with its talons as it roared. The blue Dragon that had landed earlier opened its mouth and breathed a massive stream of fire. The Gryphons twisted out of the way, flying back to avoid the attack while shrieking. Heart pounding, Alex kept her eyes locked on Emrys. A roar of pain escaped him, but he was still in the air. Then the third Dragon, this one with pale purple scales, dove towards Emrys, striking him with the full weight of its much larger body.

There was a horrible sound, crunching, cracking, and screaming all at once. It hit Alex in the chest. Her magic pooled and flowed down her hands. Emrys fell, his form casting a shadow that rapidly grew in size as the three new Dragons and the Gryphons launched themselves at each other. Alex didn't watch them fight; her eyes were fixed on Emrys as he raced towards the ground.

24

Latest Generation

2 01 B.C.E. Gulf of Morbihan, Brittany

Morgana rather liked their new home. The weather was pleasant enough, and the people shared many aspects of the culture of her childhood. Nothing would ever be exactly like her homeland, but this was close enough to make her happy. Her cloak fluttered in the gentle breeze as she gazed down into the large bay. The cliffs and hillsides almost wholly encircled the water with islands scattered across the calm blue surface. It was a beautiful, protected area that smelled of the sea and had plenty of fish to keep everyone satisfied.

It wasn't home, but standing on the rocks of the hill almost made her feel like she was back at the village she'd spent so many years with Airril in. Unfortunately, the Fae had decided that the area was rather lovely as well. When or how they had made their way off the northern islands, Morgana did not know. She imagined them hiding under blankets in boats as they made their way across the channel.

The last hints of the winter were fading from the coast, and the dry heat of the summer would soon be upon them. At least, that meant shorter nights for the Fae to use for their raids. The sound of someone moving behind her made Morgana tense. Then she relaxed, hearing the gentle thump of Merlin's walking stick.

"Find anything?" he asked.

"No. I tried scrying, but I haven't gotten a clear location on where the Sídhe are living. It makes me miss the obvious mounds back home."

"Or the tunnels. Those were usually easy to find."

"Sometimes, I recall a few well-hidden ones during the war." Her lips twisted into a small smile. "Not that it saved them."

"No, it didn't. But on a positive note, the Fae seem to be settling now that we're in the area. There have been no disappearances in the last fortnight."

"Perhaps," Morgana frowned at the statement. "But I'm not sure they aren't mustering. Some of the Fae creatures... their ancestors may have been innocent, but the toll of being in this world is affecting them. Those creatures we saw last time are vicious, almost feral."

Merlin shuddered. "Yes, I remember."

"And that one that splashed in the puddles of blood?" Her stomach turned at the memory for multiple reasons. "It didn't flinch back, Merlin. They are developing a resistance to iron!"

"Some of them, some," Merlin stressed. "Not all, Morgana. Iron tools effectively repelled several of the Fae. I understand your concern, but we'll sort it out. And we have some help this time."

"I suppose so. How are they doing?" Morgana asked.

"No visible magic yet, but they're learning how to sit still." The old man sounded exhausted, and Morgana chuckled. "Coming to find you was a welcome break."

Turning around, she found Merlin leaning on his staff and looking out into the water. "It is nice here. I can see why you slip off to the shore."

"I do like it here," Morgana agreed. "It would be nicer if the Fae were gone."

"They've been warned." Merlin shrugged and gestured for her to come with him. Morgana didn't argue and joined him on the small path that led towards the village and their current home. "And we're here to put an end to these raids."

"Yes, but then there will be another tribe of Fae that acts up, then another and another."

"Morgana, we agreed that hunting them down was a waste of time and would only trigger panic. We don't need all the Old Ones and other types of Fae uniting against us."

It was an old argument. Merlin had a point, and she hated that. As much as part of her hated letting beings from other worlds live in the Iron Realm, she recognized killing them wasn't an answer. Too many of the Fae were the descendants of slaves who had taken the chance to flee their oppression. She didn't blame them for that. The Old Ones were banished here and couldn't go home, and some of them were helpful. She just wished that the descendants of the Sídhe would stop causing problems! There wasn't a simple solution to any of this.

"How are our little mages doing?" Morgana asked.

"Nothing so far, but I have faith. They always connect to their magic. I'm confident that we'll have them trained up before the Sídhe make another move."

"I hope so. They're very young, but at least there are three of them. That's a bit easier. Each mage and set of eyes helps."

"I wonder why there are sometimes more of them," Merlin said.

"More what?"

"Mages." Merlin nodded at the trio. "Arto had us, of course, but Lokpal was the only mage in the area despite the great danger. Gofiben had Bran. I simply wonder about the different numbers."

"It may be a case of death in childhood," Morgana suggested. "You and I both know how frequently children die. Even magic can't promise health and long life." The words were more bitter than she meant for them to be, but the unfairness of it was a dark knot in her gut. "I suppose I was born as a mage to serve alongside Arto. After all, I wasn't born this way."

"No, you were not."

Merlin's tone betrayed nothing, and Morgana briefly wondered what her life might have been like if the Sídhe hadn't taken her. For a moment, she allowed herself to imagine Merlin coming to the village and discovering both her and Arto and teaching them together. He'd only taken Arto away because of the danger she brought down upon them. If she hadn't been taken, she wouldn't have done that, and she and Arto could have trained together. They could have stayed with their mother while learning magic.

It was a pleasant dream, but she pushed it aside. Life had unfolded very differently. The Sídhe had taken her as a young girl, and through foolish luck, her Changeling had survived long enough for them to be merged. She'd lost her human nature that day. Now here she was, centuries-old, and still walking the realm of the living. Arto and Airril were long gone, but she was still here.

"Morgana?"

"Just wondering if there might have been another mage born around the same time as Arto and I who died."

"It's possible. The Sídhe took you. We might have lost other mages in similar ways, or they might have been killed." Merlin shook his head.

"I'm not sure. Magic may run in the blood. It seemed to be in my family to an extent, and you and Arto both had magic."

"Perhaps, but Galath did not."

"No, he didn't." Merlin shrugged. "I don't know why some are born mages, and others are not." He smiled and nodded at the small group waiting for them. "We should be grateful that we have two mages alongside the Iron Soul. It will make things easier if they have each other to turn to."

They were so young. Morgana couldn't help but grimace when she looked at the three of them. Merlin suspected Brennus was the latest incarnation of the Iron Soul. There was nothing absolute about the Iron Soul that made identification easy, but Morgana found that there was often a sense of recognition. Morgana was inclined to agree with Merlin's assessment, but they'd agreed that the boy didn't need to know about that yet. He was only fourteen years old. Maybe he'd never need to. Brennus was a fairly small lad with brown curls and curious dark eyes. Morgana was already fonder of the boy than she wanted to be. He was clever and already proving himself the leader of this new generation of mages.

Judoc was the oldest of the three, roughly a year older than Brennus, but thankfully a patient sort who didn't mind Brennus' leadership. He wasn't the brightest boy Morgana had ever met, but he was very observant. Judoc's brown hair was long enough to be tied at the back of his neck, but small bits of hair kept escaping and tickling his skin. His brown eyes were closed tightly, and his nose wrinkled as he tried to find his magic. His expression made the corners of Morgana's mouth tilt up.

Morgana's favorite of the young mages, however, was Rozenn. It was nice to have another female mage, even if only for a few years. Rozenn's mother had been a little too happy to hand her over to Merlin and Morgana in exchange for a few gold bracelets, and at first, Morgana had been deeply suspicious. Thankfully, the girl was not traumatized by whatever had happened at home, and her mother's quick acceptance seemed to be based on the recent loss of her husband and having too many children to feed. Rozenn was also a very spirited child in Morgana's opinion and was always asking questions. Merlin found her a touch exhausting, so Morgana found her very amusing.

"Did you have a pleasant walk, Morgana?" Brennus asked. His eyes twinkled, and Morgana eyed him suspiciously.

"I did," she agreed. "I no longer wish to hit you over the head."

The boy had enough sense to at least appear bashful. Merlin chuckled and shook his head. Rozenn was watching the pair of them with adoring eyes as her fingers drummed on the ground. She wouldn't be sitting still much longer.

"Sorry," Brennus offered.

"We're just excited!" Rozenn jumped up and rubbed her hands together. "When will the magic come?"

"You already have magic," Morgana reminded her. "There was a Connection when we met you. That doesn't happen without magic."

"But when can we use it?" Brennus whined.

"You need to control it," Morgana said. Her patience was already wearing thin, and she'd only just returned. Maybe it had been for the best that she and Airril couldn't have children together. "It will come; it just takes some time."

The three younger mages all exchanged looks. Judoc pouted a little, but Rozenn nodded seriously. Merlin leaned on his staff and gave Morgana a look. She almost laughed but nodded.

"That's enough for today," Morgana said. "We'll keep working on it. In the meantime, there are chores to do."

"Can't you just use your magic?" Brennus asked. "It might help us to see more magic."

"It might," Morgana agreed. "But there are limits. The amount of magic available to each of us is limited, overdoing it leaves a person weak."

The three younger mages exchanged glances. Morgana held back a sigh. They were going to do something foolish. This was the problem with mages in the throes of puberty. They had no common sense. It was true that they were all hard workers, but their excitement over learning that they had magic hadn't faded yet. That made them potentially dangerous.

Three young mages at the same time. This was going to age her. Rubbing her forehead, Morgana held back a sigh and reminded herself that she aged slowly. Over the past decades, her appearance had barely changed. There were a few more wrinkles than when they'd been training Gofiben, and she had the feeling that these young mages were going to give her a few more. Merlin was smiling and had already sat down on the ground once again, with the young mages crowding around him. He was so much better with children than she was.

"Let's head for home," Merlin suggested. "We're all tired."

"I'm not tired," Brennus protested.

"You will be. Sitting still and trying to focus on one thing seems to be a challenge for you," Merlin teased.

Brennus blushed, and Rozenn giggled at his expression of defiance. Thankfully, he didn't argue further after Judoc yawned. The larger young man clamored to his feet and stretched. Then his stomach grumbled. The young man looked both sheepish and expectant at the same time. Morgana nodded towards the pathway. She and Merlin had taken on the responsibility of looking after the young mages, and this was just another part of it. Merlin chuckled and smiled at her.

"Arto was always hungry after training."

"Training. They didn't even summon magic." Morgana raised an eyebrow at Merlin.

"They're still growing, even Rozenn. I expect the boys will each gain at least a few more inches. Maybe even before summer arrives."

"Lovely. I remember when Altan was in his final growing years." Morgana shuddered. "The boy tried to eat his weight in food every day."

"Arto was much the same at that age. I remember despairing any time that we were traveling between villages. The boy would complain about the rations and still being hungry."

Morgana smiled a little. Over the years, it had become easier and easier to hear Merlin speak of the years she'd missed of her brother's life. It had been so long, but sometimes, his ghost still hung between them. And yet, he also united them. Merlin was the only one alive who remembered Arto, the real Arto, and not the tales that they heard from time to time.

They followed the path around the hillside to the small fishing village down the slope. A small dock was empty, and Morgana could see the usual boats out on the water. Small houses surrounded an open area, and she could see people milling about as they got closer. Animals were pinned up in yards at the edge of the village, but most of the flocks were further out. Villages like this were similar to the one she had grown up in, but there were small changes here and there.

It was unwalled for a start, and there were no guards. Even the recent Fae raids hadn't been enough to scare the locals into defensive measures just yet. Morgana had mixed feelings about that. On the one hand, she preferred them not to live in fear, but on the other hand, it made trying to protect them that much more difficult. They passed a farmer with an iron axe over his shoulder, and Morgana eyed the metal. Even centuries later, it was strange for her to see iron being used as simple farm tools.

The villagers looked at them with hints of suspicion. Morgana rolled her eyes and kept moving. It wasn't worth the effort to worry about what the locals thought. They were frightened by the threat of the Fae, but uneasy about the mages in their midst. She missed the old days when Merlin had been so respected as a priest. Looking back, she hadn't appreciated it enough.

Their three students stayed close to her, still chatting amongst themselves and looking rather pleased. Brennus waved to another young boy watching them from a doorway. The strange boy blinked in surprise, but managed a wave back and smiled. That was good, Morgana decided. She and Merlin were newcomers. They'd plucked Rozenn from a village a few miles away and Judoc from the next village over while Brennus was a local. If they didn't cause trouble, then hopefully they'd be accepted.

People went back to their business after a short, cautious look at the newcomers, and Morgana relaxed. There was plenty of daylight left for them to return to their home outside the village and tend to the garden. She'd prefer it when they could grow their own food and be less dependent on the locals. If they could have used their magic without risking exhaustion with the low magic levels, she would have. Turning to speak with Merlin, Morgana found he had moved off to speak with a woman selling vegetables out of baskets and that Brennus had wandered off.

She located the young man standing a few feet away and talking with a pretty young woman about his age. Her dark hair was braided over her head, and she was smiling brightly at something that Brennus had said. Morgana studied the girl. She was dressed like most of the locals in a simple plant dyed dress and carrying a basket of vegetables, likely from the market. Something about her seemed familiar, but she couldn't place it. There was nothing special about her. Brennus laughed, and the young woman giggled.

"Morgana?" Merlin called. "What do you think of stew for dinner?"

Shaking her head, Morgana put the young woman out of her mind. There was nothing wrong with the mages making friends in the area just so long as they understood their duty to the Iron Realm. Still... Morgana looked back at the young woman, her frown deepening as she tried to unravel what it was about the girl that seemed so familiar. It was similar to the odd familiarity that Brennus inspired, and Gofiben had inspired before him. Shaking her head, she checked on the other two young mages who were talking to each other before moving to join Merlin in selecting some produce for dinner.

25

Change of Plan

Alex was frozen in place. She couldn't even cry out as she watched Emrys fall. He wasn't dead. She could see him trying to twist his body and flap his wings, but as he tried, the torn skin was only ripped further into shreds. It was surreal. For an instant, her mind was stuck on stunned disbelief that she was watching a Dragon fall from the sky.

Then he hit the ground. The impact rattled the world and almost sent Alex tumbling. Dust swirled around them, and the sound had deafened Alex. There was a heartbeat where she didn't move. Then her eyes jumped to the sky to see if the fight had stopped. It hadn't. The three Dragons and the Gryphons circled each other high above Alex. A Gryphon was shrieking and diving towards the wing of the nearest Dragon.

Spinning towards Emrys, Alex eyed his wounded wing. It wasn't healing. Her chest tightened in the realization that he was mortal once more. They had left Earth. It was impossible to know what changes would and wouldn't stay with him. She couldn't risk it not after he'd suffered so much and then come so far with them.

"Chalice!"

Alex rushed to the fallen Dragon, leaving the others to get the Chalice out of Bran's bag. Emrys was groaning in pain, loud hisses escaping him with every movement. There was only a brief moment of hesitation when Cuthbert ordered her to be careful, but Alex was used to ignoring him. Laying her hand on Emrys' snout, Alex tried to wet her dry mouth and struggled to speak.

"The Chalice is here," Alex managed. "Stay still."

"Have to stop-"

"You need to be healed," Alex said. "You don't just heal anymore, Emrys."

The Dragon shivered beneath her hands. His scales scraped against her fingertips, the edges of them hard and smooth like manicured nails. Alex swallowed. What was pain, real pain like after centuries of healing quickly? He'd had to rip apart the White Dragon daily in a Dragonic twist of the Prometheus punishment just to keep it contained.

"They said- they ordered the Gryphons to surrender," Emrys groaned. He tried to twist his neck so he could look up. "They warned that more were coming." Alex frowned at the words. More threats must have been exchanged in the skies. A pained whimper escaped the Dragon, but thankfully he didn't try to stand. Alex shifted closer to him, making soft cooing sounds to calm him. She had no idea if they had any impact on Dragons. "The Dragons are invading." His shock radiated off of him. "My people... how far have they fallen?"

Alex didn't have an answer, and thankfully, Bran was at her side the next moment with the Iron Chalice. It was sloshing with water, and the metal was glowing softly. Alex gently took it from him with a brief, grateful smile. Emrys lowered his head and opened his mouth so Alex could pour the water in. There was nothing elegant or graceful about the movement, but the water got into his mouth.

A horrible thought that it wouldn't work hit Alex moments before the wing began to knit back together. A strange grinding sound echoed in her ears, making her shiver as the broken bones shifted back into place, and new flesh rolled across the exposed muscle. The thin skin of the wing stretched to fill in the holes with a faint shimmer dancing over the flesh. Sighing in relief, Alex swayed, and Bran caught her arm to keep her steady.

"Emrys?" Bran asked. "What should we do?"

"I don't know." The words were almost impossible to hear. While the Dragon's groans of pain were done, something else had taken its place. "They- they aren't afraid to start a war."

"Do you think they are running from the Darkness?"

"I both hope they are and pray they are not." Emrys stood slowly and stretched the healed wing carefully. "I fear what has happened to my people if war is their chosen response."

His words were simple, but heartbreak and anguish echoed in them. It occurred to Alex for the first time that despite the law binding him never to return home, Emrys might have been holding out a hope that it would be possible. Much could change in centuries, and perhaps he'd hoped that the law had. In her modern life and her memories of their past, the Dragon had always been a calm figure filled with determination to do his duty. Now she had to wonder how much more simmered beneath the surface.

She kept a hand on his neck, her fingers automatically brushing over the smooth scales, as she looked up into the sky. Emrys tensed, and she hissed in understanding. A pair of Gryphons were ripping into the wings of another Dragon. The Dragon was barely keeping itself in the air and lashing out with its tail to slap one of the Gryphons away. The blow was hard enough that they heard it on the ground.

The Dragon with the ripped wings was struggling in the sky, swerving towards the east as it fled the Gryphons. Alex eyed the other two Dragons who moved to cover its retreat. That gave her some hope, but then a Gryphon fell from the sky. The Gryphon stopped moving partway down. Unlike Emrys, it didn't manage to aim for the clearing and struck a nearby tree. Limbs impaled the corpse, sending pale red blood spurting out. The massive feathered wings were mangled, and Alex started to move forward with the Iron Chalice, only to stop when she saw that the Gryphon wasn't moving. It was several feet above her in a tree and completely still except for the way that gravity was pulling it further down onto the tree branches. Her stomach turned at the gruesome sight, and she looked up into the sky.

"I need-" Emrys started to move.

"No," Alex said.

"We aren't strong enough to get in the middle of this," Morgana said.

"But we can't just stand here," Nicki insisted. "They're trying to kill each other!"

"The Gryphons are defending their home," Morgana said. "They clearly see these Dragons as a threat. It is no different than how we dealt with the invading Demons."

"I might be able to mediate the situation." Emrys began to spread his wings.

Alex clamored up onto his back before thinking it through. Hands tried to grab her, but Emrys was already starting to flap his great wings. Grabbing onto the lowest horn, Alex tightened her legs around the ridge of Emrys' back in an attempt to stay steady. Her left arm wrapped tightly around the Chalice to keep it safe. Morgana shouted her name, but Alex didn't look down. Emrys was flying up to the others.

The injured Dragon fell in the distance with a mournful cry as its wing finally gave out. A Gryphon dived past the two remaining Dragons and slashed at it. Alex was too far away to see what effect it had, but she feared that the death toll was rising. The Dragon fell from the sky into the forest a few miles away.

"Stop!" she shouted. But the beating of wings drowned her out.

"Stop this!" Emrys tried. "Stop!"

The large blue Dragon snarled and lashed out its tail at them. Emrys pulled back, making Alex's stomach swing up as if she was on a roller-coaster. Reacting on instinct, Alex gripped the horn tightly even as she pulled on her magic. She didn't let go of Emrys but released the magic towards the Dragon with a firm image of pushing it away. The air shimmered with dark gray magic, and the Dragon roared before yelping as it was shoved across the sky.

Gryphons descended on it with raw fury. The two remaining Dragons opened their mouths, revealing glittering sharp teeth. Fire exploded into the air, forcing the Gryphons to dive away from the attack. Emrys turned in the air to meet the flames with his chest, which protected Alex as he also moved away from the Dragons. Alex clung tighter to the Dragon at the change in position.

"Stop!" Emrys shouted again. "We must speak peacefully! There is much you need to-"

But the Dragons were moving off, flying to the east at a far greater speed than Emrys could manage. She heard him huff, and the vibrations traveled down to Alex's bones. Licking her lips, she swallowed and wondered if that was it. The Gryphons followed the Dragons, but only for a few moments before it became clear that the Dragons could cover more distance. Watching them grow smaller and smaller, Alex frowned as she noted that they didn't land to find the other Dragon.

Still, it wasn't completely over. The Gryphons were collecting themselves and gathering together in a terrifying flock. Anger radiated off of all of them, and Alex didn't like the looks that were being sent Emrys' way. Emrys headed for the clearing, his body tense, and head low. When they landed, the Dragon released a long sigh, and Alex climbed down as the others rushed to join her.

"Alex Adams!" Morgana snapped. "What were you thinking?"

"I didn't want Emrys up there alone," Alex answered. In truth, she hadn't been thinking clearly. It had just been a reaction. "I'm okay, and so is he, but I'm not sure about the Gryphons."

The Gryphons were landing at the far edge of the clearing, and Alex was struggling not to stare at them. Things had been fine until today, but now more Dragons had appeared in their world who were clearly hostile. Given Morgana's record with being warm towards species who had threatened her in the past, Alex didn't have much hope for their reaction.

"Okay, does anyone else find it weird that as soon as we came into this world, the Dragons opened a portal?" Nicki hissed. She cast a nervous look towards the Gryphons. "The timing is strange."

"We don't know how time works between worlds, so we can't make assumptions," Bran said gently. He was calmer than the rest of them. "Their passage opened near the Darkness. They might have been moving alongside it to find a weak point."

"So, you don't think it was Cathanáil?" Aiden asked. He grimaced a little. "No offense, Alex."

"If it had been Cathanáil, then it would have triggered when or where Alex used the sword," Morgana said. "It's been in the sheath for days. The Sword usually doesn't open portals on accident."

"It did in India," Alex said. She hated even saying the words. "It was knocked out of Arthur's hand and ended up near Mumbai." Against her back, Cathanáil's weight was comforting despite the topic at hand. "But depending on what Arthur was thinking about, he might have activated it. His hands were..." Alex swallowed. "They were covered in my blood. Remember? He took it to help him control the Sword. The whole situation with the Demons might have been his fault."

They didn't have time to finish their debate. The remaining Gryphons swooped down and landed, surrounding them. There weren't enough of them to cage the mages, but the hissing Gryphons formed a rough circle around the mages and Emrys. Alex swallowed and braced herself. Morgana stepped closer and grabbed her right hand while Bran gently pulled the Chalice from her grasp.

"What trap are you seeking to spring on us?" The leader snarled at Emrys. "The Nest Leader agreed to help you, and this is the thanks we get."

"Trilan," Emrys pleaded. "Calm down. I have not had contact with my homeworld for hundreds of years. This turn of events pains me greatly. Everything the mages said at your Nest is the truth."

"We didn't know that the Dragons were coming," Alex said. "I swear on my world. Emrys wasn't trying to help them. They attacked him; you saw that."

"And yet, he is now whole!" Trilan stamped a foot on the ground, curling their talons into the soil. "A ruse to seem innocent."

"No, we used our magic," Alex argued. "We can-"

"You will do nothing," Trilan hissed.

"Your Leader wished for you to take us to the Darkness," Morgana reminded them sternly. At least the Pendant's magic was working.

"He is a Dragon," Trilan snarled. "They have declared war on us!" The Gryphon's gold eyes landed on Alex. "You cannot expect us to trust the beast!"

"Emrys has been an ally of ours for a long time," Alex insisted. "He came to this world with us to help stop the Darkness. That goal has not changed. Please, he doesn't know what has happened any more than you do."

"The Dragons and the Gryphons warred long ago," another Gryphon said.

"That was long before any of us, Raydin," Emrys said. His tone was guarded and gentle as he tried to calm the Gryphons down. "Please, we are almost to the source of the Darkness."

"This might be a trap. Those scouts came through," Trilan growled. They gestured with their head at the two dead Gryphons. "There may be even more waiting for us there. Perhaps this Darkness opened a path for them, and the main force waits to strike us down."

Alex wasn't an expert in Gryphon body language, but what she was getting wasn't good. The Gryphons' anger over their fallen comrades tainted the air around them. She found herself taking a step back. It wasn't that she didn't understand. Betrayal was familiar to her and loss even more so, but she couldn't let that stop them.

"I'm sorry this happened," Alex said. "But we don't have time to argue. We need to mend the path the Darkness is using before things get worse. Then we need to go to the Dragon world. If we stop the Darkness there, then maybe we can keep a war from happening."

She wondered if there was anything here or on the Dragon world that could be used to make something like an Iron Gate. These two species didn't seem to get along whenever they met. Maybe a gate would ensure they had time to cool down. Still, that wouldn't help them now, not with the way that the Gryphons were looking at them. In the corner of her eye, Alex saw Bran securing the Chalice in his make-shift bag. He might or might not be translating, but the body language probably gave away a l ot.

Flexing her fingers, Alex pulled on her magic. It fluttered in her chest, but it was weaker than it would have been if they were on Earth. But it was there. The other mages crowded close to her, which let Alex feel stronger. The Gryphons were speaking softly and glancing towards her, likely trying to ensure that she didn't hear them. Emrys whined, the sound impossibly soft.

"We will return to the Nest," Raydin said. They shifted their wings and puffed up their chest, making themselves appear larger. "Dragon, your wings will be clipped, and you will walk with the humans overland."

"That will take too long," Alex protested. "If we can't fly-"

"None of us shall bear you, the risk is too great, and the Dragon will not be permitted into our skies, not now. We will leave it to the Nest to determine if you can be trusted in light of what just happened."

"I'm sorry," Alex said. She swallowed, her mind reeling with the knowledge of what she was about to do. "We came to help. I promise that."

She waved her hand, concentrating on a memory of an attack that Merlin had used. Right now, it was the best option she could think of. Dark gray patches appeared on the ground beneath the Gryphons who didn't immediately notice them. Beside her, Morgana made a sound that was torn between surprise and glee.

After seeing Merlin do this so many times, it was easy for Alex to visualize vines bursting up through the ground. They exploded forth, sending dirt showering across the ground and began to wrap around the surprised Gryphons. Silver light flared in the corner of Alex's eye, and more vines appeared, wrapping themselves around the middles of the Gryphons, holding them in place. She swayed, her chest burning with a warning that she needed to stop. Strong hands on both sides grabbed her and pulled her further back from the Gryphons.

"Get on Emrys," Alex ordered. "We need to go."

"Alex?!" Bran gasped. "Are you sure-"

"We can't turn back!" Alex didn't look at the others. The screaming in her head left her dazed as it was. "The Darkness is close. We need to keep going if we're going to help anyone. Emrys, I'm sorry, but you'll have to carry all of us."

"I have you," Emrys assured her. His defeated tone was fading in the light of a new mission. "We'll stop in a few miles and get all of you properly secured. Hold on tight for now."

"They might come after us," Morgana shouted.

"Then we'll stop them again. We have our mission."

Alex didn't look back. There was guilt over restraining the Gryphons, but they didn't have time to worry about this. If the Dragons were worried about the Darkness enough to come here and try to start a war, then they needed to go there quickly. Heart racing, Alex leaned closer to Emrys' neck, ignoring the horns in an attempt to give the others more room. It was unsteady and crowded, but they clung to each other. Emrys snarled at the Gryphons, grabbed the net with their supplies still tightly wrapped up, and launched himself into the air. Alex didn't look back and kept her eyes locked on the Darkness ahead of them as she tried to come up with a plan.

26

The Chain

Stormy winds battered Emrys' wings, but the Dragon kept flying forward. Alex searched the ground for a place to land, knowing that eventually, they'd need solid ground beneath their feet. Everyone was crowded too close together for anyone to move much. Alex at least had the horn to hold on to. Being further back must have been terrifying, and she experienced a sudden jolt of guilt for their rapid flight.

Still, there was nothing she could do now. Narrowing her eyes at the Darkness up ahead, Alex took in the details that she could see. The rip in the sky was more visible now, and she could make out the purple sheen of the Darkness as it dripped through the tear. Lightning flashed around the edge, and Alex was sure that it was this world trying to fight back. They were still too far away for Alex to see what was below it, but she was certain that it was a black dead spot like those that had haunted Akule.

She felt sick. Alex thought she could hear the Gryphons screaming behind them. It wouldn't surprise her if they were being chased. She was confident that right now, Emrys could move faster than them, but if they landed, they might be vulnerable. Doubt crept in, but it was too late to change what she'd done.

"Hold on!" Emrys shouted. A powerful gust of wind hit them, and the arms around Alex tightened. She gripped the horn and clenched her legs against Emrys' side. "I need to land."

Alex nodded, even if the Dragon couldn't see. She didn't dare open her mouth to shout. Something like thunder, but in the wrong pitch, rumbled across the sky. Emrys took them down. His whole body quivered under them as the winds tried to throw the Dragon back. Below, Alex could see an open patch, but her heart jumped when she caught sight of the black spot beside it.

Trees were bent over, crumbling as the Darkness seeped into the ground and killed their roots. It was already larger than what she remembered from Akule's life. Then again, Akule had only gotten this close one time. Swallowing, Alex didn't know where to look to settle her nerves. The sky was alight with the war of the Darkness against the world, and the land showed the scars. It was the same and different from what Akule had seen all at once and reminded her sternly that this was a different world.

They landed with a soft thump that was out of place with their rapid flight and the battering storms. There were grumbles behind her, but everyone eagerly got off the Dragon. Emrys made a sound of relief himself, and Alex worried that they'd overtaxed him. Their net of gear had been dropped on the ground and was sinking into the mud. Aiden and Nicki ran forward and pulled the net up onto a mass of vegetation. Everyone was here, and neither Gryphons nor Dragons had swooped down on them.

Raising her eyes to the rip, Alex exhaled slowly and told herself to calm down. The ache in her chest was sharp and radiating down her limbs. She'd let her emotions rule her magic against the Gryphons, and now she was paying for it. There was a slight hum beneath her feet, but it wasn't nearly enough. This world wasn't hers. There was something here, below the surface, something that was trying to help, but it wasn't quite right.

"Alex?" Bran reached for her but stopped himself from touching her. "Are you okay?"

They hadn't been able to really talk while riding Emrys. The storm had blurred their words, and all their focus had been trained on staying seated. Now, the others had questions, and Alex didn't know how to even start to answer them. The voices were whispering. All of them had different advice, but Akule was the loudest. His experience made his words of encouragement shine through.

"I need more magic," Alex admitted. She turned to look at the others. "Holding the Gryphons took most of what I had left."

The others didn't argue. Morgana didn't look happy, but she nodded her agreement. Nicki was staring up at the rip, her expression caught between terror and awe. Alex didn't blame her. It was beautiful in a way until you remembered what it was. Aiden nudged Nicki's arm, and Nicki blinked in confusion.

"Oh, magic. Yeah, right. That makes sense."

Nicki's distraction lightened the mood a little. It wasn't much, but the pressure in Alex's chest eased a bit. Morgana didn't waste any time; the eldest of them grabbed Alex's hand and called on her magic. As the silver glow sparked around Morgana's hands, Alex gently pulled at the magic and smiled as it shifted to gray. Some sank into her body, easing the burn a little, but most of it threatened to dissipate.

Moving quickly, Alex closed her eyes and focused on the wisps of magic. Calling to them, she gathered all the stray power into an orb, which she let float beside her when she opened her eyes. Aiden went next, giving her a cheeky grin that didn't reach his eyes. Still, Alex was grateful for his show of optimism. More magic slipped into her chest, wrapping around her heart and giving her strength. The orb grew larger, and the dark gray color became deeper.

Bran stayed back with Emrys, rubbing the Dragon's neck and speaking to him softly. Alex didn't call him over. She was stronger now and gathered only a little magic from Nicki, cautioning her friend against giving too much. It was best if they weren't all exhausted. Just in case the Gryphons caught up with them, or more Dragons appeared. Her stomach twisted.

Without a word to the others, Alex turned and looked up at the Darkness. Dizzying uncertainty took hold. Akule had built a Medicine Circle to help him. He'd had the benefit of a solstice. She might have her fellow mages, but their power was limited. Closing her eyes, Alex breathed slowly and did her best to calm down. Panic and fear wouldn't help her. Alex opened her eyes and told herself to get to work.

She watched the churning sky. It was as if the clouds were trying to push against the rip, trying to force it closed, only to be ripped apart as droplets of Darkness fell into the world. Lightning flashed, and the smell of ozone was a comfort to Alex. That she understood. That smell was hers. Her fingertips twitched, and the pattern of lightning shifted. Energy thrummed across her skin. Her hairs stood on edge as more energy drifted towards her. It was almost enough to make Alex smile as a soft tug on the flickers of power made the dark gray orb grow.

"Now what?" Bran asked.

Swallowing, Alex kept her eyes on the sky. Behind her, Emrys was growling softly, and she knew they wouldn't have much time. Either the Gryphons would find them or more Dragons would show up. That was just their luck. She needed to figure this out quickly, but she didn't have the aid of a medicine wheel or an alignment day. They couldn't waste time building a circle or waiting to figure out whatever days were most potent here.

Then, like a bolt of lightning zooming across the sky, it suddenly occurred to Alex what she needed. A hole was waiting above her to be fixed, to be stitched back together, or to be bound up. She nearly slipped in the mud in her haste to reclaim her backpack. Nicki was eying her strangely, but the redhead helped Alex detangle the wet, twisting rope that made up the net so she could get into her bag.

Alex's hands dove into the backpack, digging to the bottom where the greatest weight had settled. The surrounding noise grew muted and distant. Too many thoughts were racing through her head. A small part of her recognized she wasn't in any condition mentally to be trying to do this, but there wasn't an option. Under her shirt, the Iron Pendant was warm against her skin.

The voices were a mess of noise. Everyone was shouting and trying to be heard over the others. Whatever advice or caution they were trying to offer was lost. Only Cuthbert's voice stood out, and he was sneering, telling her not to be stupid, not to make another rash decision that would get her friends killed. Alex shivered when her fingers wrapped around the first piece of the broken Iron Chain. Cuthbert's voice only got louder.

'Don't be stupid, girl. Go home now while you can. You aren't going to save anything. They don't deserve the effort.'

She ignored him and pulled the Chain out of the bag with her right hand as her left hand searched for the other piece. When her fingers curled around, Cuthbert's voice took on a different note. It was fearful this time. If she died here, what would happen to the Iron Soul? What would happen to him?

The memory of Cuthbert's death replayed. He'd been in his early fifties and sick in the Caribbean, so sick in fact that he'd been bedridden in the hotel room that he'd stumbled into. The view out the window had let him see the sea and his ship sailing off as they gave up on him. His anger and fear crippled him. Cuthbert had never been a religious man, as happy as he was to use biblical passages on slavery to justify his trade, but as his end approached, he'd called for a priest. The man hadn't wanted to die. He would have traded all of his money and his ship if it had meant living.

And now they were in danger. Alex pushed all of his baggage away. She had enough of her own without his fear and mistakes. As the two pieces of the broken Iron Chain left the bag, she turned her eyes up to the sky. The fabric of this world was fighting back in a way that Akule's memories showed the Iron Realm hadn't. Small storms were flashing along the edges of the sky where the Darkness was pouring in. It was gold, purple, and black, all mixing in a chaotic swirl. It meant death for a world, and yet it was still beautiful.

Pushing her magic into the Chain, Alex felt the flicker of power that remained from Cuthbert, reaching up to meet her. He'd never had control over his magic. Cuthbert's time had been plagued by many evils, but an outside threat to the safety of the world hadn't been one of them. Magic had been at low power, but years of his desire to bind the slaves he took to his will and keep order on his ship had seeped into the Chain. Time and a slow flow of magic had achieved for him what years of training and an afternoon had done for Arto. She might hate to give Cuthbert any credit, but the man had forged an Iron Artifact, and today, it was just what she needed.

It wasn't quite right. Something in the magic's flow was off. It should have been stronger, Alex knew that in her gut, but there wasn't time for refining. Keeping a tight grip on the metal, Alex inhaled and exhaled slowly and focused on ensuring that the magic didn't slip away. There was too little at her disposal for her to waste it.

Then she sensed it — that thread of power that ran through the Tree of Reality. Just at the edge of her vision, it was shimmering. She could almost taste it. Alex could hear and feel the hum. The power was just out of reach. She couldn't fully connect, but there was power there. The smell of it wasn't exactly like the magic of Earth. It carried a hint of this world, and the realization made her dizzy as something tried to come together in her mind. There were pieces of a puzzle in her grasp, but the final picture was just beyond her reach.

Still, the magic radiating from the thread was something she could reach. Alex called to the power, urging it to come to her, as she would have called the power of her fellow mages. There was only a bare hint of resistance. Alex closed her eyes and watched the brilliant white power change course. Rather than dissipating into this world, it rushed for her. Alex could see the line of power now, glowing just beneath the surface, giving the ground and all the vegetation a slight shimmer. It was so similar to what she'd seen on Earth, and the similarity nagged at her, urging Alex to figure it out.

But the Darkness was the priority. This didn't matter right now. Alex could hear the others. As her magic flared, her awareness of them grew and reassured her she wasn't alone. If something came, if they were attacked, she knew they would protect her. Another rumble of thunder shook the sky. The Iron Chain shuddered in her hands, the metal creaking at the sudden pressure of magic.

Unsure of what else to do, Alex pushed all the magic into the Iron Chain and imagined the sky knitting back together. Akule's memories guided her. His voice was soothing, encouraging her as more and more magic pumped into the rapidly heating metal in her hands. Exhaling,

Alex released the magic in a singular rush into the sky. Her knees buckled as the weight of the Darkness hit the magic, instantly ripping through most of it. Alex pulled on the lightning, pulled frantically on the faint heartbeat of this world that wasn't quite right, while soft assurances that she wanted to help fell from her lips.

Alex grit her teeth as the magic threatened to collapse against the press of the Darkness. The weight of the Darkness pouring into this world crashed onto her arms and shoulders, leaving her muscles with a sharp ache, and her knees quivering. Alex didn't stop. She pushed more magic through the Iron Chain, begging the magic to close the sky, to overcome the Darkness and heal the wound. To bind the power of this world to her will and to chain the sky closed. Cuthbert's tool of evil would serve h er.

The Chain shook. The old iron rings clinked together at the ends. A howling wind picked up and burned cold against Alex's cheeks. She opened her eyes but did not move. The sky was shimmering. The storm was growing worse. A flash of lightning blasted across the sky, and a large patch of dripping Darkness vanished. Alex smiled. The air churned. Leaves rattled in the nearby trees. Vaguely, she heard shouting, but didn't know if it was her fellow mages or Gryphons or Dragons.

Something gave. The pressure was gone. Alex was weightless. She nearly fell, and air rushed into her lungs, inflating them. Suddenly aware that she was faint, Alex closed her eyes and shuddered. Thunder was still rolling overhead, but the tone had changed. It was weaker and distant now. The sharp tang of ozone was fading. Alex didn't dare open her eyes yet. In her hands, the metal links of the Iron Chain were hot, but it was soothing rather than painful.

Someone was holding her shoulders from behind, supporting her and helping her stand. Gratitude swept through Alex, but she didn't thank them. She couldn't speak. There was no moisture in her mouth, all of her muscles were locked in combat, and there was no turning around. Then she heard a triumphant laugh from Emrys. It rumbled around them like thunder, but warm and welcome. Her heart beat a little faster as hope bloomed. Alex opened her eyes and looked up.

There were no clouds to part. The storms had been all energy clashing. Yet the clouds were metaphorically parting, letting the sky lighten, and the winds die down. A grateful groan escaped Alex as her knees gave out. Her fingers were still clutching the pieces of the Iron Chain as she guided her body down. She slipped to her knees, and from there, let gravity take over. The jarring pain heightened her awareness, and Alex looked down at the Iron Chain. Where she'd expected to find two pieces, one in each hand, she instead found the Iron Chain repaired, the pair of broken end links rejoined and glowing.

27

Nothing Changes

1 99 B.C.E. Gulf of Morbihan, Brittany

Humming filled the small main room of the home Merlin and Morgana shared outside the village. Over the years, they'd expanded the house to grant them more living space. The main room was the size of a traditional roundhouse and served as their sitting area, dining, cooking, and central storage area. In the back, they'd constructed a bedroom for privacy from their students. It was comfortable. The architecture of houses in the area was beginning to change towards the square shapes she'd seen in other places, but Morgana was fond of the house they'd created. It was a place that Morgana didn't mind thinking of as home at this point.

She was tidying the main room while Merlin prepared a meal in the oven that he'd recently finished building. He'd cheated and used magic to help him though he was still pretending that he hadn't, much to Morgana's amusement. She didn't understand why he cared.

The house was also different from the ones she'd grown up in thanks to the door. Instead of an animal skin covering the opening, it had a solid door that swung on wooden poles that truly opened and shut. That did make heating a lot easier even with the hole in the roof for the smoke and later the chimney that Merlin had constructed. He was making noise about switching to the oven full time and closing up the hole. Morgana was hesitant about the idea. She'd lived places with other house designs but she wasn't in a hurry to throw away the style of her childhood, at least the happy parts of her childhood.

A knock on the door of her and Merlin's cottage pulled Morgana from her musings. Merlin was at the oven, pulling out a fresh loaf of bread with an impressively perfect golden crust, and Morgana rolled her eyes. He'd better not be using magic to improve his baking, but she was suspicious. Quickly, she went to the door and opened it. Brennus greeted her with a smile and held up the basket he was carrying.

"I bring an offering."

"Thank you." Morgana stepped to the side. "Come in; it's chilly outside."

"I'm the first one here?" Brennus glanced around the main room. "I would have thought Judoc and Rozenn would be here before me."

"We haven't seen them today," Morgana answered. She tucked a stray strand of dark hair out of her face. "They'll be along soon. Please, sit down."

Brennus nodded and sat down on a woven mat covered by a thick fur that was next to the fire. The young man relaxed and smiled as he turned his gaze into the small fire that was burning in the stone-lined hearth. He rolled his shoulders, stretched out one leg, and made himself comfortable. That wasn't surprising; the lad had spent a great deal of time in and around this house. Morgana chuckled and looked into the basket, smiling when she found some smoked fish they could add to the meal.

Brennus had grown on Morgana over the past two years. She did her best to convince herself that it was because she liked his curious nature and how new things made his eyes light up. He hung on her every word whenever she told stories of her past, and the places that she'd seen, and the attention made her feel warm inside. Yet, she couldn't help but suspect that his climb in her esteem was because she saw a bit of her brother in him.

Merlin was correct about him being the Iron Soul. After spending so much time training the young man in using his magic, she no longer doubted he was the current incarnation of her brother. Such thoughts always made her happy and sad all at once. It was good to be reassured that something in Arto was immortal, that part of him remained in the world, but the burden of protecting the Iron Realm was not the part that she would have chosen to stay.

Lokpal and Gofiben had been good men, but there was a spark in Brennus that made her feel closer to him than the others. Maybe it was his smile or the small features of his face that were similar to her brothers. Or maybe she was different now. With Gofiben, she'd been resistant to him and what he signified, and Morgana could admit that to herself now. It was easier now.

Brennus was talking with Merlin about nothing important while Morgana tucked the fish away. There was some gossip from the village, and while Merlin laughed, Morgana ignored it in favor of finding the jar with her dried herbs. The news of the locals never appealed to her much. Merlin was much better at dealing with them. What got her attention was another knock on the door. Brennus leapt up despite her telling him not to and opened the door to reveal Judoc and Rozenn.

Judoc stepped inside and hugged Brennus with a warm smile, as if they hadn't seen each other only yesterday. In the course of their time together, Brennus had gained a few more inches in height, and while he still wasn't as tall as Judoc, the difference was no longer as startling. It was becoming a joke between the young men that soon Brennus would pass him. With Judoc's stronger build and having met his father, Morgana rather doubted that Brennus would ever catch his fellow mage. Brennus was nearly seventeen now and unlikely to grow much taller, even if he was still filling out his broadening shoulders.

Leaning down, Judoc kissed Morgana's cheek in greeting. She smiled a little at her student and nodded before he hurried to the fire with Brennus. Rozenn met her eyes and shook her head with a small smile. The only other female mage had grown a little herself but was petite compared to her male counterparts and a few inches shorter than Morgana. Her hair was in a long braid, and there was a twig caught high up her hair. It made Morgana wonder what the young woman had been up to today. Ever since she'd moved into a house of her own at the edge of the forest, Morgana knew less and less about Rozenn's daily life.

Despite her affection for Brennus growing, Morgana remained very fond of Rozenn and enjoyed having another female mage around. So frequently, they were male, and she had yet to determine an acceptable reason for this. Morgana felt it might be down to girls in some places being treated so much worse than their brothers and dying young. Given that they had basically bought Rozenn from her family, it was a strong possible explanation.

It could also be that young women were married and had children before she and Merlin had the chance to meet them. They well knew the dangers of childbirth. It was sad to consider that they may have lost mages to the natural process of birthing children, but it was a likely reason for the imbalance. She somewhat liked that reason more than the first.

Morgana joined the others at the fire alongside Merlin. Platters of baked bread, smoked fish, some sweet spring berries, and a large bowl of rabbit stew were passed around. Rozenn greeted Brennus with a soft kiss to the cheek, and he asked what she was so busy with that she hadn't been to the village in a few days. The conversation rolled over Morgana, relaxing her and grounding her in the moment. Merlin caught her eye and smiled warmly.

It was odd. It was rather like having grown children visit. In the past, their times with Iron Souls were intense and frequently brief. They'd grown past the mistakes they'd made with Gofiben and stayed close to the younger mages, but at the same time, the children had built lives separate from magic. If it hadn't been for Lokpal's example that such a life was possible, Morgana would have been much more concerned.

"How is your smith shop?" Rozenn asked Brennus.

"It's good," he smiled as he answered. "I'm getting more business now, which is good. I suppose people finally accept that I'm an adult now." Morgana rolled her eyes, and Merlin smiled into his food. "I like it."

"Working iron comes naturally to you," Merlin said. His eyes brightened warmly. "Always has."

Brennus nodded slowly, but said nothing in response to the words. Morgana doubted that he even believed in the Iron Soul. Rozenn however, looked interested as always. She opened her mouth to discuss the Iron Soul and one of the past lives, but Judoc jumped into the conversation.

"And the new house? It's comfortable?"

"Very, Judoc," Brennus answered. "Maela is happy with it."

"Good," Judoc said.

"What about the farm?" Brennus asked.

"Good. Not much to report. Everything is planted now." Judoc shrugged. "I just have to hope that the Fae don't start any fires this year. Being outside the blood protection spell last season was rough."

They all hissed at the memory, and Rozenn shook her head in disapproval as if the Fae would care what she thought. Merlin cleared his throat and dipped some bread into his stew. Whatever he was going to say was lost when a strange sound outside made them all pause. It was soft, but another high-pitched giggle alerted them all to the coming danger.

In a mad scramble for weapons, they all rushed to the doorway, and Morgana eyed the walls carefully. Red Caps attacking their home was nothing new. She and Merlin now slept staggered to ensure that they weren't taken by surprise in the night, but night had yet to fall. Then the smell of smoke hit her nose, and her eyes widened.

"Fire! They've set a fire!" Brennus shouted.

"I'll put it out," Merlin bellowed. "Take them out before they can move to the village."

Morgana reached the doorway as flames licked through one wall of her home. Green sparks settled across the surface, helping snuff them out as she stomped outside with a silver glow surrounding her hands. Red Caps giggled from the shadows of the trees. Rage and frustration rose in Morgana's chest, twisting and turning in a violent mess that resulted only in the urge to hit something hard. No wonder Brennus was frustrated. No wonder Maela was growing impatient. Years of these small attacks and no end in sight.

Growling, Morgana threw her right hand forward and pulled on her magic. Silver sparks leapt off her fingertips and formed a familiar silver whip. She twitched her wrist, and it lashed through the air. A pair of nearby Red Caps hissed and darted to the right, but one failed to get far enough away. Her magic ripped through the flesh, and the creature died with a choked scream.

The Red Caps turned, snarls and hisses escaping the small gray creatures with their blood dyed clothing. Morgana had never understood the viciousness of these creatures. At the back of her mind, she'd always feared that their resistance to iron had caused true madness as a side effect. With shrieks of anger, the Red Caps double backed and attacked the mages head-on. Several climbed into trees, leaping down at Brennus, who threw up a shimmering shield of magic to protect himself. His pale blue magic was almost impossible to see in the dying light of the day.

Rozenn released a series of brilliant violet bolts that blasted into the treetops, sailing through newly budding branches to hit Red Caps still holding their positions. Morgana glanced towards Judoc, who was further behind and using his orange magic to drag the Red Caps towards him. The earth rose in two places as sharp spikes to spear Red Caps before they could reach Merlin. Turning her attention to a small horde of Red Caps rushing her, Morgana spun her hand, and her whip turned into bolts that mowed the advancing creatures down.

A scream broke Morgana's calm. The last of her group of Red Caps fell, and she spun around, searching for the source of the very human scream. Rozenn was holding her side and stumbling back from a Red Cap as a wave of violet magic pushed it away. Merlin rushed to the young woman, grabbing her shoulders and pulling her away. Brennus and Judoc moved to block the Red Caps that foolishly decided another assault was in order. The hail of red and green sparks made Morgana smile viciously. But she couldn't focus on the shrieks. Merlin was easing Rozenn to the ground. Trusting that Brennus and Judoc would protect them, Morgana knelt beside the girl and reached for her magic. Her skin hummed as she gently laid her hand over the wound and closed her eyes. Healing was always draining, but Morgana's heart raced with a desperation to save her student.

Skin slid back together with a pale line of new flesh forming at the seam. A delicate sob escaped Rozenn as the fear eased. Only two tears slid down the girl's face, and Morgana kissed her forehead as her body swayed. Exhaustion weighed on her, but she kept herself upright. Merlin's hand on her shoulder kept her steady, and she breathed slowly to ease the burn in her chest.

"Well done," Merlin said. Gratitude rang in his voice.

"You need more practice at healing," Morgana said.

"When healing is needed, I prefer the master to see to it." Merlin kissed her cheek, and Rozenn slowly sat up.

Morgana checked around them, but the Red Caps were gone. The tree line was littered with the rags that the creatures called clothing and dust from their bodies was being blown away by the wind. Stillness surrounded them. There were no giggles or snarls. Another group of Red Caps had been stopped. She turned to look at her house and frowned. Part of the west wall was black from the fire. At least Merlin had kept it from spreading.

"How long do we live like this?" Brennus asked.

The question surprised Morgana, and she looked over at him quizzically. "What do you mean?"

"Well... Maela and I have been talking about having children." Judoc tensed and glanced worriedly at Brennus. The other man didn't notice and smiled sweetly. "I don't think I want to be fighting the Fae with children on the way."

Morgana opened her mouth, but no words came out. Swallowing, she looked at Merlin, who was frowning sadly and seemed no more ready to answer that question than she was. Inwardly, Morgana cursed the day that Maela and Brennus had married. They were too young, and that girl was too wild. Morgana had never put her finger on what bothered her about Maela, but it was there, always there whenever they came face to face.

"You are a mage," Merlin said. "You will be a mage all your life. We've done well in keeping the local Fae from raiding the villages and causing trouble, but it doesn't truly end."

"Never?" Judoc asked. His eyes were downcast. "So, this is our whole lives."

"They told us that when they started training us," Rozenn said. She leaned towards the men; her features uncertain. "You knew that."

"It was different then," Brennus said. "I was just a boy then."

"You're a boy now," Morgana muttered. "You're too young to be considering children."

"No, I'm not." Brennus wrinkled his nose as he protested.

"Maybe not," Morgana conceded. He looked too young to her, barely out of boyhood. "This life, it isn't always easy, but it's easier because we have each other. And your families," she added at the last second. "Brennus, the blood protection spell keeps the Fae away from the village, but not the Red Caps. What would have happened if we weren't here to fi ght?"

Brennus nodded and lowered his eyes. Sensing that she'd pushed enough, Morgana backed away from them to gather up the rags left behind by the death of the Red Caps. She stayed close enough to hear anything more that might be said out of simple concern for her students.

"I understand," Judoc said. "If I was married to a woman like Maela, I'd want to make her happy too."

"Yes, but..." Brennus gestured at the iron dagger in his hand. A sigh escaped him. "Morgana's right. We can't leave. We can't leave normal people to do this alone."

Holding back a sad smile, Morgana watched Brennus straighten his shoulders. Something like pride bubbled in her chest, but she kept her lips sealed together. At least Brennus understood. That was the most important lesson that every mage had to accept, and it was even more critical for Brennus as the Iron Soul. Still, Judoc looked like he wanted to say something. He reached for Brennus' shoulder and opened his mouth, but a moment later, he shook his head and dropped his hand.

Satisfied that her students were alright and balance was restored, Morgana turned her attention back to Rozenn. Merlin insisted that she stay the night only for Rozenn to remind him that there was only one bed, blushing while she did so. Morgana quickly joined them, adding her own firm stare to the power of Merlin's and watching as Rozenn surrendered to their combined force. Still, something nagged at the back of her mind. As if she'd forgotten something, but Morgana couldn't put her finger on it.

28

By the Firelight

Alex was in shock. That much was clear to Bran even if nothing else was. Maybe they were all in shock. Well, not actual medical shock where they needed to elevate the feet due to circulatory issues. No, they were all stunned with Alex having it the worst of all of them. Today had been insane, and Bran's mind was reeling as he struggled to process everything.

He wasn't sure what the hell had happened under the Darkness. So great was his confusion that Bran felt as if he'd lost time. Yet, the sky was clearing, and the slow drip of the Darkness had been halted. Glee filled his chest, filling in the empty spaces where his magic had been drained away, and the shot of adrenaline kept him upright. The initial rush of happiness and relief had faded when he finally noticed what was in Alex's hands.

It was the Iron Chain. He'd thought it destroyed, but there it was. Except that rather than being broken in half, it was whole. The oddly melted together links were a bit like a scar where the flesh had knitted back together, but the result was the same. Cuthbert's Chain had been repaired by whatever Alex did. Alex's eyes were glazed over as she studied the Iron Chain in her hands.

There hadn't been time for questions or to sort everything out because Emrys had insisted on flying them further from the area where the Darkness had been in case of Dragons or Gryphons. Morgana had agreed immediately with the plan, pointing out that something would come to investigate, and there was no need to make it easy on them. But the Dragon had been slow and uneven in the air, betraying his exhaustion, and they'd settled for camping alongside a rocky hillside with outcroppings roughly an hour away that provided some shelter from the wind and would make them a little harder to spot from the air.

Bran wanted to get Alex back onto solid ground and hopefully get her near a fire to warm up. She had yet to react to them, and even while riding the Dragon, her grip on the Iron Chain hadn't eased no matter how many times Morgana tried to carefully pry it from her fingertips. Their worry coiled around all of them, tightening like a noose and threatening to strangle them if they couldn't distract themselves.

When they landed, Bran, Nicki, and Aiden had all leapt to action. Nicki had circled the area to find wood for a fire while he and Aiden prepped the campsite. Neither of them had much magic nor much energy, but they were in better condition than Alex, who was led over to a rock to sit down by Morgana. The older mage hovered close by, helping Bran with only one of the small tents before returning to Alex's side.

Emrys had stayed awake just long enough to pull two downed trees closer to camp to serve as seating before stumbling to the cliff. With a burst of fire, Emrys had heated a patch of rocks and promptly collapsed on them, folding his wings close to his body. Bran had considered taking the Chalice over, but he really didn't want to wake a sleeping Dragon.

Currently, Bran was setting up Alex's tent, having found it near the top of Alex's backpack. He'd been surprised to find Galahad in her bag as well and had quickly pushed the stuffed dog out of sight. It felt inappropriate somehow that he'd found the stuffed dog as if he'd too closely seen a vulnerability of Alex's. He felt foolish for the rush of guilt, knowing that Alex likely wouldn't care half as much as he did.

"Are you alright?" Morgana asked. He looked up and blinked when he realized Morgana was talking to Alex. His friend seemed a bit more lucid now, and Bran glanced down into her lap. She was still holding the Iron Chain, and Morgana was staring at it with an uncertain expression. "I thought Merlin had destroyed that."

"No." Alex smiled a little, and Bran sighed in relief. "I'm okay. A bit... you know that feeling when you're tired, but you've had too much caffeine."

"I'm familiar with it."

"It's like that," Alex said. "I'm exhausted." Her shoulders slumped as she spoke, and Bran barely kept his focus on the tent he was setting up. "But at the same time, there's still power in me, and my mind is racing."

"So, you didn't exhaust your magic?"

"I don't think so." Alex took one hand off the Iron Chain and flexed her fingers. "It feels like I could still act if I needed to."

"Good. That's good," Morgana said.

Bran agreed wholeheartedly and finally glanced towards the others. Nicki had returned with wood and by the looks of things, some of the local berries that they'd eaten successfully. Aiden was building a small fire ring out of stone at the edge of the rocky outcropping. It would let the smoke escape into the open air, but still keep the fire partially protected if it rained. But a look at the sky made Bran smile. The clouds were vanishing, and he could see the light of the setting sun.

The dying light, more than anything else, got Bran moving. At least the storm had been artificial, and there had been no rain. He was too tired to deal with being wet. His muscles ached with the faint burning sensation that warned him he'd used too much magic. A shudder went through his body as he remembered the mass of magic that had flared around Alex. The air had rippled with power. It was a minor miracle that she was awake at all. He'd expected her to slip into a coma like Aiden had years ago.

That thought was terrifying. Bran stopped what he was doing and found the Iron Chalice. It was still bundled up in the cloth belt sling along with his water and a granola bar. His stomach rumbled, reminding him that lunch had been completely missed. Had they even had breakfast? The day was a blur now with the attack of the Dragons and the sealing of the rip standing out most vividly.

Shaking his head, Bran checked all the tents and made sure that backpacks and sleeping bags were in each. He dug out his flashlight and glanced towards Alex. She had finally moved away from the rock she'd been resting on and was over by the fire that had been lit. Relief flooded through him before he reminded himself that Morgana might have guided her over, but he was optimistic. Nicki came out of the darkness with a flashlight and one last armful of wood. She stacked it near the fire and sat down on a log. The tents were all up; they had wood, and Bran's legs were quivering. It was time to sit down.

The others were all gathered around the fire ring. Alex's eyes were clearer now, the gray color shifting back to the normal stormy tone that Bran associated with her rather than the dull stone shade it had been earlier. Everyone was safe, and the hole in this world had been fixed. It wasn't perfect, but things were better than they had been even four hours ago. Five hours? He wasn't sure at this point.

"Hey," Bran greeted. He sat down beside Alex and noted with relief that she glanced over at him and smiled a little. The Iron Chain was gone, and its absence made it easier to breathe. "You okay?"

"Just thinking." Alex shook her head. "Sorry that I clocked out for a while."

"You were exhausted," Bran said gently. "But you had us worried."

"I needed to crawl out of my head, I guess."

"Are you okay now?"

"I'm okay. Bit hungry."

"I'm working on it," Aiden huffed. "Tents were the first order of business when we landed. Then gathering wood and getting a fire started. It's a lot harder when you don't use fireballs."

"Poor baby," Nicki teased. "Glad you're okay, Alex."

"So...?" Aiden started. "What's the plan?"

"I want to return to Earth," Morgana said. "We've proven that we can close the holes, and we've confirmed your theory." Morgana straightened up, raising her chin a little, and Bran braced himself for an argument. "But we can't leave Earth undefended. The Iron Realm is our primary responsibility. We can take quick trips out to other worlds from time to time now."

"That's not enough," Alex said. A frown took over her features, and she met Morgana's gaze without flinching. "Besides, it can't be a good idea for us to open portals too often. That will bring the worlds into conflict."

"Yes, but leaving the Iron Realm for too long isn't a good idea."

"We left the Old Ones to watch over it," Alex argued. "Morgana, it hasn't even been a week. I'm sure that everything is fine."

"I'm uneasy with our absence."

"Don't you trust them to protect the Earth?" Alex frowned at Morgana, and Bran held his breath. "Don't you trust them?"

"I do."

"Then what's the problem?"

"I trust them, but it isn't blind trust," Morgana snapped. Then she sighed and shook her head. "They aren't bad, but if something goes wrong and one of them becomes corrupted-"

"It doesn't happen that fast, but even if it did, Shiva has the Trishula," Alex insisted.

"So, what is your plan?" Bran asked carefully.

"The Dragons are invading here. That means that the Darkness has reached them," Alex said. "That's the next stop."

Nicki finally spoke up. "So, you're going to keep going from world to world, sealing the holes?"

"What did you think we were going to do?" Alex raised an eyebrow, channeling way too much of Morgana for Bran's comfort.

"I didn't know how long you'd be willing to stay gone," Nicki said gently. "I understand why you want to keep pushing."

Nicki's patience seemed to help Alex settle. She exhaled slowly and closed her eyes for a moment. They all stayed quiet, letting her process everything that had just been said. When Alex reopened her eyes, the color had shifted to hard steel, and Bran knew they would not sway her. He wasn't sure that he even wanted to try.

"We have to stop the Darkness as much as possible," Alex said firmly. "I really don't want to see what an invasion force of Gryphons and Dragons would look like. There'd be no hiding that."

Morgana chuckled and nodded. "You aren't wrong." She reached over and squeezed Alex's hand. "I'm not going to stop worrying... and it isn't from lack of faith in you. It's just that I'm a mage. Protecting the Iron Realm is what I was born for. Being away from it, even if the plan is to get ahead of the threat, goes against all of my instincts."

"I understand," Alex murmured. "Thank you for coming with us. Thank you for not making me do this alone."

"I'd never let you run off to another world without me," Morgana said. They stared at each other, small soft smiles on their faces. Bran dropped his gaze, suddenly aware that he was intruding. "I'm proud of you." A shocked laugh shook the night. "You sealed the breach. The Darkness has stopped. You halted the destruction of this world. I'm proud of you and... and I'm sorry that it took me so long to realize that you were right. Merlin and I..." Morgana trailed off, and Bran saw a wet sheen in her eyes. "We should have listened more."

No one knew what to say to that. Bran looked at Alex, but she seemed calm if sad at the mention of Merlin. He wondered for a moment what the old mage would have thought of all this. Thousands of years old and yet, Merlin had never left the Iron Realm. Morgana had been raised outside of Earth, but Merlin had never crossed that threshold. The knowledge that he'd done something that Merlin, the Grand Mage, never had was overwhelming. His brain threatened to stop working.

"Uh, thanks for the help earlier," Alex said. Bran turned his attention back to her as Alex straightened up and cleared her throat. He blinked and tried to clear his mind. "Sharing your magic. I remember pulling on a lot of energy to close up the hole."

"I'm glad to hear we helped," Aiden said. "It was mostly you, though."

"What did it look like?" Alex asked.

"Like you were on fire," Nicki answered. She poked some coals with a stick, her eyes meeting Alex's over the flames. "There was this aura around you. I've never seen you like that."

"The pillar was similar." Aiden grimaced as soon as he said it and gave Alex an apologetic frown. "When the Light was in control. It made this pillar of power. It was sort of like that, but it was shifting like it was alive."

"I wish I knew if that was good." Alex sighed loudly. "I wish I knew if the Iron Chain being repaired was good."

"It's an artifact," Bran said gently. "It's what you do with it that matters. That artifact has never been used for good. Seems about time it was." He grinned and gestured up at the sky, which was now dark and filled with stars. "And today, that was definitely an act of good."

Nicki and Aiden nodded in agreement. Morgana sat down on a nearby log with a small smile. Alex relaxed a little and smiled broadly when Aiden started dumping a couple of packets of backpacking food into a pot of boiling water, along with some of the local food that the Gryphons had given them. He started humming softly as he stirred it all in the collapsible pot.

"So, what's the plan tomorrow?" Nicki asked. "Onward to the Dragon world?"

"Yes," Alex said. Morgana nodded in agreement.

"And the Dragons that are already here?" Aiden kept stirring the pot as a very nice, if odd, meaty smell tickled Bran's nose.

"Leave them to the Gryphons," Morgana said. "We'll do more good getting to the root of this problem, and I'd prefer not to get pulled into any more Gryphon matters."

Bran and the others nodded their agreement. Part of Bran couldn't help but worry about the changes this world might make to the Dragons, and he silently wished the Gryphons luck. They were a bit too paranoid for him to want to stay and help. They were lucky that they'd gotten as much distance between them and the Darkness scar as they had. Without it, they probably would have been found by some investigating party. Or maybe the Gryphons had been more concerned with chasing the Dragons.

They managed not to cheer when Aiden announced that the "stew" was ready. Mess kits were eagerly gathered from packs in a rush of movement. The thick, meaty concoction was loaded up onto everyone's plates. It was thick and brown with bits of backpacking meals, including meat, corn, peas, potatoes, and the local berries and roots mixed in. The tastes weren't very balanced, and every bite confused Bran as his brain tried and failed to determine the flavor. Still, it was warm, filling, and settled pleasantly in his belly. The tension around the fire melted away and even Morgana insisting that they keep watches tonight couldn't detract from the tired sense of victory they all shared.

29

Once More Unto the Breach

Dawn came too fast for Alex. She was stronger now and more aware, but the urge to curl up in the sleeping bag and ignore the light outside was even stronger. Only the knowledge that anything that came to investigate the area around the giant black scar that marred this world would find them made her throw one arm out of the sleeping bag. She wasn't really that comfortable. There was no mattress beneath her and little insulation from the cold ground. But sleep was easier than being awake. Being awake meant going outside and getting ready for another very intense day. Alex rolled onto her back and sighed as she stared at the roof of her tent. As it happened, that was only a few inches above her. It was a good thing that she wasn't claustrophobic.

Despite her wishes, she was awake now, and her mind started reviewing the previous day. Akule's excitement and pride radiated through her, comforting, and stable. Arto, Lokpal, Gofiben, Thor, and many of the others were congratulatory. Cuthbert was silent, and she didn't mind his absence. Michel softly reminded her to check on Emrys before they got too ambitious for the day, and she had to agree.

Emrys was their key mode of transportation as callous as that sounded in her head. Their interactions with the Dragons yesterday weren't a guarantee that all Dragons would be like that in the Dragon world, but it was a warning. If things were so bad that the Dragons who, according to Emrys, had always been firmly against going into other worlds, were doing so now, then caution was needed.

She shivered at the notion of a Dragon invasion. Those creatures had made Emrys look small. While modern weaponry on Earth could harm them, their immortality would make them impossible to destroy. No, her decision to press on had to be the right one. If they could put an end to the influx of Darkness in the Dragon world that was pressing them to leave, then she'd be getting ahead of an invasion.

It made Alex think of the Iron Urn. They'd left it back at Morgana's home, what used to be Merlin's home to await the next winter solstice. It held Merlin's ashes and was due respect, but she now wished that she'd moved his ashes to something else and brought the urn with them. Collecting some of the Darkness might be the best way to stop the Dragons if they invaded Earth.

But that idea made her stomach turn. She wanted the Darkness gone, not to be stockpiling it as a weapon. Alex shook her head and opened her sleeping bag. With some flailing and a great deal of wiggling, she got into her clothes and packed up her bag. She paused long enough to kiss Galahad's head before packing him up. Then it occurred to her that she'd slept the whole night through; no one had woken her up for a watch. Alex wasn't sure if she was grateful or annoyed by that and reviewed the watch rotation they'd agreed on. Unsurprisingly, it had been Morgana who decided against waking her.

Crawling outside, Alex scanned the area and noted that a small fire was going, and Nicki and Bran were sitting side by side on one of the logs. They were talking with Emrys, who was partially curled around their makeshift fire pit area. The Dragon's eyes were bright and alert, and she saw him tilt his head and listen for a moment.

"Morning," Alex greeted as she pulled on her boots.

Nicki nodded to her in greeting, but her attention was on a small bubbling pot with fabric wrapped packets in it. For a moment, Alex thought it was tea, but Morgana closely guarded their supply.

"Uh? What are you doing?" Alex asked.

"Experimenting with some of the food," Bran answered. His notebook was in his lap, and he seemed amused by whatever was happening. "Nicki is trying to test some of the edible leaves that the Gryphons liked for tea."

"Those white trimmed ones," Nicki explained. "The purple berry plant. They ate them, and the small creatures do too."

"You're trying tea?"

Nicki shrugged and peered forward to inspect the water. Alex looked up at Emrys, but the Dragon simply tilted his head and studied the brew. Honestly, Alex got more of an impression of a witch over a cauldron than a human trying to make tea. Then again, she supposed that all foodstuffs in their world started with experimentation.

"Don't poison yourself," Alex sighed. She really didn't know what else to say. Bran lifted the Chalice into view, and Alex felt a lot better about this experiment. "Morgana asleep?"

"Yeah, when I got up, I told her to get some more rest," Bran said. He closed his book and put his attention on Alex. "How are you feeling?"

"Stronger, more alert." Alex focused on Emrys, leaving Nicki to spoon some of her mixture into a mug. "How are you, Emrys? I'm sorry that we pushed you so hard yesterday."

"I am well," Emrys said. "And the fault was not yours. Circumstances conspired yesterday to make our path difficult, but I congratulate you on your victory." Emrys lifted his head into the sky. "The scent of the air is clearer now. The hint of decay is fading fast. I can only hope that the Gryphons appreciate what you have done for them."

"I'm just glad it worked." Alex blushed at the praise, and her mind wandered back to the Iron Chain. She didn't want to think about it. "What about your wings? Are you sure they're okay? Those winds were vicious, and then you flew us here right after." She didn't remember that part clearly, but Alex knew that it had happened.

Emrys stood up and stalked out into the small open space beside the cliff, balancing delicately on the mass of rocks that had slid down over the years. Emrys stretched out like a great cat, his front paws reaching out while he raised his haunches. Then he spread his wings, letting Alex reassure herself that they were undamaged.

"Are you sure?" Alex asked once again. "We were talking about going into the Dragon world today." There was no easy way to say it. "Given what happened."

"That is..." Emrys sighed and shook his head. "It is a wise decision. I have faith that the Gryphons of this world will hunt down the rogues that have come through, but we cannot allow the situation to escalate enough that they keep coming or worse, try for your world. It seems that the honor of Dragons has declined in my absence."

"What if they decide to kill you?" Nicki asked. She shared a glance with Alex.

A soft chuckle escaped the Dragon, but Alex felt it in her bones. "They might, but if the situation is truly so dire, then I will not be their greatest concern."

"You didn't heal yesterday," Nicki said. "So, are you sure that there are any changes that will stay with you? What if the law wasn't really about the fear of permanent changes?"

"I don't know. It is possible that I would have healed, just more slowly than I was used to on Earth, or it may be something completely different." Emrys shifted uneasily and Alex had the impression that he was frowning. "Or the Darkness may have changed something. We cannot say for sure, but we must go. I will deal with whatever comes. Should they decide to kill me, then I shall be grateful to have fulfilled my duty and be home."

"As you wish," Alex said. "Thank you." Her throat threatened to close up, but somehow she kept breathing and stayed upright in the face of Emrys' impossible calm.

They packed up quickly, and Emrys vanished for a short time to find some food for himself. The lack of large mammals thus far made Alex worry the Dragon was starving himself, but she could hope that there was better prey for him in the Dragon world.

"Hey, this is good!" Nicki's shout made Alex spin around. Nicki was holding up her mug and grinning widely. "A bit strong," she said. "But a nice sweet taste."

"Congratulations," Bran said. Then he shook his head and stood up. "If we are going to head out, I should wake up Aiden, and do some scavenging."

"I'll help," Alex said quickly. She needed to be of help to the others beyond using her magic. Last night, they'd set up camp and made the meal without her helping.

"Stop it." Nicki was giving Alex a stern look. "You were wiped out last night. We took care of you. That's what a team does."

"Exactly," Bran said. "Besides, you closed the hole in this world."

"Let's just hope it holds." Alex inspected the golden sky over them, marveling at the soft, warm shade. Night had been dark blue like their own world, so there was clearly something in the air that was colored by the rays of the sun differently than on Earth. "I'd like to think we're improving things as we go."

"Me too," Nicki said. "Uh… one thing, we've been here several days, and I haven't felt different. I always got the sense that the Sídhe and other creatures were in pain because they were in our world."

"Maybe the Darkness is affecting it," Bran offered. He set the Chalice near Nicki's feet. "Or… maybe the world is reacting differently because we're from the trunk. Maybe the effect only goes one direction."

Alex frowned, the possibilities humming in her mind. The others weren't able to offer any insight. She was further now than any of them had ever gone before. Another idea nagged at her, but it was a scary one. Maybe this world knew they were there to help and wasn't attacking them. The level of the sentience of magic had always been a lingering unanswered question in the Iron Realm, and Alex didn't know how it might be here.

They still had power. There was energy beneath the surface that aided them rather than attacking. Bran's theory about them being different because they were from the trunk might have merit. She just couldn't be sure. But there was only a flicker of fear and doubt. At this point, Alex had lived years with questions that she doubted she'd ever get answers to. This was one more, and so far, it had been in their favor. She'd happily take it.

"What's that smell?" Morgana's voice was a touch slurred from sleepiness.

Alex turned on the log and smiled at her teacher. Morgana was dressed, and her hair was in its usual braid, but she looked sleepy still, wrapped up in a Ravenslake University sweatshirt. Morgana plopped down next to Nicki and leaned over to inspect the pot.

"Tea with native leaves," Nicki said proudly. She refilled the mug and handed it to Morgana. "It's pretty good."

Morgana wrinkled her nose suspiciously, but took a drink. A strange expression took over her face, a mixture of pleasure, surprise, and doubt. Raising an eyebrow, she turned to the surprised Nicki, who only grinned.

"Did you get into my tea?"

"No," Nicki laughed. "I swear. Straight local leaves."

"We'll gather some of these," Morgana said. She took another sip, ignoring their chuckles.

Aiden stumbled out to join them next, and they passed tea around along with the last of the fruit they'd gotten at the Gryphon city. Alex missed bacon, but wasn't going to complain. There was nothing for it. At least they had fresh food to go with the rations they'd packed. It didn't take long to get everyone to agree to scavenging until Emrys returned.

Staying in pairs with Morgana back at camp packing everything up, the mages stripped everything useful they could find in the immediate area. Thanks to Emrys, they knew a good deal about the Dragon world and could be assured that there was water and wood to use, but food would be a question given the Darkness.

The memory of the attacking Dragons made them all cautious, and water was put through filters into water bottles and taken back to camp to be boiled. Alex and Bran bundled up small lengths of wood that would be enough for a small fire. Berries and roots were gathered and tucked away into anything the mages could find to contain them. The wrappers from last night's backpacker meals were very useful on that front.

Alex couldn't help but smile as Emrys flew overhead and called down a greeting. But his greeting was quickly followed by a warning that he'd spotted scouts in the distance. Bran and Alex finished grabbing what they could and rushed towards camp with full arms. Along the way, they spotted Nicki and Aiden pouring berries into a collapsible bucket.

Most of the camp had been packed up. Morgana was pouring the last of the boiled water into a water bottle when Alex and Bran returned. The tents were gone, rolled back up and tucked into packs. The net had been spread out, and Emrys was delicately arranging the edges. Things descended into strange, controlled chaos. Morgana fit the camping pots and pans back together and hooked them onto the back of her bag. She pulled on her coat and took some of the bundled food from Alex to stuff in the pockets. Nicki and Aiden came crashing into camp and handed out berries as everyone pulled on coats.

Then the last of the supplies were in the net. A rope was tied around Emrys' neck as a hold. The fire was put out, and the shovel was hooked onto Aiden's bag. Bran secured the Chalice to his belt via a bandana, and they climbed onto Emrys' back. Alex's heart was racing so hard and fast that it echoed in her ears. Fear overcame everything else, and her hands threatened to shake as she pulled on her gloves. Emrys waited patiently for them to settle and all get a grip on the rope. Her legs ached from the stretch, but Alex reminded herself that they were lucky to have Emrys so willing to carry them.

After a last check, Emrys launched himself into the air, the mages on his back, and the net of supplies grasped in his front legs. Alex's stomach swooped at the sudden movement, and for a moment, she was on a roller coaster. The Dragon quickly smoothed out his movements as they rose over the trees. In the distance, Alex could see a few more shapes flying over the landscape and tensed.

Bran nudged her, and Alex leaned forward, keeping one hand on the rope and reaching for Cathanáil. Behind her, Bran helped her pull the Sword free and then wrapped his arm around her waist to hold her steady. Leaning forward, Alex closed her eyes and focused on the air being drawn into her lungs. The air pulsed. It wasn't quite right, the slight differences making her skin tingle.

She didn't know what the Dragon world looked like, but she remembered the massive shapes of the Dragons. The way they cut through the sky, their fear, and their aggression. Alex could feel Emrys shifting beneath her and concentrated. Her magic flared to life, filling her chest and limbs and driving away the odd sensations haunting her. She pushed the magic into the Sword, and Cathanáil's soft hum changed to a song, ringing in her ears and soothing the fears trying to take hold. Alex had to trust her magic, trust Cathanáil to know her intention as it had on Ear th.

Cathanáil sliced through the air. Electric shocks rolled up Alex's arm, and she opened her eyes. A small cut had been made in the sky of the world, and beyond it was a dark horizon. Alex could see nothing more. No one spoke, and Alex swallowed painfully. Emrys shifted back only to surge forward as the opening widened, throwing them into another world.

Light shimmered around them. For an instant, Alex thought she caught sight of the Tree of Reality and its great glowing trunk. It was just a flash, but the mass of Darkness was now clear to her. It loomed like Death over the bed of a dying man. A terrible pressure crashed into her chest, forcing the air from her body and pushing her back. Her grip on the rope tightened. The air rippled. She was stretched out.

They burst into a dark sky, thick with clouds and the smell of ash and decay. There were faint outlines, through what seemed like smoke, of mountains and trees, but Alex's eyes were already stinging. Something flared to her right, glowing amongst the shrouded world. A dim river of energy flowed beneath them, beckoning to her and pleading. Alex saw it for only a moment before her eyes settled far in the distance in that direction.

She couldn't see the Darkness, and yet, Alex could feel the cruel creep of the Darkness there as the power of this world reached for her and begged for mercy. Keeping her grip tight on Cathanáil's hilt, Alex leaned as Emrys turned back to the opening and brought her Sword up to close the path they'd come by. The sky struggled against her magic, fighting to keep the rip open, but slowly, with flashes of dark gray magic, it was closed, and they were surrounded by the stench of a dying world.

30

The Cursed Lovers

1 *97 B.C.E. Gulf of Morbihan, Brittany*

The smoke was beginning to clear. The fires had all been put out though Morgana didn't know how many homes had been lost. The death count had been low, she supposed she should be grateful for that, but the wailing was still audible at the edge of the village. Searching the packed earthen street for any lingering threats, she basked in the warmth of the rising sun but did not allow herself to relax.

There was no calm to be found for her — no rising relief. As the situation sunk in, anger was the only emotion taking hold. Rays of sunlight spilled across the surface of the buildings, making the packed mud between the timbers glow gold. There were fewer shadows now, fewer places for her enemies to hide, and Morgana eyed the patches of bright red blood on the ground. It was almost gone already, sinking into the ground, and she regretted that it wouldn't serve a purpose. They'd hoped that the blood spell would at least keep this village safe, but it had f ailed.

She searched her memory, trying to find the reason, but there was nothing. The young mages had performed admirably on that day. She'd been proud. Shaking her head, she sighed and turned away. Those small

Fae creatures were much more resistant than she'd thought, or the spell had been far too weak. Given recent events, she was inclined to believe that one. Arto's spell would never have failed like this. His spell still protected her former home.

The comparison made Morgana stop. Hands trembling, she thought back over the events of the last day, and her heart turned cold. Her stomach dropped, and for a moment, she was certain that she'd be ill. Somehow, she wasn't and started walking again. Her pace was slower now, her body moving without her thinking about it as she followed the well-worn path that led to her and Merlin's home outside the village. Brennus had been taken there. Rozenn had been firmly against taking him to his house.

As her small home came into view, tears prickled at Morgana's eyes. The last few years had seen her gain some happy memories here. Now bitterness was already creeping in. She looked around, searching for Merlin, but there was no sign of her counterpart. Still, she knew that he'd be nearby. He wouldn't wander far, not now, not after what had happened. Bracing herself, she opened the door of the cottage.

Rozenn was crying, sobbing over the body on the bed. A blanket was draped over it, hiding the dried blood and terrible wounds. Brennus was gone. Morgana had known that, but seeing the body covered and still made it real. She should be used to death, and yet somehow, it was always a shock to her. Swallowing, Morgana focused her attention fully on Rozenn. The young woman's hair was a mess, and blood was smeared on her arm. Frowning, Morgana crossed the room and bent down to inspect the wound. It was a deep slash, and blood was still oozing from it. Rozenn didn't seem to notice.Morgana was almost grateful for the distraction. Gently pulling on what magic she still had into her hand, she reached forward and exhaled. Rozenn jumped a little when Morgana touched her arm, but sniffed and returned her attention to Brennus' body. Keeping her eyes on the wound, Morgana imagined the two sides of the skin knitting back together. The silver glow of her magic sank into the flesh, giving it a strange pale tint, and slowly, the wound was pulled back together. Heat flashed in Morgana's chest, warning her she had little power to use. But it was enough. The flesh smoothed over, leaving a thin pale line across Rozenn's skin. It might scar, but at least it was healed.

Swaying, Morgana leaned against the wall and closed her eyes. Her chest burned. All of her magic was gone. Between the Fae making one last desperate assault on the village and healing Rozenn, she had nothing left. She needed rest. Morgana knew it, but ignored it. Creeping towards the door of the small house, Morgana flinched with every sob that Rozenn made. Torn between wanting to comfort her one remaining student and wanting to find something, anything, to hurt, Morgana was struggling even to breathe.

Everything hurt. Another tragedy. Another senseless loss. Most of the Fae in the area had long since scattered over the past few years, but a few, a vicious few with a greater tolerance for iron, hadn't been willing to run. They renewed and inflamed Morgana's hatred of the Fae in a way that it hadn't been for centuries. She'd become soft. They'd made her hard again.

Gritting her teeth, she looked back at Rozenn. The young woman was distressed but safe enough here. Another series of sobs gave her pause. The grief was raw in the air, crashing over Morgana, and she wondered if she had missed something. People weren't her greatest talent and Rozenn....

Rozenn had never married. Despite being of age, she'd never married. Brennus had married- Morgana didn't even want to think about that woman now. Judoc hadn't married, but they'd thought he would soon.

Now all of his romantic babbling and lovestruck looks took on a new meaning. Morgana snarled and, with renewed strength, marched to the door of the house.

The cooler air of autumn hit her face. She was grateful for it and inhaled greedily. It soothed the burn. Not a lot, but enough that she could think. Her mind whirled with new ideas and connecting prior events that had meant nothing. The affair must have been going on at least a year if Judoc's dumbstruck sighs were anything to go by. She was suddenly certain that Rozenn's feelings for Brennus hadn't been the warm sibling-like affection that he had for her.

It wasn't fair. If she'd known, then maybe she could have guided events down a different path. This was too familiar, bitterly so, and somehow, she hadn't seen it coming. Talented in scrying, hundreds of years old, and a mage and yet she had missed it, the most important thing that she needed to see to protect her new life and she hadn't noticed. Now everything was falling apart.

The local Fae who had been causing problems for years had been punished and were scattered, and the people who had been suffering raids were safe. They'd be turning all of this into stories in no time, and people would forget it ever happened. But her life, this little piece of purpose and companionship she'd carved out was over. They'd been here for too long, taken too long to address the threat because Morgana had let herself become attached. It had been so similar to home, echoes of her native culture around her and children that wormed their way into her affections. If she hadn't let herself get so comfortable, then maybe she wouldn't have been so blind to the real threat.

She felt Merlin approach more than heard him. The soft thump of his walking stick against the ground allowed her to track him as he came closer and closer. Remaining by the house, she closed her eyes and swallowed back the rush of bile trying to choke her.

Memories of all the little things she'd dismissed replayed behind her eyelids. All the looks between Judoc and Beladore that she'd assumed were shared amusement at Brennus' antics. She was a fool. Brennus hadn't even suspected and had been as happy as ever with his odd little family. Her heart ached. It was so similar, too similar to Arto's fate that the old wound of her brother's death was bleeding once more.

"Morgana," Merlin called.

"Rozenn's arm is healed." She opened her eyes and didn't bother greeting him. This wasn't the time for manners.

"Are you alright?" Finally, his voice betrayed his exhaustion and grief.

"Tired," she admitted.

"I understand."

"Any sign of the Fae?"

"No, I think... I believe it might be over. Let us hope so."

"Yes, given that we are down two mages." The last words came out as a snarl. "Any news of Judoc?"

"No, I doubt we'll ever see them again." Merlin sighed loudly, sounding every bit his years. "You know he didn't mean for this to happen."

"Strange, don't you think?" Morgana tilted her face towards the sun. "This is all so familiar. The wife and the best friend leaving right before a critical battle."

"Morgana-"

"I'm sure you've noticed the similarities."

"It's not the same."

"Of course not. It couldn't be exactly the same, but it is similar enough to make me think. To take me back. Rozenn is mourning for Brennus, who died because we were down a mage. If Judoc had been here-"

"He still might have died. You know that."

"I know no such thing," Morgana snarled. She turned her head to give him a withering look, daring him to interrupt her again. "Judoc watched Brennus' left side. That was always his weak side. Brennus was used to having support there, he expected it, and with Judoc gone, he didn't know how to compensate." Exhaling, she finally voiced the thoughts that were aligning in her mind. "It was them. Judoc and Beladore are Gwenyvar and Luegáed! They were reborn."

"That's madness."

"Madness?" Morgana laughed, the sound of it rough in her throat, and she heard the hysterical note it carried. "Merlin, we are centuries old! We have magic! We guard this world against things not meant to be here and guide a soul that has already returned several times. You would call two other souls returning madness?"

"We don't know-"

"No, we do." Morgana's fingernails dug into her skin. She welcomed the sting. The hint of pain kept her fixed in this point in time and space. "It was them. They came back, just like Arto did."

"Morgana, just because this happened-"

"Don't lecture me!" Morgana grabbed his neck and slammed him against the wall. The old man didn't fight her, and his expression betrayed only a tiny flicker of surprise. It just made her angrier. "It happened again, Merlin. The events played out the same."

"It wasn't exactly the same."

"Arto- Brennus learns that his wife and best friend are having an affair. It destroys his concentration, and one of those wretched creatures slashes his throat." Her hands trembled. The events replayed in her mind. The small gray Fae was grinning and splashing in the blood before she cut it down. "Their betrayal led to his death again!"

"It is similar," Merlin said gently. "But Morgana, we've never…" He shook his head, and Morgana eased her grip. "Why now? Why would this happen at all? There's no purpose to it. I don't believe that the magic of the Iron Realm would want to see this tragedy repeated."

"I don't know." She hated the words as they slipped from her mouth. Releasing Merlin's neck, she stumbled back as weakness washed over her. "Maybe… maybe some part of Arto's magic brought them back, just later. You know that he always wanted peace. Maybe he hoped to make peace with them in another life." Tears were prickling at her eyes. It was silly. She was fond of Brennus, but her grief was more than she imagined she'd feel for him. "Or maybe it is some lingering magic from the Queen, a means to destroy the Iron Soul."

Merlin didn't believe her. He was too calm, but at least he seemed thoughtful. Stepping away from the wall, he bent down to collect his staff. Morgana hadn't noticed that he'd even dropped it. Shame flickered in her chest, but she ground it down. She would not apologize, not under these circumstances. Merlin wouldn't expect her to.

The older mage walked past her, looking towards the east where they'd last seen Judoc and Beladore ride off. Morgana's rage returned, burning away her guilt. Judoc, one of her own mages. A boy that she helped train, who knew the importance of keeping the Fae at bay. Who had been a friend to Brennus for years and yet-

Her anger towards Judoc was nothing compared to her anger for Beladore. She'd known that girl was trouble from the first moments she'd met her. Brennus' adoration had been too familiar. They'd known each other their whole lives and no one had been surprised when they married. Morgana had ignored her unease, and now she could only regret it.

"Merlin, it was them," Morgana tried again. This time, her voice was softer. Defeated. "It had to be."

"I don't know. You may be right, but... what do we do if it was?"

There was the most important question, but she didn't have an answer. She knew what she wanted to say, but it would horrify her counterpart. Regret for never hunting down Luegáed and Gwenyvar took hold. Maybe if she had, she would have seen or felt whatever terrible magic caused this and been able to stop it.

"We watch for them," Morgana finally answered. "When we find anyone that we think might be the Iron Soul, we watch those around them and be ready to destroy them if necessary."

A sharp inhale from Merlin was his only reaction. Under better circumstances, Morgana would have been proud to render him speechless. Today, however, it gave her no pleasure. Stepping away from him, she marched back to their home and went inside.

Rozenn's crying had softened. The woman had pulled back the blanket and had cleaned Brennus up the best she could. There was no hiding the damage to his throat, but the blood had been cleared away, and his eyes were closed. He was dead. Morgana wished that the grief churning in her chest was only for him, only for the bright man she'd known for the past few years, but it wasn't.

She only saw Arto on that bed. There was only her poor brother, who had been so lovely, compassionate, and strong. Arto, who was still the best of the Iron Soul incarnations in her mind and who would always be the true champion of the Iron Realm. The others were shadows, but now the shadows carried the threat of his fate. Her fingers twitched with the urge to reach out to Rozenn and comfort her, but she didn't know what to say.

Merlin came inside, and in the corner of her eye, she saw him look her way. She had said all that she planned to say to him. Sitting at the small wooden table, Morgana positioned herself so she could see the door and Rozenn. She folded her hands to keep herself from pulling out her scrying mirror. Tracking Beladore and Judoc down now would do no good. At least now she knew what threat to watch for, what to be on guard for, and she would be vigilant. The reborn souls of Gwenyvar and Luegáed would not be permitted to harm any of her charges ever again.

31

The Outpost

The sky lightened as they flew, but only a little. Aiden couldn't tell if it was day or night and couldn't see the sun even to try to orient himself. Without a sense of time or place, they flew in the direction that Alex had indicated. He hoped when they landed that she had a good explanation. His eyes burned from the smoke that surrounded him, and Aiden squeezed his eyes shut for a short time, but that only made his stomach turn as Emrys moved them through the air.

In his spot at the back, Aiden shivered as the wind raced around his exposed backside and snuggled closer to Nicki. He thought he heard her chuckle, but it was difficult to hear anything for sure. Leaning to the side, he tried to see Alex, but could only see her leg and a bit of braided blonde hair when Emrys turned them. The Dragon's large wings blocked most of his view as he was stuck behind them today, but he didn't think there was much to see.

The dark sky stretched out. It was thick, and Aiden couldn't help but think that an ash cloud like this one had sent Earth slipping into an ice age millions of years ago. He hoped that he was wrong and that it was just the weather, but he doubted it. A few low mournful cries escaped Emrys as they flew that even the wind couldn't muffle.

Aiden kept a tight grip on the rope and turned his head to look over his shoulder. Thus far, the skies were empty except for them. Emrys had taken them lower, and what looked like a burned-out forest was below them. There were no signs of birds or, more importantly, Dragons. Aiden wasn't sure if he was hoping to see some or not. His excitement for the idea had died very quickly when the other Dragons had attacked them and the Gryphons.

The sky continued to lighten a little as they flew, and Aiden grew a little optimistic. Below them, he could see signs of life in soft rosy vegetation that had only the barest hint of green. There were still large patches of trees and ground that were blackened, but it seemed that the whole world wasn't that way.

With the smoke lessening, Aiden could see further and eyed the mountains with caution. The high, sharp peaks were blackened from smoke and ash and made the Rocky Mountains look small and eroded. His mind spun as Aiden tried to process and understand what he was seeing. It occurred to him that the fires that seemed to have ravaged the area might just be because of the Dragons and not related to the Darkness at all. Then again, why would they cause so much devastation? Aiden wished he could shout the question to Emrys, but knew the Dragon wouldn't be able to hear him.

Emrys suddenly swooped down past a mountain. Aiden hissed as the rocky slope became all too clear, with no warning. The Dragon tilted, and he clung to the rope with both hands. He heard the others gasp, but everyone stayed in position. Looking around frantically, he searched for what had caused Emrys to change course so suddenly, but saw nothing. There were no Dragons flying towards them, but then up ahead, he caught sight of something. It looked like a massive ruined building perched high on a mountain cliff. Emrys was heading straight for it.

The ruins were shockingly similar to something Aiden would have expected on Earth. Walls were clearly outlined, although many had crumbled into piles of stone. It easily eclipsed the football field at Ravenslake University, leaving Aiden to estimate that it was at least six-hundred feet long and five-hundred feet wide, made up mostly of large size rooms. In the dim light, he almost mistook the walls as constructed by stone bricks, but as soon as they landed, he realized his mistake.

There were no individual bricks. Everything seemed to be carved from one massive seamless stone. The rock was smooth and dark, reminding him of obsidian and the notion that Dragons might pile up stones and then melt them with dragon fire teased at him. They'd never tested how hot Emrys' breath was, an oversight that he now regretted. A dark stone floor seemed to be intact beneath their feet, but something that looked like red moss was growing over much of it.

Everyone slid off of Emrys' back, and Aiden's knees nearly buckled when he hit the ground. His lungs filled with air, and a soft sigh of relief escaped him. The air was still smoky, but it was easier to breathe now. It was a pity they hadn't considered this and brought masks.

"How is everyone?" Morgana asked.

"I'm fine," Aiden said. The others followed suit in assuring Morgana that they were alright despite the long flight through the smoky air.

Emrys hadn't moved. Their supplies were still in the net and had barely escaped Emrys landing right on top of them. Still, the Dragon's shock was apparent, and no one rushed forward to grab their bags. Aiden's eyes swept through the ruins, eying a broken wall that was taller than him and trying to imagine how tall it must have stood to facilitate numerous Dragons.

"Emrys?" Alex called softly. She touched his neck, running a hand over his sharp scales with no hint of fear. "Do you know this place?"

"I did." The Dragon's voice was haunted. He nodded towards the nearby peak which had an odd-looking dome-like section that was distinct. "I know that mountain. This was an outpost where... I was stationed here for many years in my youth." The Dragon turned his head to look down the steep hillside. "There were caverns down there and a tunnel leading down from the outpost."

"Looks long abandoned." Alex dropped her hand and walked to one of the nearby walls. "It must have been impressive."

"Not really. Not compared to the capital, but it-" Emrys cut himself off and shook his head. "No matter, it simply surprised me. I can take us a bit further still."

"It may be wise for us to get our bearings," Morgana said. She gestured down the hillside. "This area seems to be recovering from a fire."

"Nothing unusual about that," Emrys said. He shifted back from the supplies and sat down, folding his wings close to his body. "Given that all Dragons breathe fire, such things are common in this world. The ash fertilizes the soil. Even more so than in your world. Plants evolved in this world to reproduce due to fires."

"Like pine cones," Nicki said. Aiden smiled, but Alex and Bran gave her an uncertain look. "They explode and scatter seeds when fire heats them up," Nicki explained.

"Plants in this world do not require pollination," Emrys offered. His tone was still distant, but the conversation seemed to pull the Dragon back. "When I first learned of your bees and the purpose of some birds in your world, I was fascinated."

"So, are there flowers here?" Nicki asked. "If pollination isn't a thing, do you have flowers?"

"No. There is no need for them. Plants grow, and the heat of fires allow them to scatter their seeds. Animals and the winds also help move the seeds, but that is all. It is a simpler system than those in your world.'

"Sounds like it," Aiden agreed. The mood settling in was calmer, and his heart was finally beginning to slow down. He cast his eyes around, searching for a new topic of conversation, but there was only the ruins. "You sure we're heading the right way, Alex?" He peered up into the sky. "It's not as easy to see the Darkness here."

"I'm sure." Alex carefully climbed up onto a pile of stones and pointed further into the mountains. "When we crossed over, my magic reacted to the Darkness." She paused and swallowed, struggling with something, and Aiden held his breath for the bad news. "It's hard to explain, but it felt like the energy in this world reacted positively to us. Like it was asking for help."

Aiden didn't have to look at Morgana to know that she'd have an eyebrow raised. Still, he glanced over, and as he expected, Morgana was studying Alex with a raised eyebrow and a frown. Alex turned back to them, a picture of composure despite her braid being an utter mess from the wind. There was no doubt in her features, and Aiden realized with dawning hope and worry that she was completely convinced.

"What does that mean for us?" Bran asked thoughtfully. It was the sort of question that he didn't expect an answer to, which was good as Aiden didn't have one. "That leans into the theory that we haven't suffered negative effects yet because this world wants us here." Bran shook his head. "But that takes us back to the question of sentience."

"Alex might be projecting a little," Nicki added. Her smile was a little forced, and it was Alex's turn to raise an eyebrow. "But that's good either way. If we know where to go, then we can hopefully avoid any delays or battles."

"This might not be the time to ask," Nicki said softly. "But do you have any advice about dealing with Dragons should more of them attack us? In case we can't avoid a battle.

Judging from the expression on Nicki's face, she knew how dark the question was even before Emrys' body tensed and then slumped. Despair, it turned out, could etch itself on the sharp, scaled features of a Dragon just as easily as it could the wrinkled flesh of a human. Everyone held their breath, and Aiden braced himself for Emrys to push back or worse, decide that he'd had enough and leave.

But the Dragon merely sighed, a thin trail of smoke escaping his mouth and turned towards Alex. She offered him a sympathetic frown and stepped forward to touch his face once again. Aiden glanced at Bran, wondering if his previous life gave him any insight as to what sort of friendship those two had, but even Bran was watching them sadly and curiously.

"We don't really have weak points," Emrys said. "And I can't speak to all Dragons now. The ones that attacked us were much larger than most I knew. I was on the larger side of average in my time." The Dragon sighed loudly, more smoke curling out from his mouth. "The wings are the best place to attack. You can knock a Dragon out of the air, and they are very sensitive. It won't kill, but it will cripple."

Aiden swallowed. The word cripple brought up too many memories for him, including his first meeting with Bran back when his friend had used a brace and cane and Aisling as a child when her body had needed extra support just to move thanks to her cancer. Killing had become easy over the last few years, even if that spark of guilt deep inside his chest over killing the Fae who had been bound by the Iron Chain would never go away. But being here, in another world where they were the invaders, changed things just enough that killing was uncomfortable. The thought of crippling something on purpose was even worse. He had too much baggage.

"Let's approach it as stopping them so we can try to talk," Alex ordered. "Rather than trying to maim a living thing. After all, we're the visitors here."

Emrys relaxed. It was a tiny motion in his wings and the shoulders, but Aiden knew Alex had said the right thing. The calm had all but faded under the weight of the conversation, but he hoped they might get it back.

"If this was an outpost, are there any records that might be intact?" Morgana asked, her voice oddly loud in the stillness of the ruins.

"Records would be useful," Nicki agreed. "As the primary stronghold fell, Dragons might have left things down there."

Emrys hesitated, but the Dragon nodded. "There may be something below."

Standing, Emrys moved to a nearby wall and examined it. Aiden assumed he was trying to get his bearings. While the wall towered over him, it seemed far too short to support a roof tall enough for Dragons to navigate under. He briefly remembered Nicki telling him about Romans using stones from the Coliseum to build other things, but dismissed it. There weren't separate stones here. Time and potentially other forces had worn down this fortress. It was a terrifying idea.

While Emrys looked around, Aiden moved closer to Alex, who was watching the Dragon with cautious and sympathetic eyes. Morgana's hands were limp at her sides, but the tension in her shoulders promised that she was ready for any attack. Bran had already pulled out his journal and was taking notes. Aiden wasn't sure if Bran was really trying to record everything for posterity or if it was a way for him to feel a little in control.

"Is it always this smoky?" Nicki asked. She coughed delicately and averted her eyes to look into the sky. "I know you said fires are common, but is this normal?"

"Smoke is common in this world," Emrys said. "But there is more to this. I fear the fires are no longer controlled. If things are as bad as I fear, then Dragons likely fight for the last of the resources."

Alex spoke up next. "This world isn't dead yet." Her gaze swept across the stony ground. "Can we help you with this, Emrys?"

"The above-ground entrance is collapsed," Emrys announced. "Filled in with stone. The lower cavern entrance may still be available."

"So, your people really lived in buildings?" Nicki asked. Aiden could have groaned. "You carved buildings and lived in them?"

"My ancestors lived in natural caverns, much like yours," Emrys said patiently. "But there were only so many. We took to carving homes for ourselves. We dislike getting wet as much as you do."

"How was the fortress built? It looked like one melted stone. Did you carve it with fire out of the top of the mountain or pile up stones and melt them down? Can you touch lava without danger and mold it into shape?"

"Nicki," Morgana chided. "Not now."

A soft chuckle escaped Emrys at the exchange, and he saw Nicki's lips curl into a smile. She caught his eye, and Aiden nodded in approval. His approval didn't last long when Alex told everyone to grab their packs so they could go down the hillside. With a soft groan of token protest, he grabbed his bag and helped Nicki hand the net to Emrys.

While he didn't love hiking down the hillside with his pack, he had to admit it had been a good precaution. Emrys flew low, darting around the rocky slope below them and occasionally getting the net tangled in burned-out treetops as it was. And it was kind of nice to stretch his legs and move on his own power, though he wasn't going to say that out loud. They made their way down in good time on what looked like a game trail. It didn't look commonly used, but it was there, narrowly navigating around rocks and the large reddish ferns that were growing out of the blackened soil. Alex was right about this world, not yet being dead. There were still enough large animals to make game trails.

"Here!" Emrys called to them. The Dragon was near the base of the steep slope, standing on a small patch of flatter land with his wings folded down. "This tunnel seems open."

Scrambling down with the others, Aiden looked up at the sky and tried to find the sun. The haze was too thick, and he was left uncertain how much more daylight they had. When he reached the flattened ground, his knees quivered for a moment while he caught his breath. Emrys was staring into a large, dark opening. It wasn't a hole, but a tunnel with more of the shaped stones creating an archway and supported walls. Some large red plants with vines were growing around it, managing to obscure part of the entrance, and Aiden couldn't help but wonder if that was by des ign.

"What do you think?" Bran asked, voicing what everyone was thinking.

"Emrys, do you smell anything?" Alex asked.

"Ash and the sweet vines," Emrys replied. He nodded at the red plants. "Nothing more."

"Let's take a look then," Alex ordered. She adjusted her pack and freed Mjǫllnir from its place at her side. Cathanáil was firmly wedged between Alex's back and the pack. Alex cleared her throat and held Mjǫllnir loosely in her right hand. "Remember, try not to kill anything."

No one argued. Emrys didn't wait for instructions and ducked his head below the vines to enter first. Alex followed him closely, almost walking alongside him. Aiden and the others formed the second row, the wide tunnel that had been built for Dragons was more than large enough for them to walk side by side. Nicki had her flashlight out but kept the beam focused on the floor.

Darkness quickly surrounded them. The angle of the tunnel's entrance ensured that no light came in. Aiden reached out, trying to find a wall to follow, but the space was too large. He almost fell, his sense of where the others were deserting him as he fumbled for his own flashlight when Nicki's light was all but swallowed up by the empty darkness.

Aiden tried to find the others again as he reached for the side pocket of his pack, but it was too dark and the cavern too large. There was a flash of dark gray magic, and a glowing orb appeared. Aiden's breath caught in his throat from both relief at the light and panic that Alex was exposing her position. He didn't have time to process that thought. The light glittered off pale blue scales roughly thirty feet from them, revealing the form of a large Dragon that began to rise.

32

Here There Be Dragons

The realization that there were Dragons in the tunnel didn't send Alex into convulsions of panic or terror. She heard cries of surprise from the others, but she stayed silent beside Emrys and firm in her footing. Something about the creature made her hesitate as it rose to its feet with wide eyes. The pale color was odd and appeared mottled in places near the eyes and around the mouth, tugging at some memory from Alex's past. It drew back, wings pressed tightly to its back, and Alex heard a low rumble escape Emrys, but it wasn't a sound of fear, it was of pity. There was a faint glow of red, silver, yellow, and blue against the smooth stones in front of her, warning Alex that the others were preparing to attack.

"Hold!" Alex snapped. She held up her free hand and hoped that the others got the message. No magic flew past her, though the glow remained. "Wait," Alex said in a softer tone. "Wait."

The cavern stilled. Sounds of scales moving against the ground alerted Alex that there were more Dragons in the shadows as the one in front of her wasn't moving. Its bright yellow eyes were jumping between her and Emrys with confusion winning out over fear. Once again, she remembered it had probably seen nothing like her and that helped brighten her mood.

Around her neck, the Iron Pendant was warm and solid. Thus far, it had served her well, and she hoped it would help at this moment. Emrys was silent, guarding her side and not speaking to the other Dragon. It was larger than him, but its body language was frightened and submissive, keeping its head low and wings down.

"I'm sorry if we startled you," Alex said.

The Dragon's gaze was back on her in an instant. But before a conversation could begin, there was a deafening roar that echoed through the cavern and set all of Alex's instincts on high alert. Hairs stood on end, her feet pressed down against the stone, and her muscles tensed. The blue Dragon only had time to turn before a smaller Dragon with reddish scales, and three horns came tearing around the blue Dragon.

Moving in a blur of red, Emrys cut off the smaller Dragon's charge. It was less than two feet shorter than Emrys, but their ally struck the other Dragon soundly in the chest with a quick lash of his tail before head-butting the attacker. Before the reddish Dragon could recover, Emrys knocked it down and coiled his body around it in what could only be a smooth law enforcement move. Alex's magic tingled over her skin, but there was no need to use it. The smaller Dragon tried to free itself, but Emrys' legs refused to be moved, and his claws dug into the stone floor with a metallic hiss.

"Stop!" The pale blue Dragon roared. The word echoed around them. "They're only a child!"

Emrys kept his hold on the smaller Dragon, but Alex noted with relief that he wasn't holding teeth or claws against the mottled red scales. Next to the rich red of Emrys, the child's scales were dull and malformed with the odd white spots highlighting strangely shaped scales that didn't seem to fit.

"I have no intention of harming him." Emrys' deep voice rumbled around them. "Tell him not to struggle, and I will release him."

"What are these creatures?" the pale blue Dragon asked.

"They are under my protection and here to help our world." Emrys made a low growl when the smaller Dragon, apparently a child, tried to move. "Will you behave if I release you?"

"Alex?" Nicki whispered behind her. "What's going on?"

"I think we're okay," Alex answered. She barely caught the young Dragon begrudgingly promising not to attack. "Just stay calm."

"Please," the pale blue Dragon pleaded. They lowered their head even more, and the younger one snarled.

"Don't start a fight," Emrys told the younger one. Then he shifted his weight, easing his torso off the younger Dragon.

Hissing, the younger Dragon slithered out from under Emrys and spun. A noise from the pale blue Dragon made it stop. A low growl rumbled from the young Dragon's mouth, and a thin curl of smoke rose into the air, shimmering in the magical glow of Alex's orb. The attempted display did not impress her and judging from the way Emrys unfolded his wings and let his claws scrape against the stone, Emrys wasn't impressed either. The terrible sound rattled Alex's teeth, but she stayed still and quiet, waiting for the confrontation to settle.

The pale blue Dragon moved closer to the child. In the darkness beyond her light, the sound of more scales and claws against the stone warned her of the approach of more Dragons. Emrys settled back, relaxing his posture when the young Dragon leaned against the pale blue Dragon. Alex stayed where she was, debating the best course of action.

"They smell tasty," a high-pitched voice out of view said. "Smell of mammals, but only a little fur." The pale blue Dragon and their child frantically moved back. Emrys' calm vanished in a split second, and he lowered his wings and arched his back. "So hungry."

"These creatures are sentient," Emrys announced. "And they have the power to protect themselves. We come in peace, do not attack."

Emrys turned his head to stare to the right. Alex waved her hand, pushing more magic into the glowing orb. Its glow expanded, spreading warm light further across the stone floor. A large dragon head came into view, pale orange eyes narrowing against the light and a sharp hiss escaping a mouth that was missing part of its lower jaw. A set of rotting teeth stood out against dark green, scarred flesh that had smallpox like marks where scales had been. Alex's stomach fluttered with warnings of nausea, but she held it in. Tightening her jaw, Alex flexed her fingers. Her magic jumped across her skin.

The Dragon lunged forward with a snarl. Emrys started to move, but Alex was faster. She threw up her left hand, releasing waves of dark silver sparks that surged forward to encircle the Dragon. Her right hand rested on Mjǫllnir, ready to draw the Iron Hammer if it was necessary. The Dragon roared and struggled, but the dark gray magic formed lines that tethered themselves to the ground. As it tried to twist away, the magic merely entangled the Dragon further. Whispers and small cries reached Alex's ears, but no other Dragon attacked.

"Now," Alex huffed. She didn't release her magic, but pushed more into the orb, making it explode with light and illuminate the far reaches of the cavern. Pillars of rock cast long shadows over the ground, and six more Dragons were revealed. "I am not here to harm any of you," Alex announced. "But I will defend myself." She cast a side-eye at the green

Dragon. "The Darkness, the force that is killing your world, is something that I intend to stop."

Soft words echoed in the cavern as the Dragons whispered to each other. Alex gave them a moment to process her bold announcement, but she meant it. The Dragons moved closer, and Emrys stepped protectively in front of her. Shaking her head, Alex stepped around him once more to stand beside him and rested her left hand on his leg.

"The Darkness is infecting many worlds," Alex continued. "It threatens mine and others. I want it gone, and I can help." She took her right hand off of Mjǫllnir and gestured towards the others. "We can help. All we want is some information on what happened and any advice you can offer on the area where things are the worst. Then we'll be going."

"Please, listen to her," Emrys said. He glanced at the bound Dragon. "They can help our world.'

"You're small," the young Dragon hissed at Emrys. "Why should we listen to you? You're no older than me."

"I am centuries old," Emrys answered in a measured tone. "I left this world a long time ago; I fell into a distant world where I was trapped for a long time until Alex freed me." He nodded at Alex, and she was grateful that he didn't go into the full story. "When I left this world, my homeworld, Dragons were all about my size. The world was much lusher, and the sky was not so dark. Much has changed."

In the corner of her eye, Alex saw three of the Dragons, who were slightly larger than Emrys, look at each other. Their eyes were full of excitement and curiosity. She hoped that was a good sign. "But that is not important now," Emrys added. "We came down here seeking information. We were looking for records, but anything you can tell us would help."

"It was already happening when I was born," the old Dragon grumbled. Everyone looked at them, and they slumped on the ground, their body creaking. "My mother used to speak of her own childhood when things were not so bad and said that years ago, the world had been healthy."

"Yes," Emrys agreed. "I come from that time."

"Can we go to this other world?" one of the small dragons asked.

There was a mess of voices as others spoke up in support of that plan. Panic flared in Alex's chest, but she reminded herself that portals were difficult to open. The other group had been piggybacking on the path of the Darkness, which couldn't be safe. Swallowing, she took a slow breath and waved her hand at the bound Dragon. Her magic vanished, and Alex called the remaining flickers of power back to her.

"No." Emrys shook his head. "There are painful side effects when you enter a world that isn't yours."

"Painful-" the blue Dragon snorted. "Look at us. Look at you. Our scales are dying the moment we are born. The world is tearing at us!"

The protests grew. Alex's panic was fighting for control. Her eyes scanned the Dragons as they came closer. They were larger than Emrys, perhaps an evolutionary attempt to help them fight other Dragons for resources, but the coloration, their eyes, and the way they held themselves all screamed of illness. Emrys was trying to calm them, but if he were to tell them that the Iron Realm made it so they could not die, they would have a riot on their hands. They almost did now, and Alex took a step back.

"Maybe the Chalice would help them," Bran suggested softly in her ear. "It would help them immediately and prove that we have the power to stop this." He put his hand on Alex's shoulder, and she turned to face the others, her spine prickling with warning as she turned her back on the Dragons. "It might be the solution here."

"We've never tried the Chalice on birth defects," Morgana whispered. She glanced over at the Dragons, her shoulders tense and her eyes narrow. "If it fails, then they may distrust us."

"Maybe not if we're honest about not knowing if it will work." Alex licked her lower lip nervously. "I get why you're not sure. I don't remember ever using the Chalice like that, not even back when it was made, but we shouldn't assume that something is impossible."

"Alex." Morgana hesitated for a moment, swallowing and then sighing. "We don't know how long the magic will last here. This is another world, and if the magical items have only so much power, then I'd rather save that power for our use."

"The Sword recharged in the Gryphon world."

"That was a world closest to Earth," Morgana pointed out. "We can't assume that the same is true here."

Arguments rose into Alex's mouth, but she kept herself from voicing them. Morgana had a point, she reminded herself and her sense that this world wanted their help didn't mean that their magic would recharge. Yet, in the corner of her eye, she kept glimpsing the thread of energy underneath the surface of this world that linked it to the Tree of Reality. It was dim compared to the one in the Gryphon world, but it was there.

'Careful,' Arto whispered. 'You don't know what it means.'

'Trust your instincts,' Akule advised. 'You've been right so far.'

'You can beat the Dragons,' Thor added. His glee for that course of action made Alex's lips twitch, but she didn't smile.

She'd be just as happy to avoid fighting Dragons where possible. "We need to try," Alex insisted. She might have to fight Morgana. "Some of the issues may be recent."

"We don't know how the Chalice will hold up against a taint from the Darkness," Morgana huffed.

"But it's not really the Darkness," Nicki pointed out reasonably. Alex could have hugged her. "It's messing with the environment. That's a different issue completely. I agreed that it's worth a shot, and while the Chalice is great, we have our own magic for healing if need be."

"That doesn't fix everything," Morgana whispered.

"We're sorry we couldn't save Merlin," Bran said softly. Everyone held their breath. "He was gone too fast to even try the Chalice. That could happen again, no matter if we do or don't do this."

"Bran's right, it could prove that we mean well."

Morgana curled her nose, and her brow furrowed, but she didn't argue. Emrys snapped Alex's name, warning her as the Dragons closed in further. Raising her hands, Alex released a wave of dark silver magic. The Dragons shrank back as the pressure wave struck them. It wasn't enough to harm any of them, but it gave the mages space. Alex's hands trembled, a warning to be mindful of how much magic she used.

Bran had the Chalice out in moments before the Dragons could rally their anger at her use of magic. The air was thick with tension. There were too many ways this could go for Alex to predict the most likely outcome, but a calm settled over her. Beneath her, around her, the soft hum of this world whispered to her. Different and yet achingly similar to home. She stepped forward, directly under her light orb, and held up the Chalice.

"This is an object from our homeworld," Alex said. The Dragons quieted and turned towards her. "It has the power to heal. We don't know if it will work in your world, but if any of you are willing, we will try to heal your injuries and the trauma inflicted on your bodies as a show of goodwill."

The chatter was near deafening as the Dragons shouted questions and voiced their disbelief. Those that had questioned Emrys suggested the mages should all be eaten before she used any more of her powers on them. It was the old Dragon that Alex had bound earlier that stamped its foot loudly. The ground trembled at the impact, and Alex turned her gaze towards the creature.

"I'll try. If it harms me, it won't be the first thing to eat away at me." The Dragon's maimed jaw twisted into almost a smile. "I've seen too much of the Death or Darkness, whatever you want to call it." The creature leered at her. "You think you can do something to help; I'd like to see you proven right."

The challenge was obvious. The other Dragons stopped talking, and Alex knew this Dragon had influence. Without taking her eyes off of the Dragon, Alex fumbled with her water bottle only to have Nicki step up to help her fill the Chalice with water. Stepping towards the Dragon, Alex pressed her hands tightly against the iron of the Chalice. It warmed beneath her hands as the magic sprang to life. Pushing a spark of power into the Chalice, Alex inwardly pleaded with the magic to work properly. This wasn't the time for surprises.

"You need to drink this," Alex explained. "We'll start with one cup full and go from there."

"I assume that's a cup," the Dragon huffed.

Her cheeks warmed, and Alex reminded herself to be careful about assuming they had compatible terms. The Dragon opened his mouth as she approached. Ignoring a flash of fear, Alex reached forward into his mouth and poured the liquid in the Chalice straight onto the Drag-on's tongue. The liquid shimmered as it fell, reflecting the glow of the Chalice. When the Chalice was empty, Alex withdrew her arm from the mouth and stepped back. Moving away from the long teeth was a relief, but her focus immediately turned to the Dragon.

For a moment, there was no change. Dragons began to mutter, and Alex started to turn for more water, wanting to try again before the creatures could get angry. But then the old Dragon groaned softly. Slowly more color appeared in the old scales, darkening them and smoothing out the tone. Alex's eyes focused on the jaw, hope rising as she remembered Bran's leg being healed. The flesh rippled, the Dragon groaned and tilted his head as the bone and muscles suddenly expanded to fill in the gaps. New small scales grew across the surface, smoothing out the Dragon's body.

A soft gasp echoed in the cavern, and more Dragons leaned into the light to get a better view. Alex felt Morgana tense beside her and knew that the older mage was studying each Dragon, each potential enemy closely. There was a new rush of eager voices. Emrys imposed himself between the Dragons and them, spreading his wings and ordering them to calm down and form a line. A rich laugh escaped the old Dragon, who stood a little straighter and folded his wings against his back. Bright orange eyes swung to meet Alex's for a long moment before he moved back and stretched out his body.

"Well," the Dragon said. "That works." It was Emrys he looked to next. "What do you need from us? How can we help?"

"Well, we'll need more water after doing this," Alex said. It was the only urgent thing she could think of. Several dragons nodded at her request and she breathed easier.

Reaching up, Alex gripped the Iron Pendant tightly, letting her skin be molded against the metal spiral shapes. The iron hummed gently with her magic, soothing her frayed nerves. The Dragons were forming a line at Emrys' command. She handed the Iron Chalice to Bran and Nicki, who quickly refilled it. Morgana gripped her shoulders in silent support, and Alex's vision blurred as relief crashed over her. Somehow, with the help of Morgana, Alex stayed on her feet and kept smiling as one by one, the Dragons were healed by the Iron Chalice.

33

Passage of Time

1 58 C.E. Tarraco, Roman Empire

An odd feeling had been hanging over Morgana all morning. She wasn't sure what to think about it. There was a sense that she'd forgotten something since the moment she woke to sunlight streaming into her small home. The sounds of the city had greeted her when she opened the shutters, and nothing had been obviously amiss. After washing up, she'd left the small home she rented made of pale bricks that were shining in the light of the sun.

Morgana had no plans for the day beyond entertaining the idea of going to the public baths and then using her magic to cheat at games for some money. Merlin would disapprove of the use, but supporting herself as a single woman wasn't as easy as she would have liked. As she crossed the road and moved closer to the city square, Morgana had to stop when a trio of Roman soldiers marched past, their armor gleaming in the sun.

Morgana both liked and disliked the Roman Empire. On the one hand, she loved being able to find goods that reminded her of the exotic treasures she'd seen in the northern islands as a child. Styles had changed, and bronze was no longer the currency, but there was still a strange nostalgic comfort in it. She enjoyed many aspects of the culture that enfolded the city and attended many performances at the theater. The warm breezes off the Mediterranean kept the weather pleasant most of the year.

But she wasn't always at ease with the notion of Empire. Seeing soldiers in armor patrolling the city reminded her a little too much of the Sídhe. Hearing citizens talk about the glory of the Empire and conquests that would expand it brought back too many memories of the court. Corruption had long since seeped into the colonial governments, but the city, in general, was still pleasant enough that she could usually ignore the bad parts.

This was where she had found herself after wandering for a time. It was the fourth city she had settled in since she and Merlin parted ways, and she'd been here only two years. Roman law wasn't bad to live under, and women had enough rights to property that she could make her way. Still, it might be time to move on soon. Maybe she would go north towards her homeland next and see how things had changed.

Pushing such thoughts away, Morgana smiled and soaked up the sunlight as she walked through the streets. She enjoyed becoming lost in the people. The city hummed with life around her. Smells wafted through the air, reaching out and calling her in different directions. It was exciting, and she smiled softly as she kept walking. People were shouting at each other. Bright colors accented the buildings as the laundry was hung out to dry. Painted statues and murals decorated the city, ensuring there was always something to look at.

It was good to be reminded that there was more to the world than her magical battles. A group of children ran out into the street, laughing and tossing a small ball to each other. Their rapid speech flowed over Morgana. She only understood about half of it and didn't bother using her magic. Most people spoke at least some Latin, but local languages were mixed in amongst the noise. Watching the children play until they were out of sight brought back a familiar ache.

Having children wasn't something that she wanted exactly. As a little girl, her mind and perhaps her soul had been too obsessed with the Sídhe Queen to want something for herself. The realization that her split nature left her infertile had been a relief during the war alongside her brother. There had been too much to do, too much to worry about, and after the war was over and she'd finally gone back to her husband, she'd been emotionally wrung out.

She didn't regret raising Altan with Airril. He'd been a good boy, a good son, and a good leader. After she'd left the village, she'd been pleased whenever she heard news of him and had given in to temptation a few times and scryed for him. Still, it was probably for the best that she and Merlin could not have children. Caring for the occasional orphan was more than enough. It was too easy to care about them, even when they were not blood and would die long before her.

Pushing away those silly thoughts, Morgana went to the next merchant and purchased the softest loaf of bread she could find. The merchant looked ready to snarl at her as she examined the wares, but said nothing. Once she was satisfied, Morgana paid and wrapped the bread up to protect it on the way home.

She was passing by a fountain when she caught sight of the water rippling across the surface. Stopping, Morgana eyed the ripples with a frown. It wasn't from the wind, as this small square was protected from the sea breeze, and the ripples were against the expected flow of water. A child pointed at it and tugged on their mother's arm. Suspicion took root in Morgana's gut, and she quickened her pace to head for home. Keeping her focus behind her, Morgana listened for any shrieks of shock and hoped that if she was correct as to the source of the water disturbance that they would wait a little longer.

On her way back to her small home, Morgana paid little attention to those around her. She kept her eyes and ears open for any other strange occurrence nearby. Returning home, she closed the door tightly behind her and closed all the shutters, leaving the house dark and still. A sigh of relief escaped her, and Morgana conjured a small ball of light to illuminate her entry.

The oddest thing about Morgana's small home was the large basin of water she kept on hand in the corner of her kitchen. The basin was three feet across and almost two feet deep. If she ever had guests who saw it, they would likely assume it was for washing, and from time to time, Morgana did use it for bathing when she didn't wish to go to the public baths or for laundry, but that was not its purpose. The basin required filling several times a week to keep a decent supply of water, but it was a comfort to know that it was there. The wooden basin had been carefully carved by Morgana herself and sealed with a thin layer of sap. It was uneven in spots, but it held the water she needed to feel secure.

She sat down at her table and watched the water. It was still and calm. Unwrapping the bread, Morgana tore off a piece and ate it viciously. Just as she was beginning to think that she'd rushed home over nothing, the water bubbled. Sighing, Morgana took another bite of her bread and tapped her fingers on the table impatiently. If she was being sought out, then something had happened. Scrying took effort, and Cyrridven had clearly been trying to track her, which was even more difficult.

The water swirled into the air and settled into a humanoid form. There was only the barest hint of water at the bottom of the basin when Cyrridven was done forming. The Old One smiled gently at her, the soft glow of her circlet illuminating her beautiful bronze features.

"Cyrridven," Morgana greeted shortly. "What's happened?" The Old One was an ally, not a friend, and Morgana knew she wasn't the person who Cyrridven would seek first. For a brief instant, fear gripped Morgana's heart as the notion that something had happened to Merlin hit her.

"Greetings, Morgana," Cyrridven answered. She didn't seem worried, and Morgana relaxed a little. "I bring news from Sif."

"Yes?" Morgana blinked in surprise. She and Sif had not kept in contact over the last decade. The region was at peace due to Thor long since having destroyed the Jǫtnar and the Dvegers having locked themselves underground. Thankfully, the Dvegers had all been male and would die off soon enough, so she wouldn't need to worry about them. "What is the message?"

"Thor passed away."

Morgana swallowed. The words weren't a surprise. The news shouldn't be a surprise. It had been decades since Thor had crafted the Iron Hammer and proven himself a decent mage. Of course, he'd have grown old in the years since she had seen him. And yet, Morgana's breath caught at the idea of her wild student being gone.

"Was it peaceful?" The words slipped out.

"Yes." Cyrridven was smiling gently at her. "Sif was with him. She said that there was no pain at the end. He simply let go."

"Good." Morgana nodded to herself. "Good. I'm glad that he had a full life."

"He did," Cyrridven agreed. "His health had been failing since the start of winter. Sif was prepared. She has left their home and is planning to slumber in the waters."

Ignoring the questions she had about how often Cyrridven visited the couple, Morgana focused on the most critical issue. With Thor's death, the Iron Soul could once again be reborn. There had been a few incidents with the Fae over the last few decades, but thankfully, nothing serious. She and Merlin had enjoyed a chance to rest. Stories of Thor had spread across Europe, so much so that he was held as a godly figure in some parts, to her great amusement. His death might make some factions bold once mo re.

"What of Mjǫllnir?" she asked.

"Sif and Thor made plans for it. She took possession upon his death to seal the Hammer away."

A protest burned on Morgana's tongue. Rage simmered in her gut at the gall of Sif to do such a thing, but she stopped herself from speaking. It wasn't fair for her to judge. Sif had been Thor's wife. He had trusted her, and despite Thor aging as a mortal man, Sif had proven loving and faithful. It had been her with him at the end and not Morgana.

Besides, it wasn't the first time that an Iron Soul had entrusted an Old One with an Iron Artifact. Lokpal had given the Trishula to Shiva despite her and Merlin's protests, and no evil had come of that. Her gaze fell to Cathanáil, where it was secured at Cyrridven's side. She and Merlin had done the same.

Cyrridven's expression softened. "You and Merlin must tend to the living. Let us who love this world protect the items of the fallen."

Fallen. Morgana hated that word. It was the right one. Arto, Gofiben, Lokpal, and Thor had been outstanding and bright young men. She was proud of them and their efforts, but they were gone. Gofiben had not been Arto, and Lokpal had not been either of them. Now Thor was gone. She braced herself for the next incarnation they would need to find. A soft sigh escaped her, and she nodded.

"Do you know where Merlin is?" Morgana asked. "Have you told him yet?"

"I found him yesterday," Cyrridven said. It didn't surprise Morgana that she went to Merlin first. "He took the news calmly."

"Where is he?" A sigh escaped Morgana. "I suspect that we've been apart long enough."

Cyrridven smiled at the words, beaming at Morgana as if she was a small child who had done something she approved of. Feeling her cheeks warm up, Morgana tossed her braid over her shoulder and straightened her back.

"It won't take me long to pack." She turned and stalked away from the basin. There was a hint of guilt and embarrassment, but Cyrridven merely laughed sweetly behind her. "We'll need to find somewhere else to make a tunnel."

"Of course," Cyrridven agreed.

Morgana ignored the fact that she had an Old One waiting for her as she began to pack. There was something unsettling about looking around your home and realizing how little you cared about. In truth, there wasn't much Morgana needed to take with her. There wasn't much that she wanted to take with her. She retrieved her ancient brooch that was now kept in a leather bag lined with the softest cloth she could find to keep the present from Airril safe. Beyond that, she packed two changes of clothing into a large leather bag and gathered up all the coinage she had and some trinkets that might be valuable to trade.

Walking back into the main room, Morgana stopped and searched the room. Nothing else called to her. Cyrridven was watching her silently and without judgment. Morgana was grateful for that. Her landlord would check on her soon and find her gone. She'd vanish again, moving on to avoid people noticing that she barely aged. At least this time, she was going to find Merlin. That thought warmed her chest a little.

"Are you ready?" Cyrridven asked.

"I have what I need, but we need more water than is here." Morgana frowned and surveyed the jugs available to her. "It's probably easier if I just go down to the water."

"Give me your cloak."

Then Cyrridven stepped out of the water. Her feet were bare, but the droplets of water settled into the form of simple blue slippers before she touched Morgana's floor. Morgana had seen her out of the water before, but even now, her understanding of Cyrridven was tied to the Old One's close connection to the waters of the Iron Realm. None the less, she nodded and handed over her old green cloak that was far too hot for this climate. Cyrridven took it without a word and draped it over her shoulders and pulled the hood up to hide her face.

They left the house behind without a second thought. Morgana didn't even look back. She spared a few glances at the surrounding buildings. This had been a nice place to spend a few years. Her emotions were unsettled. News of Thor's death and the knowledge that she would see Merlin soon had left her teetering between grief and excitement. She couldn't feel guilty for it; Morgana knew that Thor would have been amused.

The sun was high in the sky by the time they made it to the outskirts of the city. Walking along the beach, they said nothing to each other, and Morgana debated over what to say first to Merlin when she saw him. The sounds of the city had faded behind them, and as they approached a rocky cliff side, Morgana's heart beat faster with the knowledge that Cyrridven could create a tunnel here.

"He'll be happy to see you," Cyrridven said. She stopped and shrugged off the cloak. With great gentleness, she handed it back to Morgana. "Thank you."

Swallowing, Morgana nodded and stepped back, clutching her cloak and her bag. The warm ocean breeze was flowing over her skin. Cool water was lapping at the sand as Cyrridven raised one hand.

"Are you confident that you can do this?" Morgana asked.

"I made a point of learning." Cyrridven chuckled softly. "Besides, you don't know where Merlin is."

Morgana had to concede to Cyrridven's logic. She didn't say as much out loud, but let her silence communicate her agreement. Cyrridven's lips twitched into a small smile, and she turned her attention to the water. Focusing her attention on the sea, Morgana searched the waves for any sign of Cyrridven's magic. At first, there was nothing to see. Water kept washing up on the shoreline, darkening the warm sand before sweeping back into the sea. Boats dotted the deep blue waters in the distance, and Morgana glanced around to double-check that no one on shore could see them.

Then, with a roar, a wave spiraled into the air and began to spin. It was so sudden that Morgana took a step back in surprise. Cyrridven laughed melodically. The swirling water moved faster and faster. Shifting closer, Morgana held her breath as the churning calmed a little. Images flashed over the surface of the water. Some were familiar; some were not.

Cyrridven extended her hand and smiled. It was a sweet smile, reassuring, and gentle. Morgana took Cyrridven's hand without a second thought. The Old One's smile widened at the sign of trust. They stepped into the water. Small waves lapped at Morgana's feet, soaking her sandals, and she extended her left hand forward.

Falling into the water was the only way Morgana could describe it. Cyrridven kept a tight hold of her hand. Light flared around them, visions of strange places flashed past her, and they rushed forward. Water churned around them, but they stayed dry. Light poured in before Morgana, brightening the tunnel.

Her feet hit solid ground. Water splashed around her ankles, and warm sunlight hit her face. Everything was cooler here, and Morgana shivered. They were on the shoreline of a small mountain lake. Cyrridven released her hand as Morgana stumbled onto the shore.

"He lives just over that hill." Cyrridven pointed to the east. Then she folded her hands delicately in front of her. "I wish you well, Morgana."

"I'm sure that we'll speak soon." Morgana offered Cyrridven a small bow. "Thank you."

Her thanks earned her a soft smile from Cyrridven before the Old One sank below the surface of the lake. Morgana didn't wait to watch her completely vanish; she headed straight for the hill as she pulled on her cloak against the chilly wind. Trees with thick trunks and familiar leaves that were turning red surrounded her. It wasn't their homeland; it was much further north, and the scent of the earth beneath her feet was wild. This was no city. To her surprise, that thought didn't bother her.

Over the hill was a roundhouse like the one she'd grown up in, surrounded by a large fenced yard that held a few grazing animals. What looked like a small forge stood at one corner of the yard in a three-sided hut. Outside the fence at the front of the roundhouse was a healthy-looking garden with ripe vegetables. Home. It looked so much like the place she'd thought of as home so long ago that Morgana's knees trembled, and tears pricked at her eyes.

Then a figure came out of the house and headed for the garden. His back was to her. He was carrying a basket and dressed in simple, dark clothing. Morgana moved a little closer and smiled when she heard humming. Her chest tightened, suddenly stretched too far by the raging emotions. Closing her eyes, Morgana exhaled slowly and ordered herself to calm. It helped a little, and when she opened her eyes, Morgana called out to her old partner.

"Hello, Merlin."

Merlin jumped and spun around to face her. His surprise faded in an instant, replaced with an understanding smile. Of course, he wasn't surprised that she'd gotten in contact. She just hoped that he wasn't upset with her leaving her current life.

"Merlin," Morgana greeted again. It felt good to say his name.

She couldn't keep herself from checking him over intently with her eyes. He'd put on a bit of weight, and there was a healthy flush to his skin. Around him, the plants of his garden were a verdant green, and birds chirped from the nearby trees. His walking stick was leaning against the small house beside the door. This wasn't how she expected to find him, but the situation oddly suited him.

Merlin smiled tenderly. "Morgana." He set down the basket and walked towards her. "It's good to see you, my dear."

She accepted his hug, inhaling the familiar earthy scent of her partner and the new ones that clung to his clothing. He smelled of herbs and smoke. It was a settled scent, and she felt a pang of regret that she disturbed him, but there was nothing for it.

"It's good to see you too, Merlin." The words were shockingly true. She kept her head against his shoulder and listened to him chuckle. Then Merlin kissed her forehead and stepped back. "Looks like you've stayed out of trouble."

"I've done a decent job of it," Merlin agreed.

They stared at each other, and Morgana braced herself for a renewed Connection after nearly a decade apart. But it didn't come. While there was magic in the world, it was weak and calm. She took it as a sign that the world was peaceful at the moment, at least in those terms. Merlin nodded to her, and she expected he knew her thoughts. His lips twitched, and she narrowed her eyes suspiciously.

"Please, come inside," Merlin said. He gestured towards the small house. "I suspect we need to talk."

Then Merlin offered her his arm. His soft smile was welcoming in a way that Morgana wasn't sure it ever had been before. It promised her and reassured her that she had been missed, that he was happy to see her. With a soft smile of her own, Morgana took his arm and allowed Merlin to lead her into his home.

34

On Healed Wings

A triumphant roar echoed in the cavern as the young reddish Drag- on watched his scales darken and a bend that Alex hadn't noticed in his wing straighten. Aiden and the others backed away at the sound, but a mere moment later, the Dragon bounced around like an eager puppy. Bran looked at her, his mouth twitching as he fought back a smile or a laugh. Nicki dug another bottle of water out from their bags while Morgana frowned.

They wouldn't have much water left when this was done. Alex was mentally counting the bottles as they were emptied. Nicki and Bran had cut back on the amount of water they were using in each goblet full, but they also didn't want to make it so the Chalice couldn't work. The glow of the metal illuminated each mouthful of teeth as they poured it in. Bran never hesitated as each Dragon approached him. He smiled gently and held the Iron Chalice reverently, letting its glow illuminate his face before pouring the water.

"What is your name then?" the Old Dragon, who had threatened to eat them, asked Emrys. Even healed, he was still bent lower to the ground than Emrys, but the shine of his scales and the richness of their color assured Alex that the Chalice had worked. "Who are you?"

"These mages know me as Emrys. My story is a long one."

"With some secret you don't want to share?"

"It is not important now." Emrys shook his head.

"Emrys isn't a real name." The old Dragon looked even grumpier now.

"My birth name is Corixlynicarnic," Emrys answered. Amusement sparkled in his eyes when Alex gaped up at him. "As I told you, the names of my kind are difficult for your kind to pronounce." Emrys turned a bit more serious. "It is a real name where these mages are from. This one is called Alex. The red-haired one is Nicki. That is Bran, that one is Aiden, and the old smelling one is called Morgana." He was nodding to each of them in turn.

"This one understands us," the gruff old Dragon huffed. He was peering at Alex curiously. She was fairly confident that he wasn't going to try and eat them. "But the others don't."

Nicki was creeping forward, her eyes bright with interest. Alex held back a sigh and extended her left hand, allowing Nicki to clutch it. The old Dragon's eyes narrowed on the gesture, noting it, no doubt.

"She has an item that allows her to understand us and us to understand her," Emrys explained.

"Interesting." Alex didn't like the way the old Dragon was looking at her. It was too sharp and pragmatic even if it wasn't threatening. "There isn't much I can tell you about this Darkness. It's been plaguing our world for a long time. It was here when I was born. Records are limited at this point. My mother told me that the unified government that used to rule collapsed after the first century when their efforts to stop the Darkness failed. After that, things got worse as warlords started carving out kingdoms. The more the Darkness spread, the darker the sky got, and the less and less healthy land remained to fight over."

"How far is it to the Darkness?" Alex asked. Nervous energy built in her limbs and stomach. "The original point it entered? The closer we can get, the better."

"Not very far, across the mountains and across what remains of the Klaxeon Forest." Emrys made a sound of sorrow. "This is one of the last areas that are safe near it."

"Why are you here, then?" Nicki asked. "Why not be further away?"

"And now she understands!"

"I'm touching Alex," Nicki explained. Glee radiated off of her. "Why are you here?"

"This is a protected space," the old Dragon answered. "But this land is almost dead. The warring groups don't fight over it."

"How bad is the situation?" Emrys asked seriously.

"Bad. Most of the forests have burned in the wars." The Dragon turned his head towards the others. "Many of these are my kin, and others are too weak to survive in the middle of the wars. Falling back to places like this is dangerous, but it keeps us away from the fighting." He eyed the mages. "I don't suppose you can stop that too."

"The first thing to worry about is the Darkness." Alex hoped her expression was neutral. They couldn't start making promises about stopping a war. Worry was already gnawing at her stomach that it was too late for this world if Dragons were hiding in nearly dead areas. "Thank you for the information."

It wasn't what she'd been hoping for when they came down here to find records. She knew the direction of the Darkness already. All this had done was to leave her unsure of what happened after they sealed the breach. Even worse, they'd put the idea of escaping into another world in the mind of the Dragons. No wonder Morgana was frowning at her with her wrinkles standing out starkly.

"We need to get to the Darkness," Alex said. She reached up and tied her braid into a quick bun. "As fast as possible. We can take stock later, but I don't think there's anything more here that can help us."

"Agreed." Emrys was eying the younger Dragons who were talking in hushed tones and looking towards them. The red one was watching Emrys with an expression Alex couldn't get a read on. "Gather your things. How much water is left? We need to get more before leaving this area if things are only going to get worse."

"There's a spring nearby," one of the young Dragons said excitedly. Their scales were now a rich violet color, and a long scar on its side had healed over. "You can get more water there." This Dragon's rumbling voice was higher than some of the others, and Alex wondered if it was female.

Then again, she had no idea how reproduction even worked for Dragons. Maybe there was only one gender, and internally thinking of Emrys as a male had always been incorrect. Thankfully, Aiden and Nicki had their heads in the game and gathered the empty containers. Morgana moved to follow them, only to stop herself and linger beside Alex. Tension all but radiated off of the older mage. Alex reached over and gently touched Morgana's free-hanging left hand with her right hand, squeezing her fingertips gently.

"Thank you for the help," Alex told the assembled Dragons. "The information you gave us was valuable."

That was a stretch, but no one had been eaten. When dealing with Dragons, Alex was certain that it was a win. She didn't dare ask if the Chalice had dealt with any hunger they had, lest she remind them that they were all tasty meat sacks, but she hoped that its magic had eased any pain that they were dealing with.

When the others returned, everyone headed towards the entrance. No one knew how much time had passed, but if they were lucky, they could get closer today. Smoke tainted air wafted into the cavern, and Alex curled her nose. The scent of burned wood usually made her happy, but the thick smell outside was a reminder. Behind her, several of the Dragons were following them out. Her skin prickled with warning.

"Prepare your things," Emrys said. He moved outside onto the ashy ground. "We have a long way to go."

"I'll carry you," the old Dragon said. Alex blinked and looked at the Dragon in surprise. He turned slightly, exposing his side to Alex. "Can't be easy for him carrying all of you. It's a long way, but you'll make better time with help."

"Are you sure?"

"I'm old, but my wings are working fine now." The old Dragon eyed her. "Thanks to you." Something on her face must have given her away because the Dragon chuckled. "I'm not going to eat you. Given what you did in the cavern to heal us, you might be able to stop the Darkness after all. That's worth more than one small boney meal."

"I can't imagine there is much to eat around here," Alex said. "One boney meal might be too tempting."

Rather than being offended, the old Dragon's eyes sparked with amusement. "I'll pass. You'd probably taste sour."

"I'll help too," the young violet Dragon said.

More chimed in. The young red one tried to speak up, but the blue Dragon stepped in front of him and pushed him back into the cavern. Emrys was stretching his wings, pleasure radiating off of him, and Alex smiled as they put their things back into the supply net. Morgana's eyes were wide with horror or surprise. Alex didn't know which and tried to figure out a way to counter Morgana's argument.

It never came. Instead, worry mixed with resignation swept over Morgana's features. With a soft sigh, she moved to Emrys' side and climbed onto their Dragon ally. Frowning, Alex watched the silent defeat, all the while feeling like she needed to say something. But her words were gone. What energy for eloquence she had, she'd used up talking with the Dragons. Bran caught her gaze and shrugged helplessly. At least it wasn't just her.

Nicki's hands flared with blue magic as she started talking with the purple Dragon. Aiden gave her a quick warning as he waved to a green Dragon that had volunteered to help. Emrys moved to the edge of the open area, clearing room for Nicki to mount her Dragon.

"Well?" the old Dragon asked. "Are we going?"

"One second," Alex said. Walking over to Emrys, she reached for her backpack and unzipped the top. "I need something first."

"Alex?" Emrys asked.

"The Iron Chain," she answered. Mjǫllnir and Cathanáil hummed against her hip and side. "Just in case."

Her fingers brushed the soft fur of Galahad before she found the cold iron she sought. Pulling it out, Alex's eyes once again fell on the new melted link that had reconnected the Chain. Magic thrummed against her palm, and the metal instantly warmed. A whine echoed in her skull. Her body swayed as the scent of saltwater and sweat hit her.

"Alex?" Morgana's voice broke through the flashback.

Shaking her head, Alex secured her backpack and folded it into the net. Emrys took it with delicate claws. The weight of many eyes was on Alex as she clumsily wrapped the Iron Chain around her waist. She shoved both ends into her pockets to help secure it. The weight was uncomfortable, and the setup was awkward, but it would have to do.

"Well?" the old Dragon huffed. "You ready now?"

"Yeah." Alex told herself that they didn't have time for hesitation. Her excitement was dying down, and worry was creeping in. "Thank you." The old Dragon stayed still as she climbed onto his back. "What's your name?" Alex asked as she settled into the dip behind his neck.

"Just call me Ty," the Dragon sighed. "It's the first sound in my name."

They launched into the air, the smoke wrapped them in a veil of hazy gray and made Alex's eyes sting. Beneath her, Ty snorted, but he flew straight as if mostly unbothered by the filth in the sky. Her heart raced, that odd swooping feeling like being on a roller coaster made her light-headed for a moment. Clutching the horn in front of her, Alex wished they'd stopped long enough to talk to the Dragon about ropes or something else to hold on to. As their flight evened out, Alex carefully dug into the pockets of her coat and found her gloves. It was difficult to pull them on while keeping one hand on the horn, but with her teeth, she managed.

A loud whoop drew her attention to the right. A dark blue Dragon that had Aiden on its back came into view and Aiden was grinning like a fool. Alex turned and counted the others. She could see everyone now as a bright green Dragon with Bran on its back rose above the smoke. Emrys slowed ahead of them, Morgana on his back and the supplies hanging from his feet to allow Ty to fly up beside him. They exchanged quick shouts, though the wind meant Alex could barely make them out. Ty lurched with a burst of speed and pulled ahead.

They kept flying, the steady beating of the wings strangely reassuring. Far ahead, Alex found a dark spot in the sky. There was no storm here like there had been in the Gryphon world. No great winds battered them; no lightning flashed in aggravation as the Darkness irritated the very nature of the world. Alex cast her eyes down to the ground, leaning as far as she dared to look below. Here there were no burned-out trunks of trees;

it was just bare dead ground that was stained with black. Beneath the surface, she could find only a tiny flicker of power and grimaced at the sight of it.

If it was so weak here, then it would be even worse closer to the Darkness. Alex bit her lower lip, casting her thoughts back to the Gryphon world and examining what she could remember. It was a blur, but she'd pulled all the surrounding power. She'd drained the lightning in the sky and called on the power that the Gryphon world could offer.

The wind ripped across her skin. Without the burden of carrying all of them, the Dragons were moving fast through the air, cutting through the clouds and smoke. As they approached the dark spot ahead of them, the smoke lessened, and instead, there was a strange smell in the air. It was bitter and musty.

Time slipped away from her. Mountains framed the dark spot that was growing larger and larger. The Dragons kept flying. Dizziness swept over Alex, and her fingers tightened on the horn, fear fighting to keep her aware. The voices in her head burst into worrying questions that were too much of a mess to mean anything.

Alex flexed her fingers, aware of the soft pulses of energy circling her. The magic of this world was reaching for her. Unlike her world that fed her magic to confront threats, this world was trying to help an invader. Exhaling, Alex released her right hand from Ty's lowest neck horn and pulled on the power fluttering in the wind.

The wisps of energy gathered in her hand, their shimmering shades of color fading to her dark metallic gray. Alex smiled at the change. The dark color had bothered her once upon a time, but now it reassured her. She was iron; it was in her soul, in her magic, and in her deeds. The power condensed into a tight, small orb in her hand, and Alex didn't stop. She reached further and further, inhaling and exhaling slowly as she gently tugged on the power flickering beneath the surface and in the air.

Far below her, something shifted in the land. The stream of power grew brighter. Her eyes slipped closed, a soft melodic hum reaching towards Alex. It was there, right there, a long-dead channel fighting its way back to life. Her soft gasp was lost in the wind. More and more magic flared to life, rising into the air in tiny sparks of light.

The effect stretched out across the black plain, highlighting the fractured lines of energy that broke apart like a river delta. Ty kept flying forward, not reacting to the effect at all. In Alex's hand, the orb swelled in size. She touched her fingertips to the Iron Chain. Magic leapt off her fingertips in tiny arcs of lightning, shifting from the orb into the Chain. Its hum changed, settling into a slower melody rather than the whine.

Emrys swooped up beside them. Morgana leaned forward, and Alex smiled. She saw the older woman's lips move but didn't understand. Shrugging weakly, Alex turned her attention frontward again. Tiny collections of magic hung in the air like stars against the bleakness of the black land. She beckoned. They came, and with a thought, Alex stored them in the Chain as her confidence rose. The threads of power below were fading again, but Alex knew that this world wasn't dead yet. It could still be saved.

Ty turned, his body shifting all of his weight as he slowed. The rip was clear now. The light had changed; the sun somehow emerging from the clouds and smoke to grant them golden rays that made the edges glimmer. Darkness churned, flashes of a faint purple hint catching the light. It was hauntingly beautiful. In her hands, her Iron Chain turned hot, already detecting her purpose, its new purpose.

"Don't land!" Alex shouted. She hoped Ty could hear her. She kept her left hand wrapped tightly around the horn, feeling her body try to slip off as he changed his angle in order to hover. "Stay in the air!"

"I wasn't going to land," Ty shouted back. "The land's poisoned!"

He wasn't wrong. Below them was a gaping hole that the Darkness had cut into the world. What had once been a mountain, by the look of the surrounding landscape, was now a gaping hole with jagged bits of rock-forming a warped ring like a broken crown. Deep grooves were cut into the mountains around it, forming deep valleys, tunnels, and strange peaks.

The land was burned away, leaving a black blanket of dust and ash that made it all but impossible to see what was Darkness and what was still land. Her eyes searched around and noted with a sinking heart the effect was widespread with other eroded mountains, as if the hole had been shifted. Alex remembered that Hawaii had formed from a hole in the tectonic plates that shifted. Had something like that happened? Had this world fought off the Darkness only for it to retear the sky only a few miles away?

'Stop staring,' Cuthbert snapped. 'Either fix it or go.'

Smirking, Alex took her left hand off the horn. She'd have to trust the Dragon on this one. The Iron Chain pulsed with power in her hands, fully charged from the gathered magical energy. Overhead, the sky churned threateningly as if knowing her intentions. She glared at the rip, her eyes finding the edges easily and trying to see beyond the Darkness. There was nothing to see, the thick, dangerous liquid dripped again, sending a large droplet hurtling towards the ground.

Magic rushed out of the Iron Chain, surrounding her hands and arms in a deep gray glow. Alex narrowed her eyes at the rip, her heart jumping as magic swirled wildly in her chest. Keeping the Iron Chain tight in her hands, Alex pushed the magic forward and willed the tear shut. The sky rumbled as the magic hit the first layer of the Darkness. Dark gray sparks vanished along with droplets of the poison. Power clashed against the raw destructive force!

Ty moved; Alex had to grab onto the horn to keep from falling. The magic was flowing, moving around the rip in the world and forcing the Darkness back. Flashes of red, blue, silver, and yellow at her sides made Alex smile. She pulled on the magic of the other mages, letting the streams of power rush to her. The sparks turned to dark gray and burst into the sky.

Alex closed her eyes. She exhaled. The Iron Chain turned hot in her hands. In her mind's eye, she could see it. The edges of the rip slowly knit together, strands of magic joining the pieces of the sky like a needle and thread. Pressure hit her chest, compressing her lungs, and the wind tore at her skin. Alex swayed, weakness advancing, but the Iron Chain kept pulsing like a heart in her hands.

The smell in the air changed. She smelled the scent of ozone after the smoke cleared. The pressure released, magic backlashed into her chest, and sent an electric shock up her arms. Forcing open her eyes, Alex looked into the sky. The rip was gone, and a faint glow was rapidly fading. Her lips turned upward into a smile. The Iron Chain was heavy in her hand, and she leaned forward, trying to balance herself.

She brought her hand up, still clutching the Iron Chain, and held it against her chest. Her forehead rested against Ty's neck, just to the side of his neck crest. There was a clink of metal on metal as the Iron Pendant slipped out from her shirt and tapped against the Iron Chain. Electricity exploded across her body, burning her heart, and claws sank into her. They reached into her magic, digging into her lungs and pulled hard.

35

Find the Path

Magic pulled Alex apart, stretching her limbs too far and ripping the air out of her lungs. She was blind in pitch blackness until flashes of color exploded around her. There was a flicker of the image of the Tree of Reality in front of her, but it was gone just as quickly as she slammed her eyes shut. Her stomach rolled over, and her jaw tightened. Then it stopped, the pull suddenly eased, and Alex gasped for breath.

Exhaling, Alex focused on the wild fluttering of her magic. It was trying to go every which way, threatening to pull her apart once again. Slowly, she opened her eyes, fear crawling up her neck at what she might find. Alex was floating inside the Tree of Reality with soft flickers of light dancing around her in the blackness. Her eyes swept up the trunk, finding Earth easily, and then slid down towards the mysterious base. The lights were there, and Alex knew one was that strange hall.

A strange rumble drew her attention to one of the branches. The worlds hung on the thread of light like tiny, fragile pearls. Flickers of light illuminated the edge of the Darkness as it rolled forward. Dense waves washed across the connecting light, dimming it, but Alex could see that even in the thick of the Darkness they weren't extinguished. Her magic pulled her forward. Darkness loomed ahead of her, and Alex's heart jumped.

"No!" she shrieked. "No! No!"

Then she passed through the layer of Darkness. Her magic shuddered, but it held her tight and kept pulling her forward. No new thoughts entered Alex's brain. Terrified and relieved shock choked her. The violent pull eased as she came closer to a dark world. Darkness was swirling around it, covering everything that she could see.

Alex's feet hit solid ground. She stumbled and blinked, looking around and trying to get a grip on her flaring magic. As her eyes focused on the landscape, she gasped out loud only for ash to hit her tongue. She knew this place.

A dark violet sky overhead was filled with rubble, likely from a destroyed moon, and the ground was nothing but piles of ash. Small hints of a ruined building poked up in one spot a few feet from her, but it was long buried. It wasn't exactly the same place she'd been before, but Alex knew this was Sídhean. A low rumble made her look back up into the rubble and search it carefully. It didn't take long for her to find the rip in the sky. Droplets of Darkness fell from it, glittering in the dying light.

She took a step forward. Her foot sank into the thick ash, and Alex glared up at the rip. Why was she seeing this? She already knew that Sídhean was a dead world, and the damage to the planet is what had turned the Sídhe into a brutal expansionistic culture. The Iron Chain shifted in her hands, and Alex looked down at it in surprise, only to realize that she still had Cathanáil, Mjǫllnir and her Pendant as well as the Chain. Tightening her fingers around it, Alex turned her attention back to the tip of the building roof that she could see. Part of the highest point was exposed, and that was it. There was nothing helpful there. Turning back to the rip, she tried to estimate how far away it was. The plain stretched out before her; there were no mountains left and no other signs of buildings. There were only small black dunes scattered across the landscape.

"There's nothing here," Alex said. "Nothing at all."

Her chest burned, Alex crumbled to her knees and cried out. It was strong and hot and violent. She pried her eyes open, unsure of when she'd closed them. Around her was a halo of light that shimmered and split into flashes of the colors of the rainbow. Confused, Alex reached out and tried to draw the magic towards her. It didn't respond and instead spread further around her. For an instant, everything was still.

The voices were muted. She could hear only their whispers in her mind. Alex swallowed, ignoring the racing of her heart and climbed to her feet once again. She took a step forward. Wind rippled the ashes beside her, shaping small dunes that collapsed seconds later.

"What do you want me to see?"

Ashes spun into the air, and Alex held back a cry. Clapping a hand over her mouth, Alex narrowed her eyes and tried to watch what was happening even as instinct demanded she turn away. The ashes gathered together, forming a towering building in front of her with a spire that reached towards the tear. It wasn't solid, but the shape blocked out the sun and cast a long shadow over her. Dark gray sparks zipped amongst the ashes like lightning, only to explode up into the sky, forming a beam of light from the building.

Her eyes widened. The ashes drew back to reveal the rip in the sky and then illustrated the spire falling. Screams echoed in Alex's ears, making her jump and her hairs stand on end. Waves of ashes drew up from the ground, forming running figures that collapsed into dust mere seconds later. The building fell, and her magic flashed towards her in a bolt of lightning, striking her outstretched hand.

Alex snapped back to her body. Her shoulders screamed as they twisted too far. Sweat was rolling down her brow and the back of her neck. Gasping for air, Alex leaned forward and stretched out her torso as she fought to slow down her breathing. Someone's hand was on her shoulder, but she shivered, and they thankfully removed it.

The others were nearby. Alex's eyes were closed, but she could see them with their bright outlines of magical power. It was clearer now than it ever had been before. Her limbs trembled with weakness, but power from the flow of the Tree of Reality was reaching for her. It wasn't perfect. It was a poor match to Earth, and Alex knew it. Still, she called to it and felt the energy twist and shift into something closer to what she wanted. Wisps gathered together and sank into her skin, cooling her off and filling the void in her chest.

"Alex?" Morgana asked. The heat of a hand radiated onto her exposed skin as Morgana reached for her again, but thankfully didn't touch her. "Can you hear me?"

"Yeah," Alex croaked. Her tongue was heavy and tasted of ash.

She opened her eyes. Everything was too bright, and she slammed them shut. Someone moved beside her, and the plastic tip of a water bottle straw was at her lips. Keeping her eyes shut, Alex inhaled one more time and then took a long drink of water. It helped, and she licked her lips as she moved her mouth away.

"I'm okay," Alex said. "I'm okay."

She was on solid ground; she could feel it beneath her. Alex did not know when that had happened. She didn't know where they were. Opening her eyes, Alex turned them up to the sky and smiled softly at the sight of the rich blue color. It wasn't exactly like the sky at home, but it was close enough to be comforting, and stars were beginning to appear. So very different from the debris-filled sky.

"Alex?" Nicki called. "Honey, what did you see?"

"Well... I figured out where the Darkness is coming from," Alex said. She tried to make her voice teasing, but was sure that it fell flat. "We were right. It's a hole in the..." Alex struggled for the right word. "Side of the Tree?" A small shrug was the best she could do, and her body protested that. "There's this wound, and the Darkness is pouring in. I'm not sure of its source, but it's not from any world and is killing them all."

"So, it's an outside force, after all." Bran exhaled and knelt beside her. "Do you know which branch, Alex? Where do we need to go?"

Alex turned her head to look at Morgana. The old mage was hovering over them, impatient, pleased, and nervous expressions were battling for dominance on her face. A weak chuckle bubbled up in Alex's chest. She almost started laughing at how ridiculous it was.

"It seems that the story is coming full circle," Alex said. Morgana raised an eyebrow, and Alex mimicked the movement. "The hole is right beside the Sídhe homeworld. We've got to go to their branch."

Morgana stilled. Her face went carefully blank, revealing nothing and giving Alex not even a hint of what Morgana thought of her declaration. She already regretted how she'd revealed the news, but there was nothing for it. There was nothing she could say that would make it better. Of all the mages, only Alex and Morgana had ever been into the Sídhe tunnels, and only Morgana had ever been at the heart of the Sídhe civilization.

Everything they'd learned about the Darkness and the Sídhe's flight for survival didn't change what Morgana had gone through as a child. All the sympathy Alex could muster for a race that knew their world was dying and started a culture of conquest didn't change what those actions had led to. Morgana rarely talked about it, but Arto had enough memories of the first war with the Sídhe that she knew the terror that had filled daily life. Alex knew children were taken and groomed as sexual slaves;

she knew people were cut down if they had no value and that the Sídhe had infested all the worlds in their branch.

Yet they'd never revealed the Darkness. The Queen and her fellow rulers had always kept it a secret. If it was a desperate attempt to deny what was happening or if it had been a matter of propaganda and politics, she didn't know. And she shouldn't care, but Alex's stomach turned when Morgana slowly nodded. The woman's face was still hiding her emotions, but they were there beneath the surface.

"Are you sure?" Nicki asked softly.

"Yes." Alex nodded. "Yes, I'm sure."

"Was it natural?" Bran glanced cautiously at Morgana. "Or did they cause it?"

"I'm not sure." Alex had to admit that Bran might have a point. If the Sídhe had already been an arrogant race that wanted to expand and pushed the wrong way when trying to reach another world, then maybe this could be the result. Her vision hinted that the fallen tower had been connected to the rip, that the Sídhe had done something, but she couldn't be certain. "It doesn't really matter," she decided. "It isn't just about their world."

"So, we have to go to Sídhean?" Morgana frowned at last. "From your visions, that is a dead world. We may not be able to get there directly, especially if the Darkness has consumed it."

"Then we get as close as we can." Alex finally took her eyes off of Morgana and looked up into the sky. It was bright and clear once more. There would be scars on the land from the Darkness, but they would fade, and the sky was already mended. "I don't know if the Darkness is just what is beyond the Tree naturally or if it is something more, but it is a threat."

Morgana nodded slowly. Alex knew that this wasn't the last time conflicted emotions would come forth, but they had to go. She turned her attention to the others. Bran, Nicki, and Aiden were all huddled close to her, but Alex could still see a few of the Dragons peering over their heads. A soft giggle escaped her at the ridiculous sight. That more than anything seemed to reassure the others, and they gave her a little more space.

"Uh, where are we?" Alex looked around in confusion.

"Ty found a mountaintop that was in okay shape," Nicki said. "Don't worry; we tested it before setting down."

That did make her feel a little better, but it was a tight fit between the Dragons and her fellow mages. Slowly climbing to her feet, Alex let Aiden help her stay stable and looked around curiously. They were indeed high on what was left of a mountain. Deep ravines had been carved out below them, creating an ugly crisscross that made a chill roll down Alex's spine.

Bran had moved to the edge of the mountain. He was holding the Iron Chalice carefully in his hands and looking down at it thoughtfully. She wasn't sure when he'd gotten it out, but if she collapsed while on the back of a Dragon, it was understandable that the others had been worried. Reminded of that, she turned to Ty and smiled.

"Thank you for keeping me safe," Alex said. "When I passed out, I mean."

Ty blinked in surprise. The old Dragon's eyes softened, and he nodded. "You're welcome. Thank you for closing the sky." His voice was a mix of resignation and happiness. Alex could understand that. The tear was closed, but the devastation remained.

"Hey, Aiden, can I get some more water?" Bran asked.

Aiden tossed him one of the water bottles, and Bran studied it for a moment. Alex slipped past Nicki and joined Bran at the edge. Below them, a sharp drop made her a head spin in alarm. This column they were on was stable, but she was now aware of the enormous fall if they moved wrong.

"Bran, what's up?"

"I've been thinking." Bran rubbed his thumb over the Chalice and handed Alex the bottle of water. "I want to try something. Will you fill the Chalice?"

"Try something?" Alex took the top off the bottle and poured a couple of inches of water into the Chalice. "Bran?"

"In the myth of the Fisher King, that myth that somehow connects to me." Bran shrugged and fixed his eyes on the Chalice as a soft blush appeared on his cheeks. "The land gets healed."

"Yes, but-" Alex stopped for a moment. "Bran, that might not work. That was a story that someone who had a vision once created."

"It was a hint, part of a hint that let us find the Chalice. Maybe it also is a hint that the Chalice can do more than heal people."

There was no harm in trying. The danger was how much magic it might take to achieve what Bran was after. But the flicker of the thread of power in the corner of Alex's eyes softened her worries. Beneath her feet, the ground quivered with pain, and the magic of the world was stretched too thin after helping her seal the Darkness.

"Just be careful of how much magic you use."

Grinning at her, Bran turned his body to the cliff and exhaled. The Chalice glowed softly. For good measure, Alex reached over and touched her fingertips to the metal just above Bran's hand. The metal was warming at their touch. She offered Bran a small smile as Nicki asked what they were doing behind her.

Bran tipped the Iron Chalice, and water spilled off the rim. The first droplets hit the ash below them and were immediately absorbed. A small stream made it a few inches, but no further. Alex held her breath. Nothing happened. Her heart sank, and she heard Bran sigh. Nicki poked her head over her shoulder.

"What are you- whoa!"

A reddish plant burst from the dark soil, stretching up its leaves as if conjured by Merlin, and turned towards the hazy sun. The ground shimmered in a dark muted gold, the combination of Bran's yellow and her dark gray, and more plants burst forth. Alex's breath caught. It spread, it spread further than the Chalice's water had reached. Beside her, Bran laughed triumphantly and tossed out more water further from the cliff. Alex poured more water into the Chalice and called on the flickering magic still left to her.

"Bran, what-" Morgana gasped.

Cheers erupted behind them. Emrys said something, but it was mostly lost to the shouted questions of the Dragons. Reddish plants were spreading across the surface of the ground, small pale flowers appearing, and thick dark green vines were burrowing into the layers of ash. Above them, the sky was already clearing. The tear was gone, and the rich color of the sky was shining through the smoke. Closing her eyes, Alex breathed out slowly and reached for the energy thread. It was there, weak, but it was there. Someone pulled the water bottle from her hands, and eager voices rolled over her. She didn't listen; she followed the soft pulse of this world's power and found it there below. The glow was muted, but it was growing stronger. The soft hum changed, fading from pain to relief.

Then the sound of Dragons singing filled the air and a soft sigh of relief escaped Alex as she opened her eyes. Long, smooth notes drifted into the sky and blended together as the sun fully broke through the haze. Sunlight spilled across the landscape and the blanket of growth was spreading out before her like an unrolling carpet. It was slowing down, but she could hear Bran and Morgana discussing doing some flights to spread the water with the Dragons. Something like pride settled in her chest as her past selves whispered their congratulations. There was much to do and a long way to go, but the first leg of the journey was complete, and she knew the way forward.